Sweet Journey Home
By
Wayne Luckmann

Sweet Journey Home

Rate of Exchange, Volume 2

Wayne Luckmann

Published by Wayne Luckmann, 2022.

SWEET JOURNEY HOME

First edition. December 10, 2022.

ISBN: 978-0463461952

Written by Wayne Luckmann.

At the end of June 1958, his first year in Long Beach, California while attending college, Felix Fist lived on Anaheim Avenue in a drab, pale green room he climbed to over worn, scruffy stairs in a pale green, smog-stained building set among deteriorating houses, crumbling sidewalks, grassless curb strips of packed dirt. Alone in that dingy room with pale green walls from which he often wandered the streets at twilight beneath the neon signs and street lamps, he passing dingy stores with fly-specked windows, storefront Godshops with joyful names, dark dim-lit taverns from which issued blaring music, sudden shouts and riotous laughter, on one occasion a group of laughing, dark-skinned women emerged commenting on his pale complexion, teasing him, glancing with wide grins at their men who followed. Felix answered with a friendly tone and walked on leaving them jiving on the curb before they piled into a Cadillac and screeched away from the curb, shooting past him, shouting and waving through the open windows as he walked on toward his room.

But on another night during one of his wanderings he was stopped by a patrol car. He leaned toward the uniformed man who lounged in his seat and spoke to him through the open window, the man's hairy arm resting on the door; the other officer, the driver, studied the traffic and the aimless crowds wandering along debris strewn sidewalks bathed in the glow of neon lights from the multitude of liquor stores and pawn shops, taverns, and an occasional small café that lined each side of the street for miles.

"You live around here!" the officer challenged.

"Yes, sir, just down the street."

"Where!" the man challenged again.

Felix gave the man his address, pointing toward the pale green, stucco building that rose above the neighboring derelict dwellings he could see from where he stood. Across the top of the building a block of huge, black letters proclaimed: SINGLE ROOMS FOR RENT — LOW COST — DAY-WEEK-MONTH.

"You work around here!"

"Not around here. But I work."

"Where!"

"Morey's Chevron Service in Belmont Shore."

"Oh," the officer said, relenting. "So you know these people then."

1

"Sure," Felix answered. He felt a slight tinge of pride at seeming to be set apart outside the circle of fear and insecurity that this dark-clothed, official looking man seemed to signify, even though the man himself seemed casual, lounging, slumped in his seat, his hairy arm resting on the edge of the open window.

"Well, there's been a few knifings around here lately."

Felix felt uneasy on hearing that report.

"Some sailors have been coming up here and causing trouble," the officer continued. He looked through the windshield but directed his words through the open window at which he lounged. "So we question anyone who doesn't appear to belong."

"Yes, sir, I understand," Felix replied and surveyed the teeming, scrap-strewn streets that were darkening toward evening.

"Well," the officer said, "sorry to bother you."

The driver put the car in gear.

"Be careful," the officer said out the open window.

Then the patrol car slowly swung out into traffic and crept away leaving him to walk through gathering darkness the short distance to his dismal room. Made nervous then by dark shapes studying him lurking on scrap-strewn, urine-stained door stoops of small abandoned stores or startled by the sudden burst of laughter flung out at him from open doorways of taverns, he reached the small café beneath the pale green building that held his room.

Here in that café he on occasion had coffee greeted by the enormous cook, the stained apron tight across the man's huge belly, his coarse, dark, round face, his thick, dark arms. Felix drinking coffee from a scarred, stained plastic cup, he listened to low, mournful music from a radio while watching the quiet, unhurried movements of the enormous black man who seemed to have accepted his being there within the grungy light gleaming off the grimy windows and walls. Felix relaxed from the man's friendly smile, the polite questions, the seemingly genuine interest on the man's part as the man responded engaging Felix in casual conversation as if the man, unlike the police, hadn't noticed Felix's pale coloring and apparent displacement.

Felix in turn felt his own genuine interest when the man talked about himself: his divorce, his schooling, his hopes for business success, his hopes of eventually reaching Ghana, an emerging nation that had gained independence from the United Kingdom the previous year, the man telling Felix the new nation was sending out pleas for help from developed countries. Felix found himself amazed to learn that the man had done graduate work at UCLA, and Felix felt envious of the man's sense of purpose, the man's sense of strength from having a goal that seemed genuine and real, so unlike Felix's own indecisive, aimless wandering, floating on the surface of existence.

"Well," the man had offered, "you're attending college. That's a start. Just keep on with what you've been doing. You'll find your way."

Returning to his room, tiring of the pale, dirty walls, the emptiness, the lone dresser, its dark stained veneer softened by bare patches where the wood had been gouged, Felix shut off the hanging, bare lightbulb, the streetlight outside his ghetto room casting its yellow-orange glow into his warm, close room. He watched the throbbing neon of the tavern he could witness from where he stood at the open window. He watched the movements of people as they entered or left, some congregating on the concrete walkway to jive. He watched the passing traffic.

Felix didn't walk abroad as much after that incident with the police, and at the start of summer at the end of Spring semester in June, sooner than he expected, he had moved out of that pale green room on Anaheim heading for Oregon:

June 25, 1958

12:00 am

In 15 seconds I shall be 21. In the time it took to write those words the 15 seconds have passed. Well, I have finally arrived at that age when a whole new field of activity should open to a person but somehow I feel no excitement. The past year has been rather filled with the creating of many memories, some good and some not so good but all rather worth having.

In a few short hours I shall be leaving for Arlington, Oregon. My plans are to travel by hitching rides. I rather hope that I have little trouble and that my trip is a good one.

It is my purpose in this sitting to outline the log I intend to keep of my trip chronologically. I shall list my time of departure and the point at which I may be at every hour during my travel time. I also propose to make notations of the people I meet and the incidents that occur, when and if they should. This log shall also include my trip back to Milwaukee, Wisconsin my hometown. And a log shall be kept of all travels that I shall make from this time forth. It is late and I must rest for the long journey ahead. Until the next entry then.

Later that morning Felix woke surprised that despite worries of what he might face on his trip ahead he had slept soundly without troubling dreams. The bright early morning sun filled his room cleansing the walls, warming him, filling his spirit compelling him to rise, to pack and leave—just like that. Taking the duffel bag he had borrowed from Hank, leaving his key, descending for the last time the bare worn stairs to the cracked concrete walk alongside bare earth patches and empty, freshly washed streets, he saw bright morning sunlight dazzling on store fronts, the silver towers of the oil refining plant he had seen glow through billowing gaseous vapors in the night, its reeking odors of eons of decay pumped from the earth. He saw the wide streets as suddenly vast by the absence of traffic. He breathed rank exhaust from a passing car. Then, suddenly, someone stopped, and he was underway.

On his trip north, he seemed suspended, perhaps because of his keeping a log of his journey, he addressing it as a person, beginning to find his voice. Abandoned at a service station after a quick, silent ride with a taciturn businessman, picked up by a Hollywood film editor who raced madly across The Grapevine talking endlessly about film making and working with film stars Felix only knew by name or seeing them in films the man had edited, he and Felix roared across semi-desert flatlands stretching to the dark hulks of mountains, Felix waiting along side the road as the colors of those mountains changed from the setting sun while he studied the grass among the gravel along the roadside, the long dark line of freight train against glowing sunlight, a lone figure lounging in the open doorway of the slowly moving boxcar, the man waving to him as he passed.

June 26, 1958

My birthday. I am now of legal age. Somehow it doesn't seem too very different or exciting, but it may be because I have not as yet used my new power that came to me last night at 1 minute after 12. When reaching the age that I am now, the question arises in my mind. When is a man really a man? I wonder if and when I shall ever find a true answer to this question?

Fist paused in his reading to consider how many roads Felix had been down before he had stumbled upon an answer. Then he read what Felix had written later:

Time of departure Long Beach, California: 11 A.M.

Well I'm under way. At this time, I am seated along the side of the road on Highway 7 heading out of L.A. I stopped long enough to have the doughnuts that Carl Kedslie's neighbor wrapped for me.

I had to walk about a mile along PCH [Pacific Coast Highway] before I was able to get my first ride with a young fellow in a 51 Ford. He took me as far as Avalon Blvd. And this is where I was at 12:00P.M. In a few minutes I received a ride in a 53 Ford that took me as far as Redondo Beach. The driver drove wildly and said little. There were other hitch-hikers that were let out at the same time that I was.

I started walking up the street when a truck driver walked out of a service station and asked how far I was going. I told him and he said he could give me a ride as far as Culver City. I was let out there at about 1:05. He was a middle age man with graying hair. And he told me how he was about to start drilling for oil on his 40 acres of land. Wishing him luck and he wishing me luck I left him. That is it for now.

9:37 PM The depression that I usually have from lack of rides doesn't seem to be as great as on previous times that I have traveled as I now do.

I am sitting outside a filling station in Goshen, Calif. some 187 miles for L.A. As it is plainly seen I'm not making very good time. There is still a very long ways to travel.

Since my last writing, many interesting things took place which I shall outline at the present time.

Soon after my last writing – I no sooner put you to rest within the dark fullness of your carrier when a man – I would say about 30 years of age asked me how far I was going. He had seen me writing to you and I could see him glance towards me from the station at which he was making a phone call. He gave me a ride as far as Ventura Blvd. We talked some, mostly of the usual things; where I was headed. If and where I went to school, what was my major – with this came the usual comment that traveling would give me good experience. He was rather congenial and the time with him went rather quickly. One last comment on this man: at the same time he drove up and asked me how far it was that I was going I was eating the cookies that Carl's neighbor had packed for me. Upon entering the car I offered him some of the remaining cookies and he laughed and took one.

At 2 o'clock I was still at the spot where this man left me out and at about 2:15 I received a ride from a colored man driving a lumber truck. The usual questions came of where I was headed but the interesting thing to note was that each time I would answer his question he would laugh and say "oh yeah". The conversation was limited for we were going through the Santa Monica Mts. The road meandered extremely and the hills towering above the road were very beautiful in the haze that surrounded them. In this same section I could see men working in the hot sun building a new freeway through these rugged hills. The road in places was cut through solid rock and the patterns of the cut created an effect as if they were etchings.

The colored man let me out in Sepulveda about 5 miles from 99 a few minutes after 3.

At 4, I was still waiting for my next ride. The day had turned out exceedingly hot and the Sun beat down on me with little pity. My mouth was very dry from too many cigarettes and little water and this along with the sun began to wear on my resistance to depression.

I was just beginning to mutter to myself when my next ride came along. He waved me into the car and we shot away unto the road. The same questions came. He offered me a cigarette. I accepted. The conversation was very intermittent with periods of silence. The time was now around 4:15.

I would say the man was around 25, black hair, hooked nose and very short patience for we stopped for gasoline shortly after he picked me up and he kept muttering "Come on Buddy" to the attendant with phonograph like insistence while he purchased 10 gallons of Ethyl and we shot on our way.

I rode with him as far as Gorman, and the country we traveled through defies description. This section was part of the Angelo Nat'l forest, and at places we reached an elevation of 3200 ft., the plateau and bluff covered with shrubs of a variety I had previously seen but knew little. The land held a breathtaking silence and was helped along by the lack of conversation.

The mesas towered above us and here again the road in places was blasted through reddish rock, the cuttings making diagonal parallel etchings.

Just out of Gorman the car began to act up, but we made it to a service station where the man informed me that he was going no further. I grabbed my gear and out I went. I had a coke at the station and the cold drink stung my parched throat. After this I hoist my bag to my shoulder and start walking towards the highway a couple blocks away.

Standing on the highway I could look down at the place I had just left, for it was set in a gully. There were three stations in the same place also a restaurant. I could see the people going about their own ways and the feeling of loneliness came to me. But 2 three more cars coming so out went the thumb.

About 15 minutes later a car stopped and I could see a number of small children as I ran to the car. They seemed friendly from the moment I settled myself back against the seat when immediately the girl who sat next me in the rear seat of the 57 Chev station wagon started telling me about her classes in summer school and what she had made for her mother in arts and crafts.

The time with them went very quickly and was filled with a constant flow of words from all three of the children (there was a younger girl) they told of their fighting forest fires and their school. This was intermingled with occasional interjections by their father. All in all I rode with them about 30 miles.

Sitting by the road outside the station in Goshen, Felix watched as another station wagon, this one dark green with Oregon license plate stopped for gasoline, he returning to catch up his log, suddenly surprised when the driver, a man probably in his late twenties, dark hair and soft features, short and somewhat overweight in baggy jeans and t-shirt having finished fueling his auto, approached and asked Felix where he was headed.

"Arlington, Oregon." Felix replied, closing his logbook.

"That's in the eastern part of the state. Why you going there?"

"I'm going to meet some friends who will help me find a job harvesting wheat"

"Well, we're from Milwaukie just outside of Portland. We can take you that far if you feel like riding with us. I got a couple of kids that will talk your ear off. If you can handle that, we'll stow your grip behind the back seat."

"That would help a lot!" Felix replied pushing himself to his feet, moving his legs to shake out the stiffness from his prolonged rest beside the road. Then he grabbed his bag and followed the man to the waiting car.

The ride to Portland was long, but now that Felix knew he had a ride most of the way to his destination, he relaxed and began to enjoy his exchanges with the family who had opened their circle of personal space to help his passage through country he had never seen with the names of some places that seemed exotic: Rogue River (the river of no return). Medford, Grants Pass, Roseburg, Eugene, Salem, Portland (Felix wondering why some names were the same as places on the East Coast), Milwaukie (Felix thinking the name surprising, the spelling strange, wondering who might have settled it during westward expansion in the previous century). Felix spent the night with them sleeping in the lower bunk of the boy who proudly gave up his bed to a new friend.

Before they retired for the night, the boy's father invited Felix to join him in exploring the town, leaving his wife resigned to minding the children and spending the evening alone, a situation that Felix guessed happened all too frequently for her. That evening Felix observed the man invite two women Felix guessed were underage to accompany them to a park where they were offered beer and Felix watched the man negotiate with one young woman to accommodate the man's need while Felix without any success attempted to converse with the other younger woman who obviously bored with the whole scene appeared totally disinterested in Felix's attempt at nothing more than conversation, he having received clearly the young woman's signals that she couldn't be bothered about any of what was taking place and repeatedly complained to the other young woman that she just wanted to go home.

The next morning after having breakfast with the family, the children and even the wife expressing regret at seeing Felix go, the husband gave him a ride north to US 30, wished Felix luck, then turned back, leaving Felix again on his own. Several other rides took him east to Arlington, a small town set on a bluff above the Columbia and a dated restaurant of vinyl counter tops and chromium fixtures where he sat drinking coffee and smoking until a car, an equally dated '38 Buick loomed before the plate glass window, the grille and headlights filling the frame, and there were Hank and Amy and Bud who had a Sunday break from harvesting.

Having found him with the green duffle bag he had borrowed from Hank that had helped Felix get rides, they began swapping stories of their travels, took up his cause and carried him into the back country of wheat ranches, talking excitedly as they went, telling him of how they would help him find work, depositing him finally along with his bag at a faded red barn that he would sleep in for a night. Then they disappeared, the high, square back of the '38 Buick receding before a billow of dust. Driving off, they called back a promise to see him soon shouting as they left. They would camp along the river, spend free time together on Sundays.

Then they vanished into the summer twilight, and Felix found himself alone amid the heat heavy darkness waiting for his first harvest hoping he might pull off having bluffed his way into being hired telling Stolz, the wheat rancher whom he had called seeking work,

"Sure, I've done harvesting before!"

The next day rising at dawn, Felix soon learned what he had been hired to do and discovering that nothing he had ever done came close to what he endured that day, he required to drive a ten-speed dump across undulating hills, pulling alongside the combine to take off wheat from the hopper while the truck and combine climbed side-by-side over ridges, tipping precariously on hillsides, jolting across rough terrain. His dump brimming with grain, he would have to drive back from the fields to the ranch, unload the wheat into a bin with a conveyer belt run by a small engine he would have to pull a cord to start, the belt carrying the grain up into the barn. Then he would have to hurry back to the fields before the combine hopper was full.

Having learned all he had to manage, Felix grew uncertain and uneasy understanding Stolz's skepticism when Felix had phoned. But, as Hank and Bud and Amy insisted, the man had taken Felix at his word. So with his friends having helped him find work, they repeatedly assuring him, and since he was now here after traveling all that distance from Long Beach by hitching rides, he felt compelled to follow through on his bluff and tell himself he would learn by doing what he had to do.

The next day Felix readily enjoyed the fresh morning of dry chill and early sunlight on yellow fields of uncut grain, the sky clear and pure—all that he had dreamed of seeing when he had imagined them from a distance, so unlike the Los Angeles area. Felix, of course, suffered his typical shyness entering the tall, balloon-frame ranch house set among wheat fields, he a complete stranger sitting at the large table with the other hands who appeared to know each other well; the wheat rancher Stolz with wire-rimmed glasses, black hair combed straight back exposing his high forehead, his way of speaking sounding formal, learned, distinct from the others at the table who sounded regional from dialect. Stolz's wife, still a young woman in jeans and loose, flannel shirt with nothing beneath studied Felix the new hire as she moved around the table serving them, he self-conscious from her inspection while appreciating her lithe movements and youthful beauty and hints of bare flesh; the other harvest hands raw and lean, burnt by the sun, all of them strangers to Felix, nodding to him as he entered. The other men matter-of-factly going to the table where they sat and began passing around food then begin to eat, Felix followed their lead. Settling in his place, suddenly subjected to questions from Stolz, Felix paused in serving himself and answered as honestly as he could about his previous experiences of what he considered harvesting. Felix grew uneasy from Stolz's studied inspection.

The morning of his second day as he lay in the chill of the weathered, dusty barn crowded with spare or redundant implements encroaching but allowing a space for his bunk, he thought of those other times of bright mornings when just edging adolescence he had risen early and pedaled on his stripped down bike to the soft black fields pungent and wet from dew where he had worked pulling, bunching, crating radishes, carrots, onions, carrying the crates of produce to the truck with staked sides where an adolescent boy, a true colossus (so he seemed to Felix at the time) wearing a spotless cowboy hat and practiced swagger, jazzing all the young girls, mostly *mestizos* obviously impressed or fearful while the young swain tallied the amount of produce Felix and they had bunched and crated.

Felix the summer of his last year at Prairieville High had ridden behind a green and yellow tractor regulating the stream of seed that spilled along dry furrows of harrowed earth, the long hours of work from early morning into evening having tired him, but he enjoying the softening light on his face as the sun sank through clouds burnishing the tractor with golden light, the rich leaves of green trees bordering the fields, the rich, loamy soil spreading away on all sides. Then in twilight becoming dark, the small lights of the tractor sweeping along tall grass beside the packed earth path leading him to the farmyard and his prime chariot, a '48 black Ford sedan earned by the sweat of his adolescent brow.

He thought about the hot days among towering thick, broad-leafed plants rustling above his tall frame as he walked between green rows searching for ripened corn, the blue sky above the tall, green plants, billowing summer clouds high and radiant that seemed so far away. Surrounding him, the close, almost invisible world with its own harvest of stirring life within soft, green light beneath tall corn stalks splaying large, green leaves, glittering movements on sandy soil, a kaleidoscope of color from insects in among leaves, frothy spume on stalks and ears of corn, spiral rows of yellow kernels, silky red hair fanning in warm summer breeze beneath blue sky with billowing clouds.

All those splendid experiences were nothing like Felix had experienced the previous day when he had gone out to meet unforeseen disasters: Steep hills made the truck tip. He had stalled the engine, failed to judge the speed of the combine, and let the wheat spill to the ground. Stolz had stopped the combine (Felix winced from remembering) climbed into the truck cab forcing Felix to move aside, parked the truck under the combine spout, then bolted from the truck, climbed back up on the combine to run off the heaping wheat from the hopper into the dump of the truck.

The young wife brought the noon meal to the fields. They ate seated on the scarred brown earth among the stubble strewn with chaff using the silent trucks and machinery for shade. The food hot and filling, Felix felt too exhausted and too worried to readily eat.

"Well, how do you like real harvesting?" Stolz had asked in his formal manner, his dark eyes hard behind wire-rimmed glasses. Felix had felt humbled by the man's question but tried excusing his ineptness by joking. "It's nothing like what I've experienced." His attempt at humor lame, no one said a word.

The afternoon had been little better than the morning, he always having trouble starting the conveyer belt that carried the grain up into the barn. Yet Felix thought he had begun to learn, better at judging the speed of the combine so that he could drive alongside while the wheat spilled evenly into the dump of the truck. One time or two he even made it back to the field in time to immediately take off another load.

Today he was sure he would do better. Fully awake now after exhausted sleep from the dream that still troubled him and having lain within the light of the barn among the odors of grease and dust, Felix crawled from the cot then dressed in clothes stiff with dirt and sweat.

He studied the green duffle sitting at the end of the cot still tight with his possessions. Uncertain of what he would be facing, arriving late, he had put off unpacking. Finding himself alone in what seemed another foreign place, he had stood at the barn door studying the fading light above the rolling hills, gazing at the perfect globe of light, a wanderer, the same as he. Across the deepening twilight haze, twinkling lights of the small town among the shimmering trees along the river, a fast string of lights of a passenger train, its faint horn as it raced through crossings, reminding him of watching another as a child standing at the edge of the Great Plains in Iowa. After it was gone, he had heard the far away barking of a dog. Behind him the still sounds of the barn as it settled into night, he worried about what he would face the following day, his first, and as he had feared, a disaster.

Now as he stood alone shivering in the early morning chill studying the full duffle then inspecting the incongruous, antique, mirrorless bureau set on the dusty concrete in the hollow of the barn, he finally decided that if he unpacked only essentials, a few fresh things for evenings and weekends, they would be sufficient. Unlacing the duffle, he undid the flaps, then dug into the bag unpacking a few selected items, placing them in the barren drawers surprisingly clean and lined with fresh paper. He set his comb and brushes and shaving gear in one of the small top drawers. He let the rest of what he owned remain in the duffle, redid the flaps, relaced the bag, then set it at the end of his cot.

"Just like home," he said to himself. He studied the green duffle sitting at the end of the cot still tight with his clothing, the letters of Hank's name, rank, and serial number faded.

The barn door shot back banging against the metal stop of the transom. Felix checked his startled, conditioned response, suddenly sweating from the effort of controlling himself in reaction to the sharp, loud bang that sounded like gunfire. Stolz entered and as if searching for a tool began rummaging among the pile of implements scattered on the bench at the other end of the barn. Then Stolz suddenly turned, came forward, and Felix suddenly found himself challenged:

"You apparently misrepresented yourself when you applied to hire on here," Stolz accused in his stern, formal voice.

Felix stood stunned searching the man's face, the hard, angry, dark eyes behind wire-rimmed glasses. "I told you yesterday that this is different," Felix pleaded.

"Well, I don't have the time nor the inclination to train you! Plenty around here have the needed experience!" He dug in the pocket of his faded denim jacket buttoned against the morning chill. "Here's your time for what little you did yesterday!" He handed Felix the folded yellow paper. "My wife will take you back to town as soon as you're ready!" Then the man left letting the barn door stand open.

Felix found himself within the pickup beside the young wife who remained silent all the way to the small town where Felix was deposited with his bag before the café from which he had called two days before. Then he watched as she drove off without a word and stopped up the street. Felix watched another man climb into the truck. The truck drove off, and he found himself alone.

So that was that: one day of work after his long trip hitching rides, his longer expectations of harvesting under the open sky, the assurances of those who had picked him up at a café on the highway along the river telling him he would easily find work:

"It's easy!" the three had exclaimed almost as a chorus. "All you have to do is tell them you've done it before! They'll take your word!"

Now here he was alone without work after only one day, and those others miles away working without problems, having worked during harvest before. Felix sat on the bench before the Victoria Café, the only one in town, the large stuffed duffle beside him. Inspecting it, he felt dejected and exposed. He had brought too much, he now decided. What else could he have done? He should have dumped some at the bungalow in Naples before he had left Long Beach. Well, too late now and he having to haul all of it any place he found himself, and if he decided, all the way back to Milwaukee and then back to Long Beach. What had he been thinking?

Avoiding the curious inspection of those entering or leaving the café, he watched the slow movements of the few people in this small, wheat-country town. He studied buildings from the previous century, the high full oak beside the closed tavern across the way, the stirring oak leaves that caught the soft morning light, beyond the tavern, the slow moving line of railroad cars hauling wheat.

Then he rose, entered the café where he ate breakfast, cashed the local check for what seemed a meager amount, went back out to the glass and metal phone booth beside the concrete steps of the café and tried the number he had been given by Amy. When he reached her, she expressed surprise from his call then abrupt in expressing her disappointment. That was too bad, she declared, short in response. She was busy, had no time to talk. She had so much to do helping to prepare meals for all the hands on the ranch where she had hired on. She would talk to Hank. Perhaps he would know where Felix might find work. Then the line went dead and Felix was left alone, the phone still in his hand outside the café in the small Palouse town he suddenly felt closing in on him.

Considering what he should do next, wondering whether he should try to find work then wondering who would hire him if they surely by now had learned of his inexperience through reports of men with whom he had worked his only day, he scanned the small main street. Certainly there was nothing for him here. Then as he sat on a bench beside the phone booth deciding his next move, he watched a tall, stout man approach, coming straight at him. Felix braced himself as the large man planted himself before Felix who inspected the man's somewhat typical apparel: dusty, straw Stetson, plaid shirt, faded, sagging jeans beneath a large paunch. Then Felix noted the man's scruffy, hightop canvas shoes.

"You from these parts?" the man demanded.

"Not exactly," Felix hedged. *Who was this guy? What'd he want? Why the third degree?*

"Didn't think so. Don't remember ever seein' you around much. Though I expect you've been away for a while." The man nodded toward the large green duffle at Felix's leg. "Soldier, huh."

"Once," Felix offered.

"How long you fixin' to stay? Lots of strangers here this time of year. But they're easy to take. You can see right off they're ranch hands. They're not hangin' around on Main Street midmorning. Those not workin' seem to stick right out. Just as easy to tell those who haven't been anywhere near a wheat ranch."

"I've worked on a ranch," Felix offered in defense

"That right?" the man asked. "I guess sometimes you never know." Then he added abruptly, "Hope you enjoy your trip wherever you're headed." He moved off toward the steep concrete steps of the café in his Stetson and hightop sneakers.

"Thanks!" Felix said to himself. Then suddenly desperate, he called after the man. "Hey!" The man stopped, turned back facing Felix. "How do I get to the main highway?" Felix asked.

"Just follow this road straight down. It'll take you right into Lexington and Heppner." Then he turned up the stairs to the café.

Felix felt even more desperate from losing his one contact.

"Hey!" he yelled again. Again the man turned. "You know where I might find work?"

The man came back down the steps of the café and treaded back to Felix in his hightop sneakers, rising on the balls of his feet with each step. "So you lookin' for work?"

"You bet." Felix said.

"Now that's a different story," the man said. "Puts a different light on things. You should have said that right off. I guess I must have seemed unfriendly. But folks here get uneasy with strangers idlin' around not doin' anythin' durin' the day. Specially so many of those kinds that's been passin' through lately."

"Sure," Felix said. "I understand."

"So you lookin' for work? Ever cut before?"

"Just finished working for Stolz," Felix gambled.

"Is that right? You worked for John? Well, let me think." He studied the ground. Felix waited for him to ask why in the middle of the day during harvest he no longer worked for Stolz. "Maybe we can help you at that," the man said raising his head. "You got change for the phone?"

Felix dug in his pocket for a coin and offered it. The man turned from Felix to use the phone booth next to the steps of the café. He dialed, greeted by first name the person who had answered as if he knew the person well, asked if Lloyd was still looking for help, then shoved the receiver at Felix who found himself talking to a woman who asked him the question that Felix thought he now could answer with more honesty, risking the same answer he had offered the stout man who waited. Felix hung up the receiver and turned to the man in Stetson and sneakers.

"I'll start in a couple of days," Felix told the man, beaming. "They'll pick me up here." He offered the man his hand. "Thanks!"

"Glad to help someone who's served our country," the man said, accepting Felix's hand. He studied the ground again then raised his head. "You probably need a place to stay until you begin cuttin'," he said., "Two blocks straight down. Can't miss it. Big white fancy place. Lots of frills. You'll see. Nice place. Don't cost much per night for a room. You'll like it."

Felix thanked the man again, overwhelmed by this new unexpected gift and watched as the man turned in his hightop sneakers, settling his Stetson, talking to himself.

"Like to help the boys who done somethin' for us here," he said more to himself than the world. Then the man went up the steps into the café.

July 3, 1958

"I know it has been a while since last I wrote. I must confess that I was again feeling lazy and not at all like writing, but until this time I have been rather busy.

A number of things have taken place that has shown me new ways of life and new experiences that have had a definite affect on me. I hope I have the ambition to bring you up to date on my experiences. I rather hope I don't become restless in my tale as I usually do and quit again. I have little excuse now for now I have plenty of time to write. Perhaps it is time I start.

My last entry was cut off suddenly by my getting a ride—quite unexpectedly—by a family from Oregon. I better outline more precisely at a later time for now I must bring you up to date and to the time I was at the service station in Goshen, California.

After leaving the children and their father I was soon able to catch a ride in a 57 or 58 plymouth station wagon. This ride took me six miles on the other side of Bakersfield. The driver was a film editor who worked on short features but had done some work on Mike Todd's Around the World in Eighty Days. The man was very talkative and a very fast driver and we quickly arrived in Bakersfield. He stopped at a liquor store and let me out—as I said before—six miles out of the city.

It was getting to be late afternoon and I was anxious for another ride that would take me a longer distance than the previous ride. I had to wait almost 2 hours in the hot sun with no shade anywhere and soon I became depressed, tired, hot, thirsty and a number of other ways that made me feel all together miserable. At around 6:15 a late model Studebaker stopped and I climbed in thanking the man for I had felt ready to collapse from the heat and lack of water and I recalled my having sunstroke when I was 8 or 9 from standing hours in the sun waiting for the Jackson Park pool to open.

The driver was a young man in his late 20's or early thirties his destination was Tulare about 55 miles distant. During my time with him we exchanged tales of our travels. He told of his travels through Kansas, Nebraska, and Oklahoma and I told him of my own similar trip the previous year. He had an accent that I placed to be from one of those states. He also told me of the passing away of his wife from double pneumonia and how they had planned to be free of debt in August (perhaps he had given a ride to a stranger to whom he could tell his story and help him deal with his sense of loss), but his wife's death had taken its toll. He informed me of the convention he was going to and how he would be taking his state exam for his minister license (Of course, I had never in my life knew that you needed a license to be a minister. Wasn't God supposed to take care of that?) Before I left him he gave me his card and told me that if I was ever in Lancaster, Calif. I should look him up and if I was ever hungry he would feed me. I guess he was trying to live by his faith and be a good Christian.

We were in Tulare at 7:00. I waited along the highway but no cars seemed to want to stop, I knew that daylight wouldn't be with me too much longer and from past experience I knew how difficult it was to receive a ride at night.

How lonely one begins to feel when out along the highway at sunset. The cars rush by and the people in their moving mass of steel stare out in wonder and defense at the lone figure out in the middle of the vast expanse of nowhere. I wondered about these people. Where they might be going, what lives they led. What kind of living they had left and what kind of life they would lead when they reached their destination. The cars passing by weren't as bad as the trucks with their thundering load, the head long flight along the hard ribbon of road. Their passing created an endless blast of wind and dust that made me close my eyes and stagger under the force.

Growing hungry and thirsty, I walked back a 1/2 mile to a little eat stand where I had a hamburger and large orange drink. I was tired and overheated from the labor of having to carry my bag this distance and the coldness of the drink made me gasp..

After lighting a cigarette I was once again under way. At 8:00 an Oldsmobile stopped. This ride took me as far as Goshen. The driver was a man in his forties. He began pumping me with questions about school and my destination and I learned that he was working for his doctorate at the College of the Pacific and wanted to start a private practice as a psychologist after his schooling. By the time we reached Goshen it was nearly dark. I walked to the station bought a coke and started up the road toward the place where there was a light. This place was chosen so that the cars could see me. I waited for an hour and 20 minutes, smoked a number of cigarettes and became very thirty. I walked back to the station to have another coke. Then I sat down to bring you up to date. I shall have to continue at a later date. I feel very restless again. I don't know what is wrong with me. My desire to write burns hot within me and yet when I sit to put down my thoughts I become restless. Perhaps it is the conditions that I am now subjected to. I'll explain later. Don't fear that I will forget and not being able to tell you, for I could never forget—especially not an experience as being fired. Until then.

Later in the day

I begin again hoping that I will not weary as easily. For about the third time I have come back to my room in Ione, Oregon. Being restless I took a walk through the town. It is an interesting town from the standpoint of the people and the lack of activity. How apart from the rest of the world these people seem. Set in the middle of the wheat land many miles from another town, these people go from day to day in a quiet, lazy atmosphere. I would soon go mad with nothing to do but talk of farming and harvesting and auto repair and things that are important to them, but for me I find it hard to become part of all this. My restlessness would soon drive me out of my mind.

I wonder who is better off; as I have said before, they seem unaffected, but what of their worries and fears and other things that go into making up a person's life.

Are they better off for having found what they want and are content to remain as they are or is it that they know nothing else. Could there be some who wish to break away from this life. (I think this could be a plot for a story) There are so many things—when I think of it that could dislodge the tranquility, a severe storm that would ruin the wheat crop. A fire. Fugitives from the law taking over the town as a sanctuary from their pursuers. Oh, so many things.

Ione is a town of about 200 permanent residents. This number increases when harvest hands come through looking for work, but they do not stay very long if no jobs are available. The town itself consists of a main street with service stations. Chevron, Texaco, Shell (a surprising number for such a small town), the Victoria Café where I find myself spending most of my time and from where I have recently returned. Two grocery stores one of which is owned by a bent over man old before his time with many wrinkles etching his weather and time molded face. He can be seen constantly wandering out to the street in front of his establishment and then back to the cool dimness of his large sparsely stocked store. All this movement is done with snail-like speed while his shoulders sag, his legs spread and bowed slightly, his green trousers sagging from his thin waist.

Ione also has one post office, one tavern, one insurance office, and a few other battered and run down buildings that are in use but with a great deal of disorder. Farther on down the road a small park, a small church, and still farther out the grain elevator, but I would have to be stretching it a bit if I want to include these as part of the town. Oh, yes, I forgot to mention the Railway Express office and the chemical store across the way from the cafe. On the whole the town is no more than two blocks in length. Set back from the main street are the homes of the inhabitants. Some are old and in a state of collapse and in badly need of repair, others quite new and seemingly out of place among the rest. Last of all, is the large victorian type house immaculately white surrounded by a neatly trimmed lawn and a gray iron fence with a gate of the same material crowned by a wood trellis covered with dying roses. This is where I have my room. I have failed to tell you how I came to take a room but I shall again leave this when my courage is strong enough to recall that sordid event. I guess I am really a coward at heart (most likely because of my father's attitude toward failure). The real reason is that I wish to describe my room at this time for various thoughts about its furnishings came to my mind.

The room contains a very high and ancient bed, rather hard with about as much spring as a hardwood board. That bed has a reading lamp attached to the iron wire head board. Next to the bed is an old wood table covered with a white cloth. On this rests an ash tray advertising some firm in a small Iowa town (how it came to be in this room puzzles me) against the wall opposite the bed is an old desk, this too covered by a white cloth. Next to the desk is a waste basket then a window an old knawed up looking chair then the door. This presents another puzzle for there is a slide bolt on the inside but no lock without, almost as if the lock was not to keep people out but rather to keep people in. Next to the door is a sign written in ink by a very neat hand upon a piece of index card. I read as follows:

1. Checking out time
is 11:00 am—
Otherwise be charged for
another day.
2. Please pay when
accepting the room.

All this held up by a thumb tack and hanging on a wall covered with wallpaper having a pattern of some undistinguishable flowers against a pale blue background. Next to the sign is a large closet and then a dresser with a mirror then a window and we are back to the bed. I forgot to mention the thermometer above the table next to the bed. It probably hangs there to tell a person how warm he should feel and how much he should complain about the heat (as of yet I have little to say about the weather).

It seems that I have also failed to tell of the calendar above the desk and the drapes that hang before the windows. No surprise the calendar is out-of-date (as most rooms I have slept in haven't had an up to date calendar) this one with a picture of the Ione High School football team with all its members looking youthful and smiling with a few looking more as if they wanted to fracture the lens of the camera with their manly stare.

The drapes are like all the others I have seen, faded and worn looking with a huge flower pattern that fails to blend with the wallpaper. I again failed to mention that there are two throw rugs, one rectangular in shape and the other an oval. With this I believe I have covered all and now it remains for me to explain my taking this room, but I must see about the job I supposedly start tomorrow so once again I shall have to put it off. Sorry to keep you waiting so long, but maybe the waiting will make it better and I shall be more objective concerning the whole matter. See you soon."

The two days Felix spent in town were endless and dull. At first somewhat curious about the large rooming house where he stayed, Felix, almost to the point of exhaustion, observed the large, gray enameled porch reaching to the door with oval window of beveled glass; the cavernous hallway and dark stained floors with carpeting of rose design on the stairs that led to his room; the large room itself of faded blue wallpaper with indistinguishable flowers; a double bed with iron frame; a dark spindle-legged table with an embroidered linen cover; an out-of-date calendar on the wall with a picture of the local high school football team; a white enameled closet door he never opened. The whole house seemed mysterious and haunted, filled with hushed noises from beings he never saw, presences he was aware of only through sounds and traces: the quiet movements on the creaking, carpeted stairway; the quiet noises in the common bathroom: a sudden flushing; beads of water on tiled shower wall, in the large, claw-foot tub and ceramic sink; a radio blaring suddenly then squelched followed by a brief curse; a quietly closing door, then footsteps descending; the latch of the front door, then silence.

He sat within the room listening until the quiet stirring sounds made him restless compelling him to flee down the carpeted stairs with rose design to the oval window of the white door to the gray porch with knobby, lathed pillars, down the gray steps to the walk, the picket fence with white trellis, climbing rose vine, the graveled walk and asphalt road. He roamed the two-block main thoroughfare of the town both ways, east toward mountains passing the implement store with an array of colors and machinery, the small park with empty wood tables and benches beneath tall oak where a few houses began and the road angled sharply over railroad tracks leading to the towering concrete tubes of grain elevator and beyond toward distant

Lexington and Heppner. Then back again through Main Street exploring the other side: the general store almost barren with mostly empty shelves tended by a thin, bent man with silver hair, wire-rimmed spectacles, and green, sagging pants. He passed the service station, grease stained, smelling of oil and gasoline; the green, wide-windowed Victoria café, the tavern with dark wood siding closed during the day; he passed another service station, this one with a single antique pump on a graveled drive; a concrete block garage, the last building in town before the road disappeared around a curve, ascending into low hills.

Back again to the Victoria café, he climbed the steps, went through the screened door into the high ceiling room to the counter, the stool, the coffee and cigarette, the idle chat with the old woman with gray hair and sunken mouth who waited on him, chatted with him, wondering about him, where he was from, what he was doing here. He revealed enough to keep her talking.

"Worked for Stolz, did you? Good man!"

Felix nodding being agreeable, what point in revealing his own assessment? He told her he was going back to work for the Morgans.

"Oh sure," she remarked. "You'll like those folks—nice people—sweet children—fair wages, too, from what I hear."

She left him then. He sat nursing his coffee listening to her chatting with the other men, one of them the man with the Stetson and sneakers who greeted Felix as someone he knew well:

"How you doin', friend? You'll be workin' soon!" Then he turned back to the other men who, like Felix, were waiting out their days. Felix had nothing else to do but wait.

Sometimes he sat on the concrete steps of the café or on the bench beside the phone booth watching the intermittent traffic from the comings and goings of ranch wives, the quick stops of harvest truck drivers hurrying into the café for cigarettes then coming back out ripping off the red cellophane strip as they hauled themselves back up into the truck. He sat watching the stirring leaves of tall oak trees next to the closed tavern across the road, the slow passing boxcars beyond the tavern where the railroad nudged the edge of town running along the base of low hills with steep sides.

Late afternoons he roamed the dusty graveled side streets past old houses bordered by white fences to the large field and the high school with cyclone fence around the pool where he went to watch those using the pool during the heat of the day, the boys not yet adult in their obvious adolescent manner courting girls the same age self-conscious in bathing suits exposing pale thighs and legs, the girls and boys along the side of the pool, the older folks watching from outside the fence who now and then inspected Felix, an obvious stranger, getting used to him. When he grew tired of watching them watching him watching them, he turned, crept back to his room where he tried to read while avoiding the calendar with high school football team reminding him of his own lost days, reminding him of the cool scent of pool water and the dry hot night beneath the dark wheat-covered hills rising from the narrow valley above the school. He avoided the thought of young women in bathing suits he had witnessed at the pool.

July 1958: while Felix Fist was in Oregon failing at one job and waiting for another, Eisenhower established NASA reviving Felix's interest in the possibility of a future exploration of space Felix had fantasized during his reading science fiction when he wasn't reading material that stimulated his prurient interests readily available from his father's cache of *Playboy* or Jack Woodford novels or Mickey Spillane crime novels Felix with some feeling of shyness and a sense of committing an illicit act had purchased with his scarce resources during lunch break while attending high school in Prairieville. Reading those potboilers of either sex or crime or both with garish covers, Felix tried concealing them within a textbook in Study Hall, but they too often were confiscated by the gray-haired man assigned to monitor the large room filled with quivering, hormone-driven adolescents. That large man with bloodshot, baggy eyes from whom Felix would endure a class in physics returned to a desk raised on stage for better surveillance, set his big butt and middle-aged spread behind the desk, and proceeded to read with interest the prurient material he had confiscated from Felix who silently mourned his loss of limited resources and prurient reading, one more reason he never liked that study hall with its windows covered by wire screens overlooking the asphalt PE playground where he felt caged observing pubescent girls in gym clothes. He preferred the large, airy, brighter room with tall unscreened windows that overlooked Grand Avenue with its vault of green-leaf ancient oak and the whump of car tires over redbrick roadways, their steady beat prompting him to day dream prurient fantasy of finding himself up close and personal with one of the blossoming lovelies he eyed immediately surrounding him while he pretended to study. No surprise that he had never done well in Geometry proving Euclid's theorems.

The two days in Ione finally passed. The morning he would start his new job he woke early, rose, packed, quietly descended the carpeted stairs with rose design relieved he was descending the last time, and went out the white door with oval, beveled window, closing it quietly behind him, went down the gray enameled steps to the walkway beneath the arbor with wilted roses and out the gate. He walked to the café where he would wait for a ride to his new job, he hoping this was his last morning of waiting as he reached the main street with buildings still dark except for the lighted café.

The morning was already heavy with heat even before the blue gray color of the dawn mingled in the trees when he came out of the early morning darkness, up the stairs, into the warm yellow light of the cafe'. Rich fragrances of frying eggs, strong coffee, sweet sizzling bacon met him as he swung his bag before him through the screen door that banged closed behind him shutting out the frantic insects foraging. A lone bare bulb hung from the ceiling by a long cord shedding its yellow light that faded into shadows at the rear. Thick blue smoke billowed through the light. Bacon spattered on the grill; hotcakes bubbled and browned; eggs turned white with crisp brown edges. Old men in bibbed overalls, plaid shirts, and scuffed leather high-tops sat hunched on stools at the counter talking in soft tones while the heavy woman moved down behind the counter along the line of men dispensing refills.

Felix straddled a stool at the end of the counter near the door and set his green duffle beside him on the floor. The woman having come to recognize him from the two days he had spent in this small, wheat-country town brought him coffee while smiling a weak, sleepy, early-morning smile. She took his order, turned, and moved back down behind the counter to the grill where she tended the orders that sizzled in bacon grease. He relaxed with the warmth and comfort of the coffee listening to the hushed voices, the scrape of dishes until she returned, set the steaming plate of food before him, stood back, wiping her hands on her stained apron before taking up the money he had placed on the counter, just enough of what was left.

She nodded toward the bag. "So you 'bout to go back cuttin.'"

He chewed his food, then swallowed before he could answer with a bit of pride, "Going to work for the Morgans."

"Oh, yes, so you said. Good people."

Then she turned up along the counter to pour coffee. Her remark seemed addressed to the others as well who became silent, sipped at their cups, chewed their food, nodding their head in agreement. Felix finished his plate and sipped his coffee while he waited. He added a last cigarette.

Then someone called. "Here's your ride!" the man in Stetson and sneakers exclaimed.

Felix turned toward the large window to see the dusty brown town and country wagon pull up before the café. He gulped his coffee, slipped from the stool, turned to those who had banked to watch him leave.

"Thanks," Felix called and waved. Then he grabbed his bag, went out the screen door, down the concrete steps to the dusty brown car. He bent to peer in the open window at the heavy set woman in the driver's seat.

"You Felix Fist?" she asked.

"Yes," he answered.

"Come along, Felix," she invited.

He turned for his duffle, heaved it with his leg toward the car and the rear door that he opened, heaved in the bag, slammed the door, opened the front door, and dipped into the front seat beside the woman.

"I'm Diana Morgan," she said. "We spoke the other day. You ready to help cut wheat, Felix?"

"Yes, Ma'm!" he said and meant it.

He looked ahead as they pulled away from the café aware of being watched from behind the broad window by the cragged face of the man in Stetson and sneakers. The green leaves and lawns of the town became the yellow hills that rolled away in waves to mountains. He watched the road that cut between the hills. He watched the shadows of the clouds that moved across yellow fields. As far as he could see the wheat lay golden and ripe in the early morning light. He had never seen anything quite like this before, and he marveled at the richness and the softness of the earth mellowed by the endless fields of golden grain. Then they turned off the glowing asphalt onto the white gravel road that led up a canyon between small rugged hills following the dry bed of a stream. Along the way, dusty cows grazed in the heat on the short grass and shrubs of the hills. He turned back to watch the road that cut between the hills along the dry arroyo.

"Have you been cuttin' long?" the woman asked.

"This is my first summer here," he said, hedging his reply.

"Oh," she said. "But you have worked harvest before."

The car slowed as if responding to her hesitation.

"Sure," he said. "Just finished helping John Stolz.

"Oh, yes! So you said the other day on the phone!"

The engine roared as they regained speed.

They drove for a time in silence. He felt uneasy. He should say something to keep her talking. He felt awkward knowing he would be living with her, working with others who would be strangers, living with her almost as family. Yet he didn't know exactly what he wanted to say, not wanting to reveal anything more about himself than needed, but she seemed satisfied enough to remain silent the rest of the way to the ranch except for one brief comment she made, "We're almost home," as they turned off a red dirt road onto a long cindered lane that lead to a weathered, two-story, balloon-frame farm house set on a level among low, yellow hills.

They passed a young woman with hair down to her lower back, her hair the color of the horse she rode without a saddle, her bare, tanned legs in cut-offs pale against the dark color of the broad back beneath. She waved as they passed, and the woman returned the young woman's greeting.

"That's Ginnie," she said. "She's the oldest. Two more young ones, a boy and a girl, around somewhere. They'll most likely pester you to exhaustion even though I've told them not to bother hands while we're cuttin'."

She stopped the car beside the house. He climbed out and set his bag on the grayish red dust of the yard. She stood on the other side looking at him, shielding her eyes from the bright morning sun.

"It might be a while before Jeff comes in with a load. How about somethin' cold to drink before I show you where you'll bunk?"

"Something cold would be great," he said and followed her through the gate of the white fence that separated a green lawn from the thick reddish dust of the yard. Two border collies came to greet them, their snouts scanning his shoes and legs. He set his bag beside the concrete stairs before he followed her up into the house. The collies inspected the unknown green bag.

The house was still and cool. An air-conditioner hummed from somewhere in the house. The porch on which he stood was dim from the shades that kept out the sun shimmering off the bright, hot hills. He waited in the doorway as she went into the kitchen.

"Make yourself at home!" she called.

He heard the sound of cupboard doors, the sound of the refrigerator door opening, then closing. He heard the sound of ice clinking into a glass and the sound of the glass being filled. He sat himself at the large, round oak table on the porch as she came in, handed him a glass, went around to the other chair with her glass, and sat.

"You'll be livin' with us for a while," she said.

They drank, and he suddenly knew how thirty he had become. He nearly drained his glass then set it on the table. She fanned herself with her blouse.

"It's hot!" she said. "And still early. Better take in lots of liquid. Those trucks get nasty with the sun bakin' them on the open fields!"

"Does it always get this hot?"

"Always," she said, "'least in summer." Then she noticed his empty glass. "Here, let me get you more."

She rose, went into the kitchen, came back with a pitcher, stood beside him, refilled his glass then hers, went back to the kitchen, came back and reseated herself across from him. He drank more slowly now, his thirst quenched. They sat in silence. He heard the hum of the air-conditioner, the far away clatter of machines.

Then she gazed beyond him through the screen door behind him across the yellow hills to the mountains. "Are you from these parts?" she asked, looking at him again.

He shook his head. "Midwest," he said. "California more recent."

"Of course," she said. "So many of you are from there." She drank from her glass. "I've been to California, northern part mostly. We don't get around too much. We stay pretty close to home."

"You like farming then?"

She searched his face as if he had asked a compromising question. "We think of ourselves as ranchers," she corrected, smiling pleasantly. "But you know, I've never even considered whether I like the way I've lived my life. I can't remember doin' anythin' else. When I was just a girl I use to come out with Daddy once in a while and ride with him on the thrasher when he worked the fields. When I was old enough about Ginnie's age I hired out as a cook's help. Now I've got my own place to keep."

"You must enjoy it, then, or you wouldn't have stayed."

"There is somethin' about this life and where we live. These yellow fields and hills, especially when the wheat's ripe and not yet cut. And the clouds. How I love to watch the clouds. They come across the river from the mountains. And this is my home, my land, my people. I've never thought whether I like ranch life. I'll just probably stay here just as my parents did and their parents did and their parents before them, she said wistfully. "And now my family keeps me busy here at home."

He watched her as she talked. She seemed to be talking more to herself than to him. Then he heard the roar of a truck and her eyes went to the screen door. She rose from the chair and moved around the table to take up the glasses.

"Here's Jeff," she called back as she disappeared through the kitchen doorway. Then she returned. "I guess I better show you where you'll bunk. You can store your bag and settle your things later. Jeff will probably want to show you what you'll be doin'."

He followed her out of the house into the hot sunlight, down the concrete steps, grabbed his duffle, and followed her around the side of the house to narrow concrete steps that led down to the cellar beneath the house. The room cool and dim beneath the bare joists of the floor above, a bare mattress against the wall on a low, wood platform against the concrete block wall, an empty fruit crate rested beside the bed. Diagonal from the bed, a washer and dryer beside raw wood stairs that led up to the kitchen. Beside the stairway against the wall opposite the bed, a toilet and a shower with a drain in the concrete floor and a circular metal rod with a plastic curtain.

"It's not much," she said. "But you won't spend much time here with the long hours you'll be workin'. I'll leave some clean sheets and a pillow case for you to make up your bed." Then she led him back up the concrete cellar stairs and through the gate of the fence before the house into the thick dust of the yard.

A tall, young man with trim muscular build came around the front of the truck backed against an incline leading up into the barn. He stood at the front of the truck watching them come across the yard. Felix wasn't sure, but he thought he recognized the man from the photograph of the high school football team on the out-of-date calendar in the room he had languished in for two days waiting to begin the work he now anticipated.

"This here's Felix," the woman said to the man. "He'll be takin' your place.

Jeff offered his hand. "You ready to help cut wheat?"

Felix met the young man's strong grip and his steady inspection. "Ready as I'll ever be." Felix said with some truth but mostly conviction.

"I'll leave you two get to what needs doin'," Mrs. Morgan said then turned back toward the house and the two men turned toward their task.

As he had guessed, Felix learned that Jeff was from a local family and that he was leaving because he had promised to work for another rancher. Jeff had been helping out until Lloyd Morgan could find a replacement, and because Felix had been hired, today would be Jeff's last day.

"Lloyd was glad when Riley called about someone in town lookin' for work," Jeff said.

"Riley? He the guy with the Stetson and hightop sneaker shoes?"

"That's Riley. He's the local busy body."

"Well, he helped me. And I'm grateful."

"Sure. But best we get goin'. Lloyd's probably waitin' with a hopper load of grain wonderin' where we got to."

With all that Jeff showed him, Felix wasn't sure he'd remember everything, and recalling his lack of success from his previous job, he felt a bit anxious as he watched Jeff climb into the cab, start the truck, put it in gear, and back up the incline into the barn over heavy wood grating in the concrete floor. Jeff yanked on the handbrake, climbed out, went around to the back of the truck, grabbed a heavy block of wood cut at an angle from along side the barn wall and shoved it under the dual wheels on the left side. "That's just to make sure the weight of this beast doesn't cut loose. But you got to remember to remove it before you drive down the ramp. You forget, the truck will tip and the dump with take off the barn door!"

Jeff went to the cab, climbed in, revved the engine, and pulled on a lever beside the seat. Felix watched the dump rear, the full load of grain begin to slide.

"Release the gate!" Jeff shouted against the noise of the truck engine and the sliding grain.

Felix pulled on the latch of the dump allowing the weight of the grain to push open the steel flap of the dump. Felix watched the shower of yellow kernels stream through the grating. Jeff revved the engine again, the dump rising higher until the stream became a trickle. Then Jeff released the lever and the dump lowered and banged to rest on the heavy steel frame. Jeff slid from the cab and climbed a wood ladder nailed on the barn wall, reached a gray control box where he jammed a red button. Felix heard a motor whirl to life. Jeff came down from the ladder and stood over the wood grating. The two men watched the grain swirled by a large screw suck down into a concrete pit.

"Let it run until most of the grain is gone!" Jeff shouted over the noise of the motor and the whirling screw. "Then go back up to stop the motor! You can do that now to get you goin'!"

Jeff went to remove the chock from the wheels while Felix climbed hand over hand up the ladder to the control box and jabbed the red button. He peered through the small open window at the heap of grain and the slow trickle of kernels from the spout. Then he climbed back down and went to the truck that Jeff had let roll down off the incline, the steel gate banging to rest. Felix climbed up into the cab.

"So you about set?" Jeff asked, gazing through the windshield at the yellow hills.

"You bet!" Felix said.

"O.K. Let's go cut wheat!" Jeff looked at Felix and grinned. He put the truck in gear, spun the wheel, stomped on the gas. The engine roared as he turned the hood toward the low hills and the black earth trail that led up into the flowing fields of ripe, golden grain.

Throughout July 1958, Felix helped harvest wheat and barley for a ranch family who hired him after he lost his first job, he apparently never returning to his log to record that shameful experience he wanted to but was unable to forget. Amy and Hank having gone east to Wisconsin, Bud having gone back to Long Beach to join Marilyn, Hank's sister, Felix eventually having learned his job became close to the family, especially the children. After a long day of harvesting beneath the hot sun on vast, open fields, Felix spent evenings passing on to the young boy and younger girl who grew fond of him and he of them what he had learned of the cosmos in his Intro to Astronomy class, his up close and personal connection with the older daughter compelling him to leave with reluctance when he hitchhiked back to the Midwest along US 30, getting most of his rides with truckers who logged him in as a relief driver, thus allowing the trucker to drive longer hours than those limited by DOC regulations.

He would be leaving soon; the harvest was nearly over. As he came down from the fields with the last load of the day, he saw the wasted fields, the farms already harvested. He saw the stubble, the earth scarred from truck wheels and the iron cleats of the tractor that pulled the thrasher. As he drove, he thought of his first fresh days of harvest. He thought about his inexperience, about his errors: how he had let the wheat spill. Cursed by the stern man with the wire-rimmed glasses, made the butt-end of jokes by the others, then let go, he had found this job where he had redeemed his previous faults but committed others by driving too close to the hopper spout of the thrasher and damaging the spout. Yet having been forgiven, taken in, finally accepted almost as if he were part of the family, now, each day of harvest was one day fewer.

Tired and dirty from bouncing all day on the dusty, cracked vinyl seat of the 10-speed dump truck, he hung his arms over the steering wheel and watched the rocks and cows and dry stream in the arroyo that followed the road down to the highway. The road was gravel, and as he drove, the truck tires raised clouds of dust that billowed back along the way. The arroyo wound down through small, rugged hills that were rocky, and stones lay white and bare along the dry stream bed. Along the way, dusty cows grazed on the short grass of the hills. The dust billowed and churned, and the brittle wheat grass along the way swayed in the rush of air from the passing truck.

The sun now low in a cloudless sky, the heat having begun to fade, as the sun sunk lower, he relaxed his squint and enjoyed the cooler light. The last load of wheat golden in the sunset shifted with a quiet hiss in the back of the truck.

At the towering concrete tubes of grain elevator rising from surrounding fields of yellow grain beside the railroad spur outside the town, he drove onto the large wood scale, waited for the sign from the man behind the window, then pulled on the lever beside his seat and gunned the engine raising the dump that poured the shower of grain onto the large grating of the pit and the whirling screw that sucked up the grain into the massive concrete tube. Seeing the man sign again, he lowered the dump, drove off the scale, stopped, climbed from the truck, walked back to get his ticket, helped himself to cold water, then climbed back in the truck and left.

Going back, the trip was even slower. The truck labored up the road that followed the arroyo, and he had to keep shifting to a lower gear when the truck lost speed. Then he sat beating his hands softly on the wheel while the truck roared against the pull of the incline. So as he slowly climbed, he watched the white gravel of the road, the churning clouds of dust that rose behind him, and as he climbed, he thought about the first time he drove down to the elevator and climbed from the cab immediately after the dump unloaded and he was yelled at to get back in so the weight of the truck with him in it would be the same as when he arrived with a full load of grain.

Felix thought about his setting off for where he found himself now on this dusty, cracked seat of the slowly moving ten-speed truck. He thought of the dingy room with pale green walls from which he had wandered nightly in twilight beneath neon signs and street lamps at the edge of the ghetto passing dim-lit taverns. On occasion he had sat in an empty cafe drinking coffee, listening to the low, mournful music from a radio, watching the quiet, unhurried movements of the enormous black man who had accepted his being there.

He thought of the bright morning sun waking him, filling his spirit, compelling him to rise, take his bag, leave his key, descend for the last time the worn wood stairs to the cracked concrete walk beside bare dirt patches and start up the empty, freshly washed street appearing vast from the absence of traffic until suddenly someone stopped, and he was on his way.

On his trip north, several rides took him to a small town set on a bluff above the Columbia and the dated restaurant of plastic counter tops and chromium fixtures he had sat in until the grill of their car loomed before the window. Having found him, Hank and Amy and Bud took him up carrying him into the backcountry of ranches, depositing him along with green duffle beside a faded red barn where he had spent the night alone in darkness heavy with heat waiting for his first harvest. He had changed jobs. Hank and Amy having finished theirs had gone to Wisconsin, they stopping to say good-bye. He again had watched them go, the old Buick disappearing before a cloud of dust.

Bud remained. Felix didn't feel close to Bud who was Hank's friend long before Felix arrived in Long Beach. Felix had met Bud once at night in town after Hank and Amy left, and Bud seemed to have warmed to him once they shared their ambitions. Felix confessing wanting to write and develop his art, Bud showing his large, perfect teeth, grinning at Felix from behind plastic-rimmed eyeglasses beneath a blond buzz cut had reminded Felix in his West Virginia accent that he was already an artist and worked harvests to raise funds allowing him leisure the rest of the year to do his real work. Bud would be leaving soon. Felix would meet him again that night before Bud went south to rejoin Marilyn, Hank's sister, at her bungalow in Naples, Long Beach. Felix again would find himself alone.

Felix reached the fork in the road and turned the truck up the last hill. Then the road leveled onto red dirt and the truck began to gather speed. Ahead of him the land lay yellow and flat stretching for miles then rising and falling over foothills. The sun was behind him low in the sky, and the shadows moved across the yellow land deepening the land to a gold that would become purple before it became dark. To the side of the road a small graveyard lay among wheat fields disturbed by the ground of a fresh grave. Some other flattened graves had cut flowers at their markers, bright orange and yellow and red against the deepening sky. The headboard markers cracked and gray and faded from the years of rain and sun had crumbled with decay that worked at the graves. Tall wheat grass covered the graves and hid them from the open sky. A weathered fence surrounded the graveyard. Near the road a few pickets were gone leaving wide holes between the gray boards. On the other side where the graveyard met the vast field, a whole section of fence leaned to the ground.

He saw all this as he passed; and as he passed, he wondered how the fence had fallen and why no one had fixed it. Then he turned back to the road that disappeared into the darkening hills. He slowed, eased the truck in at the cindered drive, and barreled for the yard. He rounded a curve and passed the young woman riding the bareback horse, her cut-offs tight against the broad brown back, her tanned, trim legs along the broad sides. She waved as he passed. He smiled and waved admiring what he saw but sped on caught up in the thought of the night ahead in town.

When he reached the yard, he backed the truck in between the fuel storage tank and the weathered barn, shut down the engine, leaving the key in the ignition. Then he scrambled from the cab slamming the door. He hurried through the gray red dust into the neat green yard around the house.

The dogs barked and jumped on him. He reached down to pat them as he brushed them off. He went down the concrete stairs into the cellar.

He shaved standing naked before the mirror. He watched the path of the razor that cleaned his face as he shaved. Then he rinsed the razor beneath the faucet of the metal wash sink, placed the razor on the shelf under the mirror on the cellar wall, and turned to adjust the shower. He stepped beneath the spray and pulled closed the plastic curtain. The spray felt hard and soothing after the hot day beneath the sun in the dusty cab of the truck. He relaxed enjoying the shower that drenched his body and washed away the sweat and dirt of the fields. He soaped himself, dunked his head under the spray, and rinsed his mouth. He turned the shower cold. He shuddered, slapping his body against the shock of the icy stream. He shut off the water, looked at his feet watching the water running between them down the drain.

He thought about the graveyard and the yellow wheat grass and the fresh brown earth of the new grave. He thought of the night ahead in town, about Hank and Amy who had left, about Bud who would be leaving soon. He thought about the young woman on horseback. He watched the quiet stir of the sack between his thighs.

He heard the basement door open above him. He heard the sound of a light step descending.

"Felix?"

He knew her from her voice that seemed too rich and deep for someone so small. He heard her quickly close the door behind her and start down the stairs, then stop, her hand on the raw wood rail, hesitant.

"You goin' into town tonight?"

Not waiting for an answer, she came down to the cement floor of the basement. She surveyed the neatly made bed against the cellar wall, the orderly arrangement of his things in the apple crate.

"If I can get your Pa's pickup."

He grew chilled and shivered from the coolness of the drops of water on his body he wiped down with his hands. He stood behind the curtain aware that he was standing naked with only the thin plastic between them and he felt his flesh begin to fill.

"Could you take me in with you?"

She stood on the stairs running the rubber soles of her canvas shoes over the edge of the raw wood step.

"Sure, I guess I can, if your parents don't mind. Be kind of late. "Wouldn't your Pa mind your staying out late?"

"Not if you bring me home. Daddy wouldn't mind me goin' in with you, even if it were late."

"Have you asked?"

"Not yet. I will right now."

"O.K., I'll see you at supper."

He reached for the towel hanging over the side of the shower. He scrubbed his hair.

She rose and turned to climb the stairs. Then she stopped and leaned against the hard edge of the raw rail. She watched the curtain move and listened to the sound of him drying his body. She listened to his humming, caught up in his own thoughts, unaware of her still there listening to him, watching his movements behind the vinyl curtain. His flesh tingled from the shower and the brisk rubdown from the dry towel. He felt refreshed and relaxed, and he thought again about the night ahead in town. He thought about the taste cold beer would have in his parched throat. He shot back the curtain and stepped out of the shower.

She looked at him, looked at his face, and her face flushed pink. He wrapped himself in the towel.

"Shouldn't you be upstairs?" he asked, studying her.

She looked down at the stairs.

"Your mother doesn't like you down here when I'm here. I've heard her say so."

She kept here eyes down, turned, and hurried up the stairs.

He watched her supple bottom in tight cut-offs disappear behind the closing door. He felt his flesh stir, begin to fill, and he thought of how long since he had been with a woman. He stroked his tumescent flesh then turned to dress.

When he climbed the stairs to the kitchen, the fresh jeans and t-shirt warm and soft on his clean body, he quietly closed the door behind him and stood with his back to the door as Diana passed in front of him with a steaming pot.

"Hungry, Felix?" Short with a round, smiling face and dark hair and eyes, she looked up at him.

"Yes, Ma'm," Felix answered.

He towered above her, young, virile, his hair leached from the sun. He watched her from the door as she poured the steaming water from the pot into the sink using the lid to hold back the contents. He thought of the daughter, her small, trim body, and he knew he'd never want to see her when she was as old as her mother.

"You goin' to stand there all evenin'?" Diana teased.

"Ma'm?"

"Go sit, Felix, we're ready to eat!"

He stepped away from the door and walked through the kitchen onto the sun porch framed by screened windows open to the lingering light. He chose the seat he always used, the one he had sat in when he first arrived, and he settled at the round oak table fingering the napkin and silverware. He felt uneasy, self-conscious sitting there alone, not related to them, no matter how much he liked them or how much they seemed to like him, no matter how kind they had been taking him in after his being fired from his previous job.

Then the two younger children came in, Josh, the boy reflecting his father's thin, sharp, raw features still softened by youth; Gerry, the small girl with corn-silt hair and bird-like bones. Josh threw himself in place, wriggled into position, and reached for the muffins in the basket covered by a blue-checkered cloth until his mother called a warning from the kitchen, and the boy quickly retracted, sat contrite, and fidgeted, while The younger girl settled into place.

"Play with me tonight!" Gerry demanded, confronting Felix.

"Can't, Pumpkin," he offered. "I'm going into town."

"You said!"

"I didn't say tonight, did I?"

"You promised!"

"Tomorrow for sure."

He reached for her to touch her, comfort her, maintain the bond they had formed over the previous weeks, but she drew back pouting, deliberately avoiding his eyes, punishing him, ignoring him, hoping to wound him, to make him relent.

Then Lloyd came in through the kitchen, red-faced and lean, with a section of pale skin above the ears where the skin had been protected from the sun. Lloyd wrung the last moisture from his hands and took his place at the table, his back to the wall of windows.

"Went pretty good today," Lloyd said. He picked up the glass of iced water. He drank while looking at the younger man.

"It did," Felix said, feeling more at ease now that he could move as the others were gathering around the table. He took up his napkin and spread it over his legs.

"Hope the weather lasts," Lloyd said. He took a muffin and passed the basket to Felix who took a muffin and reached for the butter. Lloyd offered the basket to the boy who lunged for a muffin.

"It certainly was hot today," Felix said watching the boy tear into the muffin. "Those truck cabs really get scorched. While waiting to take off another load, I had to sit on top the cab to get any breeze."

Lloyd cocked his head as if he understood and went on chewing in silence.

Diana came in with a bowl of potatoes and went back into the kitchen. Ginnie came in with a dish of green beans and set them before her father. She took a seat across from Felix. She kept her eyes lowered. Felix looked at her then looked beyond her through the window to the plum tree and the tethered horse grazing on a patch of grass beneath.

"I understand you're talkin' about goin' into town tonight," Lloyd said, breaking the heavy silence. "You'll most likely want the pickup."

Felix nodded. "Yes, thank you, if you don't mind. I was going to ask."

The little girl sulked.

"Keys are in it. Make sure you've got fuel before you go. Don't want you runnin' out middle of the night."

"I'll be sure it has enough gas."

"How you fixed for cash? You need any? You can't have much with all your travelin' and your time in town before you hired on here."

"Some would help."

"We'll settle up when we figure your wages at the end."

"Thank you." Felix glanced at Ginnie and considered saying something about her asking to ride in with him, but he remained silent.

"My daughter said somethin' about goin' in with you. Says she wants to visit with friends for a bit. You mind if she rides along?"

"Not at all. She asked me when I was coming in from the truck."

He looked into the man's fierce blue eyes and lied. Out of the corner of his eye he saw Ginnie raise her head to look at him. Then she quickly looked at her father.

"I told her it was fine with me if I could get the pickup," Felix said, telling the truth.

"Wouldn't be any trouble for you? Lloyd asked. "I don't like her or the younger ones pesterin' you. You work hard all day. I appreciate that. You're a good man."

Felix started to thank the man, but the man continued

"So I don't like havin' her or the other two botherin' you when you're tired from a long day."

"No trouble," Felix said. "I'm grateful for using the pickup. As long as I'm going in, she can easily ride along."

He sat back as the older woman placed the roast and took her seat at the table between Felix and her two daughters. They passed the food in silence.

"How much work you think we have left?" Felix asked.

"Don't really know," Lloyd answered. "Maybe another week or two if the weather holds, more if the fields not yet cut don't ripen as they should. Could be the end of the month."

Thinking of what the man had said, Felix watched the deepening shadows on the low surrounding hills.

"What you goin' to do when we're through?" the man asked.

"Sir?" Felix asked. He turned from looking at the hills, the man's bright, fierce eyes searching his face.

"What you goin' to do when we're through cuttin'?"

"I've been thinking of going home."

"Oh?"

"I haven't been there in almost a year. So I've been thinking of going. But I don't know if I will. Not much there, I guess."

"You're kind of young to be away from home. Don't see why you'd want to leave."

"Well, there was school for nearly a year and I wanted to come up here to such beautiful country. Personal reasons mostly make me want to stay away."

"That so?" the man said, looking off toward the hills. "I guess I must be gettin' old. Can't get use to these changes. When I was young, I worked everyone else's fields around here. Never went very far, not like you young people today. Fact is, I sometimes pass the house where I first saw the light of day. Shame about that old house, though. Nothin' much left of it. Sits alone among the fields in the sun and wind and rain. Always wanted to buy it. Fix it up."

"I might just keep going and try more harvesting," Felix said. "I hear in town that the wheat's ripening across the river. Should be lots of work over there if the wheat's ripe once we're done here."

"Yep. Almost think of it myself sometimes. Maybe we ought to get up a team. Go over there and show them what real cuttin's like."

Felix studied the lean weathered brown face of the man across the table. He liked the man. He almost wished the man really meant what he said about going together across the river into the fields beyond. "Never work, though," the man went on. "Wife here wants to take off after we're through. Vacation time, then. And I've about had enough cuttin' for one season."

Felix nodded. "I would think so," he said, and looked at Diana whose smile filled her round face. Then they went on eating.

When he came out of the house, the night felt mild after the hot day. He came down from the porch, moved away from the warm yellow light of the sun porch, and walked into the darkness. He looked up into the night and the deep sky overhead filled with stars. Then he reached the truck parked by the fence that closed in the yard around the house, climbed into the cab, and started the engine. He pulled the truck up to the gate and sat in the cab with the motor idling. He watched insects fly in the beam of headlights.

When she came out of the house and hurried down the stairs to the truck, he leaned across the seat to open the door. He looked at her face in the dash light, but she avoided his eyes. He sat straight and quickly used a cloth from beneath the seat to wipe off the dust that had settled on the seat. She softly thanked him, climbed into the cab, and slammed the door. He put the truck in gear and they started down the long, cindered driveway. He turned the truck onto the red dirt road picking up speed toward the white gravel road that led down to the asphalt highway that would take them into town.

They sat silent on the way into town and watched the lights of the truck on the road ahead. She looked at his tanned face and sun-leached hair in the dim light of the dash then quickly looked away at the road that raced beneath the cone of light from the headlamps and back beneath the wheels. He glanced at her long, brown hair hanging free around her shoulders. Her face seemed pale against the slight rouge of her lips. A white blouse tucked in her pale-green summer skirt spread upon the seat, she sat with her hands upon her lap. As they passed the cemetery now shrouded in night, she watched the sweeping light upon the grass beside the road then looked out across the dark fields to the distant lights along the river.

They saw the town through the trees from the highway as they turned from the white gravel road onto asphalt, bounced across railroad tracks, then passed the small park overgrown with grass and thick with towering trees. The buildings of the town were dark, including the café he had been in so often, but the red neon light of the tavern shone out across the dark road. Across the street from the tavern, the service station nightlight gleamed dully. Farther up the street, one or two lights shone out from dark houses. Beyond the glowing sign in the hardware store, the road led off into the night, up into dark hills.

He angled the truck in front of the tavern and set the hand brake, and shut down the engine. "How long you think you'll be?" he asked.

"Not long," she said, clearing her throat. "Mom said she wanted me home early."

As she spoke, he noticed again her voice soft and quiet. He finally admitted now that he always liked to hear her speak, the sound of her voice so rich and deep.

O.K.," he said. "I won't be long. I'll just step in here to talk for a while with a friend, have a couple of beers, if that's all right. Come around when you're ready to go."

"I will," she said. "Thanks for bringin' me in."

"Sure," Felix said. "My pleasure."

She climbed from the truck, straightened her white blouse and fluffed her light green skirt. Then she walked away up the side street. He sat looking after her until she disappeared into the darkness underneath the heavy leaves of summer trees. Then he slid from the truck and went up the bare weathered steps into the tavern.

He came in from the dark and stood inside the door waiting for his eyes to adjust to the light while he searched the room. Bud was seated on a stool near the door talking to a tall, slender man who stood leaning forward with his thin arms on the bar. The man's face was thin and drawn and etched with wrinkles. A straw Stetson rested on the back of the man's head with thinning hair.

Behind the bar, John, the huge bartender, tall and weighing at least three hundred pounds, stood before two men seated at the far end of the bar. Even in the heavy heat, John wore an open flannel shirt exposing gray hair above the sweat-stained t-shirt. The sleeves of the flannel shirt were rolled showing thick, hairy arms. The flannel shirt hung loose over a huge belly.

A large mirror covered the entire wall behind the bar reflecting the men at the bar and the circle of men at the card game beneath a hanging, shaded lamp in the dark corner of the room. The men at the game in the corner were silent in the heat. One player, a straw hat pushed back upon his balding head, wiped his neck with a bandana. Another player had a large wet circle where the sweat had soaked through on the back of his gray shirt. One man stood with legs spread, arms crossed, watching from outside the bright circle of light on the men at the table. Large billows of smoke curled up through the lamp to churn in the darkness among bare rafters.

Felix walked to the bar. The tall man with wrinkled face stopped talking and looked up as Felix put his hand on Bud's shoulder. Bud spun on his stool.

"You're late," Bud said in his soft, West Virginia accent. "This here's a friend of mine," Bud explained to the man beside him.

The man nodded to Felix, offering his hand. "It's a pleasure. Jody's the name."

"How you doing? Felix asked as he took the man's hand.

"Jody's workin' with me up at the Morrison's."

Felix nodded.

"How come you two ain't cuttin' together?" Jody asked.

"Couldn't hire on together," Bud said.

"He started up here before me," Felix added. Then he stepped to the bar and looked up toward the end where John stood talking to the two men. "I can certainly use a beer! How about you two? You ready for another?"

"Sure. Why not?" Jody answered. "Make sure I don't get away without buyin' you one back."

The two men drained their glasses and emptied their bottles into the glasses and placed the bottles in the trough at the inner edge of the bar.

Felix called to John.

The huge man turned and saw the empty bottles. He moved away from the end of the bar swaying on his massive legs. His huge belly carried him forward as he moved. He took up the empty bottles, set new bottles in their place along with a bottle and glass for Felix, took up the bill Felix had placed on the bar, turned, rang up the amount, turned back, laid the change, then went back up along behind the bar. Felix let the change lie in the wetness from the cold sweat of the beer. The men filled their glasses.

Jody raised his glass toward Felix. "Here's lookin' at you!"

Felix nodded lifting his glass before he drank. The beer was cold and bitter and stinging against the dryness of his throat. He set the glass on the bar, wiped his lips on the back of his hand, and looked at the reflection of the men playing cards underneath the lamp on the other side of the large raftered room.

"Been cutting long?" Felix asked.

"Pretty long," Jody said. "Sometimes, I think, maybe I've been cuttin' too long. Can't recall when I first started."

In the mirrored wall behind the bar Felix saw Ginnie come suddenly into the tavern to escape the unwelcomed attention of adolescent boys who annoyed her. The loose green skirt settled as she stood for a moment inside the door. She tucked in the white blouse. Felix watched her in the mirror as she looked around the room at the dark wooden walls, the large men red from sun, raw from wheat chaff. She studied the card players in the billowing smoke beneath the green, shaded lamp.

"You ever think of giving it up" Felix asked. He leaned on the bar allowing him to watch Ginnie as she walked to the counter at the end of the bar and looked down at the items in the glass case. Then another girl came into the tavern, glanced at the men along the bar, at the card players underneath the lamp, said something to Ginnie, then turned and left. Felix saw the faces of adolescent males who peered in briefly from the door.

Felix turned and waved to John.

Jody took another drink of beer. "Sometimes," Jody nodded in answer. "Sure, sometimes, lots of times, I've thought about givin' up cuttin'. Never seem to do it, though."

"You usually work the whole season?" Felix asked.

"Plenty times. Best years I had those that I worked the whole year."

John stopped before them to take Felix's order while Jody talked. Felix watched as John tipped his bulk to reach down into a cold storage chest beneath the bar, tipped back up, removed the cap with an opener, then moved in his slow massive fashion to place the wet bottle of orange drink on the glass counter.

Ginnie reached to take it up. She stared at the man's heavy jowls, his flushed face, the sweat beaded on his forehead. Then she watched as he turned and moved past Felix, pausing to pick up with two fat fingers one of the coins Felix had left on the bar, moved to the cash register to ring up the sale, then moved down to the end of the bar to his station before the two men who had watched him in his slow ponderous mission there and back. Ginny held the bottle to her lips as she looked at Felix leaning on the bar. He raised his glass saluting her. Jody and Bud turned to see why Felix had raised his glass then turned back.

"Now isn't that a tight little piece." Jody said.

Felix felt himself flare at the man's remark then held himself in check as the man continued his narrative.

"Yep," Jody said. "Must of started — let's see — must of been pretty near the end of May when I started down in Texas. Followed the cuttin' clear up into Canada—Alberta, Saskatchewan — gorgeous country. Near the end of October before we quit."

"That's a long time cuttin'," Bud said.

"Sure is," Jody said. "But I sure made a load of money that year. Took all that money — must have more than five thousand dollars — course that be a lot more now, probably double — even triple."

Bud shook his head grinning in disbelief.

"Yes, sir," Jody insisted. "Near six thousand dollars, maybe more. Took it and went to all kinds of places — New York City, Chicago. I got myself a little place for a while. Got myself a little something to keep it for a while just about like that one who just come in. Pretty nice at the end of that season." He paused so long the pause seemed almost as if he was reliving that year again. "I ended up in Texas, just about in time to sign up on another crew."

"Must have been tough, though," Felix said. He glanced at Ginnie who remained standing at the counter sipping her drink watching the men at the bar and in the room. Jody searched Felix's face then turned to look at Ginnie at the counter.

"Pretty little thing," Jody said. "Friend of yours?"

"Daughter of the rancher I work for."

"Sure is cute. Wouldn't mind tryiin' some of that."

"A tad too young," Bud said.

"I suppose," Jody said. "But she sure looks ripe. You know, that's always the hard part of this kinda work. Always movin'. Never havin' a woman. The rest of it though is mostly just work. So it weren't tough — least not always. Most the time bed and grub furnished. Mostly clear money. Same as now. Clear money for when cuttin's over. Then you can get yourself somethin' like that," he said, nodding toward Ginnie at the counter. "Sure would be nice, so sweet and tender, ripe for pluckin'."

Felix again squelched the flare of jealous anger he felt at the man's comment and watched with the others as Ginnie set the empty bottle on the counter, turned and moved toward the door until she saw them in the mirror watching her, she studying Felix before her friend came in again and pulled at her as she turned and followed her friend out into the darkness. Felix watched the fading image of her white blouse, loose green skirt. He heard the yell of an adolescent male, a shrill answering scream.

"That the only year you done it that long?" Bud asked.

"Yep," Jody answered. "My woman didn't like it. Said I was gone too long. Course she never knew about the tight little extra fluff I had before I went home. Now I just come cuttin' to get away."

"It's hard to stop," Bud agreed.

"It sure is," Jody said. "Summer comes — just seems a man's gotta go cuttin'. Gettin' tougher, though. New machines comin' in. Don't need so many truck or tractor drivers now. Only combine men."

The man lifted his hat and ran his fingers through his thinning hair, scratching his scalp. Then he set the hat back on his head. They drank in silence in the thick heat and smoke of the tavern. They sat looking at the displays behind the bar. Then the man finished his beer and squared his hat on his head.

"Well, I have to be goin'. I need my sleep. Long day tomorrow. How about my buyin' you one before I leave?"

"Thanks," Felix said. "Maybe next time."

"All right, then. You remind me."

"I will," Felix said, knowing how unlikely his meeting the man again.

"Nice talkin' to you," the man said to Felix. "I'll see you back at the ranch," the man said to Bud.

Felix took the man's offered hand. Then the man turned and sauntered out into the dark. Felix filled in the space the man left at the bar. Bud called to John, finished his beer, and set the empty bottle at the edge of the bar. John came in his own good time and took the empty bottles while putting full ones in their place. He went back up behind the bar and labored onto his stool. In the mirror, Felix saw Ginnie appear in the doorway. He saw the light on her back, the swirl of the green skirt as she disappeared into the heavy darkness pursued by adolescent males.

Ginnie sat waiting in the truck watching the rustle of the dark leaves of the tall oak beside the tavern. She watched him as he came out and stood talking to his friend, saw him shake the man's hand, saw his friend walk to another truck parked beneath the tree, climb in, drive away with a short hit of the horn. She watched as he came around the front of the truck.

Feeling light-headed and flushed from the beer and the heat and the smoke of the bar, Felix pulled himself into the cab, slammed the door, started the engine. He sat for a while, letting the engine idle while looking vacantly out over the hood of the truck until the tavern lights went dark along with the glowing beer sign. Felix backed the truck out onto the roadway, resting his arm on the back of the seat behind her shoulders so that he could guide himself by turning his head to look out the rear window. His arm so close to her, he studied her in the light of the dash as he straightened the truck onto the road. He breathed in her warm fragrance and studied her profile, her long, loose hair. Then he pointed the truck toward the road that led up among the dark fields.

"Tired?" he asked, breaking the silence, turning the truck up the white gravel road that ran beside the dry arroyo.

"No," she said softly in her rich voice. "I'm not tired."

"Probably keeping you out too late."

"It's not late," she said. "John always closes early on weekdays durin' harvest."

"Oh," he said. "Well, I'd like to stop for a bit, if it's all right with you."

She looked at him, his face in dash light, his eyes meeting hers until she quickly looked away.

"The graveyard," he explained. "I've passed it for over a month always wanting to stop but couldn't. Maybe it's too late.

"It's not late," she said quietly, watching him.

He said nothing more on the way up the arroyo road. He thought of Bud moving away from him into the dark hills on the other side of town. He thought of the Stolz ranch near the one the other man, Jody, was driving toward, of the barn that he had slept in, the ranch house, the young wife in loose flannel shirt with nothing beneath and the recent dream of seeing her fully exposed in bright moonlight as she stood at the doorway of the barn where he had slept and he suddenly joining with her upon the ripe, warm earth of harvested grain fields. He thought of waking from that dream with his flesh firm and his lying awake in the dark cellar thinking of Ginnie asleep in the house above and how he had stroked himself to release. He felt his flesh stir, begin to fill, and almost missed the burial ground. Without the moon to help him, he could not see the darkened fence or the dark headboards of overgrown graves, but he caught a glimpse of orange flowers in the headlights as he passed. He brought the truck to a stop in a spray of gravel and dirt and backed the truck off to the side of the road among the tall, dry, wheat grass and shut down the engine.

"Ever been in a graveyard at night?" he asked. "Maybe you might want to wait here."

She pulled up on the door handle, swung open the cab door, and before he could come around the truck to help her, she stepped down into the shallow ditch at the side of the road.

They stood together in darkness, she waiting for him to show her what to do next. Then the noise of the engine died in their heads and the silence that followed was heavy and dark. Tall weeds along the side of the road rustled in a light, warm wind. Far away along the river, a train moved through the night, a small, fast line of lights and a thin horn lost among the dark bluffs along the river. Far away along the river the lights of a town flickered in the light wind among tall, full trees. He moved away from the truck into the graveyard. She followed.

He went through the wheat grass dusty from trucks, darkened by the night. He moved through the graveyard, past the fresh mound, to the fence on the other side where the graveyard met the yellow fields that stretched across the land to rolling hills beneath the starry night.

When her eyes grew accustomed to the dark, she watched him from where she stood at the mound of the fresh grave as he turned from the fence at the other side of the graveyard where the fence leaned to the ground. He knelt at a grave. He stayed that way, almost as if praying, kneeling among the orange flowers in among the long yellow grass. He searched the headboard, running his fingers over the carved letters. Then he rose and came to her.

She watched him move toward her through the tall grass. She watched as he reached her, stood looking down at her as he knelt before her burying his face in the soft loose folds of her light green skirt, his hands behind her thighs gently holding her. She placed her hands on his head and waited in the stillness of the cooling night, looking toward the grain fields, gazing at flickering lights along the river. From far away, she heard the lone, long howl of a dog.

Going home, she sat with her hands together in her lap watching the tall grass along side the road in the headlights. Then she gazed through the dark across wheat fields that spread to rolling foothills and beyond to mountains snow-capped even in summer hidden in night. They reached the yard. He pulled the truck along the fence and shut off the lights, gunning the motor once before he turned it off. They sat in the darkness until the silence crept in to stir them from their thoughts. They sat in silence listening to the quiet, nervous movements of the dogs resettling until he reached for the handle of the door and the sound of the screaking door seemed loud as it opened. The truck door squawked again as he closed it, pushing against the handle with the heel of his hand until the latch caught.

He stood in the darkness waiting for her to come around the truck. He watched her with his eyes now used to the dark as she tried to move by him keeping her head down looking at the ground. But he reached for her before she could flee, and he held her gently by the arm until she raised her face to look at his pale image in the dark and he bent to seek her soft lips.

They stood together in the night with the bright river of stars above. Then they parted, turning from each other, he waiting while she went up the concrete stairs into the sun porch, softly closing the door behind her. He stood looking at the dark house, the dull sheen of the windows. Then he turned toward the dark concrete stairs that led him to his cellar bed.

She undressed in the quiet of the dark house. Then she lay in bed listening to the far away howl of the dog, and the far away answer, and the long lonely horn of a train from along the dark river. She thought of the graveyard, of the soft earth of the fresh grave, of the dry crackling grass, of the brilliant spread of stars above her in the deep night. She thought of how she had felt joined with him. She thought of the touch of his lips on hers. She thought of him as he, in his sound sleep, turned toward the cool dawn, the long day among yellow fields and the dust and sweat and heat of the stifling cab, the glowing sunset at the end of another long day when he would descend the arroyo road with yellow dust clouds billowing, the last load of wheat shifting with a soft hiss, quiet and golden behind him.

They waited for the uncut wheat to ripen, and it seemed as if the whole world waited with them. Each day the machines, their rattle and clang and jarring vibrations, the shouts through churning dust and wheat chaff above the roar of the machines, all were silent. Now a heavy stillness crept over yellow stubble left by whirling, swishing blades. Each day the heat remained, oppressive, dry, heavy. Each day a slight breeze barely stirred leaves of thin trees along the creek, sunbaked grass, ripening wheat, stiff stubble in fields already harvested but gave no relief.

At lunch each day they quaffed iced water to quench their thirst and cool their bodies. The air-conditioner droned endlessly on the highest setting billowing curtains. Fields outside the shaded windows of the sun porch shimmered beneath the glaring sun. The hot food they ate more from habit than from interest lay heavy in their bellies.

One afternoon of waiting, Felix searched the ranch alone looking for relief from the heat. First he tried sketching beneath a tree within the small orchard behind the gray, slat-board house set among the low hills of yellow fields. He sat with his head against rough bark gazing at the ripened plums bobbing above his head in the slight breeze. He heard the hard, lonely clang of the nearby windmill plunging into the wet darkness, reaching for deep water.

Their first day of waiting, their energy still vital, they repaired the windmill pulling up the long rods hand over hand, the rods slippery with scum, hard to handle. Felix recalled the quick commands not to let the wet rods slip as they pulled them up and out of the dark well. He heard again more quick commands as they lowered the plunger back down into the dark, deep hollow of the earth. Now the sound of the windmill slowly churned by the breeze, the quiet bobbing of the ripening plums above his head made him restless.

He rose and walked through the ranch yard toward the barn. The sun was brutal, the sky cloudless, endlessly blue. The ground was powdery, the gray, reddish dust lifting in rolling billows covering his shoes with a fine layer as he walked. Settled just inside the wide open door of the barn, he found that the shade of the barn gave him even less relief than the orchard tree. But too tired from the sapping heat, he sat with his head against the hard weathered wood, his eyes lowered to a slit to keep out the glare.

A cat slinked by, stopped at his pursed bidding, stared with fierce yellow eyes, a weaving long gray tail held high, then went on its way.

In the fallow behind the hill, a tractor bellowed and clanged sending up columns of dust toward the clear sky. He listened to the constant staccato of the diesel. A faint whiff of acrid diesel fumes carried to him on the slight breeze. As the tractor came over the ridge of the hill, he watched the harrow dragging behind, its steel, spiraling blades churning the dry soil. He watched the rattling clang of tractor cleats jerking in an endless steel chain moving the machine and harrow and noise over the crest of the hill until all that remained were clouds of gray, reddish dust rising silently toward the clear, blue sky.

The whole world settled back to stillness. The dry heat pressed down upon yellow fields. He sat with his head against the side of the weathered barn, his legs bent, his arms across his knees, his hands dangling limp. He sat waiting, resting, letting the heat soak into his body, letting the heat fill him as it moved slowly down to stir his limp flesh. He studied the yellow fields in stubble. He studied the black scars of earth showing through where the tractor cleats had slipped on the yellow stubble, dug in, bit deeply beneath the powdery surface, and finally held.

He saw the land rolling in round sensual hills, firm and dazzling beneath the hot sun. The still afternoon air lulled him; the clear sky, the heat made him numb. From behind the barn where it blocked his view, a horse and rider slowly moved out into the field and began an unhurried ascent of the hill. Behind the horse, the dog walked as slowly, its tongue long with heat, its tail limp.

The young woman with brown hair that hung long and loose upon her back rode without a saddle. Her slim bare legs wide, her buttocks in brief cut-off jeans splayed across the broad brown back, her young body tight against the strong firm body of the gelding. She seemed relaxed yet held herself straight, her small, unhaltered breasts concealed beneath a loose thin blouse. Her trim body swayed with the slow rhythm of the large animal beneath her. Her long hair, the light blouse stirred in the breeze.

He watched them as they made their way to the top of the hill through wheat stubble crackling where they walked. He watched unseen, unnoticed.

He sat within the heat of the barn, beneath the clear sky, waiting for the ripening wheat.

Finally he rose and slowly followed through the dust and stubble toward where the horse and rider and lagging dog had disappeared beyond the sundrenched hill.

He came down from the fields carrying the last load of grain in the dump of the truck. The truck tires dug into the dirt leaving deep ruts in the dark earth among the yellow stubble. A few days ago, he had seen the long stalks of wheat sway in the clear early morning air. Thrilled by the sight at daybreak, he had gazed at the long ripple of grain as the morning breeze moved across the fields softly sweeping the stalks in a long, slow wave that carried to the rolling foothills glowing pink and golden in clear morning sunlight.

Reaching the reddish dust of the yard, then the white gravel of the ramp that led up into the barn, the dual-wheel truck tires splayed gravel as he backed the truck up the ramp over the wood grating. He took the truck out of gear letting the engine idle, strained against the steel bar of the handbrake, scrambled out of the cab, and set the wood chock under the rear wheels. He hurried across the grating and started up the ladder to the top of the barn. He punched the large red button on the gray control box with his thumb and peered through the small window into the storage bin at the enormous pile of grain, the long conveyor belt reaching into the darkness of the bin, the grains remaining from the previous load beginning to spill onto the top of the pile. He hurried down the ladder to the truck, scrambled into the cab, jammed the dump lever into gear, and eased out the clutch. The dump tipped; he revved the engine; the dump reared. Then he worked the clutch, controlling the angle of the dump and the flow of grain through the grating until the last of the load slid from the dump in a rush.

He shut off the engine, placed the truck in reverse gear, and slid from the cab. He went to the back of the truck, used a shovel to scoop out the last grain from the corner of the dump then watched the last grains spill through the grating. The conveyor motor ground in the silence after the rush of wheat.

He stood rooted, listening to the conveyor, imagining the grain spilling from the conveyor onto the towering heap within the dim barn. Then he remembered the warning, hurried up the ladder to the gray control box and slapped the red button with the heal of his hand. The conveyor motor stopped, and he was through. The harvest for him was over.

He sat on the rafter at the top of the barn gazing at the pile of grain and the last small shower of yellow that trickled from the silent black belt.

One time during the cutting, a young cat — still a kitten had wandered into the barn while he was dumping a load. Shooing it away to protect it from possible danger, frightened, it had bolted, fleeing him and had slipped through the grating, hung there briefly, eyes wide in terror, then dropped even before he could move to save it. He had heard a thud, a sharp, brief cry, and the dull grind of the screw pouring grain onto the belt that carried the grain up into the dark bin. Scrambling up the ladder, he had watched the limp body drop quickly covered by grain that spewed from the belt. Shutting down the conveyor, after a pause during which he thought about the dangers (the darkness of the barn, the thick dust and suffocating weight of grain), he had fought his way over the high pile into the barn, his feet and legs sinking into the pile, the grain sucking at his legs, filling his shoes. Fighting his way to the top of the pile, he had taken up the limp body with the slight head wound, staring eyes, slightly open pink mouth showing teeth. Then he had turned, fought his way out through mounds of grain, thick dust, and chaff. The dead eyes had stared at him filled with frozen terror as he laid it on the dry grass beside the barn.

Felix with worry having revealed the incident, old Lloyd had scolded him, the man's thin face above the bibbed, striped overalls red with anger, the gray eyes fierce.

"What in heaven's name ever gave you the idea to do such a fool thing as to climb around in a bin of piled grain alone? Listen, son, people have been buried in grain bins, and no one found them 'til it was too late!"

Felix had stood looking at the hills, saying nothing. Now he eased himself from the rafter at the top of the barn and went down the ladder to the truck. He released the chock, remembering with a brief rush of shame the time he had forgotten. The truck had tipped, ripping off the barn door. He had worried for days, wondering how to tell Lloyd, remembering how such accidents had led to his losing the first job he had found when he had first arrived. Finally, somewhat to Felix's relief, Lloyd had discovered the accident himself.

"How'd this happen?" Lloyd had asked.

Felix explained.

"You should have told me sooner," was all Lloyd had said.

Then in an interlude while they waited for another section of grain to ripen, together they had repaired the door.

Felix released the handbrake. The truck rolled down the gravel of the ramp onto the powdery dust of the yard as he switched on the ignition, put the truck in gear, and popped the clutch. The engine caught. The steel dump banged down on the frame. The tailgate flapped and banged. He eased his foot from the clutch, revved the engine, shifted into low, and went up through the yard where he backed the truck in between the large, round fuel storage tank and a tool shed, set the brake, turned off the ignition, leaving the key. He slid from the cab, slammed the door, and went up through the dust to the house.

The sun beat down upon the hills and the yellow fields of stubble. He went in through the gate of the fence that bordered the house with green lawn set out among the brown hills and fields of yellow stubble. The dogs came at him barking, wagging their tails, their whole large bodies shaking from their greeting. He reached down to pat them as they jumped. He shook them off and started for the steps that led down to the cellar. Diana Morgan came to the sun porch door as he passed. He stopped when he saw her.

"Hello, Diana!"

"Through cuttin', Felix?"

"Yes," he said. "I guess it's finished. Lloyd's stripping down the thresher. He should be in soon."

"Fine," she said. She looked at him squinting up at her with the hot, midday sun in his face. Several weeks before she had picked him up in front of the cafe in town, he sitting in the café at the counter waiting, the large, green duffle on the floor beside him when Riley in Stetson and hightop sneakers had yelled to him that his ride was there. He had hurried out to the car. How relieved he had seemed when she leaned over the seat to peer out the open window.

"Felix?" she had asked as he grabbed his bag, then paused.

"Yes?"

"Come, Felix," she had said.

Then they had come out to the ranch, and he had lived in the cellar, sleeping, showering, climbing the stairs into the kitchen, always standing polite and self-conscious until she had shooed him out onto the sun porch where he had sat at the round, oak table always in the same place surrounded by windows that looked out at the brown hills and yellow fields he had worked every day until the sun burned red and low in the sky.

She looked down at him now as he stood squinting up at her. He was trim and healthy looking, his hair the color of young wheat.

"How about somethin' cold to drink?" she asked.

"It has been hot," he answered. "Something cold would be welcome."

"Come on in," she invited, knowing he wouldn't follow unless she asked.

"Thank you," he said.

He climbed the stairs by two's, then stood inside the door waiting while she went into the kitchen for the drinks. He looked out the back windows to the orchard where he had picked fruit for her during one lull while they waited for a section of wheat to ripen. He looked beyond the orchard to the windmill turning slowly in the still air. The windmill creaked each time the long rod reached through the derrick, plunging into the dark earth. One day during the first lull, he and Lloyd had hooked up the rod after the blades had turned useless for years. Josh, Lloyd's young son, had come along but gotten in the way. Lloyd had cursed, surprising them, banishing the boy to the nearest hill where he had sat and watched while the two men struggled to link the rod to the blades.

Diana Morgan came back carrying a large pitcher with ice cubes tinkling off the glass pitcher sweating in the heat. "Why don't you just sit, Felix?" she ordered.

He took the seat he used at meals. She set the glass before him, then reached around him to fill the glass, hovering, hunched over him, almost touching him. He thanked her as she poured herself a glass and sat down across from him. He quaffed the drink shocked by the sudden cold liquid. She refilled the glass and he drank slowly then set the half-empty glass on the table.

"Where's Josh?" he asked.

"Went to town with the girls."

She sipped her drink, then lowered the glass and held it between her two hands on the table.

"I think it's been real nice the way you've taken an interest in them," she said. "Especially Josh. He's been so happy since you've been here. He's never acted like this in other years. He gets so excited from the way you tell him things."

"I've enjoyed sharing with him. He's a neat kid," Felix said, embarrassed.

"No, no!" the woman insisted. "Lloyd's said somethin' too. We've tried to make the boy leave you be. You've been working hard. Lloyd's mentioned it. Said you're one of the best he's had. Workin' hard all day, a man needs his rest. We've tried to keep him away so you could relax in the evenings the short while before bed. But that boy! Soon as we weren't lookin', he'd be at you, followin' you around, askin' so many questions you always took time to answer."

Felix nodded, self-conscious, moved by the woman's words about a man needing his rest. He recalled the nights he had sat with the boy on the hood of the truck telling the boy about the starry heavens above that curved out endlessly above them, dark and deep, still and passionless, beautiful, serene, sublime. Sometimes the youngest girl, Gerry, would come, too, insisting on being told about the stars the same way her brother had been told. So he often found himself telling them again. But that hadn't seemed to matter to them. They seemed as interested in hearing what he said the second time as they had the first.

One night they had seen a glowing light suddenly move from below the horizon, fast and steady, unlike anything he remembered, unlike anything they had ever seen, moving against the jade-colored sky high above the rim of the dark hills. They had watched it pass, disappearing into the coming night, and he had felt a thrill along his spine as the glowing object vanished, leaving him alone with the young girl, the young boy in total darkness.

"Gerry's in town?" he asked.

"I'm about to fetch her home with Josh and Ginnie."

He nodded. Hearing the older daughter's name, he thought about the afternoon of waiting he had watched her ride out among the yellow stubble of the fields, how he eventually followed, how he found her cooling herself in the small stream, how he joined her, how her small body felt cool against his under the open sky beneath the dazzling sun. He thought about their night together beneath the stars. The images of both times stirring him.

He looked at the woman across the table studying him and wondered what she would say or do if she could see the images he had conjured of her daughter and him together. He sipped at his sweet sour drink and listened to the creak of the windmill.

"What you goin' to do now?" she asked, breaking the silence. "Now that cuttin's done, I expect you'll be movin' on."

He thought about an answer, but none came to him. He felt suddenly confused. He liked it here. It was comfortable, almost safe, and he felt that he would feel sorry to leave. These people had been kind to him, and he had enjoyed the boy and the youngest girl, even after the long day in the fields in the hot, stuffy cab of the truck. And, of course, he had enjoyed the young woman for whom he felt a growing regard and desire. How he loved to see her move, her young, trim body lightly clad or sheathed in cloth that revealed her soft, blossoming shape.

"I don't really know," he said. "I haven't thought about it a lot. Maybe I'll hire on someplace else and work more harvest."

"Cuttin's about done around these parts. You'll have to move on across the river."

He thought about the high, billowing clouds, the vast, blue sky between, the distant land across the river that stretched far away, undulating and endless, made vast by distance. He thought about the barren hills along the river, the dry river bluffs that he saw as he had stood on the cab of the truck waiting for a breeze that might help to relieve him from the heat. He thought of how one day stirred by the heat and idleness waiting for the thrasher, on impulse he had stripped off his clothes, threw himself onto the soft, yielding pile of ripened wheat in the dump of the truck. Having become at once fully firm, his flesh probing the grain, his seed coming in a sudden rush, when he rose, kernels clung to him, forming a crown. Then he had hurried into his clothes and gone off to find the machines and their human crew watching for his truck while the machines stood idling, the hopper brimming with grain.

Finishing his drink looking at the ice cubes in the bottom of the glass, he set the glass on the table. The glass left a wet ring he wiped away with his hand.

"I've been thinking of going home," he said, finally.

"Oh, yes," she said. "I remember, now. You mentioned that before. Probably be nice for you to do that. Be nice for your mother, I expect."

"Maybe. I'm not sure how much time we've ever had for each other." He shoved back from the table. He rose. "Guess I better get cleaned up," he said. "Thanks for the lemonade, Diana. Thanks, really, for everything."

She looked at him, her eyes suddenly sad. "You're not gone yet," she said. "You sound so final, as if you're ready to go out the door this minute and vanish. As if you're half way across the river by now. Wait until you're ready to leave. Lloyd'll be in soon. We can figure up your pay. Then we can worry about good-byes."

She rose, gathered the empty glasses, the half-empty pitcher. She went into the kitchen, leaving him alone on the porch. She heard the screen door close quietly as he left.

Folding his clothes, stuffing them into the green bag, having kept out clean clothes for after his shower, he took his personal items from the wood crate against the cellar wall of the house surrounded by wheat country and placed them in his bag. He set the bag on the bed and went up the cellar stairs into the warm sun. He went through the gate heading toward the large shed. The dogs came at him slowly sapped by late summer heat, lazily wagging their tails. The dust of the yard covered his shoes as he walked.

He found Lloyd working on the thresher breaking down the cutting head for repair, maintenance, and storage. Lloyd's face was still dusty from working in the fields throughout the morning, white skin protected by goggles circling his eyes, his high forehead starkly pale covered by the battered Fedora hat he had pushed back as he worked.

Lloyd inspected Felix without raising his head, twisting it to the side. "All cleaned up, are you?"

"Yes," Felix answered. "I certainly enjoyed the shower."

"Must be about ready to go."

"Just about. Bag's fully packed."

"Where you headed?"

"Haven't made up my mind," Felix admitted. "I've thought about going home. I haven't been there in a year."

The older man bent to his work. "How you goin'?"

"Hitch rides, most likely. Saves my hard-earned money."

"Well, you have worked to get it, that's for sure."

He finished loosening the bolt, then climbed down to work on the lower bolt that held the cutting head to the thresher.

"But I don't know if I'd hitch rides," Lloyd advised straightening to make his point. "Could be dangerous. I did it once. Last time, too. The fellow that picked me up pulled a gun. Waved it at me. Warned me I better not try anythin' funny. Well, I took the ride, but after that I thought that if I couldn't afford to pay my way I'd just stay home."

Felix remained silent. He thought it strange that this man would ever have been young enough or spirited enough to hitch rides anywhere. He watched as the man bent again to his task, the man's rough, thin hands working the wrench in loosening the bolts. He saw the dark, burnt neck, white where wrinkles had protected the skin from the sun. The man somehow seemed as solid, as serene, as settled as the hills of black dirt and yellow stubble that surrounded the barn and the house with its patch of green lawn. He had seen this man work for hours on the thresher, always looking out over the fields to the river, looking at the vast blue sky with towering clouds that moved above the yellow land. He had seen this man sit for hours on the tractor, plowing, turning under the yellow stubble, exposing the dark, rich earth. He had watched the man walk among a vast field of yellow grain, bending to gather a handful, crushing the kernels in his rough, hardened palms, lowering his head until his tongue touched the kernels testing them for ripeness, then blowing them away while he straightened to look out over the fields of swaying grain that swept away to the horizon.

Lloyd finished unhooking the cutting head. Then he bent to separate it from the thresher. Felix moved to help the man without being asked, and they lowered the cutting head to the ground beside the machine. They stepped back, looked once at the dismembered machine, turned, and started for the house.

"Well, guess that's it" Lloyd said as they walked through the dust of the yard. "Let me get cleaned up. After that, we can settle on what you earned."

"Sure," Felix said quietly. "There's no rush."

They reached the house and went in through the gate where the dogs quietly greeted them with their snouts against their pants legs.

The older man went down into the cellar, and Felix watched the windmill send the long rod reaching into the earth. Then he looked out past the weathered buildings to where the dark tire tracks led up into the yellow hills, and he recalled his first day when Jeff whom he had replaced showed him what to do as they made their first pass of the thresher explaining how Felix should stay close alongside the machine but adjust his speed to spread the spilling grain throughout the dump of the truck. Then they let the thresher move on by and Felix took over for the second pass, Jeff climbing up onto the thresher to take Lloyd's place and Lloyd climbing down, climbing into the truck, offering his hard hand and his friendly greeting then instructing Felix on how to avoid overusing the clutch to control the speed of the truck, and Felix briefly worried that perhaps a report of his inept only day at his former job had followed him.

Recalling his first day there, he recalled his first midday meal with the harvest crew, so unlike his first job when the crew ate out in the field seated on the ground among stubble, their backs propped against the quiet, hot machines. Here, when he climbed the cellar stairs and went around to the house and up the stairs into the cool sun porch that overlooked the low surrounding hills and the reddish gray dust of the yard, the weathered barn that stored the grain not trucked to the concrete tube silos outside town, Felix found the other hands already there seated for their midday meal.

Living in town, they went in each night at the end of the day, returning for breakfast before the next day's cutting began, that meal and their lunch included as part of their daily wage. He took the empty seat at the round table. Then as they passed him plates of food from which they had already served themselves, Felix, the new hand on the crew, quietly greeted the others around the table:

Roy was younger than Felix by a couple of years yet more self-assured, self-important as a newly promoted driver of the tractor that pulled the aging thrasher. A new straw Stetson christened with wheat chaff and dust hung on the back of his chair; new leather gloves were laced through the shoulder loops of his kaki shirt as if he were an officer of rank, Felix eventually accepting the young man's adolescent jibes at Felix's sometimes inept moves when he first started.

Clarence was a sharp contrast to Roy, almost too old, heavy with large belly and gray, thinning hair, a puffy, sagging face dominated by an enormous red nose pocked and painful to look at with broken veins under the skin.

Interested immediately by the man's age, because the man reminded him of others like Riley that he had seen in town, Felix had watched Clarence throughout the long day as Felix pulled the truck along side the machine underneath the hopper spout. Impressed by the man's ability to hold up under the heat and flying dust and long hours on the machine, Felix had watched the old man guiding the whirling thresher blades at just the right level above the ground to catch the grain stalks at the proper height no matter what the changing contour of the land.

Clarence in bibbed coveralls over a t-shirt brown from wheat chaff, dust in his hair powdering his huge nose with broken veins, circles around his blood-shot eyes gave him the appearance of wearing a mask, Clarence had washed before the midday meal, holding his head underneath the outside faucet, spraying water in all directions, coming up dripping. His eyes closed, his hair soaked, his fat hand groping for a towel with thick fingers, finding at last the one Felix offered him, burying his face in the cloth, Clarence came up scrubbed and shining. Reaching inside his coveralls, he pulled out a kerchief from which he shook small clouds of dust. Then he blew his painful looking nose — once, twice — and stuffed the cloth back into his coveralls. Felix had followed as the man slowly climbed the stairs into the sun porch for lunch, the man thick and stiff and bent from too many summers on the thresher, controlling with the strength of his arms and the skill of his years the whirling blades that swept beneath the antique machine just the right height above the golden grain.

Felix had not been surprised that Lloyd had learned of Felix's inexperience from the other hands that came out from town during the day. What had surprised him was Lloyd's acceptance of the report with a shrug after his study of Felix's worried face. "He's doin' all right now."

Woke from his daze when Diana suddenly drove up returning from town with the children, Felix saw the excited faces of the two younger ones through the windows of the car as it came off the cindered driveway into the dust of the yard, sending up billows, stopping next to the white fence that surrounded the house. The younger children were out of the car almost before it stopped, their mother shouting after them as they raced through the gate. The dogs barked and ran jumping. The older daughter hung back to help her mother with the groceries. She avoided Felix's inspection.

Felix went to help carry in the supplies from town. The children followed at his legs.

"Play with me!" the little girl cried.

"Play with *me*!" the boy demanded.

"You said you'd play with *me*!" the little girl cried. "You promised!"

"Let me help take these inside," Felix said, "and I'll play with you both."

The children shouted in glee and ran away around the house chased by the barking dogs.

Felix followed the women into the house with bags of groceries. Then Lloyd came up into the kitchen from the cellar, clean and red from the shower, running his hands over his damp, thin hair, watching as the women unloaded the bags. He went into the sun porch and sat at the table. The older woman followed him with a pitcher and two large glasses and poured the man a cold drink.

"Like some water, Felix?" she asked.

"Thank you," Felix said. He sat down across from the man, leaned back in his chair while the woman placed and filled his glass. He sipped the icy water.

"Well, now," Lloyd said, "guess it's time we better think of settlin' with Felix for all his hard work!"

"Yes, I guess you're right," the woman said. She went into the kitchen and came back with a calendar.

Lloyd took the calendar and began counting off days. Then he settled with pencil and pad to tally. "Looks like we owe you this much," he said. He moved the pad across the table so Felix could see his calculations. "That seem about right?"

Felix looked at the pad, then at the man. "Whatever you decide."

"Don't forget his half-day of pickin' plums," the woman said. "He worked hard that day."

"Well, now," the man said, the tone of his voice joking, "seems like you should pay him out of your pin money." But he added the sum to the bottom of his tally. Then he sat back with his hands before him on the table. "You think that's a fair wage? Lot of money there, son. Make sure it's right."

"Seems more than I've ever had," Felix said looking at the man. "Don't forget the cash you advanced me for the times I went into town."

"You'll never get anywhere that way," Lloyd advised while bending again over the paper, figuring again, the pencil tracing the dark columns.

Felix watched him, then looked out toward the weathered barn and the bright hills.

"Well, here you are," the man said finally. "I think that's fair." He handed Felix a yellow check with black ink.

"Thank you," Felix said. He folded it without looking at the numbers on the check and put it in the pocket of his shirt. "I guess I better think of getting ready."

"Plenty time," the woman said. "How about somethin' to eat? You haven't had anything since breakfast."

"I sure could use somethin'!" Lloyd exclaimed. He seemed in a good mood now that the grain was in storage and the harvest was done for another year. "Seems like I worked up an appetite since this mornin'."

"I'll fix somethin' right away," the woman said. She went into the kitchen and began rattling pans. Lloyd rose from the table and went out and down through the yard.

Felix followed him out of the sun porch. He sat for a while on the concrete steps, then rose and went across the dusty yard to the shed. Lloyd looked up as Felix came in out of the sun, his image blocking the light. Then the man bent back over his work and went on straightening and patching a damaged hopper spout.

"I'm sorry that happened," Felix offered. He recalled the curses roared above the clatter of the machines as the man had leapt to the ground to confront Felix for his driving the dump truck too close to the thresher.

"Forget it. It's past."

Lloyd went to smooth the edges of the patch. Shivering from the shriek that played at his spine, Felix watched the sparks fly from the metal until the man stopped and held the spout against the light, leaning over and turning the spout to inspect the patch.

Felix cleared his throat. "I was wondering if maybe I could get a ride to the highway?"

Lloyd looked up from where he bent over in the light examining the repair. He studied Felix's face, the man's fierce eyes holding him in their gaze.

"Sure. I have to take care of some things in Heppner for next year's planting. My bank's there. Probably be a good time for you to cash the check."

"Yes, good idea," Felix agreed, then fell silent.

The man filed the patch. The air in the shed was hot and close, smelling of grease and dust.

"I've enjoyed it here," Felix said.

"Have you, now?" Lloyd said. He straightened to study the young man's face. "Strange you should enjoy workin' so hard. But I guess there is somethin' good in this life. Glad to hear you enjoyed it. Enjoyed having you." Then he added, "You've been good for the children — good for everyone, it seems. Strange how one body can have such an effect. Haven't seen folks so riled around here in quite some time. Can hardly get anyone to eat—specially the young ones. Can't hardly get them to bed. You've been good with them, playin' with them, talkin' with them, even after a hard day's work. Good for the older girl, too, takin' her around, haven't ever seen her so sociable."

Then the man paused, his bright eyes locking on Felix's who waited wondering what was coming next. "Look. I've sensed somethin' goin' on," Lloyd said, "but I've been too busy with harvest. Seems that the children have been taken with you. Well, if you'd like to stay on for a few days, we'd be glad to have you. I know it'd be all right. The Mrs. would love to have you stay. The children certainly would. Stay as long as you like."

Felix felt the hot, closed air of the shed. He recalled the long Sunday in town after Amy and Hank and Bud had left, the stores closed, the tavern closed. He had roamed the town alone, sick with idleness. He, almost in desperation, had joined two young boys who took an interest in the tall stranger roaming the town closed down on Sunday and had invited him to spend a long, dull afternoon in their shanty beside the railroad tracks, their parents never present, almost as if the boys had been abandoned. What would he do around here on the ranch all day without the long hours of harvesting? Of course, there was his involvement with the children, and he thought again about the older daughter and his joining her at the creek. But what would happen now with Lloyd no longer distracted by the long hours of harvesting? Then, too, something seemed pulling at Felix, drawing him away.

He met the man's study. "One day you said your wife and your children might want to go somewhere once harvesting was done. I think I just better leave," he said quietly.

"Sure," the man said, bending again to his work. "I'll be goin' into Heppner after lunch."

Then the man straightened, set down his tool, left the shed, started across the dusty yard. Felix held back, letting the man go ahead then followed.

The young girl met them as they reached the gate.

"Play with me, Felix!" She pulled at his hand, trying to keep him from entering the house.

Then the boy raced from around the house and he helped the girl try pulling Felix off into the grassy yard.

"He's having lunch!" Lloyd ordered sharply.

"Tell you what," Felix said. "I'll play with you both after we eat. I promise."

The children dropped his hands, then turned and slunk off around the corner of the house followed by the dogs.

Felix followed the man up the stairs into the sun porch.

They ate in silence. Felix avoided looking at Ginnie. Once he met her glance, but she looked away. The children sensed the mood and were unusually quiet. Then the meal finished, the woman rose to clear the table. Ginnie helped, and the children went to play. Lloyd rose and went to get ready for his trip to Heppner. Felix remained, watching Ginnie move around the kitchen, but she ignored his gaze, so he went out to sit on the porch steps. The boy and girl came and danced before him, pleading for him to play. He rose and went down onto the grass of the yard led by the children pulling him by both hands.

"Swing me! Swing me!" the little girl cried, and he swung her until she tumbled laughing onto the grass. Then the boy pleaded to be swung, and Felix swung the boy by the arms and then by the legs until Felix's side ached from the heavier weight of the boy, and he let the boy down as gently as he could on his hands.

Felix collapsed on the grass breathing hard. The boy and girl came to sit by him.

"You're goin' today, Felix?" the boy panted. He seemed proud, as if he knew something important that the girl didn't.

"Yes," Felix said. "This afternoon."

"NO!" the girl screamed. She looked at Felix with large eyes filled with fright. "You can't go!" she cried. "Why do you have to go?"

"Harvest is over, Pumpkin. I can't stay on. I'd just be trouble for everyone."

"No, you won't! Stay, Felix! Please stay! Who's goin' to play with me?"

"We've had a wonderful time together," Felix said quietly. "But I'd just cause trouble if I stay."

"No, you *won't*!" the girl cried then began to weep.

Felix reached for her, surprised by the sudden wave of feeling he hadn't expected. She clung to him, crying. He stroked her fine, blond hair, caressing her, soothing her.

"Tell you what," he said. "I'll be back soon. Then we can play. How's that?"

"You won't *never* be back!" she cried. "I want you to stay *now*!"

"I can't," he insisted quietly.

She broke from his arms and ran up the steps into the sun porch. The boy sat beside him caught up in the silence after the girl left.

"You really comin' back?" the boy asked, glancing at Felix from the corner of his eye.

"If your folks will have me, I'll be back. Maybe next harvest. We'll have fun, just like we've had."

He reached to rub the boy's head, but the boy shied away, rose, and went around the front of the house followed by the dogs, leaving Felix listening to the clang and creak of the windmill.

The small girl suddenly returned coming from the house, rushing down the concrete steps, throwing herself on the grass beside him.

"Promise you'll come back?" She seemed happy now and coy.

He marveled at the swift change in her mood. "Sure," he said. "I promise." He felt more certain now of his going, relieved that she was happy again, that he wouldn't have to carry away with him the burden of her sorrow.

"Will you take a present?"

"A present?"

"Yes. Somethin' from *me*."

"I'd like very much to have something from you."

"Close your eyes. Hold out your hand."

He complied. He felt her place something light in his palm. When he opened his eyes, he saw her scampering around the corner of the house, her light dress catching the air. He looked down into his palm. He held a photo of her that he would carry with him for years.

Felix rose, brushed off his jeans, went down into the cool, dim cellar for his bag.

He stood at the gate waiting, his bag leaning against his leg. Lloyd finally came out of the house into the afternoon sun.

"All ready?" Lloyd asked.

Felix followed the man to the station wagon then lifted his bag onto the back seat. He turned back toward the house.

"I'll be right with you," he said, and the man nodded knowingly, waiting beside the wagon.

Felix went up the concrete stairs and knocked. The woman came, holding open the door, looking down at him standing below her on the steps.

"You *knocked*? she asked, her face showing puzzled surprise. "Why didn't you just come in, Felix?"

She turned and went into the sun porch.

He climbed the stairs and followed her in.

"I just wanted to thank you again," he said.

He offered his hand, and the woman took it, awkward, unused to the handshake.

"God go with you," she said. "Write once in a while."

Then she surprised him by pulling him into her embrace, his response stiff and awkward.

He stepped back toward the safety of the door. "I will," he said. Then he turned toward the stairs, moving down toward the wagon and the man who stood waiting, watching as his older daughter suddenly came from the house.

"Felix!" she cried.

Felix spun from the sound of her voice.

She rushed down the stairs, ran to him, and he gave in. Stooping, he gathered her into his arms as she clung to him, her arms around his neck, sobbing, as he held her, saying nothing, unable to say anything.

He sensed the woman on the stairs behind him watching. He opened his eyes to see the man's fierce eyes watching. Then Ginnie pulled back, kissed him long and hard, and broke from him, twisting from his arms, all this surprising him.

She ran from him sobbing, racing up the concrete steps past her mother into the house.

Felix stood dumb, as if planted there, looking at the grass and the reddish gray dirt between. The woman stood on the porch steps watching him. The man stood at the front of the wagon, watching.

Felix turned through the gate avoiding the man's eyes as the man studied him from the other side of the wagon. Then they climbed in. Lloyd started the engine and put the wagon in gear.

The wagon moved along the cindered driveway leading to the road that would take them down to the highway. Felix looked back. He saw the small girl hugging the rough bark of the tall, lone oak tree that stood on the front lawn of the two-story balloon-frame house set out among the low, harvested hills. Then something caught his eye and he turned and saw the horse grazing in the lengthening shade of the tree, and he knew Ginnie was somewhere near. He looked back until the wagon rounded the curve in the drive, and the tree and the girl and the horse and the house were lost from sight.

When they reached Heppner, the ride blessedly short, Lloyd went into a supply store to ask the price of supplies for next year's planting. Felix went to the all-glass bank, strikingly modern and out of place in a redbrick, nineteenth-century pioneer town. He stood before the low counter while the young woman in stylish summer dress efficiently cashed his check and sold him traveler's checks. Then he turned and pushed through the large glass door of the air-conditioned bank. Returning to the heat and sunlight, he approached Lloyd who stood waiting at the wagon.

"There's a fellow goin' out to the highway," Lloyd told him. "Says he can give you a ride that far if you want."

"Sure," Felix said. He felt slight relief that Lloyd would not take him out to the main road. Resigned to the change and slightly chagrined at his sense of relief, he added. "Thanks again, for everything."

"Sure," the man said.

Then they stood beside the wagon in awkward silent, waiting for the man who would give Felix a ride to the highway.

Soon, a large man dressed in business suit, white shirt and tie, and polished shoes came from the seed store carrying a briefcase. The man climbed into a car and fired the engine.

"That's you ride," Lloyd said.

They walked together to the idling car.

"Here's the fellow I told you needs a ride," Lloyd said to the man, and Felix reached in to shake the man's hand.

"I'm not going far," the man said. "But you can ride along."

"Anything will help that will get me to US 30," Felix said. "I'll just get my bag."

"O.K.," the man said, and he busied himself with papers in his open case.

Felix walked back to Lloyd's wagon and reached in back to haul out the green bag. He offered Lloyd his hand.

"I'd like to come again, if you'll have me." he said. He fought to meet the man's eyes.

"O.K.," Lloyd said, finally taking Felix's offered hand then letting it drop. "Write about the end of May to see how the grain's comin' in."

"I'll do that," Felix said.

"We'll wait to hear from you," Lloyd offered.

They stood looking at each other.

"Well, I better head back," Lloyd said. "Look's like your ride's about ready to go."

Felix waited while Lloyd climbed in and started the wagon. "Good luck," Lloyd said looking at Felix out the open window.

"I'll be back," Felix said.

"Will you now? Well, we'll see," Lloyd answered.

Then he put the wagon in gear, swung the wagon around in the middle of the asphalt highway, and drove off.

Felix watched the wagon grow small. Then he reached for the green bag by his leg on the gravel along side the road. He walked to the waiting car.

"Oh, yes," the man said, looking up. Arranging his papers, he closed his case, then unsprung the handbrake.

Felix climbed in the car after settling his bag in back.

"Well, I guess we're ready," the man said.

"Yes," Felix said. "I guess we are."

The eighteen-wheeler came down from the mountains into a great basin ringed by a barrier of massive, towering rock and a range of jagged earth folded over upon itself in huge, cake-like layers the large truck labored through and left behind descending a long, steep grade in a headlong plummeting rush that seemed to Felix almost freefell hurtling them toward the distant range of high, gnarly peaks shimmering blue and purple far away at the horizon thrusting toward vast, open sky. During the night driving through a mountain rainstorm so violent that the water flowed in an incessant sheet across the windshield, the wipers on full speed laboring without effect against the torrent so heavy they were forced to stop in a rest area. The driver crawled up into the bunk at the back of the cab leaving Felix to huddle awkwardly on the cold, vinyl seat using the door as a headrest while he listened to the rain pounding on the roof and hood of the truck. He dozed fitfully, woke by sudden stillness when the torrent quieted and the man above and behind him stirred from his warm cocoon.

They moved on with the rain still falling steadily but diminishing with the dawn, the truck lights softened in the gathering light glistening on the wet road, the dawn light offering them a view of brown hills darkened by rain. Huge drenched rocks and boulders and crags jutting from the earth exposed folded layers ancient and ageless stirring Felix to marvel at their sublime grandeur. What would it be like to set out in some form either poetry or painting all that he viewed?

Now, with the rain stopped, the air clear, the world wet with browns and yellows, the sky coloring with the rising sun catching the last wisps of glowing cloud displayed in a collage of pink and gold, the large rig pulled into Little America, a truck stop the size of a small town set out in the desert that Felix was able to locate on a map. Felix followed the driver out of the cab, then watched the man walk around the rig inspecting tires. He waited while the man went to negotiate having a tire replaced, the driver pointing out to Felix how the tire was worn and that it would be better to change it now before they were up to speed on the road and the tire blew.

"Wouldn't want that," the man advised, "just be more trouble and cost more having it replaced on the road."

Then they went inside the restaurant. "Might as well chow down," the man said. "We've got at least an hour's wait.

Felix didn't like waiting now that he was underway, but he guessed he didn't have much from which to choose: wait for the tire repair or try hitching a ride with someone else he didn't know or how far the driver was going. Then he asked himself: Why the rush to get someplace he wasn't sure he wanted to be? So he chose to wait.

The interior of the restaurant they entered was a vast arena of booths and tables, and after the isolation, openness, and serenity of the mountains, the place seemed bustling with a clamor of voices and dishes that washed over them as they moved through the crowded scene. Felix and the man settled at a table, immediately served coffee, ordered from the menus they had found, and settled back to watch the steady flow of people entering and leaving the animated scene of a multitude eating and conversing.

"Is it always like this?" Felix asked, looking out across the crowded tables, the long counter in chrome and formica with matching stools all filled.

Despite its vastness, the place was jammed: Waitresses in western attire moved ceaselessly over the carpeted floor; a steady exchange of patrons, mostly truckers in their characteristic garb of plaid shirt and faded jeans and cowboy boots, the few obvious tourists in casual clothes overwhelmed by the size of the place and the size and number of truckers who came and went endlessly, their greetings and farewells, the snort of their rigs slowly exiting the vast plain of asphalt then struggling through endless gears as they pulled away onto the open road slowly gathering speed.

"What?" the driver asked. "You mean this place? Yeah, always busy. I stop here just about every time I come through."

"Not so much this place," Felix said. "I mean trucking. We've been moving almost nonstop since you picked me up way back in Idaho. You haven't slept at all except when we stopped because of the storm. How you slept through that is amazing!"

"Have to work it like that," the driver said. "Don't have much time to lollygag. Get where I have to go and then get back. Otherwise, you don't make any money."

"But how do you manage to keep going? That's got to be hard on your body."

"You want to know how I keep going?" The driver paused and sat back while the waitress came to place their food, freshen their coffee, then moved away in jeans so tight they seemed sprayed on. The two men watched her go.

"Pills," the driver said. "You know, uppers. Keep me going for days."

He sat back, groveled in his jeans pocket, came up with a small tin.

"Want to try one?" He offered Felix the open tin before he took one of the tablets, popped it in his mouth, and washed it down with coffee.

Felix faked a shudder. "No thanks. Not for me." He paused, looking around at the crowd of men at nearby tables. How many of them, he wondered, were wired on something? "And you do this all the time?"

"All the time. Most of us. Make a trip East then back out West. We stop only for repairs or weigh stations unless we can avoid them or they're closed, a bite to eat — mostly coffee. What with the uppers, I don't really feel much like eating.

"And you've been doing this how long?"

"Longer than I care to recall. Twenty years. May have to quit soon. My doctor says I have an irregular heart beat. Don't know what else I might do. I still owe on my rig. And it's due for major work. So I keep truckin' on down the road!"

"Seems like a tough life," Felix observed.

"Yeah, it's tough sometimes," the man agreed. "Decent money, though, over the long haul."

"I'm not sure it's worth what you have to give in exchange," Felix said. "You know, when I was a kid, I always thought driving long haul truck would be a great job to have — the open road, seeing places, going places. Now I see there's not as much glamour as I thought."

"Glamour!" the driver snorted. "Yeah, probably lots of people think that. Me? I got in because that's what I did in the Army. Only thing I could do when I got out. First I hired on to relieve other drivers. Eventually, I bought my own rig. Now, I'm my own boss, although I've got more debts, more responsibility. When I drove for someone else, all I did was drive. But what I do now ain't so bad. Although my wife gets pretty tired of my bein' gone all the time. And when I'm home, all I want to do is sleep."

"I can see why!" Felix offered.

The driver pushed back his plate, took a last gulp of coffee, and pushed himself up from his seat.

"Guess I better go check on how that tire's comin."

He picked up the check, waving off Felix who fumbled for his wallet.

"Forget it," the man said. "Food's on me. I'll log it as an expense for my relief driver. That's what you're doin' so I can get through weigh stations without hassle. Looks to me you could use the money you save."

He handed Felix the check along with a large bill. "This ought to cover it. You pay while I see about the tire. Don't forget the tip."

Felix watched the man move out through the crowd of tables to the double set of glass doors he pushed through to the outside.

Finishing his coffee while watching the busy scene, Felix finally rose, moved to the cashier where he paid the bill, went back to leave the tip, pocketed the change, and went to the wall of glass cases by the door. He studied the displayed merchandise wondering who would buy such stuff and why, then wandered out to the truck where he found the driver paying for the new tire. Felix groped in his jacket pocket and handed the man the receipt and the change he received.

"Guess we're 'bout ready to go," the driver said. "Time to saddle up!"

Felix followed the driver up into the cab settling into a place that now seemed his. He looked down through the windshield at the people moving in and out of the restaurant as the driver cranked the starter, the engine coughed to life; the diesel roaring and belching smoke, the driver fought the truck into gear, and the big rig slowly moved among idling trucks out onto the highway heading east toward the Great Plains.

A day later, early, Felix emerged from the hollow of the now empty trailer lugging the last sack of potatoes, dropping it onto the full pallet held up by forklift. He felt good to be working, doing something other than gazing glazed-eyed through the windshield of the cab at the endless passing scene that seemed not to change much in the day and a half they had driven across two states. Felix recalled the long, sweeping curve of the road that followed the Platte River into Grande Island where more than a century ago covered wagons had passed the other way moving west and he seemed as if he were in some great ship following a great circle of the globe moving toward the East. He recalled the continual high signs the driver gave with a casual sweep of his arm and extended hand to the drivers in the continuous flow of trucks that passed them in the opposite direction offering the same sign in return as they lumbered in their rigs toward the high country that the driver and Felix had recently left behind.

Now Felix straightened from finishing his labor to observe the brightening day, the flare of orange light on the low hills and trees opposite the distribution center warehouse platform on which he stood, the quickening traffic, some slowing to turn into the yard of asphalt where he worked unloading the trailer backed up to the loading dock.

"That's the last of them," Felix said.

"Good enough," the driver said. "I'll just run these in. Then we can settle up."

Felix watched the man maneuver the forklift and pallet into the warehouse, marveling again at the man's industry: What a life! Not only did he haul this load across three states over most of three days, he had to unload it as well, and then only after he negotiated with the warehouse manager to take the load. Felix had watched as the manager inspected the load, jabbing a thermometer into random sacks, letting it set, then withdrawing it, studying the reading, then shaking his head, pondering out loud as to whether he could accept a shipment that was bordering on being too warm. But it was good enough, the driver argued, and he slipped the manager a folded bill whose size Felix was readily able to see. Then they had set themselves to unloading the heavy, bulky, bulging sacks.

Now finished and comfortably tired from his effort, Felix moved to the cab of the truck to retrieve his jacket that he put on against the morning chill caused by the sweat he had worked up unloading the truckload of sacks. The driver returned on foot from the warehouse, pulling on a plaid shirt over his t-shirt, buttoning it as he arrived.

"Well, I guess that's it, then," the driver said. He reached for his wallet, extracted a bill, offered it to Felix. "That should be about right, I guess."

Felix took the bill and stuffed it into his jacket pocket without looking. "That's fine," he said. "I appreciate the ride and the work."

The driver offered Felix his hand. "Fair enough exchange for me. I thank you for your help. You're a good man." Then, as if he was reluctant to let Felix go, or perhaps because he didn't want to seem as if he were dismissing

Felix, "How about some breakfast," he offered. "We can get some here in the cafeteria. Won't cost as much as eating on the road."

"I could use coffee and a bowl of cereal," Felix admitted. And he, too, found himself curiously reluctant to sever the connection they had developed over the previous three days, Felix, of course, in his typical youthful fashion lingering from adolescence divulging his adventures traveling to California from Wisconsin, surviving nine months of school in Long Beach, hitching rides to Oregon, helping harvest endless fields of golden grain.

"Come on, then!" the man said, and Felix followed the driver through the warehouse past the towering stacks of produce to which they had contributed then through twists and turns of tiled office corridors leading them to the cafeteria. Felix became alert by the sudden rush of voices and the swirl of people as he and the man entered, as they went through the service line then seated themselves at one of the rectangular tables arranged in rows.

Felix watched the fashionably dressed men, the attractive, fashionably dressed young women — clean, fragrant, and soft, he listening to their chatter as they came through the foodline exchanging comments about their work, their lives, last night's TV, last night's date. He saw those going through the line eyeing him and the man seated across from him, Felix suddenly feeling skuzzy with bristled chin, rumpled hair, faded, crumpled denim jacket, and scruffy shoes.

Felix watched as the workers gathered at neighboring tables, some — one woman especially — continuing to inspect him, he returning her gaze, he suddenly thinking of Gloria, a woman he with whom once worked, and her elegant manner; others turning to their coffee, their pastries, their shared experiences. He suddenly, slightly nostalgic, recalled his own former days working in a similar setting just out of Prairieville High.

"What you think?" the driver asked, breaking Felix's reverie. "You think they're happy? Don't they look content? Look at them! How settled they are! Like cattle!"

Felix found himself surprised by the man's remarks. "They must have something going for them!"

"What? Their daily routine? They've been doing this for how long? Believe me. I've seen them. Like those." He nodded toward a second wave of workers, these more gray, dulled looking. "Look at them! You know what's wrong with them? No hope! No ambition!"

Felix recalled the supervisor of his first fulltime job. "Maybe they have what they want," Felix defended. "Or that's all they could find. Just like you."

"OK, but do they know what they want? Security? Home? Family? They're no more than zombies! Did they really ever want this! Would you ever want this?"

"I had something like it, once upon a time," Felix admitted. "That's why I left. Now I'm not sure what I want. But what about you? From what you've told me, seems to me your life's pretty much routine doing the only job you could do."

"Oh, sure. I admit I got my routine. But I can set my own hours, work when I want to. I'm my own boss. I don't have to answer to anyone."

"Except your wife!"

"Yeah! Except my wife!" the driver admitted, laughing. He finished his coffee, set the cup on his tray. "Speaking of, I better see about heading out. Have to pick up a load of toilets to take back out West. Now ain't that somethin'! Bring in a load of spuds and take out a load of crappers! Seems somethin' almost poetic in that!"

Felix's laughter joining the man's, he added his mug and bowl to the tray. Rising, he pulled his jacket from the back of the chair. "I'll get my bag from the truck."

"Sure," the driver said. "You probably can get a ride easy enough right outside the gate. Business loop traffic will take you out to the main highway."

They made their way back through the maze of vinyl-tiled office corridors to the warehouse then through the cavernous depot to the truck. Felix reached up inside the cab for his bag, set it down to take the man's hand and wish the man a safe journey home, the man expressing hope that Felix would find what he was searching for.

Felix hauled up his bag, carried it to the gated brick entrance of the warehouse lot where he set it, turning back to watch the driver climb up into the cab, fire up the rig, then pull out through the gate watching for passing cars, waving to Felix, giving a short double blast on the air horn, as the big rig moved out into traffic, heading back toward the West.

Felix turned to his immediate task, lifting his arm, his hand, his thumb in the universal sign of the road that seemed for him as natural as breathing.

A luxury car, the kind Pa had always dreamed of owning, pulled through the gate of the parking lot of the warehouse where Felix had unloaded the truck. The gleaming auto stopped. He saw that the driver whose elegant attire complemented the car was not inspecting the flow of traffic. Instead, she was studying him. He recognized the woman from seeing her in the cafeteria while he drank coffee with the trucker now long gone. Felix inspecting her trim, fully-developed body sheathed in what to him seemed elegant apparel among the more common dress of the others who had moved through the service line, she had studied him then as she did now, and he had returned her gaze, conscious of his skuzzy appearance after days on the road and then unloading an eighteen-wheeler filled with potatoes. Now she sat in her elegant auto studying him again. He again returned her gaze while watched the window slowly descend.

"Where you headed?" she asked.

"US 30."

"I can go that way," she said. She signed with elegant, polished nails for him to enter.

He grabbed his bag, pulling it in after him, setting it between his legs when he entered, thanking her.

"Where you from?" she asked. She searched Felix's face, meeting his eyes, the beauty and strength of hers having a color he hadn't seen since what now seemed too long ago, her sharp features, complexion, and expression offering a slight sense of the exotic tinged with something else, as if she harbored some hidden power. He breathed in her subtle fragrance that conjured remembrances of things past.

"All over," Felix answered, offering his usual reply. "California, Oregon."

The elegant woman turned to check the passing autos then pulled out into traffic. Felix noted the quick, powerful response of the machine after the slow start of the truck he had ridden in for days.

"You've been in the military," she offered, searching Felix's face with those brilliant eyes turning back to watch the road.

"Army Reserve," Felix admitted.

"Not much fun, huh?"

"Not really," Felix confessed.

"Don't want to talk about it," she observed. "No surprise there."

"Not much to talk about."

"But some do. Maybe a bit too much."

"Don't I know?" Felix said. "They're always the ones who give the orders."

They rode in silence, gazing out the windshield at the fleeing autos that raced before them. When they reached US 30, she pulled over to the shoulder.

"So where to from here?"

"East," Felix offered.

"You're a man of few words," she said.

Felix said nothing. He reached for the door handle that wasn't there.

"I open the door from here," she said.

Felix studied the fleeing traffic.

"I'm sure you wouldn't mind a chance to clean up after all your travel. Have a shave and shower. Launder your soiled clothes."

"It's has been a while," Felix admitted aware of his blend of ripe odors.

"You could use my place."

"Really! You wouldn't mind?"

"I wouldn't have offered."

"Of course. Thank you. I'd appreciate that."

"My house is your house."

"That'd be great!"

"Good," she said, checked for traffic, then pulled out onto the road.

Felix was suddenly struck by her manner that he seemed to recognize as similar to someone he had known about the age of this women, someone for whom he had cared deeply with a passion still lingering from what now seemed long ago whenever he thought of her. Strange, he thought, perhaps even weird, this exotic woman he had just met but suddenly seemed to know up-close and personal.

The residence where they arrived appeared more elegant than the others in the development, much like the vehicle he just climbed out of hauling his green, weathered bag. On entering the large house, Felix inspected with wonder the rich décor and doubted any other house in the cul-du-sac was anything as elegant as the one he entered following her stiletto heels, allowing him to appreciate her trim legs, her shapely bottom, her trim body, straight shoulders sheathed in elegant apparel. He viewed the massive door, the long entry way with tall columns, side rooms with well-appointed furnishings, each different with complementary décor; large dining room with crystal chandelier, long table of dark, polished wood, matching chairs with black velour cushions. She led him to a spacious bedroom with spacious bathroom and tiled shower.

"You can store your bag in here," she directed, opening a door off the bedroom.

Felix viewed a closet the size of a small room with lush carpeting, empty hangers, built-in drawers for t-shirts, shorts, socks, and accessories..

"You might stay for a while as long as you like," she offered.

Felix met her eyes with amber irises, deposited his bag, turned back to where she sat on her luxurious bed.

"Come here," she ordered quietly. When he approached, she reached for him, unbuttoned his fly, drew him out, stroked him, and lay back on the bed, lifting her thigh-length dress. "You're the perfect size. I could use a quick one," she said, pulling aside her thong. "Why not make my day."

Already firm from her stroking him, Felix moved to satisfy her need, entered her, began stroking, bringing her to a quick release that he watched while she gave herself up to her response. When she calmed, he stepped back, allowing her to rise, adjust her thong, smooth her elegant dress

"That felt good. I'll want more later," she advised, softly caressing his cheek with fingers that held her scent. "Make yourself at home. Enjoy your leisure."

Then she was out the door, Felix listening to the sound of the luxury auto speeding away. He stood with his tumescent flesh still exposed, listening to the quiet of the softly stirring house, wondering whether what he had just experienced might be only the start of something strange and equally unexpected. What had he gotten himself into this time? Maybe it was something he would enjoy.

Having finished his shave and shower, enjoying the feel of his clean flesh and the stillness of the luxurious dwelling, that stillness made more so by the quiet tumble of his clothes in the dryer located in the utility room on the other side of the house, Felix wandered back to the bedroom, enjoying the perverse freedom from being naked in the home of an attractive, passionate woman. He surveyed the well-appointed setting of the bedroom that obviously was hers — a woman of apparently considerable means. How could she afford all this, given where she worked? She must be someone of high rank and status, and he wondered why she had chosen him.

The large bed with quilt of pastel color and complementary pillows and shags and curtains, the armoire and commode with large mirrors reflecting images of the bed and its linen, the papered wall — all proclaimed taste that required sufficient means to meet the expense. He studied the large dresser of blonde wood with ornate gold pulls. He went to stand before it, his clean and powdered flesh reflected in the mirror. He opened a top drawer and, as he expected, found a rich cache of delicate garments of various bright color, all of satin or silk carefully arranged. How would that sleek material feel on his naked flesh that became tumescent at the thought. Not since he had purloined a garment from his mother had he indulged his curious impulse.

Suddenly he felt tired from all his recent activities: endless, tedious travel, unloading the trailer of an eighteen-wheeler, servicing the exotic woman who had suddenly taken him up and just as suddenly deposited him in her lare. He lay on her bed, stretched out, relaxed, breathing deeply, quietly enjoying the feel of silk garment on tumescent flesh as he slowly drifted to sleep.

Felix woke to find the woman studying him, scanning his body and his brief apparel. He returned the woman's gaze, wondering what she must think finding him so obviously exposed.

"So, you cross dress," she said quietly.

"Not often," Felix offered, expecting a damning response.

Instead, she climbed onto the bed, pulled his tumescent flesh from beneath the garment, took it in her hand to hold and stroke while she bent to cover him with her soft lips, taking him into her mouth until he was full and firm, then raised herself, lifted her light dress, pulled aside her thong, straddling him, placing him at her folds, then slowly lowering herself, pressing his long, hard flesh into her sheath, and rode him to release, collapsing on him, quivering while resting on him with his flesh still firm within.

"Oh, my!" she said raising her head. "That was really good!"

"My pleasure," Felix said, although she had taken him so fast and reached climax so quickly he hadn't been able to fully respond.

"What about you?" she asked.

He studied her.

"You want more?" she asked. "I always want more. Don't move!"

She climbed off, quickly undressed displaying her trim, well-developed body, climbed back on the bed, straddled him again, and lowered herself onto his firm flesh.

She rode him again, but this time he was fully aware. He grasped her hips and held her while she galloped, stroking him, he beginning to respond. But again she went over before he was ready.

This time, however, she climbed from him and stretched out on the bed. "Your turn!" she said. "Enjoy the ride."

He moved to cover her. She reached to hold and guide him, grabbed his waist, and pulled him in. "Now do me hard!" she ordered.

So he did.

Later, after they rested, she rose slowly and used the garment he had worn to catch all he had pulsed into her.

"You gave me quite a load!".

Then without apparel, she started for the kitchen where she began gathering items to prepare a salad.

"How about a barbeque?" she called. "Weather's perfect! What about ribs? You like ribs? They're fresh!"

Felix rose and followed her to the kitchen. He studied her shapely, trim figure fully exposed. She surveyed him standing naked in the door way, her inspection coming to rest on the part of him she most favored.

"You're well built."

"Thanks."

She studied him again while she shredded greens. "Why don't you mix us drinks? Can you do that?" She indicated the cabinet that he found fully stocked with top-label brands.

"What would you like?" he asked.

"Whatever you decide," she replied wagging her firm, shapely bottom while turning to add ingredients to their salad.

Felix mixed gin martinis, stirred not shaken, then poured them into crystal glasses. She raised her glass to his, then sipped.

"Very nice," she said. "Just the way I always like them. Where'd you learn? You're not that old."

Felix no longer feeling adolescent accepted her off-handed reference to his age. "I became legal in June," he offered casually. "But a good friend introduced me to martinis a couple years before that. They were her favorite."

"She teach you what you just did so well with me?"

"We were just good friends," he replied, wise enough not to reveal that she reminded him a lot of his former good friend.

"I see." She studied him with her amber eyes. "Why don't we enjoy our drinks outside?"

Then she took his tumescent flesh in her soft, well-manicured hand and led him from the house to the back. Sipping his drink, aware of them both so exposed to the bright air, Felix viewed the idyllic scene, more than a yard, more like a park, a verdant pasture with two mares and stallion, an adjoining pasture with bull and two cows.

"They're busy all the time," she said, smiling, nodding toward the massive creatures lounging in shade. "They're such fun to watch when the guys get it up and service the gals."

And even as she spoke the words, Felix noted the bull and stallion rouse from their torpor in the shade and amble to where Felix and the naked, well-endowed woman stood behind the open rail fence, not much of a barrier for such powerful creatures who obviously could stroll right through without much effort.

Felix tensed as the two massive forms approached.

"It's OK," she said. "Relax. Stay calm. They're really quite gentle."

She reached to stroke them both one after the other with long slow strokes as the beasts stood quietly allowing her touch and his presence at which they snorted as if somehow accepting his being there because of her stroking them. She spoke to them quietly while she stroked. Felix thought of how she had stroked him earlier, her touch having the same effect as it did when she had used her smooth hand on him. He saw their flesh begin to fill, and Felix felt himself begin to fill again as well.

"They like you," she offered.

"How can you tell?"

"I have my ways. They're quiet. I just know," she said. "Talk to them."

"What should I say?"

"Say, 'hello,' of course. You have to say it quietly and sound friendly and unafraid. And then they'll allow you to stroke them like this. Let them get to know you."

Felix said 'hello' and reached out slowly to stroke their massive flesh, firm and sleek. He felt their power and energy, their vibrant heat, and breathed in their deep scent. Now as he stroked the massive creatures, he felt their strength flowing into him, his own flesh tumescent growing with every stroke, so large and firm he did not want to stop.

"You do get addicted," she advised, inspecting his size. "Nice, huh?"

Felix met her bright eyes that drew him in and held him. "Yes," he said quietly. "Then you feel it too."

"Of course!" she said. "I've enjoyed what they have to offer."

Felix studied her not fully understanding.

"Offer?"

"I've had both," she said casually. "My sister who loves horses taught me. I'll show you how they use me, if you stay awhile. Would you like that?"

"Use you? Stay awhile?" he asked himself. Where was this going? What had happened to his urge to get where he had to go while unable to decide where that might be?

"I like you. You're strong and healthy, well-equipped, a man of few words, and you obviously enjoy sex as much I do. I respond especially well after cunnilingus. You ever do that?"

He met her bright eyes as she studied him, her interest obvious. "Some," he offered, not wanting to appear naïve to this unworldly woman.

"I'll teach you how to do it right, if you stay awhile."

Felix studied her in silence meeting her bright eyes. He somehow knew she would teach him well.

"We also have sheep," she said, turning away. "And, of course, swine. I like pigs, don't you? They seem almost as smart as people, sometimes smarter. And they're really cleaner than most. You just have to provide the right conditions. But, of course, we use them. You do like ribs, don't you?"

Felix met her gaze that seemed to pierce him. *We?* He asked himself. Why did what she had just said somehow seem ominous?

They left the massive bull and stallion snorting as he followed the woman toward the sty where they stopped to watch the penned animals stir from their slumber, rise, and approach, ready to be scratched, their grunting somehow sounding almost human.

Felix looked back to the pastures to witness both bull and stallion raise themselves upon the wide back of a ready female, their firm flesh quivering as they entered and stroked themselves to a snorting release. Felix felt wet from watching.

"So, you also like to watch," she observed and reached to grasp his gorged flesh in her soft hand. "Looks like you're ready," she added.

He said nothing. He studied her gleaming eyes."

"Follow me," she ordered quietly.

Felix followed. How could he not, she still holding him in her hand, the grunting swine complaining as he left.

She led him to her elegant bedroom where she slowly ran her hands over his body. His flesh ached under her soft hand stroking him.

"You will be so good," she said, "just like them," as she stretched out beside him on the bed, holding his flesh in her soft hand while nuzzling him, her soft lips moving over his neck, his shoulder, his chest and belly, reaching his firm flesh, thrilling him with each lingering touch of her lips and tongue.

"Stay with me, Felix," she said softly as she rose to mount him, placing him at her folds, lowering herself, beginning to ride him as if he were a stallion.

He held her hips, helping her while she galloped as she rode to a peak that shook her, stirring him as she rode on and on to another peak then over, he watching from beneath as she took him for all he had. Finally she slowed, bent over him, holding him, nuzzling him, his gorged flesh filling her.

"You're so good for me, Felix," she whispered. "Stay with me."

Then she rested on him, lying quietly while he held her, stroking her back and hips and firm, shapely bottom while studying the fresco on the ceiling, mythic scenes of rampant, carnal knowledge filled with creatures of various size and species: couplings of a white bull and a dark woman with long, black hair; a black stallion and blond-haired woman; a goat and nymph; an ape and young human female; all eager players, willing to frolic and enjoy each other.

"Your turn, Felix," she said finally. "I'll teach you how to do me right before you take me."

She rolled from him to stretch full-length while Felix turned, kneeling, as she drew up her legs, placing her feet on his shoulders, offering herself, her slick, pink groove, gaping sheath, gorged clitoris, as he bent to use his tongue and lips, she coaching him how to use his tongue to stroke her groove, her labia, her clitoris he took between his lips, she instructing him not to stop after she reached a peak and went over, he continuing until she reached a second taking longer, then reaching a third yelling her release, begging him to take her now, she reaching to grasp his firm flesh, guiding him, grabbing his hips, drawing him in, then lying back, her legs still bent back, her thighs spread, her arms above her head as he thrust in deep.

Aching from restraint while she had used him to satisfy her need, Felix stroked into her slick flesh, each stroke sending back a charge deep into his groin as he went on, his stroking growing harder, growing faster, until pounding into her with his full force, he felt her begin to tense, slowly climbing toward something greater than she had reached before, she gazing up at him, her eyes sparkling, her face filled with passion as he drove on and on and on until he felt the tension he knew well, his gland beginning to grip taking him where he wanted to go if he just gave in. But he went on, her ascending response leading the way, his gland responding as he felt a strong surge grip him, and he let go, she going with him, while she hollered and thrashed beneath him as he pulsed again and again and again so long and deep he thought he would never stop.

When they lay quiet in each other's arms, basking in the warm afterglow of their sudden release, she whispered again.

"Stay with me, Felix. You're so good for me."

And while Felix knew he would, he had no way of knowing how long.

As he waited just beyond the crossroads, all that he witnessed was immediate and clear: late afternoon heat; soft, green fields filled with broad-leafed corn rolling away in low rises to the clumps of tall, thick oak; peppered pea gravel at his feet; thin stalks of what appeared like wheat grass he was surprised to see conjuring images of recent days now lost.

The rush of air from a passing vehicle sent up a blast of air that churned the hot dust. He watched through rising waves of heat the receding image of the car that had ignored him, the hot engine whine diminishing. The long, thin stems of scattered wild grass along the gravel of the road settled to a stir, and the late afternoon heat returned.

He sat on a concrete culvert, the green bag beside his legs, his arms across his knees. He looked back up toward the crossroad. Cars flashed across the intersection, their engines roaring as they sped on through; others slowed, stopped, waited for the glowing red light to change, the air shimmering from their glaring hoods.

He hung his head between his arms and studied the wild grass and pebbles at his feet. He had been this way before, how long ago, he couldn't say for sure while on his way to retrieve his '54 blue and white Chevy with blue vinyl seats he had left behind a service station outside Ames, Iowa when he had ran out of fuel at the same time he had run out of money on his way back from California after sitting for placement tests and registering for classes. Felix recalled the ride in a convertible with its sweep of polished vermillion hood that mirrored the flashing countryside, this road he had traveled beneath the splendor of the clear sky, beneath trees through which he had glimpsed the vast blue sparkling lake, the fleeting image of the dome of Yerkes observatory, the canopy of rich, green leaves on the sweeping branches above his head, the open sky expansive with towering, billowing cumulus-nimbus clouds. Breathing the aroma of the tan leather seats hot from the sun, the silent man beside him, estranged, smothering in the details of his own life, Felix, in contrast, had felt free, setting out at last to discover for himself his own brave new world.

Yet, now he felt glum. Why should that be?

He thought of the weird, exotic woman he had finally escaped one morning after she had left for work. He had packed his bag and fled — or he had tried. For almost as soon as he had stepped out the door and it had closed, locking behind him, her car pulled into the cul de sac before her house. He waited, resigned, his bag by his leg as she drove up, sat with the engine idling, studying him with those brilliant eyes following him as he walked around the car to her door, meeting her gaze as the window slid down.

"Going somewhere?" she asked.

"It's about time I left."

"So it seems, but I already knew when that was going to happen."

"So?"

"Go get your precious bag. I'll give you a lift. Where you want me to drop you off?"

"Wherever's convenient."

He studied her as she touched the switch unlocking the car door. He went to get his bag, climbed in the car, sat looking out the windshield at the house, listening to the quiet idle of the engine, his precious bag between his legs.

She took him to where she first offered him a ride, how long ago he couldn't say.

"Some trucker might be going your way," she said.

Then after he had heaved from the car with his bag and closed the door, she had pulled into her designated parking spot, shut down the engine, climbed from the car, and strode into the building on stiletto heels without looking back. Felix again had found himself facing the open road.

Now alone with his bag, he once again suddenly conjured the iron, grated gates of open store fronts in Long Beach, the wide expanse of concrete boulevards striped with tar, the stirring palm trees fanned dark against the setting sun. Why he now renewed that image he wasn't sure. Having thrilled on his seeing the ocean at night spilling onto the endless beach, the timeless phosphorescence riding huge waves that broke with a thundering clap and then a roaring hiss of foam and pebbles spilling onto the lip of the continent, he saw again the night bound fishing pier, the row of silent shapes standing watch over poles that arched into the dark beyond dim light standards, globed, yellow light bobbing on waves of black water, thin fish lines dropping toward the swish and endless plash of ocean off barnacle encrusted pilings. He recalled the scuttle of frantic flounder, the flip of fin and body on the pier as it swung up from the void, flopping and flapping upon the gut-soiled pavement of the pier. He had watched a hand unhook it, a booted foot stomping the flat head, until the heel crushed the bewildered eyes and gaping mouth.

Walking on the dim light toward the pier's end, passing the bait store, the stand complete with glowing beer sign, fishnet, and gurgling tank, he had reached the coffee shop that he had come to know and the small, dark-haired, wiry man who owned the place, a Greek who had reminded Felix of the Acropolis, the Parthenon — Felix having recently discovered Greek history in his History of Europe class with Doc Gates — saw the shop with dim yellow lights, dark wood tables, dark wood chairs, plush green walls hung with original oil paintings that Felix had gazed at with envy — to think that someone had actually done those — he wondering at the time whether he would ever do something on his own. He recalled the honeyed Greek pastries, the bitter, black coffee served in small cups.

Then almost as if the image and the memory were lingering to creep upon him, he thought of the young, dark-haired woman with almond-brown eyes he had met in a modern dance class. Later, having shared one of the few small tables, they had walked back together along the pier observing the night's catch being gutted, and after strolling the endless beach along the crashing, hissing tide foaming onto the sand, she had come with him through the thick, swirling fog, through the quiet, closing screen door to his pull-down bed.

After that night, she had visited him often in the fog-bound dark before dawn, almost as if in a dream. He ached now thinking of her cool body warming beneath his hands, her smooth, firm thighs, taut bottom, and then the wet, electric softness of her sheath as she had straddled him, easing herself down. He flushed now, throbbing in remembrance and longing. Why had he let her slip away? Why had he left? Why was he always leaving? Just as he had left the exotic woman who had taught him so much.

Behind him now the distant ocean with endless surf roaring in upon the sand, sliding back in foam, then shooting back with spray, crashing against slowly wearing rock; the night sea sending white-capped breakers against the land far away to the West beyond harvested wheat fields drenched in hot sun. Behind him days of sweat in a stifling, dusty truck unloading a clattering thresher among golden grain that spread in soft hills rolling away to the wide, swift river. He thought of the young girl and young boy to whom he had explained the starry night above. He thought of the blossoming woman in a graveyard at night set out upon a ripening field of grain. He thought of the afternoon waiting in stifling heat with others for the grain to ripen and he had found her cooling in the creek and had joined with her under the clear, open sky. All that now behind him gelled in amber.

The night descending, he rose, cinched the cloth strap closing the bag, looked back at the crossroads and the neon that ebbed and throbbed against gathering darkness, the signal above the deserted road gleaming, changing from blaring red to silent green. He turned and started down a darkening road, the gravel crunching beneath his soles, the roadway glimmering, trees along the roadside dark and thick, green fields beyond the roadside of stirring leaves disappearing in long, close rows that swept away towards the low hills at the horizon. Above the hills, the light lingered soft and pale, the lone, bright globe, always his companion, glowing in the gathering dark.

Behind him at the crossroad, a car slowed then idled. Then as the light changed, the car started, gathered speed, slowed when its headlights caught him in their beams, then surged ahead, passing his squinting face and raised arm beside the road, the stuffed, green bag on the graveled shoulder. He turned, following the car, dropping his arm. He trudged on knowing that the increasing dark reduced his chances of getting a ride. He wondered now if he wouldn't have been better off staying near the crossroad. Yet he walked on, darkness having finally shrouded the hills and trees and rows of corn along the roadway. Soon a score of stars rose in the evening sky becoming multitude. Orion the hunter as always seemed to lead the way.

A curve in the road took him into total darkness shutting him off completely from the glow of red and green lights at the crossroad. His eyes became accustomed to the dark shapes of trees and structures that loomed along the roadside. He saw the glimmering host of distant worlds above the dark canopy of trees: Andromeda, Cassiopeia, the Pleiades.

Now and then a beam of light from behind would give him hope, but the engine sound took longer to reach him each step he took further from the crossroad. The beam of light swept the sky and tree tops before it broke around the curve and swept over him, blinding him as he raised his arm into the glaring light that exploded past him, sweeping on down the road that rose and fell in hills following the landscape. He watched it go, the headlights sweeping the road showing him the way, the flash of red taillights, the doppler engine roar diminishing as the vehicle went into the dark.

He heard the sound of his own footsteps on the gravel beneath the hard unyielding leather of his shoes until the night sounds returned, and the dark world came alive. A single cricket chirped, another soon answered, and suddenly a chorus of scraping syncopation went with him. Then a frog somewhere grumped followed by others, all joining the pulsing chorus of crickets, the night filled with sounds beneath the leaves of dark trees. He stopped. He listened, gazing at the sweeping expanse of stars above his head. He walked wrapped in darkness and undulating pulsing sound, his legs tiring as he moved along the road, his mind numb.

Darkness stretched ahead. No cars came to break the night sounds. The summer night, warm and humid, he began to sweat under the load of the bag. He walked for stretches with the bag balanced on his head to relieve his shoulders from the cutting strap, but his walking beneath the bag jolted him against the hard asphalt road. He thought of the town ahead. He knew it was there, having found it as a dot on the map as he had sat at the crossroad. Perhaps it was just beyond the next crest. Surely it had to be.

A soft glow edged the darkness, and as he moved toward the dim light, he came upon a tavern. He passed feeling even more alone and chilled, even though the night was warm. As he passed, he imagined a different kind of warmth just beyond the darkness of the wooden porch with wooden pillars. A red neon sign in the window shouted beer. In the dim light behind the window, a soft yellow light played along the chorus of bottles that ranged along the shelves behind the bar. As he passed, he saw the black shapes of autos on the gravel driveway. He crunched on. No one approached him, came out to challenge him, invite him in, or question him. He heard no sound from within.

He walked on through the soft light that spread upon the darkness until he found himself again in night, saw the tall hulks of trees, and above the broad canopies, the black sky crowded with stars. He walked on following the road that lay across the rolling countryside thick with trees. He walked with nothing else to do but walk. He thought of sleep: How nice to settle, relax, stretch, float upon his weariness until he thought of what he would have to do to uncinch his duffle, wrestle out his sleeping gear. Where would he sleep? In some ditch along the roadside? Where would he find himself when he wriggled out and stretched himself in the dawn needing to relieve himself? Some farmer's front yard? What kind of reception would he get then? He walked on. The bag began to trouble him, growing more heavy as he walked, making him wish he hadn't brought so much, having thought that everything he packed was worth trundling this dark road, up hill and down. He switched the strap to the other shoulder, relieving the burden for a spell by again carrying it on his head that soon strained his neck.

Through the faint light, he peered at an occasional tall, old house, the painted wooden sides, the high, peaked roof with wrought iron fencing, the long, darker shadows of the tall, old windows, the long driveway leading up into the yard from what he knew might come to challenge his passage through the dark. Walking quietly, cautiously, listening, searching through the darkness, he heard from far away a faint cry, the far away answer, the cries growing louder as he walked until he passed the dark shadow of an old ghostly house, and from the yard came a yowl that startled him. Then he saw the dark, moving shape sidling toward him, the head lowered; and as he passed, he felt the inquiring snout that shocked his leg, his shoe heel, until it fell back, a single-headed Cerberus permitting him passage.

No human voice ever challenged him. Sometimes the quick, frantic cry of a bird sent ahead a message taken up, answered, carried forward, long after the first sentinel he had passed slunk back to the dark pillared porch. Alone again, he thought the darkness sweet: the choir of frogs, the chorus of crickets. He was startled by the huge dark shapes of beasts behind what appeared a fragile fence beside the road. He saw them turn their heavy heads to eye him as he passed. He saw the dim barn side, recoiled from the sharp sweetsour sting of rotten, liquid barnyard.

Then he reached a hillcrest and started down the long slope that took him toward a small cluster of lights set among the trees in a valley of rolling hills. From the crest of the long slope that brought him from summer trees and midnight sounds, the bag upon his head to rest his arms and shoulders from the cutting strap and dead weight, he passed a graveyard not noticing it until the dull shapes of tombstones broke the darkness beneath the tall fir trees. A sharp, sudden sound—a call, a cry—startled him. He saw wrought iron spirals of fence, gray shapes of stones. He thought of dark hulks of houses with wrought-iron roof walks he had recently passed along the road. He shuddered recalling his terror of the night when he was young, his childish fears of lurking things beneath black, yawning stairwells. He felt the silence, the stillness as he passed, as he peered between the twisted pillars of fence at the dim shapes of gravestones prompting a thought of an uncared graveyard among wheat fields, of a fresh grave beneath the starry night and the feel of a soft, living, yielding body beneath him as he slowly stroked to pulsing release.

From the crest of the hill he saw below him with sudden relief a bright line of streetlamps as he came down the asphalt road widening into a street and he passed white wood-sided stores with tall, dark windows, the road becoming a concrete, tar-patched grid with sidewalks along storefronts raised above the level of the road.

Yet having finally reached the town, despite the dark fronts of closed buildings, he felt conspicuous. Descending from darkness to what he thought an oasis of light, he found instead a sudden challenge from a messenger of some curse sent by some angry god he must have displeased. What blasphemy had he committed deserving what he now faced? He had met others like this man, would meet others, all reminding him of Pa's demanding authority, compelling a sympathetic response to threat and anger and an urge to flee he always fought to resist. The other moved toward him along the opposite side of the street while Felix crept along the dark, closed storefronts glancing at them out of the corner of his eye while watching the shadowy figure that came to oppose and confront him.

Felix held himself in check, squelching his fear. A few more steps passing through and he'd be safe when moving beyond the town toward the freedom and the safety of the open road and the crossroad ahead somewhere lost in night. There the traffic intersecting from every part of the state would give him more chances for a ride. He would walk there. He had come this far. He could walk a little farther, even though his legs felt numb from the long walk through the night to this town with its street lamps he passed under, these store fronts he moved along, the challenge of the dark figure opposite giving him more than a once over. Felix noted the dark trousers, light shirt, both creased; the peaked hat with gleaming, plastic brim concealing the face, generalizing it, masking it. The orange light of streetlamp caught the leather holster slung from the man's hip; the long, thick club; the polished shoes. The man passed opposite still eyeing him. Felix cautiously returned the man's inspection, surprised to see how young the man seemed, perhaps no more than a half-decade older than he, even more dangerous. Felix turned away his gaze toward the dark sky above the glowing lamps of the thoroughfare.

"Don't challenge him," Felix told himself. The man would try to prove himself since they were so close in age. *"Don't ask for trouble. You're just passing through. If you don't feel guilty, you won't look guilty. You're just curious, just interested."*

He moved on self-consciously inspecting storefronts.

He had been this way before. How long ago? Somewhere along this line of stores was a place he had stopped one time traveling the other direction, a restaurant where he ate with the man in the convertible who had given him a ride to this town before the man went on without him, leaving Felix to pay the tab. That place obviously would be closed now this time of night if it still existed. But he wished he could find some place open. He could use something: a glass of cold water, a cup of coffee, a bite to eat would make him feel better. He thought of the miles to go before he slept. Now that distance seemed endless.

Here he was suspended in the night, caught in the bright row of lights that led from dim dark to total darkness, a brief oasis on the vast, stirring plain that ripened in the night. Beyond the town, ahead, behind, on either side, the country swept toward hills, toward ranging mountains, toward the distant, western sea. All that lay behind were part of him now, shaping him, taking him forward to where he reached the end of storefronts and again the gravel of the roadside. There he stopped, dropped the bag, and sat on it. His legs ached from fatigue.

He groped in his shirt pocket, found the flattened packet empty. His luck! He crushed it, threw it down, then looked back along the street. The man had turned, crossed the street to the side where Felix sat, had stopped, watching him. Felix retrieved the packet, ironed it with his fingers, folded it, stuffed it in his pocket. He cursed his blundering. Would he ever learn? He rose, hauling up his bag, walked on, reached grass that edged the gravel and concrete grid of roadway. The carpeting of lawn enticed him. He stopped. Tempted, he gave in, let the bag fall, then dropped himself.

The grass felt cool beneath him. He propped himself against the bag, studied the dark, rambling house, then looked back up the street. The man was gone. Felix felt relieved. Maybe he could stay here, rest here through the night. Then in the dawn he might find someplace open, could clean up, maybe catch a ride. Back along the road a beam of light flared the sky at the edge of the hill he himself had crested. Felix saw the row of running lights of an eighteen-wheeler descending toward the town. Perhaps here might be a ride that would carry him away from this place. But when the semi reached town slowly moving through swept by shadows and light, it passed Felix without pause. Felix watched it move off into the dark, its engine laboring through numerous gears.

Up the street, the man reappeared. Felix watched the man climb into a patrol car, start the engine, then swing the car around so that the headlights caught Felix in their beams. Felix squinted against the glare. The headlights went out. Felix waited. He watched the dark shape seated in the patrol car. Then he saw the glow of cigarette and envied the pleasure. Now he sat with his legs and body relaxed still aching from the long walk. What lay ahead? How far had he come? How far would he have to go? How much more night was left until dawn?

He sat at the edge of the prairie town beneath the orange light of street lamps scattered by the leafy canopy of trees. Felix thought of Pa who joined the police force for a time, one of the many jobs Felix remembered him having, first in the large city where Pa had lived his whole life, then in a suburb of that city, the small town where Felix spent his adolescent years and Pa a volunteer constable. Both times Pa failed at something he always wanted, the first time for accepting a free drink in a tavern on his city beat even though off duty. Having accepted a gratuity, accused of taking a bribe, forced to resign, he, again, too vocal in advocating rights for workers in a system thoroughly corrupted by those controlling it for their own benefit. Pa's second attempt at law enforcement as a volunteer constable failed when confronting two town locals he stopped for some infraction. They mocked him, taunting him to use his weapon when he challenged them with it drawn but backed away as they pounced and beat him. Felix lying in bed had listened to Pa heave in sobs of humiliation and anger while reliving his failure. Felix also felt defeated and humiliated as he did now recalling Pa's breaking voice of complete dejection. Felix never before or since had heard someone sound so weak in such despair, Felix having suffered his own at the hands of the sons of the men who had beaten Pa, they ganging up on Felix the next day at school to taunt him for his father's cowardice, Felix suffering his own defeat, they nagging him with glee, sending him fleeing home sobbing to wail his grief and anger. Why had he been cursed to become his father's son and inherit Pa's weakness!

Having dozed, Felix came awake when he heard the starter motor of the patrol car whine, the engine catch and roar. He watched the black and white vehicle creep toward him underneath the street lamps, the light gleaming off the polished hood and grille moving through the shadows in between, stopping beside where Felix sat on the lawn of an antique, balloon-frame house. As he watched the window slide down, Felix felt his bowels begin to roil, his sphincter clamp. The man leaned across the seat. Felix saw the sharp, young features, hardly older than his own. The young officer waved him over. Felix pushed himself up from the lawn, ambled to the car with studied indifference, bent toward the open window.

"You going someplace special?" the officer asked.

"I guess."

"Where you headed?"

"The crossroads," Felix said.

"Then?"

"Home."

The man glanced past Felix to the bag behind him on the lawn.

"You done service," the man said.

"Some," Felix said.

"I never did, not like I'm doin' now," the man admitted. "Get your bag and get in."

Felix's spirit sunk, then surged anxious. Yet, he turned with deliberate slowness, fighting to keep calm. He had done nothing, had nothing to hide, nothing to fear. He was just passing through. He had cash and traveler's checks. He snatched up his bag and worried it to the car. The man reached to unlock the rear door.

"Stow you gear back there. Sit up here."

Felix complied. He climbed beside the man who relocked the doors, settled behind the wheel, put the car in gear, glanced behind him, and started off. He swung out onto the road, increasing speed, every movement precise, as if by the number, carrying Felix along. The man took off his hat, reaching back without taking his eyes off the road to set it on the back seat, and Felix saw the man for how young he was and the sharp features that seemed thin, the chin peaked, the hair trimmed flat on top, fine and fair, a complement to the dark pants and light-blue short-sleeve shirt with sharp creases, the black, polished shoes.

"There's a law against hitching rides in this state," the man stated breaking silence. He offered Felix a cigarette. Felix took it with a brief thanks lighting it with his own matches. Felix, not knowing the law, assumed the man was right.

"Don't have much money. I'm trying to save." Felix offered. He noted the strange sound of his own voice, his manner of speaking in contrast to the man beside him. He seemed to have picked up the patterns of regional dialect from those whom he had left behind perhaps already rising in the dawn as he moved away from them toward day, he seeing them now as ghostly images.

"Still against the law," the man said.

Felix kept silent.

"I wouldn't think you could get many rides this time of night."

"I couldn't," Felix admitted. "I walked from the junction with US 30."

"That's twenty miles!"

"Really? Well, I didn't have anything better to do." He felt suddenly light-headed, talkative. "I thought of sleeping alongside the road, but I felt odd about that. It didn't feel right. Out West, it's different. There's more room, I guess. I've hitched rides all over the place. Slept where I dropped. Went off into the brush or the trees, anyplace there was shelter."

"This ain't the West."

"I know," Felix said.

"Every try underneath highway overpasses?"

"A good place, Felix agreed. He felt himself begin to relax. The man began to seem almost friendly.

"Seems to be," the man said. "I've picked up enough transients there."

Felix felt himself tense. He remained silent waiting for what might come next.

"And you walked all the way from the junction."

"Sure," Felix said. What kind of interrogation was this? "I wasn't sleepy. So I just started walking. The bag got heavy, though. My legs got really tired, but the walking was all right. I'm used to it. I've done a lot."

"You must be in an awful hurry to get somewhere."

Felix considered. "Maybe," he admitted. "I hadn't really given it much thought."

But having said that, he did think about the many miles that had brought him here to this place and the many miles ahead if he somehow could get beyond the place where he found himself now.

"What you got there?" the cop behind the desk asked when Felix and the young cop entered, the young cop leading the way while Felix wrestled his bag inside, setting it beside the screen door. The man behind the desk looked up from the magazine, his face still young but soft and fleshy as the rest of him, his chin obscured by jowls, his neck thick disappearing into his meaty shoulders. 'Soldier boy?"

"Transient," the young cop said. He hung his hat and club on a peg near the screen door open to the night, the light from inside splaying out across the stairs attracting large, hard-shelled insects that flung themselves against the mesh and clung there trapped, beating their wings.

Felix got his first good look at him. Five or six years older than he, the young cop seemed thin in his neat uniform, his sharp features almost delicate.

"Caught him trying to hitch a ride."

Caught! Felix thought, wisely keeping his own counsel. *Hitch a ride! I was just sitting on the lawn resting!*

"There's been lots of those through these days," the fat cop said. His fat hand leafed a page of the magazine and Felix caught a glimpse of bare skin, of naked hip and thigh and breast. He felt his own brief response while he watched the man's dark eyes sweep the page beneath his thick hands. "Where they all come from? Where they all go? You'd think they'd have something better to do then coming into places they're not wanted, bothering people."

Bothering people! Felix thought. *I wasn't bothering anyone! What's going on here!*

"Going to lock him up?" the desk cop asked.

Lock me up! Felix thought. *What for?*

"He says he's looking for a place to rest," the young cop said, his voice flat. Felix studied him and saw the other man's wry smile.

"We've got plenty of room if he wants to rest here."

The man reached the back cover of his magazine. He let it lie on the desk, then pushed back his chair and rose. Felix saw the rest of him that matched his face and hands: the meaty shoulders, porcine chest and arms and legs, and a paunch that strained his shirt and hung over his wide belt. The man saw Felix inspecting him.

"He's a young one, ain't he? What you lookin' at pretty boy!"

Felix remained silent.

"Anything doin'?" the fat cop asked, turning away from Felix, his face twisted in disgust and condescension.

"It's quiet." the young cop said.

"Think I'll take a look," the desk cop said, looking again at Felix. He hitched up his pants, grabbed at his crotch. Then he moved from behind the desk in a ponderous, rolling gait. He approached Felix to look up at him full in the face.

"Take your time," the young cop said. "I'll let you know if something happens."

"From the looks of it," the fat cop said, looking Felix over, "You won't be needing me."

"I think I can handle things," the young cop said.

"I'm sure you can."

He moved past Felix to the hat peg where he retrieved his hat but kept it in his hand. "Too hot for this," he said, as he moved slowly to the screen door and out, scattering the winged insects that whirled around his heavy form moving away into the dark.

Felix felt the void after the stout man's departure. The two young men shared the stillness, the buzz and whir of insects at the screen door, the drone of the ceiling fan that slowly stirred the heavy humid air.

"Have a seat," the young cop ordered.

Felix took a chair against the wall near the door facing the desk behind which the young cop now moved.

"You want coffee?"

Felix studied the man, surprised by the man's offer.

"Probably too hot for coffee. How about something cold? Cold would be better, wouldn't it?"

"Water would be welcomed."

"Don't have cold water. But I guess you could put ice in it. We got ice in the fridge in the kitchen. It's back there through that door. Glasses in the cupboard. Help yourself."

Felix studied the man who now sat and glanced down at the magazine that he now picked up. He held it out before him to look at the cover. Then he leaned to open a drawer, shoved the magazine inside, and slammed the drawer.

"Don't know why he wastes his time on that stuff," he said, looking at Felix who returned his inspection. "Thought you wanted water."

Felix hesitated, then pushed himself up from the chair and made his way toward the door the young cop had directed him. Inside the room, Felix found a small light underneath a cabinet above the sink, the light casting soft shadows on a brown wood table and benches on square, brown vinyl tile. He found a glass, filled it with water from the tap, then went to the small white, round-top fridge where he found ice in a metal tray. He took out two loose cubes and added them to his glass. Then he went back out to take up his station by the door. He drank and studied the man behind the desk who was reading, surprising Felix from his selection, Dana's *Two Years Before the Mast*.

The man looked over the edge of his book. "You find everything all right?"

"Yes. Fine. Thanks."

The man returned to his reading, allowing Felix to inspect the room, beginning to wonder now why he was here and what he would have to do if he were ever going to get out of this place.

"You ever read this?" the man asked, peering again over the top of his book.

Felix nodded, meeting the man's clear, bright eyes.

"Thought you had."

"A good read."

"It is." Then. "Wouldn't it be great to do what he did?"

"I have in a way."

"Really! What was it like!"

"Have you got to the places where he's in California? I've been to some of those. Stood right where he stood at land's end, where Drake once stood. You get a real sense of what's gone on."

"Sounds great!"

"It was!"

The two young men fell to a studied silence, watching each other, wondering perhaps what the other was thinking, both trying to see through the other's eyes, the one landlocked, trying to see the blue, glistening sea and pounding surf, the other remembering living in a small town similar to this one where he now found himself.

"Must be nice to be able to do things like that," the young cop said, finally. "No ties. Go where you want. See different places. I wish I could do that."

"Why don't you?" Felix asked.

"Not much chance for that in this line of work."

"Don't you get vacations?"

"Sure. But then I have to catch up on all the things around here I couldn't get done during the year. This job is twenty-four hours a day, seven days a week.

"Maybe you should consider another line of work."

"Easy enough for you to say! Oh, I've thought of that, now and then. Not sure what I'd do. Sort of just grew into this one. My dad used to be town constable all the time I was growing up and the town still small without all the recent housing developments and the regional shopping center. He loved what he did, always wanted to be what he was. He never wanted to do anything else. I used to ride along with him. Seemed an easy enough job to do. Still not much excitement around here. Steady pay. People here grow up with a respect for law and order. They know me, respect me, count on me to keeps things quiet and safe. It's not been all that bad."

"Except you can never get away."

"You're right there. Not much chance to do that. Maybe someday, though." He placed a colored, printed marker in the book and set it on the desktop

"So you're from here." Felix ventured.

"Born right here. Edge of town. You were sitting on the lawn. Lived here the whole time. Born here. Raised here. Probably die here."

"Family?"

"What? You mean married? No, not that — thank God!"

"Girlfriend, though."

"I guess, kinda. 'Cept she's gettin' ready to leave herself."

"And you'll stay."

"Of course. Have to. Got my job here. Where would I go? She don't know where she's goin'. She says she wants to go out to California and

Hollywood. See what it's like. Just wants to get out of here. Don't blame her. But I'll stay. What would I do someplace else?"

Felix didn't have a ready answer. It would be out of place, smart-alecky if he were to offer counsel. So he just studied the man who looked back studying him.

"Where you say you served?" the man asked.

"I didn't."

The two young men fell silent. They listened to the sounds of the night: the insects at the screen door, the whirring of the fan, the hum of the fridge in the kitchen, the car engine that announced the other man's return. Felix felt himself tense, bracing himself for something, for what, he wasn't sure.

They heard the engine die, the car door slam, heavy footsteps on the porch, the screen door screek, and then the man's bulk filling the door.

"You ain't locked him up, yet!" the man groused.

Felix wasn't sure if he was serious.

"You ought to lock him up."

"On what charge?"

"On whatever. Vagrancy. Hitchhiking. Anything. Keep him around awhile."

"What for?"

"You know damn well what for. Use him around here. Not often we get such a young one come through. He's a fresh one, I bet."

Felix didn't like the man's insinuations. He didn't want to begin to consider what the man might mean.

"I bet he's cherry!" The man declared, then turned to Felix. "Hey, boy! You cherry?"

Felix studied the man, not sure how to answer.

"You must know what 'cherry' means."

Felix just studied the man's smug expression.

"Well, why don't we just see?"

Felix looked at the young man behind the desk. What had just happened? Why the change once the fat cop returned. The young man returned his study.

"Come along with me," the fat one ordered. He started toward the kitchen.

Felix rose still looking at the young man behind the desk and followed the man who led the way.

"First we better have you shower. You like that? Probably need it. You smell kinda ripe. It's right back there. There's soap and towels, a robe for when you're through. We'll take your clothes until we're finished. Just leave them on the hook outside the shower."

"Why do you need my clothes?" Felix asked. He felt a bit relieved knowing most of the money he had was in traveler's checks buried in his bag. "What's going on here?"

"You don't ask questions here, boy! Anybody asks questions, it's me! And you'll see soon enough what's going on! Now get in there and clean up your stinkin' body. Get it real clean so we can appreciate how pure and sweet you are!"

Felix went through the kitchen to the small shower room. There he reluctantly undressed, hung his clothes on a wall peg, then stepped into the shower, studied the taps, then twisted them. The hot water once he adjusted it was refreshing after more than one day not having access. Then he rinsed himself, shut off the taps, let the water bead from him, then swept back the plastic curtain, and reached for the thin towel hung on a row of pegs. The peg that had held his clothes was empty. In their place hung a thin cloth robe, faded and worn. He dried himself, ran his hands through his shaggy hair, hung the thin, damp towel on the peg, reached for the robe and put it on. The cloth belt was missing, so he pulled the robe around him and stepped into his shoes.

What now?

He waited.

"You 'bout through, pretty boy?" the voice called. "Get on out here when you're ready!"

Felix in untied shoes shuffled into the kitchen clutching the robe around him, his arms pressed against his sides.

"Well, now! Don't you look cute!"

Felix felt humbled under their inspection.

"Let's see what we got!"

Felix studied the man, confused.

"Get rid of the robe!"

"What's this all about?" Felix asked.

"You know damn well what this all about! Don't tell me this hasn't happened before, someone so young and pretty! I know your kind! I knew you right away! Now just get rid of the robe, or I'll have to help you! And I don't think you'd want me to do that, would you!"

Felix pulled the robe from his shoulders and stood holding it in his hand. The man approached him and took the robe, stepping back to look him over. Felix had never felt so naked, so exposed.

"Not bad," the man said. "You'll do just fine."

They directed him to a bench with a vinyl cushion set out in the center of the room. Ordering him down onto it, he lowered himself by his arms until he lay with his belly on the smooth plastic, his vitals crushed beneath him while they pulled his arms and legs over the sides so that they splayed and they bound him with cloth belts to the cold metal legs of the bench.

"Now we're ready!" the man said. "You ready, pretty boy?"

Felix was sure without a doubt what the man meant. He knew how he would feel later, bleed, most likely, but now bound by both wrists and ankles to the chrome legs, naked and splayed, belly down on the vinyl bench, he accepted what was happening as punishment or retribution for some unconfessed crime or sin. He should have seen it coming. Now it was here.

"Get ready for this!" the man ordered.

In the narrow, tall mirror on the wall at his head, Felix saw the man knead his buttocks, spreading him. He saw the man's pale, thick, hairy thighs, the hanging sack between, and the gorged root of flesh thrusting from the groin. He saw the man lean to place himself. Then he felt a spongy firmness pressing in, making him dizzy. He felt the firm flesh withdraw and felt swept with relief.

"We better use something to help us," the man said. "You're tighter and more cherry than I thought."

Felix saw the man take up a tube, squeeze out a glob on his hand than stroke himself, making his hard flesh gleam. Then he approached Felix again, placed himself again, pressed in again, withdrew slightly, then pressed in again, deeper. Felix felt himself spread, felt himself gorged, the man forcing himself in until Felix felt himself fully impaled.

"He sure is a tight one," the man exclaimed.

Felix gripped the bench, wincing, beginning to ride with the man's movements.

"You really like this, don't you?" the man hissed.

Felix remained silent, answering by bracing himself, pressing back against the man's quick thrusts.

"He really likes it," the man said, increasing his efforts. "How come I can always tell when one of you guys likes being reamed?"

His thrusts increased to where they became vicious. Felix rode with the man's pounding, yielding to the sense of fullness, of being gorged, the weird sense of feeling complete, of having wanted what now was actually happening. Why had the possibility of such violent fulfillment always fascinated him, attracting him with its sense of vicious power? How could such a display of violence validate him, complete him, compensating for the void left by rejection? What did all this have to do with Pa?

Giving himself up to the man's steady stroking rhythm, Felix relaxed, now that the man's movements became easier, smooth and slick from ointment, and Felix felt himself begin to stir, the steady, strong stroking filling him so that he felt he might reach release until he felt the man suddenly pulse into him, grunting until the stroking slowed, stopped, the man stood with his flesh still inside, the man heaving to catch his breath, slowly withdrawing, leaving Felix straddled on the bench expecting the other to take him now that his experience with the first had released something repressed, kept under control. He thought of Fat Jack and how his former friend had used him in much the same way. He thought of his brother Sonny with whom he had come close to what he had just been through. But that time he had made Sonny stop, and they had ended as usual by satisfying their nascent urges using their usual way by straddling each other at the same time, their gorged flesh in each other's mouth.

"That was sweet!" the fat one said, slapping Felix on his bare bottom. "Thanks, pretty boy! Your turn," he said to the other cop.

"I think I'll pass," the young one offered.

"Come on," the fat one said. "You know the deal! No one has something on the other!"

"This one's different," the young one said.

"What you mean different? What you two been doin' while I was gone?"

"Just talkin'"

"Well, you got to do more than just talk!" the fat cop ordered. "You know you always want this as much as I do, so don't kid me!

"I'm not kiddin' you," the young one said, but then knelt at Felix's head at the end of the bench offering Felix tumescent flesh.

"Open wide!" the fat cop ordered.

Felix complied by taking in the young man's flesh feeling it grow full and firm as the man began stroking into Felix who remained with eyes closed, arms pressed against the cushion of the bench, his hands gripping the chrome legs, perversely fulfilled.

"Look at him go!" the fat one cried. "He really does dig this! "Don't you, boy?"

Felix knew they didn't want an answer. Instead, he focused on the feel of flesh in his mouth and throat, filling him, its firm sponginess, the slick feel of the skin as it slid back along the hard shaft beneath, the faint, warm odor from the groin, a bit of sweat, a bit fecal, he using his tongue to circle the gorged glans, the most sensitive part, prompting a soft moan from the man who stroked into him. Felix knew all this from a long time ago with Sonny and with his friend Jack. He felt the man grip his shoulders, increasing his thrusts, grunting as Felix felt the flesh in his mouth swell and then the warm, pulsing gush against his throat, pooling there as he held it, letting it gather.

"Don't save it!" the fat one ordered, but Felix knew well when to swallow, savoring the thick sudden musky flavor. "That's it!" the fat one yelled, seeing Felix's moving throat. "That's good! Take it all!" he yelled while the young one continued to pump pulse after pulse, Felix gulping the thick, ripe flow until the young one slowed, stopped, withdrew, slippery and red.

The man rose from his knees, rubbing Felix's hair. "Thanks," the young man said, and Felix felt suddenly used.

Then they released him and left, allowing Felix to gather, rise, move to clean himself, then slowly dress.

When he went into the outer room, the fat one was behind the desk, the young one leaning against the wall. Felix met their gaze, their eyes searching his face. Both studied him with wry smiles.

Then the young one pushed himself away from his post. "Come on," he said, "I'll give you a lift to the crossroads."

The eighteen-wheeler, its heavy staccato diesel thrumming steady and dull moved through the rain soaked dawn of Midwest countryside, the silent driver in the soft glow of the dash lights, and Felix nodding in troubled sleep, jostled and swaying with the forward momentum of the truck. Felix came awake as they arrived at a town on the state line, the truck slowing, the driver downshifting, the truck coming to a shuddering halt of gasping Jake brakes beside the yellow and red service station across from a café that displayed a blue and white sign indicating it was also a Greyhound bus station. Felix shouldered open the cab door, tossed his bag before him to the pavement before he climbed down from the cab, turned back to thank the driver who nodded then saluted him farewell. Felix slammed the door and stood back to watch as the huge rig lumbered away, growing smaller as it moved off, its engine winding through endless gears leaving Felix watch it go, hoist his bag, and start across the station driveway.

In the open service bay, a young man watched him approach. About the same age as Felix, most likely a year or two younger, he remained mute when Felix asked to use the facilities but pointed him the way. Returned, relieved and freshened, Felix found the young man standing where Felix had left him as if the youth were a guard surveying the line of redbrick, nineteenth-century buildings across the street, one that held the café and bus station.

Felix dug in his pocket for change that he plugged into the machine, waited for the coins to drop, made his selection, then fought the bottle from its metal frame. He pried off the cap, letting the cap fall into a receptacle, raised the bottle to his lips, and drank. His thirst relieved, he turned to join the youth in his study of the plate glass store fronts, the tall, narrow windows of the apartments above in the redbrick building across the road.

"You ever notice," the youth asked suddenly, "all these old buildings seem to look about the same?"

At first Felix didn't know if the young man was addressing the remark to him. The youth seemed to be addressing the rain soaked facades themselves. Felix wondered if the young man really wanted an answer.

"Probably because they all were built around the same time," he finally offered.

"I guess that's likely."

Then silence, while the two young men continued their survey of the building across the way.

"You come a long way?"

"California by way of Oregon."

"Really! That is a long way! What's California like!"

How many times had Felix tried answering the question the young man asked? And every time he tried, he never quite knew what to say. How could he even begin to describe for someone who hadn't ever been there what it was like? At times, it had been hard for him to grasp that what he had been living through was real, that after all the years of dreaming, seeing it projected on movie screens, and only recently on the new medium of television, portrayed in *Life* photos, a magazine to which Pa had subscribed for years and which Felix had devoured after the latest issue had been relinquished, Felix had done it; he had made it; he had arrived at last in California, unlike those left behind who would only be able to dream of what he had witnessed. He knew his answer should be brief, that those who had asked wanted a quick report, not some lengthy discourse.

"I hear it's gorgeous, warm and sunny and dry," the young man offered, "not like here and all this rain!"

"Oh, it rains all right!" Felix informed the youth. "When it does, its a downpour. In L.A. — Los Angeles — the rivers have concrete walls and bed and are dry as a bleached bone most of the year until it rains. Then the deluge turns intersections into lakes, the sewers spout like fountains, and the concrete river becomes a brown flood that sweeps everything away — trash, cars, people. It's quite amazing!"

"Sounds like it! But it still must be gorgeous when it's not raining!"

"It has its beauty, all right."

"It can't be like this place. Rain in the spring and summer. Snow in the winter. And cold. God! How I hate this place!"

Despite once having lived the same experience himself, Felix wasn't sure how to respond.

"I hear the babes are something else — all those movie stars! You see any movie stars?"

"They save their appearances for the big screen and stay in hiding most of the time."

"I'd like to see some movie stars! And go to the beaches! And see the ocean! You seen the ocean? You been to the beaches?"

Felix admitted he had seen both.

"That must have been great! I'm so sick and tired of looking at these old brick buildings! I'm just about ready to die! Ocean beaches! Hollywood! Movie stars! God! What I wouldn't give to get away from this place! Go out to Hollywood! Go to that place where all the movie stars have their names put on the sidewalk! Maybe even I'd see a movie star!"

Felix thought best not tell the young man that the actual Hollywood was quite ordinary, some places quite ugly. He could imagine the youth's response if he revealed his own sense of deflation and disillusionment on first arriving at the end of his own pilgrimage: Surveying the bus station appearing more like a castoff gas station surrounded by acreage of parking stalls, the line of redbrick buildings along Hollywood and Vine seemed so much like all the other small cities he had wandered through in the steady direction of his dream. He had studied the broken concrete walks, the debris and refuse that swept along the gutters in chilled wind at midnight, and there had been no movie stars.

Where was that Hollywood of glamour and fame that he himself had heard of, had dreamt of, had envisioned, just as this younger man, listening in wonder to the reports of someone who had been there, an accidental acquaintance who had offered Felix photos? How would the young man he stood with now respond if Felix told him that the glamorous Hollywood of movie stars was more an illusion of the mind than its actual location?

"Maybe someday you'll get there," Felix offered. He finished his drink and set the empty bottle in the case beside the machine.

"Don't I wish! But I don't think that's going to be anytime soon!"

"Why don't you just go?"

"Leave my job? I know it's not much, and I do get tired of it, doing the same thing, day after day, year after year, but I couldn't just quit! Besides, Sarah would never let me go!"

"You need permission?"

"Not exactly permission," the youth said somewhat defensively. Me and Sarah been going together a long time, all through high school. It'd be hard just leavin' like she didn't mean a thing."

"So you'll stay here and do what?"

"Not really sure. 'Bout what I'm doin' now. Maybe get my own station."

"And that's what you really want to do?"

"I guess. I'm not sure what else. I'm not sure what I might do."

"Get married? Start a family?"

"I guess. I know that don't sound like much. And I guess it bothers me some too. When I look around, seems as if everything I do in my life wants to keep me here, hold me back. I guess that's why I think California be'd so great to see. Get out of here and see what the rest of the world is like.

"So what do you all do around here?"

"Work mostly. Besides this, we sometimes help out the local farmers with their harvest once it's ready. Other than that, not much to do. There's the movie house to go to now and then, hang out in one of the local pubs, cruise around in our cars when we're not workin' on them to keep them runnin'."

To Felix, listening to the young man's account, the town seemed sealed in amber, not much beyond what Felix once lived just a few years ago living in a small Midwest town much like this one, growing up in a small circle of friends, working on cars, hanging out at the local drive-in, pursuing without much success girls flowering into women expecting marriage.

He wondered how much different he really was from this young man. Yet, he did feel different, and he wondered why. His time in the National Guard Army Reserve? His travels? His year in college? His working the grain fields in Oregon? His being uncommitted to anyplace, to anyone, surviving as best he could offering himself in exchange? Surely those experiences had reshaped his mind. He'd be moving on shortly in a matter of minutes, and the youth would go back to his study of the soiled, rain-drenched brick buildings across the way, his work in the red and yellow service station, his long-time, adolescent love, Sarah.

Rain during the night had forced Felix to seek shelter underneath a highway overpass where he had waited out the fierce storm of lightning bolts that flared in the darkness with explosive thunder claps that echoed and bounced off the concrete tube jarring Felix and filling him with awe. Now, while he and the young man talked, the sky grew darker, a bright bolt shot across the sky, a sharp crack rattling the frame and windows of the metal envelope in which they stood. Then the warm rain in a sudden torrent washed over pavements, running in shimmering sheets. The sudden squall drove them back into the service bay where they stood mute watching the rain as a humped figure dashed in, his head covered in a team jacket, cursing the rain.

About the same age, the two younger men greeted each other warmly and fell to talking about the previous night's adventures, the possibilities later that evening, and as the two friends talked, Felix felt excluded even more so by the questioning glances the friend cast at this obvious stranger in rumpled denim jacket with faded jeans and green duffle. The two friends talked dates while Felix surveyed the fronts of buildings across the street pummeled by downpour.

Then the rain eased, Felix grabbed his bag, moved out through the open bay door across the sluicing driveway. Hunching against the rain, he hurried across the street to the cafe where he bought a cup of coffee and held it so that it warmed his hands, adding a stream of sugar for nourishment. While he sipped his brew, he looked back across the street at the young attendant lost in talk to his friend, having obviously forgotten the transient with the green duffle and how he had confessed to the stranger his heartfelt dreams.

Felix suddenly felt weary, drained from his journey, the previous night's walk, the troubling assault that had revived feelings long repressed, the fitful night of dozing under an overpass during a storm of thunder and lightning. Giving into his fatigue and his doubt of hitching rides because of steady rain the last hundred miles to the city that was his destination, he bought a bus ticket and waited while looking across at the youths in the station.

The bus arrived as Felix finished a second coffee. Felix boarded, found a seat at the rear, and settled for the long ride into the city where he was headed. The dreariness of rain-soaked dawn and grayness of day seemed to match Felix's mood as he pondered his return. Now he began to wonder if returning to his origins was such a prosperous move.

Then as the bus left the town through rain-washed, overcast streets, Felix looked back at the two youths in the station bay still talking as they were swept behind and Felix swept forward on the bus. The mist rising from rain-drenched fields, dulled grass, dulled rain-steeped buildings, dulled head-hung animals, the warmth of the close, plush interior of the bus lulled him, dragging him down. Felix dropped asleep to the steady, staccato pulse of the diesel at his back.

Felix slowly woke to view passing buildings that seemed familiar. Fully awake, he looked into the face of a small, blond girl with bright, blue eyes who disappeared giggling behind the back of the seat before him. He thought of distant wheat fields and another blond-haired girl who had cried out wanting him to stay, making him promise to return, offering him a photo image of herself so he wouldn't forget. He thought of how he had tried to tell her that he had to go, even though he couldn't tell her why. What was it that had driven him from those warm, bright eyes and bright smile to this indifferent road and its now sunbaked asphalt with steaming waves shimmering upward to the now cloudless sky?

He chided himself for having fallen asleep missing the countryside that always moved him so deeply, its terrain of lakes and fields and woods of ancient soaring oak rising in swells of high, ranging hills of kettle moraine scooped out by the slow scouring press of ancient glacier, that landscape having nurtured him, inspiring him in his quest for some way to express his response to what he had witnessed. Chiding himself for having missed that passing scene, he resigned himself to viewing the familiar streets now sweeping by, the familiar storefronts, two-story wood flats that hadn't changed through all the years he had lived here and the year he had been away, their gray, slatboard siding seemed a comforting constant as he passed them in his cushioned perch looking down at people moving slowly along sidewalks going about their appointed errands as he passed through the remaining streets to the depot.

At the bus station, roused from his seat, he moved sidewise along the aisle behind other discharging passengers, stopping to retrieve his bag a porter stooped to haul out from the cargo bay beneath the bus. Shouldering his bag, Felix moved through the crowd into the waiting room that seemed unchanged he remembered from trips he had taken to the city from Sunfish, the country town where he had lived and he had missed while asleep. He went to the men's room to wash the sleep from his eyes, use the facilities with strangers along the line of porcelain receptacles, moved back through the waiting room, and out of the station to the sidewalk.

As he left, he observed how foreign people appeared to him now since he was no longer a part of their lives. Having left and now returned, the bonds from adolescence severed, now a sojourner, unkempt from days of travel, scruffy, and tired, he moved to the city bus stop. There he waited until an electric trolley bus glided up beside him. The door flapped opened, the driver peering down at him, Felix hauled his bag up the stairs, dropped coins into the fare box, made his way down the aisle swaying from seat to seat, jostled from side to side as the trolley pulled away from the curb. Felix fell into a green vinyl seat beneath his bag that he straightened on the seat beside him. Then he righted himself and gazed out the window at the passing scene so familiar from all the times he had traveled this route, but now the passing scene tinged with strangeness from the intervening years since last he rode this way on a bus. He noted slight changes that others who had remained would pass over: old stores and warehouses, relics from another era when horses pulled carts and carriages, then horseless carriages, then streetcar trolley cars moved through these streets and had vanished. Some derelict buildings remained, their windows boarded over. Felix imagined spectral images of men with thick moustaches in bowler hats and white shirt sleeves with black elastic arm bands and black heavy trousers held up by suspenders gazing out from dirt-clouded, cobwebbed windows as he passed.

The trolley bus reached the towering brick factory building of the Allen Bradley Company that made electric motors where Pa had worked for a spell when Felix was a child, the amber, ozone odor of hot electric motors still present. The overhead wires sparked and crackled as the trolley slowed to negotiate the turn up Greenfield. Now Felix was in home territory: Down a side street on 11th he could glimpse the antique dwelling where he once rented a room just before he had left for California. Over another block on 13th he caught a brief view of the rounded front of the Carnegie Library with its massive curved windows where as a child he had haunted the towering shelves of books, their leather and colored bindings, their large size and thickness holding him in awe as he struggled to heave them from their place and open them on the large varnished oak tables. Then in the holy hush he had leafed through thin pages, scanning the rich, black print, surveying the magic script and illustrations.

Why he still was so fascinated by crawling things he wasn't sure, ants especially, they seemed so orderly, so dedicated. He carrying some of the volumes he selected, placing them on the tall, varnished wood counter, challenged by the expected inquisition as to whether such tomes weren't too difficult for him, he finally able to check them out with his very own card on which the librarian typed his name and on which he had signed in cursive his name as carefully as he had been taught. From those books, he had gleaned information he then tested against his own experience, belly down, his nose to the small, grainy pile circling the hole, his gaze fastened on the quick comings and goings of the busy creatures so much smaller than he indifferent to his divine scrutiny.

The bus glided to a stop on the corner of 24th and Greenfield. He descended through the rear door. The bus glided away, its electric motor humming, and Felix found himself left alone in the quiet open air of his old neighborhood. Not knowing what he might face, he started up the side street past houses and buildings here so long, his having seen them his whole life, he never doubted they would be here, one a shanty that in the previous century had been a store but during Felix's childhood used for storing bundles of *The Sentinel* that Felix would help his older brother Sonny assemble for his morning paper route, the small, closed building redolent with the fragrance of pulp paper and newsprint. Reaching the faded, red brick alleyway, green picket fence and gate with trellis rife with roses he went under and through, he moved down the concrete walk beside rose beds bordering the marbled cinderblock foundation with small cellar windows and reached the concrete stoop and gray door paneled with frosted glass. Felix pushed the button beside the door, heard the faint, familiar buzzer within as he twisted the worn, yellow knob, pulled on the knob, finding the door unlocked, as he knew it would be, started up the steep, gray enamel steps of sun porch hauling his green bag after, and saw the short, heavy-set woman with wire-rimmed glasses in her seat at the chrome-legged table, her face slack in surprise before it flowered into a smile and dancing eyes.

"Felix!" she cried, struggling up from her chair, her flower-print house dress gaping revealing her dark gauze hose.

They met at the top of the stairs. Felix dropped his bag to embrace her then let her step back to inspect him.

"My goodness, what a surprise! Come in! Come in! Where have you been!"

"Been to college in California, Grandma. Just hitchhiked here from Oregon where I helped harvest grain."

"You've been traveling! You must be hungry! You look almost starved! Why don't you just let me get you something! Coffee? How about breakfast?"

"Cup of coffee would be great."

"You need more than that! I'll just fix you something." So she set about the kitchen, as he knew she would, beginning to prepare for him one of those meals he remembered well from the times he had spent with her when she had lived alone between her two marriages after the death of her first husband, Felix's Grandpa Emil.

Felix let his bag rest beside the doorway as he sat himself at the table. The old woman moved her short, bulky body to the tall cupboards with clear glass fronts. She took out a green fireware mug and set it on the fake marble formica table top, moved to the old gas range to take up the enameled pot, moved to the table to pour the black liquid into the heavy, pale green mug.

Felix let the coffee steam before he raised the cup to his lips. He watched the familiar yellow bird flit around its cage then rest on a perch to offer a sudden burst of warbling song. His grandmother had kept such a bird — the same species, the same color — for as long as Felix could remember, one replaced immediately after the previous one was discovered dead in its bath. Felix always enjoyed those occasions when the canary at some unknown prompting burst into melodious warbling even though caged.

"Where's Ma?" he asked after what he thought an appropriate interval.

"Oh, my, I don't see much of her anymore. Nor your father, for that matter, not since they came back from Florida."

The hot liquid burned his lips. He set down the mug on the smooth formica tabletop. "How come they didn't move in with you? How long since you've seen either one?"

The old woman took the seat across from him and sipped at her cup before she answered. "It must be couple of months since I've seen your mother, almost a year now since I've seen your father."

She rose and moved to the cupboard again drawing out a plate then moved to the breadbox from which she drew pastries and placed on the plate then set the plate on the table before Felix.

"How come they stopped coming around?" Felix asked. He reached for one of the pastries and brought it to his mouth suddenly aware of how long it had been since he last ate, his senses responding to the mixed aromas rising from the skillet simmering above the low, blue flame on the stove.

"Guess they didn't want to see me anymore."

"Didn't want to see you anymore! What brought that on! Pa has always thought this place his!"

The woman rose and went to the stove to tend the skillet. "Well, I guess he must have changed his mind."

"Why would he change his mind!"

"You know your father."

Felix had to agree, but he felt there was something else going on that the old woman wasn't telling him, something she was reluctant to talk about, and he thought that his place wasn't to push her for an answer. Besides, he most likely would find out what was going on soon enough once he found his parents, although now he didn't know how eager he was to find them.

He leaned back while the woman brought the plate of steaming food from the stove to the table and set it before him. Felix saw the yellow yolks of eggs filmed with white, the edges crispy with a tinge of brown; he saw the crinkled bacon, the toasted bread and suddenly felt his hunger. He dug into the food conscious of the look of approval from the woman who watched him wolf down the food.

"I just knew you were hungry," she said.

"You still fry up a great breakfast, Grandma."

The old woman patted him on the shoulder, went to the stove to get the coffee pot, came to freshen Felix's cup, refilled her own, sat herself once again across from him, and watched him devour the food.

"You want more? You can have more if you're that hungry!"

"This is plenty," Felix said. "It's been a while since I last had a full meal."

"It appears that way."

"So where they living now?" Felix asked.

"Above the drugstore."

"On the corner across from Tess's tavern?"

The woman nodded. Felix thought about this piece of information while he finished his food, using the bread to clean the plate of egg yolk and bacon fat.

Gildner's pharmacy was maybe no more than a hundred yards away from where he now sat. That was so much like Pa. Live close enough to the house he always claimed as his to keep it under surveillance. Felix recalled how they always had lived within a block or two of the dwelling that had been the family home long before Felix issued into the light: For a year or two, during the last years of the Second Planetary War, Felix and his brother Sonny and their parents had lived in an upper duplex flat just down Greenfield from Laynie's tavern across the avenue close enough Felix could often see his grandmother working in the backyard. Before that, they had lived at the end of the next block in a lower flat beside what was once the Abbey theater, no more than a few minutes walk down the alleyway beside the house in which he now sat and ate. Before that, they had lived across Greenfield from the place beside the Abbey in a basement flat on an alley off 22nd Street at the end of a gangway behind a two-story stucco flat facing the avenue and the movie theatre opposite. The only time the family had moved from the neighborhood they had been expelled from this house and lived during Felix's troubled adolescence in a cottage at Little Sunfish Lake near the small country town of the same name Felix had missed while asleep on his way into the city by bus.

Something seemed almost Freudian about Pa's reluctance to move from out of what some might view as his territory. Felix had read that gorillas were known to have a larger territorial range of twenty miles compared to the two or three city blocks where Felix had lived during his childhood. What was going on here?

"I guess your father got mad because of what he learned after Ed died." the old woman said, breaking into his dark reverie.

"So what did happen?" Felix asked. "What's been going on around here, Grandma!"

"It hasn't been pretty," the woman said. "Least not for me."

"Will you please tell me what happened!"

"Now you calm yourself," the woman cooed. "You're starting to sound just like your father."

Felix calmed. "Sorry," he said, stung by the woman's remark. He sat back and waited for the woman to continue.

"Well, as you said, your father always thought this place eventually would be his."

"I heard him say more than once, but I guess it's no surprise he might think this place his since he lived here most of his life, and he always talked about how he had helped Grandpa fix the place years ago. So I guess he might expect the place would eventually be his."

"Well, that's what your Grandpa thought. And that's what I wanted too"

"So, then what's the problem?"

"Well, I met Ed a year or so after your grandpa died."

"OK, so you met Ed."

"And we, well, got together."

"I remember your going out together to dances and Bingo. And I remember how Ed and Pa used to go places together."

"And then Ed moved in with us."

"And you two eventually got married. So what was the problem?"

Felix thought curious their "living in sin," given her faith and what Felix knew of her prudish victorian attitude toward sex, the conception of her two children more a result of rape. In addition, both she and Ed were well into senior status. Felix felt odd trying to image such old people having sex. Maybe they had just been companions.

"Well, after Ed and I got married, your father and Ed didn't get along. Whereas once they did things together—going to sporting events and things like that, they got into fights as to how things should go around here and who should decide."

"So you moved us out, Pa bought the cottage in Sunfish, and we didn't see you for a while. Why was that reason enough not to see you after Ed suddenly died? Seems to me that should have taken care of the problem of who would get the house."

"It wasn't that easy. You see, after you and your brother and your parents moved out, Ed thought we should have some work on the house that really needed to be done. He wanted to do some remodeling. Put in a bathroom up here so we didn't have to go down to the basement at night or use a camber pot like we had for years. Lord knows after all our years of going up and down those spiral stairs day or night and this place so old it certainly could have used some remodeling. But, as you can see, we never got around to remodeling or fixing anything."

"Because Ed died so suddenly."

"Ed's death wasn't the problem."

"Then what in the world was!"

"Now just be patient. I'm trying to tell you, but it's a subject hard for me to talk about."

"Sorry."

"The problem was that Ed borrowed money — a good sum, in fact."

"For the repairs and the remodeling."

"Well, that's what he said it was for. But he actually invested it in some scheme that someone sold him on."

"Don't tell me. Let me guess. The scheme went bad, just like Pa buying land in Florida and Arizona on speculation."

"It was never good from the start."

"He lost the money."

"He lost the money. The sticky part is that he borrowed the money from his son and signed a contract putting up this house as collateral."

"But it wasn't his! How could he do that!" Did you agree to the deal?

"I did agree thinking the money would go for repairs and remodeling. He was my husband. Half of it was his by marriage."

"But only half, yet he had you sign the whole thing over to his son as collateral?"

"When Ed lost the money, and we couldn't pay on the loan, his son claimed the house belonged to him."

"And my father has been completely aced out."

"And your aunt. Some of it would have gone to her."

"Has anyone seen a lawyer?"

"Your father and I talked to one, but we were told that what it would cost to take this through the courts would be more than what the house is worth and that we'd most likely lose the case since I signed the agreement."

"So no one can do anything."

"And your father is hurt and angry."

"And doesn't want to see you because he thinks you're to blame for his loss of the house."

"Yes, he blames me."

Felix saw her eyes grow moist. Now she pulled a linen kerchief from her apron pocket and dabbed at her eyes.

"It'll be all right, Grandma," he said, feeling awkward seeing her tears. "I'll talk to him."

"He won't listen. You know how he is!"

Felix knew, but he felt he should do something. What could he do? He certainly wasn't looking forward to confronting Pa from whom he had felt estranged and alienated long before he had left for California.

"I'll think of something," he said.

The food that he found delicious moments before now churned in his gut. What a homecoming! Why had he thought the situation might have changed! It had changed, all right! It was worse! So now what?

"Now don't you go and get yourself all upset," the old woman warned.

"Well, he makes me mad!"

"Getting mad at him won't help. You know that. You know how he is. You'll just end up getting angry yourself. He'll just be the same, and nothing will have changed."

"I know, Grandma. I know." He tried to calm. "Maybe I should talk to Ma first. See what she thinks. Surely she can't feel the same way. She must just be going along with want he wants because he's forcing her to, just like he always has."

"You can talk to her if you think that will do any good. Other times like this she's usually come around on her own without your father knowing it. This time it's different. I haven't heard a word from either of them since all this happened."

"I'll talk to her. I'll go see her now."

"You won't find her home. She's working now."

"Working! When did that happen! Pa would never let his wife work! That would reflect on his ability as a husband and provider! How'd she manage that!"

"I don't know. I only just found out myself. One day I was talking with folks at Gildner's. They asked me how your mother liked her job. I was surprised as you. But I didn't let them know. I simply told them that she thought it just fine even though I knew nothing about it. No sense letting people see us air our linen in public. Our family misunderstandings would just give them something to talk about."

"Misunderstandings! That's so like you, Grandma, always trying to put the best face on things."

"Well, better to think positive. Otherwise, you just make things worse."

"So where she working? What she doing? She never worked a day in her life outside the house."

"From what I heard, she's a salesclerk at Gimbels in South Gate."

"Salesclerk? Strange. Maybe I'll run out there and find her and talk to her first before having to deal with Pa. OK if I leave my bag here until I size up the situation?"

"Of course you may. There's plenty room here. Just me. More room here most likely than in the one bedroom apartment your parents live in above the drugstore. You just let your things here. Your welcome to stay as long as you like. Be more comfortable for you anyway. Give you more space to move about."

"You're right there, Grandma. I'm not sure I could stand more than half an hour under the same roof with Pa. He'd be ordering me around as if I were still under his command because my feet were under his table just as he had after I finished high school."

"Just leave your things here. I'll fix up the bed in the attic room for you, just like it was when you used to live here. You go along now! Go find your mother! She'll be happy to see you!"

"O.K. Grandma. I'll sort my stuff as soon as I get this other business straightened out."

"Now don't go getting yourself on the outs with your folks!"

"That shouldn't be difficult."

He rose from his seat.

"Leave your plate," she said. "I'll tend to it."

Felix took his jacket from the back of the chair where he had hung it while he ate. Slipping it on, he went to place his arm around her shoulder then leaned to kiss the top of her head.

"Everything will work out," he said.

"I know, Felix" she said, reaching back to squeeze his arm. "Go find your mother."

"That should be interesting," he said as he turned away from her, leaving his bag beside the door, descending the gray enamel steps of the sun porch with its riot of green plants, stepping down to the door with its frosted pane, then out along the walk to the street, heading for the corner where he had descended from the bus only a short time ago. Now suddenly that time seemed long past.

The trip to the shopping mall just beyond the city limits took Felix past places he knew well from childhood. Having roamed these streets as a boy mostly alone but sometimes with friends, how familiar these changeless settings seemed now as he started out walking, heading for the boulevard three blocks distant where he would catch a bus that would take him south across town to the city limits. Cross corner from where he turned from the side street heading for 27th and Layton Boulevard, he studied the tan brick pharmacy across the avenue, a contrast to the gray wood or asphalt tile sidings of neighboring structures. Above the pharmacy a row of windows for apartments, one where his parents now resided. Always curious as to what he might discover behind those dark frame windows with drawn beige shades, now he might soon find out, how much he wanted to yet another question.

Next to the pharmacy, the small beer depot where every adult male in the neighborhood bought his favorite brand of hometown beer by the case. On special occasions for one of the frequent anniversaries or wedding receptions or neighborhood block parties, someone would buy a keg. Felix remembered how crowded and closed the place seemed with its low ceiling, narrow aisles, shelves crammed with products that seemed to young Felix a riot of color, the cases and coolers from which he sometimes was allowed to select a soda, the racks displaying small cellophane packages of snacks from which on rare occasions Pa feeling surprisingly expansive Felix was allowed to choose a treat.

Next to the depot, the bait and tackle shop where Felix accompanied his father and grandfather before they on a rare occasion went fishing on Little Sunfish Lake where thy eventually lived, but Felix just as infrequently entered the shop alone when he thought he could afford real hook, line, and sinker for trying his luck at the pond in Mitchell Park five blocks from his grandmother's, he paying for that extravagant purchase from his small cache of coins garnered in a Mason jar what he had earned from running errands, yard work summers, shoveling snow winters, and birthdays, monies he once considered an abundance of wealth, and Felix suddenly aware of the cache of traveler's checks he now carried in the pocket of his denim jacket.

Felix liked the bait and tackle shop just because he had found the place such a fascinating collection of earthly delights: the large glass and wood display cases filled with glittering, glimmering, multicolored lures, spinners, and reels; a rich assortment of tobacco products: cigarette packages in gay colors lined in neat rows alongside cans of pipe tobacco. The dim interior of the place ripe with fragrances of tobacco leaf, racks of fishing rods lined the dark-stained clapboard walls. All this wealth seemed surveyed by the glass eyes of the large moose head that dominated one wall, the huge elk head on another wall near the high, scrolled, white plaster ceiling. On yet another wall behind the glass cases, a large, hexagonal clock with roman numerals ticking slowly to the steady slow movement of the tarnished pendulum that swayed to and fro through plumes of tobacco smoke.

Felix could not recall anyone else waiting on him other than the gray-haired man with square, sharp features and red, watery eyes who emerged through the door that led to the mysterious back of the building. Felix always enjoyed most that brief time after he climbed the weathered gray concrete steps and he entered the tall glass door in its dark green frame that matched the stores exterior. The small, brass bell suspended from above the door quiet, he had stood alone on the wide board floor worn bare listening to the slow ticking of the clock, watching the ponderous sway of the tarnished brass pendulum, meeting the glassy-eyed stare of the elk's head, the dead, noble gaze of the moose head, marveled again at the monstrous, dark purple crustacean almost black suspended by almost invisible wires from the ceiling. The stillness, the throb of his own blood in his head, and his being alone among all those marvelous creatures had filled him with a spooky sense of awe. Then the gray-haired man, even older than Grandpa Fist, would emerge through that entrance at the rear and take his place behind the barrier of glass showcases over which he presided with an air of gloomy resignation. Felix now recalled never seeing another customer all the times he had entered alone.

Felix passed a grocery on the corner of 25th, the store once part of the National Tea Company chain he had gone with Ma when she went looking for items not carried by the small, green grocer and butcher shop she frequented next to Laynie's Tavern Pa frequented on Greenfield between 23th and 24th. Crossing 26th, Felix came upon the church school playground where he once played with Jimmy, his Catholic friend, the tall spire of Saint Lawrence church topped with a cross. The German bakery just before 27th where, despite his recent meal, the rich aromas issuing onto the street compelled him to stop before the large window and study the rich display of cakes, loaves, and pastries. Here he had come with Pa, or often he had been sent alone to buy fresh hard rolls he never could find anywhere else. Across the avenue from the bakery, another pharmacy, this one with large, dark wood framed windows used as display cases for various products, the interior with two rows of dark stained wood booths one of which he had slid into with Sonny after Sunday School, or sometimes with his parents in the evening on special occasions, he rewarded for good grades and allowed to order an ice cream sundae with hot fudge and chopped nuts and real whipped cream all for twenty cents, a cost that now seemed enviously small. Here, Felix had brought a girl from his church school fourth grade class on his first arranged "date," paying for their sundaes with coins he reluctantly had taken from his cache of coins in a Mason jar.

Felix waited on 27th for the light to allow him to cross Layton Boulevard. Cross corner was the convent, a granite block, medieval-looking structure that always had fascinated him by its cloistered appearance with its towers, its wrought iron fence, another laurel hedge barrier behind the fence where he rarely saw any movement, any life, save for the times he had seen women he knew as nuns gliding out in long, black habits and white coifs and long, black, heavy chains from which hung heavy, silver crosses, the women moving so quietly, so smoothly, they had seemed not to have ever touched the ground.

Felix reached the safety of the opposite side then crossed the street again to stand at the bus stop before the granite block pillar corner post for the wrought iron fence of the convent. He studied the structure, curious as to why even the large, tall windows in the curved walls of the towers seemed blank shutting out the world. From where he stood, he could see back cross corner to the rounded glass block entrance of the lounge with its door trimmed in chrome. As a boy he had always been intrigued by the sounds and odors exuding from the dark interior when the door opened to reveal a row of men sitting on chrome-legged stools, blinking against the sudden spear of light that caught them in its glare as the door opened and Felix had caught the gleam of glasses filled with amber liquid.

Up the street from the corner lounge, the yellow stucco house that Felix had visited on occasion to play with Vernon, a boy from the Christian grade school they had attended next to the pile of redbrick church on 23rd. Here at Vernon's house, they had constructed elaborate fantasies they printed out carefully as they could, "publishing" them by using red rubber stamps of letters in what they considered a newspaper to which Felix with a feeling of self-importance had contributed his first nascent attempts at art. Felix could not recall their ever having distributed their publication to any of the neighboring houses so quiet they always had seemed vacant. Perhaps they had sold one or two for a nickel each to some accommodating adult who indulged a whim of promoting the young boys entrepreneurial sprit. Now Felix again wondered whatever had happened to that pale, thin, somewhat sickly appearing boy whom he had befriended as the newest kid in class when others teased and tormented the gaunt boy with thin hair that had always hung across his forehead and his eyes. The boy's lips so pale and thin, the boy's hands so delicate with fine bones, Felix thought the boy more a girl. Then Vernon had stopped coming to school because of some unexplained illness, and Felix never saw him again.

One time, Felix had boldly gone to the yellow stucco house to ask for Vernon. Going up the short, yellow walk to the low semi circle of stoop painted rose red to complement the tile roof and trim and low evergreen shrubs that nestled the windows and the pillars of the porch, Felix had used the pearl button beside the rose red door and had heard the melodious notes of the door chime. The door had opened to a woman Felix had never seen before who informed him that Vernon had moved. Felix sadly sensed the boy had died.

Tired of waiting for the bus, Felix decided to walk. He could catch a bus along the way, boarding at one of the several major intersections he knew he would have to cross on his way out to the mall.

As he started out, he passed the convent and reached the sanatorium. He always having thought that the two were somehow connected, he again marveled at the sweeping lawn and gardens, inhabitants swaddled in white blankets in white wicker chairs taking the sun. They still seemed like specters, their gaunt faces made more ghostly by the dull coloring of the chairs on which they lounged, the white stone facade of the building, the white wrought iron fence a continuation of the black fence of the neighboring convent. Felix on first seeing it had repeated the word 'sanatorium' over and over to himself, curious at the sound of the word. The place and the word that described it had always seemed spooky.

As he walked on, he studied the houses along the way. They were typical two storied, mostly built of wood, some of brick, some of asphalt tile siding, all with balconies that ran along the front held up by wide brick pillars of the porch below. Felix found curious how many variations could be played upon s basic design. The houses a part of his life from having walked this way before, how many times, he couldn't say, he knew them as ageless, seemingly more so by the elm trees that once had reached above the gables and the peaked roofs, the elms long gone from a voracious fungus now replaced by towering oak. He walked on, enjoying the scene, the full-leafed oak, the beauty of the boulevard center strip planted in seasonal flowers rich in full color, the trimmed, ripe grass surrounding the beds of dark, rich soil. Summer, the season of ripeness on the cusp of autumn, the season of decay, he took in all through his senses and felt exulted, the earlier anger and frustration subdued. Such social foibles and challenges now seemed minor and of little merit.

He crossed side streets with names he recognized — Lapham, then Mitchell, so he played the game he had played as a boy seeing if he could guess the name of the next street, all the streets bearing names of some pioneer of the area who had developed it, their names scattered in places and institutions and thoroughfares across the city. He enjoyed a childish delight when he found that he still knew all of them as he passed, his pace steady now and determined.

Some streets held significance. Down Burnham, if he walked several blocks he would reach his great aunt's house, Pa's aunt, one more source of Pa's bitter disappointment, Pa having thought he his aunt's favorite from his frequent help maintaining her house and therefore her heir but not even mentioned in her will, Felix always fascinated by his Great Aunt Vi who boasted of her travels throughout the West, tokens of those adventures she displayed in a wood and curved glass china cabinet along with photos of her wearing fringed leather western garb posed before the Painted Desert and the Grand Canyon, she assuming an attitude as if she were responsible for both. Beyond his aunt's, Burnham Public Park with its ball field where Felix had played with friends, and in winter when the field was flooded and frozen, Felix had skated for hours, then had walked back home along the same route he now traversed, his feet numb, his legs rubbery after the endless gliding over the crisp surface of the rink, he showing off on his racing skates with 16-inch blades. Felix now wondered what had happened to those skates. Most likely in a trunk in Grandma's attic. Maybe when he had time and inclination, he'd search for them. Why, he didn't know.

He reached Forest Home, a major thoroughfare where Felix viewed the cemetery Pa at eighteen or nineteen during the Great Depression had worked at one of his first fulltime jobs cutting grass among the graves of Grandma Fist's family, he having previously worked part time in a sweet shop owned by his Aunt May, the shop adjacent to a movie theater where he had met Ma. Here the broad avenue ran off to the shimmering horizon, leading to the village beside Little Sunfish Lake where Felix once had lived in a cottage throughout a troubled adolescence.

Felix now knew he had come farther than he had thought, the bus he had wanted to take roaring past him, so he walked on enjoying after days of confined travel the stretch of his muscle and his memory, filled with a strange joy at seeing again all he passed and how little changed each place seemed. Further down Forest Home, the factory named for its German founder Rundle where Pa had worked for almost 20 years before being considered redundant. Beyond Forest Home and the Heil Company where Gloria's husband worked, Felix came upon Kinnickinnic River Parkway. Through the parkway, what now seemed a small creek flowed beneath the concrete bridge where Felix stopped to gaze down at the endlessly, quietly purling water. Along these banks he once had wandered chasing frogs or turtles, dragonflies, or any other living thing that moved, breaking off cattails and using the fat, brown, furry cylinders as if they were cigars, young Felix suddenly feeling for a fleeting second grown up. Another wide, busy intersection at Oklahoma, a tavern and a bowling alley all in one where sometimes he had accompanied Pa to tournaments. Opposite, another expanded greenbelt and a rambling tan brick building, the secondary school that Gloria once had attended named for Pulaski, a Revolutionary War hero.

Felix had to hurry to negotiate the wide avenue with its steady flow of traffic. Then safely across on the sidewalk, he reached the border of South Gate, a shopping center with an enclosed mall. The row of flats and towering trees ended, the terrain flattened into a vast asphalt parking lot with striped parking and a line of stores and fast food outlets, the mall emerging from glittering black asphalt with structures of glass and polished stone and neon signs lit even in full daylight. Somewhere in all that bustle of wandering people he would have to search for his mother, and he felt surprised again that he would find her here, so far now from the neighborhood ghetto that had nurtured them both throughout their lives.

He found her with a woman customer. How strange to see her so familiar to him only in her kitchen at home now dressed appropriately for the world of work, attending, apparently with efficiency, her professional tasks. He saw she noticed him, her face showing surprise and delight, saw her turn back to the woman about her age who followed the direction of Ma's inspection, the woman listening to the salesclerk explain her sudden distraction, smiling with Ma as both inspected Felix standing there at a respectful distance, somewhat rumpled in faded jeans and denim jacket and well-worn shoes.

Felix watched as the two woman turned back to complete the sale. Then his mother came around from behind the glass case. He approached, presenting himself, knowing he would not receive her embrace, especially not here in so public a place.

"So you're finally here," she said.

Felix looked down into her face with features so much like his. "You didn't get my card?"

"Yes, of course, but how was I to get hold to you?" Felix wondered if her way of speaking now suddenly noticeable to him was an echo of her place of origin or a dialect of the region.

"You travel so much," she said. "I would have let you know."

"How did all this happen?"

"My working? I'll tell you later. Where are you staying?"

"I thought I might stay with you."

"That would be so nice. But, you know, our apartment is yet so small. And your father how he so likes his space."

"I heard about your living above Gildner's. I thought Pa probably wouldn't like to be crowded. So why didn't you live with Grandma Fist after you and Pa got back from Florida?"

"We'll talk later."

"Well, my bag's at Grandma's. There's plenty of room. She said it would be all right if I stayed with her."

"That would be good" his mother said. "She would like company, I'm sure. And we would be so close, we could visit any time I'm not here."

"Pa would let you visit? Grandma says you haven't been to see her for a while."

"Well, I've been so busy."

They studied each other. Felix should have known that seeking her here would go nowhere.

"Go get yourself settled," his mother said. "I'll come as soon as I can."

Then she moved away, going back behind the barrier of the glass counter, approaching another woman customer waiting with obvious growing impatience.

Felix took a bus back to his grandmother's. He woke from his brooding reflections regarding family "misunderstandings" by the looming shape that resolved into a bus gliding to a stop where he stood. The door flapped open; he climbed the steps, deposited his fare, dropped onto the green vinyl side seat across from the driver, allowing him to look out the large windshield and from time to time view the passing scene through the windows opposite.

On the way, he stared out at the streets and houses and trees he had just recently passed walking the other direction. How quick the return seemed — almost a blur —except for one instance when he saw a young man in rumpled denim jacket, faded jeans, scruffy shoes, unkempt hair striding in the direction of South Gate.

"You're back!" Grandma Fist exclaimed when he reached her house and climbed the sun porch steps into the kitchen.

She rose from the chrome and formica table upon which were spread rows of cards set out in a game of Solitaire.

"Sit down, Felix! Have some fresh brewed coffee that will go well with the *kuchen* I made while you were gone."

"Coffee cake! It's been years since the last time I've had anything as good as yours!"

"You just sit there and have as much as you like!"

She served him with a wide grin that wrinkled her round face and sparkled her eyes behind her wire-rimmed glasses. Felix dug in without waiting for coffee, and when she poured him a cup, he helped himself to seconds, eating it more slowly, taking it in between sips of the fresh, strong brew, he obviously enjoying both.

"Nothing like your coffee and cake, Grandma!"

"I don't get much of a chance to bake for anyone anymore."

"And they never come around at all?"

"Not at all. Your mother used to without your father knowing, that is before she started work. Now she hasn't been here for a while herself."

"Not much seems to have changed while I was gone. Ma having to sneak around behind Pa's back to do something she shouldn't have to think twice about doing!"

"She just thought it easier that way, I guess. Keeps things quieter if your father doesn't know."

"No surprise."

They sipped their coffee. Felix wondered where all this was leading. He certainly hadn't come home for all this. If he had known, if he had even suspected, he would have stayed away. But now he was here, and he felt obligated to do something, if for no one else than the woman who sat across from him at the table. Now she remained silent, pensive. As he studied her, those features so much like Pa's only smaller, fuller, and rounder, mostly due to age, he wondered what her life had been like. Despite how familiar she seemed through all the years he had known her, he suddenly understood he knew almost nothing about her. Did he know anything about anyone — especially himself? Shouldn't the psychology class he had spring semester of 16 weeks help? He set down his cup, pushed back his chair. Rising, he pulled on his denim jacket.

"I better go see them," he said. "Ma should be home by now. Maybe I can make some sense out of all this."

"Your father will be there before her. Don't you go getting yourself in trouble now."

"I'll be O.K., Grandma. I'll be back in a bit. We'll do something together like we used to."

"That would be a nice change," she said. "I don't seem to get out much anymore."

Felix went to her, kissed the top of her gray head then turned toward the door.

"Guess I'll go face the Old Man!" he said.

"Be careful, Felix!" she called after, but he was already down the stairs, out through the frosted paneled door to the concrete stoop and walkway that ran to the front gate.

Felix instead used the side gate into the red brick alleyway unchanged in decades, went up the alley to the street, then down the street to the corner, and crossed the street to the tan and pink brick pharmacy. He glanced through the large display windows to where he saw Ma involved in a mimed exchange with two other women and felt a bit relieved that he wouldn't have to face Pa alone then chided himself for his fear. He waited outside the doorway for her to come out through the double door, first the glass door with its polished brass handle, then the wooden screen door he recalled from other summers when it was continually opening and slamming to.

She looked up from bending over arranging her purse, startled to see him looming over her. Then recognizing her son, she greeted him as if he had never been away. He followed her around the corner of the building to the doorway that led to the apartments above and followed her up the narrow, carpeted stairs to a short corridor with flowered carpeting that led to three varnished doors. She stopped at the center door, turned the knob, and entered.

Felix tagged along behind into the galley kitchen and small combined sitting and dining area where Felix saw Pa's broad back as the stout man, taller than Felix, bent over the sink.

"Well, you finally made it home!" Pa said angrily without turning. He held the pot beneath the faucet, filling it, his back to those who studied him.

"I had some errands," Felix's mother said quietly, accepting her husband's complaint, as always.

"This place is too damned empty when I get here and you're not back from work!" Pa complained. He set down the pot to insert the basket and fill the basket from a tin that sat on the counter beneath blond cabinets. "There's no fresh coffee," he grumbled.

He placed the pot on the range, bending to adjust the blue flame beneath. "You'd think a man who's been on his feet all day could come home to fresh coffee!" Then he straightened and finally turned.

"You don't seem to have any problem making your own coffee." Felix offered.

"Well! Look who finally got around to coming home!" his father said through forced laughter.

Felix silently met Pa's inspection.

"Felix, why don't you take off your jacket," Ma said. "Sit yourself. Make yourself at home. We soon will have fresh coffee."

She left the kitchen carrying her summer jacket and purse. Felix removing his jacket and hanging in on a chair, he sat at the fake colonial period table.

"Home!" Pa called after her down the hallway as he joined his son at the table. "You call this a home! This cheese box!"

"Look's comfortable enough to me," Felix offered.

"What would you know! You don't live here! Nothing's as comfortable as a house! That's what we ought to have!"

Felix's mother returned to the kitchen. "Henry!" she said in a weary voice as she entered, as if she had heard his complaint more than enough. "Don't you start again!"

"Well," Felix's father grumbled, conceding to his wife. Then he turned toward Felix, as if he were displacing his bitterness. "So how's the great scholar!"

"I'm fine, Pa," Felix said wearily. "And I'm not a great scholar."

"Why not!" the older man asked, his voice sarcastic. "Then what the hell you've been doing? How many degrees have you earned so far?"

"I've only finished my first year, Pa," Felix replied, resigning himself to his father's uninformed challenge. "I won't have an associate degree until I finish my second year, and I don't really need that to transfer to a four-year school. Besides, degrees themselves don't really mean much. You don't wear them like a badge of honor. They allow you to add letters to your name that make you feel important. What you learn is more important."

"Then how do you know how much you've learned?"

"Good question! I'm assigned grades, but I'm never sure how much they indicate what I've actually learned. I get a grade. No one tells me what I did right or wrong to get that grade or what I might do to get a better grade when I think I've done better and learned more than the grade they gave me."

"So have you learned *any*thing! Why'd you go through all the trouble quitting your job, moving out to California! You could have learned just as much or just as little here!"

"Oh, I've learned plenty besides what I've learned from my classes! You better believe making it on my own, especially in California, has been nothing like what I've experienced before. Besides, the way my life was going and I was given the chance to get away from what I was doing, I thought my leaving for a new location I didn't know would help me decide where I was headed, and I think it has. But I'm still not sure how what I've learned will actually help me get to where I want to go."

"Doing what? What's your goal? How are you using your opportunity going to college as a way to better yourself! When you going to learn you can't always set out on your own in your own direction without considering where it might get you? How come no one's taught you that!"

"What about your union work? Weren't you setting out in a direction no one else wanted to follow? Didn't you take risks on your own doing what others were afraid to try? What were you doing when you were trying to organize for fair wages and better working conditions for everyone, not only yourself?"

"That's now history," Pa replied, he sounding suddenly deflated. "It didn't work out." His voice went softer still. "Nothing's worked out the way I wanted."

Felix moved to the advantage of his father's regret. "So college isn't working exactly the way I thought. But I'm still learning lots I never knew or even thought about before."

"So you're lucky. Me? I barely made it through tech school. Why would I even think of college? Look what hard times did to me with a wife and kids. What college would accept me? Too much baggage. I have no one to blame but myself."

The man seemed slumped in his chair, hunched over his coffee, cradling the cup, as if it would give him solace. Felix's mother, in contrast, straightened in hers.

"Now, Henry," she said. "You know how much you wanted to start a family! You went and got me pregnant with Sonny so we could get married."

She turned to Felix. "Your Grandpa Fist did not allow at first your father and me to marry so young."

"He just wanted to keep me under his thumb," Pa offered, regaining his edge. "The old lush! Why he cared, I'll never know! He was drunk most the time, anyway! Always taking out after Ma when he was in his cups, bitter and angry about his life and what he never was able to achieve!"

"Like father, like son," Felix mused silently. Then thinking he saw an opening, he ventured broaching the problem he promised his grandmother he would help resolve.

"Speaking of Grandma and how poorly she's been treated, why haven't you visited her since you got back from Florida?"

"She tell you she's been poorly treated by me? Well, I've been busy!"

"So busy you don't even have time to just stop in to see how she might be doing?"

"I've been busy!" Pa insisted, "She's got a phone and my number! If she needed something because of something really important, she could call me!"

"And that's it! You condemn Grandpa for his physical abuse. Yet you haven't considered what her life is like alone and you refuse to visit her? Have you considered what that might be doing to her!

"Well, smart ass with all your college, what about what she's done to me!"

"What has she done that's so terrible you no longer want to see her?"

"What she did with the house. After all that I put into it and she kicks us out because of some guy she meets at an old people's dance and moves him in, and he invests in some crooked scheme that takes all the money he's borrowed using the house as collateral and when he can't pay back the loan, his son who lent him the money claims the house is his!"

"But that happened years ago and now he's dead. Is that enough of a reason for not visiting your mother?

"You bet it is because I'm still pissed off! That house is mine! And as far as I'm concerned, that's reason enough, so don't keep at me about it!

Felix studied Pa's angry face and decided that he would have to try something else, unclear as what that something else might be.

The two men sat mute: Felix weary from his prosecution, Pa stung by the son's unaccustomed, sustained challenge from someone he wasn't sure he knew. They faced each other as if in a stalemate, neither of them knowing what move to make next.

Felix's mother seized the opportunity to establish a truce. "Some people called about you, Felix!"

"Really! When?"

"Again just the other day. Someone named Jack who said he knew you from belonging to your Guard unit and he would like to see you whenever you showed up. And someone else." Her wry smile made her seem like a conspirator. "A woman! She called too! She said she knew you well from high school."

"What she want? I haven't seen or heard from anyone since high school, except for Greg D'Amico's sudden arrival in Long Beach."

"Well, she called right out of the blue. She wanted to know where you were, and when I told her, she asked if you might be coming home anytime soon, she said she'd like to see you if you did."

"Really! I wonder why she called?"

"And one day little Nancy asked about you. I saw her one day at work."

Felix noticed how much emphasis his mother put on the word 'work,' as if she wanted to remind everyone of her new status.

"She came right up to me. 'Hi, Mrs. Fist! Remember me?' So cheery, just like always. Why you two broke up, I'll never understand."

During this exchange, Felix's father rose, went to the stove, poured himself more coffee, stood listening to their chatter, then returned to his seat ready to insinuate himself into their cozy exchange.

"He broke up with her because lover boy here met that older dame!"

Felix's mother frowned but ignored the intrusion. "I said to her, 'Sure, I remember you!' She's so grown up now. 'Whatever happened to Felix?' she asked. I told her what I knew — which wasn't much — since you never wrote. She said she's married now, just as the other woman who called."

"Sounds as if everyone's married."

"Everybody but you!" Pa growled. "Might do you some good!"

"You hear anything from Greg D'Amico?" Felix asked ignoring his father.

"No, he has never called. Whatever happened between you and Nancy? We always thought you two would marry some day. You seemed so close."

"You bet they were close!" his father said. "They were screwin' all the time!"

"Henry!"

"Well, they were! Right out on the sun porch when we lived at the lake. They'd get under the covers on his bed. I could tell what they were doing. I got ears. And a nose. Let me tell you, they were hot stuff!"

"Henry Fist! You are absolutely terrible!"

"What! For telling what's true? Then he met that married dame! What was her name?"

"Gloria," Felix offered quietly.

"Yeah, that's it!"

"Gloria? Who then was Gloria?"

"You know who Gloria was," Pa said, impatient at what he took to be his wife's slowness. "That older dame he used to work with before he went out to California!"

"Oh, now I remember," Felix's mother said. "She was anyway a little too old for you."

"That didn't work out the way I wanted."

"What you expect?" Pa said, his expression smug. "That she'd leave her husband for you? How much older was she, anyway? She hot stuff, too? How come you couldn't be satisfied with someone your own age?"

"So that's my history," Felix said. He knew not responding to Pa's insinuations would do more than offering a direct rebuttal, and if he answered, he knew Pa would dismiss his response. "So you never heard from D'Amico?" he asked his mother.

"No, nothing."

Felix sat at the table and sipped his cold, bitter coffee thinking about the report he had just received. He needed to get away from here where Pa's presence turned him sour. He wanted to get off by himself to put all the items just reported in some context. "I better get back to Grandma's. I need to get settled in."

"So when you takin' off again?" Pa asked.

"Henry! He just got here!"

"He'll be gone again before long!"

"Is that so?" Felix's mother asked.

"I don't know how long I'll stay," Felix said. "School doesn't start until the end of September, but I still have to decide how I'm going to get back out there. I need to travel cheap so I have most of the money I earned harvesting. Finding work is still hard with the recession, and I don't know if the job I had pumping gas will still be there."

"See! There you go again! You throw away a good job to do something else that's more appealing! When you going to learn you can't have everything your own way?

"Would it not be nice to have dinner together some night?" Ma offered, deflecting her spouse's revived attack.

"We could," Felix said, ignoring Pa's renewed assault. "You decide when. My treat. I've made so much money helping harvest, I should be able to afford it."

Then he rose, pulling his jacket from the back of the chair, leaving the cold, bitter black coffee in the cup on the table. He shrugged into his faded jacket and went to the door. There he stopped and turned back to those who watched him from where they sat.

"I'll be staying at Grandma's. You know where that is. You used to live there. You can find me there."

Then he went out and was gone.

Felix stood with the receiver of his grandmother's rotary dial phone to his ear checking for the dial tone then reached for the printed directory beside the phone. He leafed through thin pages, found the page, then moved his finger down the list of names until he found the one he wanted. The name seemed stark, bold, heavy. Felix used the rotary dial of the phone, listened to the ringing on the other end, then heard a baritone voice on the other end.

"D'Amico?" Felix asked.

"Which one? Father or son?"

"That you Greg!"

"Who's this?"

"Felix." he waited but got no response. "Felix Fist!"

"Felix Fist?" Silence. Felix imagined the man processing the information. "Oh! Felix!" the man said, finally. "Hey, guy! How you doin'?"

"OK, considering," Felix said. "Just got here yesterday. Finally able to call you. Thought we'd get together."

"Get together?"

"Yeah, you know. Do something."

"Do something? Like what?"

"I don't know for sure. What do you do for laughs these days?"

"Same as always. Not too many laughs. Go out for a beer. Shoot some pool. What you have in mind?"

"Nothing really. Whatever you feel like doing."

"O.K. I guess we could do something."

"Look, I don't have wheels. You'd have to come get me."

"I guess I could do that. Where you at?"

"My grandmother's. You remember the place? Twenty-fourth off Greenfield?"

Silence. Then, "Oh, yeah. I remember that place. I guess I could find it again. What's a good time?"

"Whatever you say. I don't have any commitments."

"O.K., then, how 'bout seven, seven-thirty? That too late?"

"No. That'd work. I'll watch for you."

"O.K., see you then."

That evening, Felix sat on the top step of the front porch, his grandmother behind him in a rocker he had brought out from the stifling interior. She sat in the warm evening air, her fingers working the thread and needle, tirelessly, endlessly, crocheting one of the continuous projects Felix always saw her working on, producing the delicate, exquisite patterns that would adorn someone's pillow or armchair or dresser or table. They sat quiet in the early evening light watching the traffic passing on the avenue, the coming and going of people from the pharmacy on the far corner, the steady rhythm of the screen door screeching open then slamming to joined in concert as the evening progressed by the added deeper creak of the tavern screen door on the near corner opening and closing to the gathering summer night.

Felix reached into his pocket and took out a watch, an obvious relic, his grandfather's his grandmother had given Felix that morning just after breakfast. He studied the bold roman numerals, felt the smooth, warm casing in his hand filled with a weird sense that he was seeing the numbers through his grandfather's eyes. From inside the closed, stifling house came the faint chiming of the windup, bell-shaped clock stroking the hour from its shelf above the sideboard in the dining room as it had over the past half-century or more.

"What time is that, Grandma?"

"Eight O'clock," the old woman said and kept on with her work without missing a stitch.

"Late as usual," Felix said with resignation, resetting and winding the pocket watch and replacing it in the watch pocket of his Lee's.

"What's that?" she asked, pausing in her work.

"D'Amico." Felix said. "He's been late all his life. All the time we were in high school together, he was always late for everything."

"Some people are just that way," she said and resumed her work.

Felix studied the traffic on the avenue stirred to attention by the sudden appearance of a cherry red '48, V-8 Ford convertible as it slowed then cut in front of the oncoming traffic, the whitewall wheels screaming, the engine roaring, answered by the blast of car horn. Felix watched the car start up the street toward where he rose from the stairs, started down toward the sidewalk as the car slowed suddenly, pulled in at the curb in front of the porch.

Felix stood admiring the perfectly refurbished car as the deeply tanned young man behind the wheel set the handbrake then used the mirror to comb his black, wavy hair, Felix thrilled to see again the young man's handsome, sharp Roman features.

"Some car!" Felix said.

D'Amico climbed out over the door on the curbside to offer Felix his thick, muscular hand.

"I should hope! With all the work I've done on this baby over the years!"

"Must have cost you a bundle."

"Yeah, it did. Plenty."

"How could you afford it? You must be doin' all right."

"I get by. My job pays OK. What's money for? I worked on this baby a bit at a time. Now most of it just upkeep, fixing stuff that goes wrong. But I still got it. Got my baby. The same one. Just the way it always should be. Just like new. Just the way I wanted!"

The two men stood back admiring the car. Another newer vehicle with two men passing in the street slowed to inspect the restored auto. "Looks like it just came off the showroom floor!" the passenger called out the window.

D'Amico waved, acknowledging their admiration, obviously proud, obviously enjoying the attention his baby brought him.

"So you about ready to roll?' D'Amico asked turning to Felix

"Let's go!" Felix exclaimed, pleased to be with his old friend again.

D'Amico went around to the driver's side, waited for a car to pass, the car slowing, one occupant leaning out to offer his remark. D'Amico self-consciously offered his thanks, then climbed in behind the wheel, started the engine, while Felix took the passenger seat. D'Amico revved the engine, checked behind him, then swung the car out onto the street. Felix waved to the old woman on the porch who watched them leave.

Felix felt a surge of joy as he relaxed into the tan leather seat, his arm resting on the door as the car took them smoothly past scenes familiar to Felix from his childhood, those scenes now transformed by their swift passage in the open-air car. The green full canopy of trees rushed by above their heads. The flow of air felt warm and mild, the first early evening lights brilliant and rich with color. Their passage took Felix back to years they had done this in their teens. At each stoplight, those in cars on either side rubbernecked to inspect the car, and D'Amico took advantage of their distraction. At each stoplight he roared away before everyone else, leaving them in his pungent, blue exhaust.

"So you're here!" D'Amico said, surprising Felix with his remark that seemed for the first time to display some excitement in seeing Felix again.

"Yep," Felix said. "I'm here!"

"Been a while."

"I guess."

"So how you been? You still in college?"

"You got my letter, then."

"Yeah, I did."

"I wasn't sure. I never got an answer."

D'Amico took his eyes off the road to look at Felix. His shining, dark eyes held what seemed to Felix a bit of sincere regret.

"Yeah, well, I'm sorry. Really. You know how it goes."

"Sure," Felix responded quietly. "I know."

"So how was it? Must have been rough having to work and take all those classes."

"Yeah, it was. I survived. Not everyone does. Some who live with parents and don't have to work just screw around then drop out."

"Really? Me? I never thought of doing what you done. Why try something I'm not really interested in and don't have the smarts to make it. Not like you. You always had your nose in a book.

"Not like the kind I had to read the past year. So how you've been doing? You've been lucky enough to avoid the draft."

"Yeah. More smarts than luck. I used my head like always. I stay in the Guards but only attend just enough meetings to keep me from getting thrown out and end up drafted. Your going to college and doing well must help keep you safe.

"So far it has," Felix replied and studied the handsome man at his side as D'Amico steered the car into a parking stall before a large tavern Felix had never been to set under a viaduct Felix had often crossed, had seen the tavern roof below, and had always wondered what it was like. They climbed out of the car, moved toward the tavern's large door.

D'Amico turned back briefly to check his car. Two men coming out of the tavern paused to inspect the car, admiring it. "Don't get too close!" D'Amico warned. "I don't want nobody screwing up the finish!"

The men raised a hand, heeding D'Amico's warning, shook their heads, and moved on. Felix and D'Amico entered the tavern where some of the crowd greeted D'Amico by name.

"Meet Felix, my buddy!" D'Amico shouted into the crowd above the jarring music and loud talk. "He just got back from California!"

Felix self-consciously accepted the mixed chorus of praise and condolences offered by people lining the long sweep of dark wood bar that D'Amico and he moved along until they found a space the crowd allowed. They settled into their spot and received tall glasses of foaming liquid from the man behind the bar who greeted D'Amico by given name and nodded to Felix, offering a wet hand. Felix took up his beer, the sharp, bitter taste quenching his thirst. Then he resettled his glass.

"So what you been doing since I last saw you?" Felix asked.

"You mean after I got back from California? Went back to muckin'. You know, helping dig trenches for sewers. About the only job I could find with everybody out of work."

"How come you ended up back here?"

"Well, you remember how it was." D'Amico took up his beer and turned with his back to the bar to survey the boisterous scene. His response seemed almost addressed as much to the crowd as it was to Felix. "I couldn't get work. I thought I had some relative — an uncle or something someplace — in San Diego — Corona del Mar — Chula Vista." D'Amico seemed proud that he could spin off the names so easily, showing that he, too, had traveled, he, too, had class. "I left you a note," he said to Felix. "You didn't find it?" He, again, leaned against the bar, directing his query to the crowd.

"Yeah, I did," Felix said. "I moved after you took off. I couldn't afford the place we had together, so I had to move to a room I could afford until I left for Oregon."

"Well, too bad about that. Things didn't work out too good for me neither. Turned out I couldn't find my relative — or there wasn't one. I did get a job for a while. At an auto service center — Ford, as a matter of fact. But I quit after a week. I came back here."

"How come?"

"Not very good pay. Didn't like California too much! Too busy! Too many strangers! Everybody in a hurry! Everyone going after the same thing! Fame and fortune!" D'Amico quieted. "I got lonely," he admitted grudgingly. "I couldn't make friends. Really! Me! Imagine! So I said, 'To hell with it! Why make something harder than it should be!' So I left. Came back here where I know everybody and everybody knows me."

"You left as fast as you arrived." Felix said with a laugh.

"Yeah. Just as fast." Then D'Amico became animated. "Hey! Were you surprised when I showed up at your friends' place!"

"I was. I was thrilled to see you."

"Thrilled!"

"Sure. I missed you."

"Missed me!"

"Sure," Felix said with some doubt. Perhaps he had shown too much affection. "I'd been away from here longer than I had ever been. I didn't know anyone at first."

"But it worked out better for you. You knew what you wanted. You started school. You met people who were like you — you know, like brainy — artsy. Say, you still do all that stuff?"

"Not much, lately," Felix admitted.

"So how come you're back here? You gunna stay?"

Felix considered how to answer, but before he could respond, D'Amico quaffed the rest of his beer.

"You 'bout ready to cut out for someplace else. Maybe meet some cunt?" D'Amico asked.

He started off through the crowd, pausing along the way to receive the embrace from what Felix thought a very attractive woman. Wasn't that just like his old friend — always the lover, always the ladies' man? Felix followed, threading his way through the crush of bodies at the bar, moving outside where they discovered a gaggle of youths gathered around the car. D'Amico warned them off. One grumbled a response. D'Amico flared, going at him, the biggest one, laying into the youth without warning, pummeling him with short, rapid blows, staggering him. The others moved to come to their friend's aid, but Felix at full stature stepped forward, holding them off, while he stepped between D'Amico and the one D'Amico picked as the target for his jealous rage.

The adolescents moved away grumbling. "What's your problem? What'd we do?" "We were just looking!"

"Go on!" D'Amico growled, waving them off. "You keep your grimy hands off my baby!" Then they were gone, leaving the two men facing each other in the twilight.

"The punks!" D'Amico grumbled, studying Felix, expecting confirmation.

Felix kept silent, climbing into the car while D'Amico walked around the vehicle, inspecting it. He climbed in and started the engine, ramming the car into gear.

"Were we ever like those creeps!"

Then he swung the car back in a fast arc, swung it forward shooting out into traffic with a screech of tires and odor of burning rubber met by the blare of horns and screech of skidding tires as D'Amico raised his arm, flipping them off, leaving the stalled, indignant traffic in his rich exhaust.

They drove along a boulevard paved in concrete grids striped with tar. Thick bushes flowered in the center islands of the roadway. Felix breathed in the fragrance of twilight. The sky deepening to an iridescent blue, the first bright stars and the glowing wanderer, he swept along by the movement of the machine, the thrumming engine sent back faint whiffs of hot oil and grease and gasoline. Reaching open country, the landscape growing dark, the road narrowing becoming asphalt, the yellow headlamps of the vintage vehicle casting spears of light, they arrived at a small lake bordered by the soft lights from houses spotted along the shore. D'Amico swung the car onto a gravel driveway beneath a timber gateway arch with the brewhouse name spelled out in lights, eased along the narrow drive that ran up between rough rail fences and shrubs that broke out into an area of white gravel crowded with parked cars gleaming in the blazing colored lights from the steep roof of a towering structure built from logs.

D'Amico pulled the convertible onto an area of lawn away from the other vehicles and shut down the engine. Felix wondered if they should be parking there, but he kept his own counsel and followed his friend up the rough wood steps through large wood doors into the resort. This place, too, was jammed. Smoke billowed among the high log rafters. Voices mashed with music from the three-piece band of accordion, trumpet, and drums largely ignored on a wide stage at the rear. On the bare-plank floor strewn with woodchips, rows of tables were jammed together filled with people on benches.

Here again, a chorus of shouts greeted D'Amico on their entrance from those already deep into tall mugs and pitchers of brew. As he followed D'Amico through the tables searching for a vacant bench, Felix noticed an attractive woman with blond hair coming forward, directing them toward a table at the rear. The woman seemed familiar, and Felix finally recognized her as D'Amico's former wife.

Felix watched as the woman greeted his friend in a way that suggested she still had some lingering feeling for her former spouse. But D'Amico returned her embrace with indifference, and when he brushed by her, she turned to Felix, throwing her arms around him, pushing her lips toward him. Felix stirred from the contact, having once been hot for her while she was dating and then married to D'Amico. Now he saw she was somewhat under the influence and that her embracing Felix was meant more to get back at D'Amico who rose to her baiting, growled, and moved off through the crowd. Felix saw him glom onto another attractive female. Felix knew that even if that woman was with someone wouldn't matter. He knew D'Amico would leave with a woman, even if he had to fight to take her away from the date she had come with. Felix knew D'Amico would be eager for the fight. He had seen D'Amico in action before. D'Amico loved to fight as much as he loved to score with women, as much as he loved cherry red '48 Ford convertibles.

"You see that?" D'Amico's former wife said. She threaded her arm through Felix's and led him toward a table with space enough to sit together on a bench. She leaned into Felix but still watched D'Amico bearing down on the woman he was hitting on.

"The jerk!" D'Amico's former wife snarled. "Just like him, ain't it?"

"How you doin' Carroll?" Felix asked. "What happened between you two? The last I saw you two together nothing could pry you apart, not even in public!"

"So times change. He dumped me — just like that. Said I was boring. That he needed his freedom. That he wanted to go out to California. Maybe find you."

"He did. And that's how I heard about your splitting up. I was sorry to hear that."

"What the hell! Forget that big lug! What about you? How you been?"

"I've managed. Went to school from September to June. Hitchhiked to Oregon from California to help harvest grain. I decided to come back to see if anything had changed."

"I wish I could do that — travel all over. Instead, what have I got here in this deadbeat place that never, ever changes? I have nothing! A lousy, two-bit job! This so-called nightlife!"

She waved her half-filled glass at the room then refilled it from the pitcher on the table and drank again. She offered Felix her glass; he sipped obligingly and gave it back.

"You know what?" the woman said, beginning to sound tipsy. "He didn't even want kids! And he supposedly a good Catholic. What kind of Catholic is that if he don't want kids: What good is religion if no one lives by their beliefs: What's this all about anyway? You know! This! Life! What's it all mean?"

Felix had seen this before: People have a beer or three, get a bit light-headed, they want to start discussing the meaning of life. "Maybe it doesn't mean anything," he said finally, hoping to shut down the topic before it took hold. "Maybe it just is."

"There's got to be *some* meaning? Otherwise what's the point? You're born, you live, you die! And that's *it*!"

"Maybe what it means depends on the person and what the person does."

"Is that what you think? You probably got that out of one of those heavy books you were always reading."

"Probably," Felix admitted. "Just as likely from what I've seen, most of which has not always been pretty. People out of work and struggling. People living in poverty in ghettos treated as if they were inferior animals in cages. What's that suppose to mean?"

"I'll tell you what it means," she slurred. "It's God's will to show us just how bad we are."

"Well, if we're so nasty and cruel to each other, and if it's God's will, I wonder what God is really like. Maybe we've created God in our own nasty image."

"You can't say that!" the woman breathed reeking of stale beer and tobacco.

"Can't say what?" D'Amico asked suddenly returned, curious, perhaps, as to what was taking place between his old friend and his former spouse. "What you two got so much to talk about? You haven't budged since we got here!"

"Deep, serious stuff!" D'Amico's former wife jeered. "Stuff *you* have never been capable of understanding!"

"Oh, yeah!" D'Amico snarled. "What kind of stuff: Come on! Try me! See if I can hold my own!" He drew himself back as if ready for a fight.

"We've been discussing the meaning of life," the woman said trying to sound smart.

"Oh, sure!" D'Amico scoffed. "That's typical! The meaning of life! Your life doesn't have any meaning! Look at you! You bitch! You're a lush! A whore!"

"Hey! Come on, Greg!" Felix pleaded, hoping to diffuse the anger. "Go easy! For crying out loud, she used to be your wife!"

"Yeah, sure!" D'Amico snarled. "You mean my ex-slut! Well, you can have her!"

The woman flared. She shot up from her seat, reared back, pulling back her arm as if to take a swing at the dark, twisted features of her former mate. Felix rose to block her move, turning to hold off D'Amico who had started forward to meet her attack.

Then the three of them suddenly felt the center of attention when they noticed the band had quieted, a hush had come over those who watched from among the crowded tables. Two huge security men ambled slowly toward them.

The woman with dramatic slowness lowered her arm, glaring all the while at the man who met her gaze, his dimpled chin thrust out in defiance. The woman spun away, weaved and stumbled her way on heels among the tables until she found refuge. She collapsed onto the bench, leaning into the man who circled her with his arm, pulling her to him. She nestled against the man's chest looking back at the two men she had left. The band at the rear resumed playing; those at the tables restored their chattering; the bouncers went back to their stations.

"See what I mean!" D'Amico growled, thrusting his head toward the woman who was now nuzzling the neck of the man who had given her comfort. "To hell with her!" D'Amico yelled. "You about ready to cut out of this dump!"

"I guess we better," Felix said. He looked toward the woman who had fled. "Hold on a moment," Felix added. "I want to check to see if she's all right."

"Forget her!" D'Amico snarled. "She'll do just fine!"

"No, wait. We really ought to see how she is."

"Suit yourself," D'Amico said. "But I'm not waiting around all night!"

Felix moved off among the tables to where the woman was sharing a glass with the man with whom she had sought refuge. Felix leaned to speak to her. She reached up to pat his face.

"I'm fine," she said. "But I think your jerk of a so-called friend is ditching you."

Felix looked back to see D'Amico toss back the rest of his beer, bang down the mug, then rise and move toward the door and out into the night without a backward glance.

Felix waved to the woman as he started after his old friend just as the man behind the bar called time, the band hit a final strident chord, and people at the tables began to rise, quaffing down the last of their brew before moving toward the door.

Felix was carried forward with the stream that took him out the large wood doors onto the wide wood porch and down the rough wood steps to the gravel lot. Felix searched for the place where D'Amico had parked the car. He found the space empty. He spun to see the round rump of the convertible disappear into the darkness among the trees, the red taillights flashing once before his former friend was gone.

Felix stood searching among the flow of people streaming around him to various cars. D'Amico's former spouse and the man with whom she had sought refuge passed, she waggling her fingers at him as they strolled by. Felix watched them climb into a car and join the file of cars that were funneling onto the driveway leading out to the road. Felix soon found himself standing alone, the last car having vanished. Then the floodlights of the resort blinked out, and Felix was left in total darkness.

Above the trees and the high peak of the resort, the silent night offered a bright display of constellations that had accompanied him all too often before. Now he set off again, moving off into the dark, passing beneath the dark canopy of trees and the black canvas of bright gems that expanded outward above him. Thinking all this part of a grand adventure, Felix with easy but determined stride walked back to the city alone. Orion, the hunter, again led the way.

Felix was home a week when she called again. His mother whom Felix was visiting on her day off answered.

"Hi!" his mother said cheerfully, as if she knew the caller. "Yes he's finally here. Just a second." Then she handed him the phone, a strange, thin smile on her face. "For you," she said.

She held the receiver out to him as he rose, came to her, and took it from her.

"So you're finally here!" the voice breathed in his ear, soft and sensual, a woman. "Welcome home!"

Felix didn't recognize the voice. He was puzzled even further when the woman used the name that he hadn't heard himself called since high school. He felt embarrassed being addressed with a name he now thought sounded juvenile. To think that at one time he had been proud to have those he knew address him by such a moniker.

"You don't remember?" the voice teased. "I'm crushed! And you said you would never forget!"

"That must have been some time ago!" Felix said a bit irritated. He didn't like being treated like a fool. "Either that or I was drunk."

"It hasn't been that long and you were oh, so sober! You promised," she accused, challenging him, her voice cheerful, musical.

He frankly didn't remember having promised anything to anyone since he had no idea who was toying with him. He tried to remember those to whom he had written. He recalled writing to nearly everyone he felt close to just after he left, surprising himself, admitting finally how lonely he felt, how strange his new life seemed, so severed from his past and all those he had left behind, and he remembered having said something about hoping to see them all again whenever he returned. But when his letters went unanswered, he stopped writing.

"I just got here a couple three days ago," he hedged. "I needed some time to relax, get my bearings, re-orient myself."

Who was this anyway? He looked to his mother for help, but she was ignoring him, busy at the galley counter fixing lunch, her face flat with such studied concentration on what she was doing he was sure she was listening.

"You seem changed," the woman's youthful voice said. "You sound different."

"How did you know I was in town?" he asked, ignoring what seemed like another demeaning comment. He strained to detect something that would help him recognize the voice.

"Oh, I've got my ways."

"I guess, since I didn't tell anyone except my mother I was coming."

She laughed, the music of her voice filling him with a sudden rush. "I called your mother!" she exclaimed. "Her number's in the phone book!

Felix looked at his mother now seated at the table across from him. She watched him over the rim of her cup as she sipped her coffee, the midday light dancing from her glasses. He knew now that Ma surely must be in on this. He cupped the receiver in his hand. "Who *is* this?" he whispered harshly.

She grinned, accepting her role as co-conspirator. "Jean," his mother said.

He was surprised. Why had *she* called? Then he recalled Ma telling him the day he arrived about some woman having called and being married and her having sought news of him, all that seeming even more strange now when he recalled how definite their "affair," if you could call it that, had ended. Certainly there had been a definite finality and bitterness once the initial shock had settled. Now she had called.

"Look, Jean. . ."

"You must have asked."

"Well. . ."he paused. She had always made him feel the fool.

She laughed again. "When you going to come see me?"

"Never!" he felt like saying. He didn't like being laughed at, especially by her after all he had previously endured from her, but he checked his response. "When you free?"

"Never," she said. "I'm quite dear."

He knew that to be true. He remained quiet, tired of this game, waiting to see where all this might be going. She must have sensed his mood as she once had readily.

"Well, I work evenings at an ice cream and snack stand near where I live. The kids are close. I use every penny I earn just to buy basics. I can't afford a sitter. I thought you might meet me there where I work and walk me home. I don't live that far. Not even a block from where I work."

"I could do that, I guess." Why was he being so considerate after what she had put him through? Then he surprised himself further. "How about next week? Wednesday maybe." Then with even further consideration he hadn't expected of himself, "I'd come see you sooner, but I'm busy the rest of this week. I tell you, these homecomings!"

"Oh, I'm sure," she said. "But Wednesday's fine." She sounded a little less buoyant. She gave him directions to where she worked. "Have fun on your dates," she added quietly. "I'm looking forward to next Wednesday. We haven't seen each other since we lost contact."

"Right," he said. Lost contact? More exactly, after she had dumped him for someone else, someone — according to her — more "mature." No surprise, since he had just turned seventeen.

"Look, Jean," he said into the phone. "I've really got to go. But it's been really nice talking to you. It certainly has been a while."

"Too long," she breathed, recovering her former pose.

He remained silent. The only time he had heard her sound that way was one summer night when she had almost yielded to his adolescent urge on his eighteen birthday.

"See you Wednesday," she confirmed.

He felt an uneasiness that hadn't troubled him for some time.

"Wednesday," he agreed, finally.

But she had hung up.

Between the time she called and the following Wednesday, he found himself thinking about her more than he supposed he might or wanted. After she had hung up and after he had reflected on what had happened and given the memories, sensations, and emotions her call resurrected, he wanted to forget the whole thing. He felt uneasy. Why complicate his life? He had a life now essentially and assuredly different from hers, and he considered the divergent ways each of their lives had taken. Why entangle them again: Hadn't the first time — or the second — or the third been enough?

And then there was this business of her being married! At least according to what his mother had told him, he assumed she was married, although she hadn't said anything about a husband. But she had children! For crying out loud! The last thing he wanted was some confrontation with a jealous, irate, self-righteous husband! Yet, at the same time he wondered what kind of man she had married. Would he see anything of himself in that man? Why was he even considering that as a possibility?

He felt like calling her back: He would express regret for cancelling their meeting, deliberately careful not to hurt her as she had him. He would think up some excuse, but then he had not thought to get her number. And for the life of him, no matter how he tried to recall their conversation, even asking his mother, he didn't have a clue to her married name. So how could he even begin tracking her down to return her call?

Then he thought of just ignoring her invitation: He would simply not show up. And if she called again, he wouldn't return the call. But then he thought again of his noble resolution that he seemed to wear like a badge of honor he would never deliberately hurt her. So he decided finally to go through with the whole sordid reunion. He would see her, and he would leave as quickly as he could. Having decided, he tried to dismiss her from his thoughts.

Yet during the time between her call and the following Wednesday, he found himself coming back to thoughts of her again and again. So that by the time he stood alongside the curb, purged and somewhat prepared, waiting for the bus that would carry him across town to their reunion, he thought through the whole course of their troubled "affair."

He, of course, started at the end. How long since he had last seen her? He groped back from one incident to another to the first moment of what he considered recognition when she had struck something within that had immediately attracted him to her. So as he thought more of her, thought more especially of their beginning that now seemed so distant, he felt himself soften, perhaps, just a little. But at the same time, he became aware and consequently amazed at how their "affair" had really been no more than an isolated burst of adolescent raging hormones. So he still hesitated to fully admit the depth of both his trust and having allowed himself to be taken for the ultimate fool not once, but three times.

Then he thought of the sound of her voice when she called: How warm it seemed. Was there something else? She certainly sounded friendly, perhaps enticing, her voice again seducing him, so that now as he thought of it, he began to feel an old uneasy stir creep through him settling as it always did in tumescent flesh

Where had he met her the last time he had seen her? He pondered that question watching the traffic that pulsed before him on the avenue while waiting for the bus: Cars slowing for the stoplight where he waited, crept forward until the light changed and the engines roared again, carrying away the line of staggered cars and the people who with apparent disinterest glanced at him standing beside the bus sign before the pharmacy. He, in turn, would glance at someone passing before him or investigate more fully the shapely form of the woman who stopped before the sign he stood at, settling herself, placing her high-heeled shoes just so to wait.

Felix decided the last time he saw Jean was at — of all places — Sunfish Beach amusement park. How fitting. But no — wait! That wasn't her That was Nan. He more clearly remembered now because he saw the image of a small, trim woman he bulked above, remembered the fine, sharp features, the long, soft chestnut hair, the prim blouse that only accentuated her fullness. He recalled the tight jeans that molded her trim hips and thighs. How he stirred on seeing her again; how he felt a surge as she smiled, somewhat sadly, he thought, as she asked and waited for his answer about the common details of his life apart from her now that they were estranged because of his growing involvement with Gloria, the older, married woman with whom he worked and over whom he and Pa more than once had battled over their ongoing differences from conflicting ideas as to how Felix should direct his life.

Nan was with someone else. In fact, she was with the fellow with whom she had coupled with before Felix, so meeting her again gave Felix a certain sardonic pleasure. Their meeting somehow seemed warmly up close and personal as he stood talking with her again intimately under the other fellow's gaze, the other fellow jealous, perhaps, as Felix had been learning of her first experience coupling with the other male and Felix having felt deprived and somehow cheated.

He thought again of Jean, but he held that thought as the bus loomed along side the curb, the door flapped open, and he waited for the woman to enter before him while he watched her thin ankles and the slick movement of her light, thin dress play over her full hips and bottom as she slowly climbed the steps. Then he climbed the steps himself, bracing himself as the driver took his bill, spun the steering wheel, jabbed at the coin holder, and eased the bus out into traffic as he folded the bill into the pile of bills he stuck in the pocket of his shirt, all without taking his eyes from the road and flowing traffic.

Felix clung to the smooth metal pole, dropped the coins into the cash box, then lurched back toward the rear, returning the glance of searching faces inspecting him while he looked for an empty seat. He glanced at the woman who had waited with him at the bus stop, he finally able to judge how her features matched the rest of her, but she ignored him as he passed, and he dropped onto the empty bench seat at the rear.

He gazed out at the passing scene. All he viewed again seemed essentially unchanged: the houses and storefronts that began to flow behind him appeared the same, would not seem any different to someone who had never left and would never note the increments of change that seemed to somewhat jar him now:

The small upholstery shop, for example, across from where he had stood with the woman waiting for the bus: Who would ever imagine that it was not always used for reconditioning old furniture. How many times had he frequented it in another era when it was a smoke shop, a sweet shop, a hobby shop all combined into one dimly lighted narrow cell run by a man whom Felix not unkindly always thought a bit odd: The man's paunch strained the buttons of his shirtfront where it hung over the brown, scruffy leather belt; his cheeks hung loose, almost flapping when he spoke; he seemed to speak through his nose, his mouth puckering, while his eyelids blinked. Felix remembered as a small boy peering up at the man who sometimes made faces perhaps attempting to make Felix laugh.

That man came each day to his dim cell lined with shelves of model kits of cars and planes and glass cases displaying tobacco products behind which he presided and at times retired behind a faded cloth curtain of flowery print that hung in the doorway at the rear of the cell beside the old, chipped soda cooler. For what purpose the man stepped behind that curtain, Felix could scarcely imagine and only came to know later.

Now, carried by this humming electric vehicle carrying him away to an uncertain reunion, as he thought of that man and that small shop, Felix was amazed at what part that dingy store had played in his life. How unaware he had been the many times he went there, and now seeing it so utterly transformed wiping away any trace of the man whom Felix eventually learned had turned to whiskey and magazines with explicit photos of naked women, the man imbibing both behind the faded cloth curtain.

Those days now seemed so distant they left only a fading ghostly image of the man in his narrow shop, the windows now boarded a dull tan as the bus carried Felix forward into night allowing him to renew his reconsideration of the two adolescent women he had known: What was the link that led him to recall the one from thinking of the other? Well, for one, he had left one for the other. Well, not exactly. No, he on rebound had quickly took up with one after the other dumped him. He recalled Jean's studied manner and her apparent distain when she commented to a friend deliberately right in front of him that his then current girlfriend, the other young woman, was barely a teen, she a freshman, he a junior, both ripening adolescents. Although he had noted Jean's indignant remark, he had ignored it as he had followed his new love into the yellow school bus with green vinyl seats. Why had she cared? Why should he have cared what she thought after all the abuse he suffered from her? All those times she had toyed with him only to dismiss him, Jean had played to her advantage and his dismay. Having always been so friendly after the rather long intervals between their infrequent meetings, he had always seemed to meet her someplace by chance. He certainly hadn't always intended to meet her, and she always seemed to be somewhere he least expected.

He recalled again especially well that summer day he has met her unexpectedly when he caught sight of her across the busy street as she walked along unaware of his presence, he following slowly past the wide trimmed windows beneath green and white striped awnings hung from storefronts, threading his way through the host of people flowing past him blocking his attempt at catching her until they reached a place where the asphalt street and narrow walkways widened to a bright expanse of concrete striped with tare where he had finally called her name.

She had turned, her smile and eyes thrilling him again, as always. He noticed how even more lovely she seemed, her dark hair cut short in the latest style, her blue eyes accented by dark eyebrows and lashes highlighted by mascara, her rouged, bright smile, all heightened by the mellow tan, the, long, pink linen skirt and short-sleeved, white linen blouse that accented her full figure, her fleshy arms, her tall, white heels. She had seemed slimmer, more trim and seemed to glow.

"God! You look great!" He had exclaimed almost breathless as he caught up to her. Her quiet "'Thank you," her downturned eyes, dark, sweeping lashes, her pleased, innocent blush made him thrill even more. But when he asked where she was headed, her reply gave him pause.

"You should have let me know you were coming," she responded. "It's such a shame for you to come all that way and miss me!"

He had noticed her slight uneasiness, the thin smile with which she emphasized her words. She was going to a job interview, she told him, somewhat insistent on his not accompanying her. "You'll be bored waiting for me." But when he had objected, she added, "I'm sure I better go alone. They'll be so much more receptive."

So he had yielded, withdrew, watching her walk on alone in her tight, pink skirt and white, high heels, he turning back to wander the streets feeling aimless and lost, searching store windows, stopping for a soda at a place they had frequented together during lunch hour while in school, but that time, he sitting alone feeling empty.

Outside again, moving slowly toward the five-point intersection as the afternoon light lengthened, the light diffused through a haze, filling the air and bathing the buildings and streets with a golden hue, he had stood on one corner transfixed by the aura when they passed. He knew the fellow, knew him, perhaps, too well, and she, as they passed, completely unaware of Felix standing in the crowd gathered at the corner waiting for the light to change, she studying the street before her through the windshield of the sleek convertible, her bare, tanned arm resting on the door.

He had watched as they went down the street among traffic, saw the fellow glancing in the mirror, saw her turn, startled, searching, as if afraid, Felix watching in a daze as the car had suddenly pulled to the curb halting traffic that honked in protest. She leaping out, ran back to him, tried to apologize, her movements all so deliciously romantic. He had stood dumb while she backed away, turned, ran back to the idling car, her movements made awkward by the long, tight skirt, the white high heels, her feet flailing out from side to side while the college man in his convertible had sat twisted toward them watching the whole scene, his arm over the back of the seat until she leapt in, slamming the door, and they had roared off, leaving Felix dumb and dazed.

Having conjured that scene, he recalled now that there were other incidents like that one. One time when Felix and she were at a school sock hop at the local Y, Felix involved in what might have ended in a brawl when one drunk, acne-pocked teen had confronted Felix. Even now Felix couldn't understand why, except that the fellow was another suitor whom she had rejected for Felix. The drunk was with friends who challenged Felix to step outside to settle things — to settle what, Felix still wasn't quite sure, especially why what they proposed would settle anything. Just in the nick of time the fellow in his sleek convertible suddenly had appeared, whisking them away, and Felix knew he probably had been saved from a beating.

And what about that time Felix had walked her to the stop where she would catch her bus for home? Meeting her as she was coming from the place where she worked, she again had seemed uneasy at meeting him so unexpectedly. Her uneasiness seemed to grow as they approached the bus stop, as the bus appeared, as the bus arrived, and as they started forward behind the crowd inching toward the door that flapped open, there was the other fellow without his convertible leaping down through the crowd, acknowledging Felix in a stiff, indifferent manner, taking her by the arm, helping her up the steps into the bus. The door flapping shut, Felix had stood there watching dumb and dazed again as they had walked toward him down the aisle while the bus eased into traffic, growing smaller as they sat together, turned toward each other. Then the bus had vanished around a curve, leaving Felix, as usual, at another junction in his life.

Those times were truly absurd, he readily admitted now. Yet he blanched recalling again how shocked and serious, how deliciously hurt from his sense of shame. Even now, reliving those lost times, aware of those seated near him, Felix squelched his revived sense of despair on a bus that carried him indifferently toward a reunion with her after years of silence.

Yet there had been one or two times as memorable, not quite so ludicrous, and those times recalled so enthralled him he became dulled to the passing traffic beneath his window, the red-bricked stores, the gray weathered flats with high porches and brick pillars, the streets that he had run through as a child and came to know so well he could even now draw a map from memory of that neighborhood he once had wandered so freely and now held a tinge of strangeness upon his return.

One time he had found her home alone fresh and dusted from just having bathed wearing only a soft, cloth robe and nothing else. The radio quietly playing pop tunes of young love in the heavy heat of a summer afternoon, they had exchanged pleasantries, sharing a beer which he had relished, first for its cold bitterness and then because it was illicit, they both underage.

Suddenly they were on the floor, she stretching her arms above her head allowing him to undue with awkward, shaking fingers the slowly yielding buttons of her robe that finally fell away upon the rug, she watching his face as his eyes played over her. He recalled her expression, the glow of her flushed face, the hiss of her words through clenched, perfect teeth as she lay completely exposed, willing to yield to him if he met her challenge to take her even if she resisted.

He had never seen someone so completely open to his inspection. He squirmed now in his seat as he recalled his first, halting, awkward reach to touch that luscious, soft, silky flesh, but that time, too, his hesitant deliberation stopped cold by the sudden scratch of a key within a lock.

They had bolted, so that by the time her mother came through the widely swinging door, her arms filled with packages, he from necessity was seated cross-legged on the couch, and her daughter, rebuttoned, strolled in from the kitchen with a cheery greeting for her mother.

The woman startled to see him there, he had met her half-questioning, half-accusing eyes behind plastic-rimmed glasses as he watched her set mouth that seemed to quiver as she tried to smile, as she tried to utter a reply to her daughter's greeting. Having married young, she always had been somewhat cold toward him worried about his being too serious, of something happening, her daughter ending as she had married too young with child.

Another time, another summer, a year or two later, this time in the warm, star-filled night, he recalled the dark, calm waters, the black rise of distant hills, the small, bright strip of gaily colored lights from the amusement park across the lake, the shimmering kaleidoscope of color on the dark mirroring water. He recalled the sounds that had reached him across the still water: the screams of delight softened by distance; the muffled clash and thrum of thrill rides, the subdued shock and rattle of gears and chain of the roller coaster as it slowly climbed to the crest of the first steep drop, and then the rushing roar as it went over and plunged; the wisps of music from the dance pavilion, the melody flowing in gentle undulations across the quiet, star-filled lake.

That day his birthday, he on the cusp of manhood three weeks younger than she, traveling to the county seat of Prairieville to register for the draft, picking her up in his recently purchased '48 black, stick-shift Ford, she having accepted his invitation to come out with him on that day to spend it with him and celebrate his birthday, she teasing him on his finally "coming of age." How thrilled, how intimate it had seemed to have her there in the cottage where he lived a short walk to the lake, her being there giving him a sense of what it would be like if they were together all the time, if they, in fact, lived together. What a strange, exciting notion imagining them as a couple living together in their own home. How naïve and romantic that notion now seemed as the public vehicle in which he sat and reminisced carried him toward an unexpected, somewhat reluctant reunion with a woman once the object of his adolescent dreams.

That night after the bright heat of the afternoon they had avoided by lounging on the shaded, screened-in porch now legally sharing a beer, they walked the darkened road beneath the towering arch of trees that led them down to the night-bound lake. There he had coaxed her to unsheathe down to her skin. How curious and excited he had felt to see her shrug off bra, slip from briefs, placing them on the thin dress draped over the beached rowboat, then wading with him into the dark waters. They had cowered beneath the black, rippling surface from sudden sounds that startled them. But when the night grew quiet again, he had held her in his arms, straining his firmed flesh toward the yielding softness he had seen only one time when she had lain exposed before him on the rug, and she transfixed by the aura of the night had opened to him, he pressing himself between her thighs beginning to mold her to him when halted by some barrier, unable to press in further. Had she truly been a virgin? He had wondered then, wondered even more so now recalling the college man she had "dated" having rejected Felix.

That night, breaking from him seemingly in panic, she swimming out toward the darker, deeper water, and he, startled, had followed, coaxing her back to shore, dried her, soothed her with words, while she sat shivering so wide-eyed, he could see her fright even in the darkness. Had she truly been that innocent? Why then that time had she rejected him?

Now, in the lingering hours of summer twilight, with those specters of the past having suddenly risen to haunt him as the bus carried him forward taking him across town to the district where he would reunite with her, he considered the area where she lived bordering the ghetto. Swaying back up the aisle to ask the driver, he learned that the bus he rode crossed the street on which she now lived, so he felt relieved he didn't have to worry about transferring, perhaps having to wait for the next bus longer than he thought safe, and that once he was at her street, he only had to walk no more than a block to where she worked. But then he considered that since the street would be dark by the time he left her, the neighborhood where she lived bordering the ghetto still gave him pause.

Why should he feel such unease? He thought he had left that business behind him rejecting prejudgment through focused reasoning and experience during his stay in Long Beach when he had lived in that drab, pale green room in a pale-green, dirt-stained building set among deteriorating houses, crumbling sidewalks bordered by grassless strips of packed earth, he often walking the streets alone at night passing storefront Godshops with their joyful names, dim-lit taverns issuing blaring music, joyful shouts and bursts of laughter. Thinking now of those times in Long Beach, Felix searched the street before him and thought about the neighborhood he would visit that night. He remembered it from seeing it on occasion while visiting friends of his parents who lived on its borders. How strange that so many facets of his life seemed to intersect in that location: the high-school couple he had double-dated with married because the girl was pregnant, the young couple living in an ancient, faded flat in the same area; or his parents' friends whom they crossed the valley to visit where they lived on the border of the same area, their upper flat much the same as the high school couple's. He recalled his childish wonder from the newness of that location bordering the ghetto, the dim street lamps and neon signs glowing in the chilled dark, he having fled the boredom of the stifling heat and smoke-filled attic flat he was visiting with his parents while they played endless hands of Sheepshead.

Seeing again the faded wooden facades, the houses hideously tiled with asphalt siding, the pitiful splashes of pride in trim of bright colors, the cracked, unkempt streets, scraggly trees, wind-blown, brown-stained papers scattered on barren patches of lawn, thinking of those places now, he found them more strange, more unfamiliar, more filled with the possibility of grief and fear than the uneasy, festering streets that he had roamed freely in the West. Peering at the street before him, these places that filled his marrow bones, seeping like tainted blood through his veins, how utterly more strange and distant they were then the unfamiliar places he had wandered through. Were his friends as strange? More strange than those dark unfamiliar shapes that had passed through his life and[vanished, leaving only an uneasy trace tainted by doubt? The few days he had been here had begun to make him wonder just exactly what he was doing here? Why had he returned?

He searched the passing streets for an answer. The gray, wood flats; the soot-stained, nineteenth century brick buildings; dust covered storefronts, their blank, empty windows, dim interiors with yellow, varnished desks and chairs; the black girders of a draw bridge — all flashed by. He saw the dark, roiling waters of the river beneath the bridge, and up ahead, at an angle from where he sat, the towers of the financial district, their gleaming facades checkered with lighted windows rising toward the gathering darkness crowned with a lingering, iridescent glow. Then once they roared through an area of dazzling lights from theater marquees and neon signs of stores and restaurants and tall light standards back into the dark, the driver's coarse, vindictive cry roused him to the flash of cross streets and people moving along beside him in slow motion as the bus slowly glided to a stop. This is where he got off.

Felix descended from the trolley bus and watched as it pulled away, moving up the street, growing smaller, leaving him alone. The deserted street appeared comfortably quiet with rows of autos lining both sides of the street. Full-leafed trees lined the sidewalks interlaced with high lampposts that cast large cones of light on the canopy of leaves, vacant autos, and splayed yellow light and shadows on the concrete sidewalk that Felix now started up heading for the area lit by neon he saw at a distance. He passed quiet, dark fronts of brick apartments with the yellow glow of drawn, tan shades. He glanced into dark stairwells filled with soiled paper scraps and cast off packaging.

Then he entered an area of fluorescence and neon, approached a small stand, where he stopped, waited, watching the full-figured woman with short, dark hair, blue eyes, full, rouged lips as she served people gathered before the small window. He saw that she noticed him there apart from the small group of children and adults that pressed toward the fold-down shutter that served as a counter. He saw her search his face, saw her face brighten in recognition,. She held up her hand in greeting before she returned to scoop ice cream into cups and cones. Those before the stand turned briefly to see whom she had signed to. Then after the last small child, the last adult had been served, Felix approached.

They stood facing each other, the counter and difference in elevation between them, holding them apart.

"Felix!" the woman beamed. "How nice to see you again!

"Good to see you, Jean." Felix felt strangely shy, the hiatus of years and sudden renewal of contact making him feel awkward and uncertain.

"So you're finally here!"

"Yep, I'm finally here."

"You certainly took your time coming around to see me!" she teased, taking up the persona she had assumed on the phone.

She reached behind her to begin untying her apron, preparing to close. Felix understood the script she was following, yet he still felt awkward as he talked to her over the counter as she went about closing out the register, his words punctuated and made seemingly more hesitant by the halting grind of the machine spitting out tape as she went about her task, only partially attentive to what he said.

"There were a few things I had to settle," Felix said. "And. . .well. . . I really didn't want to disturb your life. I mean. . . I didn't think your husband would appreciate an old high school friend suddenly hanging around."

She looked up from her task as he talked, searching his face, as if to see he might be jesting or even being sarcastic; then she went back to her task, finished by stuffing the folded tape and money into a deposit bag. He watched as she closed down the stand, he helping close up the shutter counter against the snack stand, sealing her in, waiting while she shut down the lights, came out a narrow door at the side, turning to lock it, then turning to meet him, taking his arm as they started up the street.

"I'll just drop this off on the way," she said. Then as they walked, "John doesn't mind your being here. And you're not exactly hanging around. We haven't seen each other in years, not since high school. Beside, I've told him all about you. In fact, he knows that you were going to be here tonight."

"Really! He knows? And it's all right! He must be quite a guy!"

"He is! That's why I want you to meet him. I finally found someone who would put up with me!"

"I'm glad for you," Felix said honestly.

"You might find it hard to believe but he's someone who can keep me in line," she added. "He'll be off work in an hour or so. I thought you might walk me home, have a beer, see my kids. John will be here soon. I want you to meet him. I want him to meet you."

"I guess that'd be O.K.," Felix said. "But why would you want him to meet me?"

They entered a small area of stores. At a small bank branch, she dropped the bag into night deposit, and they went on into an area of trees and shadows and parked cars gleaming under streetlamps. She again taking his arm, drawing close to him, snuggling against his side as she had once done, as if there had been no intervening years.

He looked down at her, saw her brilliant eyes, her full red lips, her dark hair, her suddenly familiar fragrances of powder, rouge, cologne, and he flushed with warmth.

"The two of you are really a lot alike," she beamed, her smile filling him with warmth. "But I just want him to meet someone from my past, someone who meant a great deal to me, who knew me as I was then."

Felix paused to consider what she had said as she stopped before one of the dark brick buildings that Felix had passed along the way. She turned up the stairs, letting go his arm to reach for her keys in the pocket of her uniform, unlocked the door, then started up the dark stairwell. He followed.

Felix was suddenly overwhelmed by heat and powerful odors, individually indistinguishable, but all strong and sharp and stinging, melding together into an oppressive stew that made his stomach heave. At a landing, she stopped before a paneled door, groped the key into the lock, swung open the door, releasing another wave of rank odors. They entered, stepping over scattered items, and in a low light, Felix saw the room in shadows and shambles. Jean moved trying to relieve some of the mess, bending to pick up a soiled, reeking diaper. Felix had trouble checking his rising gorge.

"Better come into the kitchen," Jean said, obviously embarrassed. "At least there's a place to sit."

Felix followed her into the kitchen where Jean deposited the diaper in a trash can, removed soiled dishes from the table, adding them to the pile already in the sink and on adjacent counters. She bent to retrieve scattered toys beneath chairs, and under the small light from above the sink Felix studied the flare of her hips, the silhouette of her briefs beneath her thin uniform.

Jean straightened, moved around him to the other room. Felix surveyed the mess that surrounded him, the disarray that obviously had not been ordered in some time: clothes and toys strewn on furnishings; the kitchen piled with unwashed dishes; all this a striking contrast to the almost obsessive, ordered cleanliness that Felix recalled of Jean's mother.

Jean returned from the darkness of the adjoining room. "Want a beer?" she asked, as if none of what he saw mattered.

"Whatever you have," Felix said.

Jean went to the frig, rummaged among leftovers, stooping again in the sudden light, allowing Felix to observe clearly the image of her form beneath her dress. She dragged two bottles from the back, straightened, handing them to Felix, then went to a drawer next to the sink, wrestling it open, rummaging through the jumble, extracting an opener, turning to pop the caps from the bottles that Felix held out for her. She took one, held it toward his. They clinked bottles.

"To old times," Jean said quietly.

"Old times," Felix returned, studying her.

"Have a seat," Jean offered. "Sorry about the mess."

Felix sat on a scarred, wooden chair at the table, easing onto it, unsure of its stability. Jean took a similar chair beside him.

"I guess I'm not much of a housekeeper," Jean said. "What with the kids and my job and everything."

"Don't worry about it," Felix offered.

"I guess I don't much take after my mother. Remember how tidy she used to be! How she'd make me keep things just the way she wanted?"

"How is she?" Felix asked.

"Older. Aren't we all? She's seemed to have gotten old suddenly after my father died. She lives alone, of course, insists on doing everything by herself, as usual."

"Your father died!" He hunched, restraining his voice, checked by the dimness of the kitchen light, the black void at the doorway, the stillness from the other room from where he heard the steady breathing of someone asleep. "I'm sorry to hear that," he added in a hushed voice. "Your mother old. I always think of her as young and full of life."

"Remember the time she walked in on us just as we were about to go all the way! Sounds quaint now, doesn't it —'going all the way'. I remember we both were so flushed, so breathless. . ."

"And you said you wanted me but that you'd fight me, and that if I could overcome your resistance, I could have you."

"I guess we had to play that game, didn't we? Since we really didn't know what to do. Neither of us had experience."

"But I was ready to learn."

"We were so full of ourselves. We thought we were so adult."

"And then your mother walked in. Were we scared!"

"It's kinda hard now to think of us as being so young. And what about that summer party you had?"

"On my birthday."

"We went skinny dipping."

"You had to be coaxed to undress."

"That was the first time we held each other that way. We came close to doing it that time."

"You pulled away at the last second."

"I was so scared!" Jean laughed. "I thought I'd get pregnant just from your touching me with your penis."

Felix heard the word explode into the room.

"And just look at me now! Married! Couple kids! Strange to think we're now almost the same age our parents were then."

"We were pretty innocent, all right. I remember how crushed I was when I discovered you were dating someone else — an older man — someone in college — that was some big deal."

"He seemed so mature. He swept me off my feet — literally," she laughed. She reached to touch him. "I didn't ever mean to hurt you, Felix," she said quietly.

He allowed her hand to rest on his bare arm. "It's past — ancient history — I survived."

"Are you ever sorry you never had me, Felix?"

"I don't ever think about it," Felix said, then saw himself again in a blue and white '54 Chevy with blue vinyl seats paused at a STOP sign watching as Jean passed in a car driven by someone he recognized as one of her former rejected suitors, the pocked-face one who had challenged Felix at a dance to step outside and settle things. Felix had followed their car, watched them pull into a "lovers' lane," watched as they embraced, obviously preparing to "go all the way," their motions now frantic, as Jean's leg came up over the seat, the man looming over her.

"I think of it, sometimes" Jean said. "I'm sorry now I never let you have me. I just didn't know anything. You didn't know anything. We were just so young. Yet, I loved you so much!"

Felix studied her, searching her face, holding on her bright eyes.

"Really!" Jean insisted.

"You were my first real love," Felix admitted finally. "When I thought I knew how love felt."

Jean moved closer to him. "You were always sweet to me. That's why I wish we had been together. I've always thought our love making would have been special."

"I remember how frustrated I always felt. We were just so close, and then you'd pull away."

"We both were so young, even though we thought we were adult."

"I'm glad that time's over. Now I wonder why we thought going all the way was so important."

"Because we didn't know. All we heard was talk. And probably because everyone was trying to keep us apart."

"Which only made us want to do it more!"

They both laughed, drank from their bottles, studied each other again, searching each other's eyes. Felix wondered where all that had come from, where all this was going. What, in fact, was he doing here!

"We could still find out how it might be," Jean said. She reached to put her hand on his arm where it rested on the table edge. She leaned toward him, offering him her lips, her breast crushed against his arm.

Her lips were as electric and as strange as the first time his had met hers years ago.

"What about your husband?" Felix asked when they sat back apart. "What about your kids?"

"I'm thinking of us now, Felix — you and me — how it might be for us! They're a different part of my life!"

She waited for him to respond, then rose, went to the frig to dig out two more bottles, the light from the frig splaying into the dim kitchen illuminating her thin uniform, her legs and thighs and groin a shadowy vee. But he declined another and she came back, reseated herself. "Don't you want me, Felix?"

"It's not a question of wanting. We're just different people now. We're not those wild-eyed, hormone-gorged teenagers we were. We have different lives."

She sat back, drank from her new bottle. "I don't blame you for not wanting me! I must seem ugly to you now spread out and overweight from having kids, living in this constant mess, so tired I often don't care about anything!"

"You're as beautiful as ever!" Felix said. "We just can't go back to what we were then, no matter how much we want to redeem those times for what we did or didn't do."

"What happened to us, Felix?"

"We went our own ways, made our own lives, had our own experiences. Things like that happen to everyone all the time."

"But we wanted so much!"

"Doesn't everyone? Maybe we finally understood that we can't always get what we want. Our choices just led us in a direction different from what we planned."

"It seems unfair in a way. When we finally come to know what we might have had, we're too late, too far beyond getting it."

Felix raised his beer as a salute. "*Asi es la vida!*" one phrase he knew well and used often: "That's life!"

He set down his empty bottle, pushed up from his chair, stood looking down at her.

"It's late," he said. "I better go. Your husband will be here soon. Not a good idea to have him walk in with us so cozy."

"He'll be fine," Jean said. "We haven't done anything." She reached for his hand. He allowed her to take it. "But if you have to go, I want you to see my kids." She rose still holding his hand. "Come with me," she said, then led him from the kitchen.

They meandered through a messy room to another decorated for children in the same kind of shambles as the others.

Felix looked down on two children deep in sleep. He watched as Jean settled their covers then led him out of the bedroom to the apartment door and out into the stifling stairway, descending toward the street.

"Aren't they beautiful!" Jean said in hushed adoration.

"They are," Felix agreed in a loud whisper. "You love them very much."

"I'm glad you can tell that!"

They reached the street, the warm night now mild after the stifling hallway, the air pure after the heavy stew of odors in the messy flat.

They stood on the sidewalk next to a parked auto, beneath tall trees thick with leaves. They studied each other in the dim light from streetlamps, he looking down into her upturned face as he had done so many times, years before.

"We most likely won't see each other again, will we, Felix?"

"Probably not."

"Drop me a line, now and then, if you get the urge."

"I will," Felix agreed, thinking now he meant it but didn't seek her address, nor did she offer hers.

He bent toward her face, she rising on her toes to meet him, just as a large shape loomed out of the dark beyond the light. Jean and Felix stepped apart, turning toward the man who approached.

Felix was surprised to see a slight mirror image of himself. Jean introduced the two men to each other, and the two men shook hands.

"Well!" Jean's husband said, stepping back, "the long lost lover returned!"

Felix remained mute, self-conscious under the other man's inspection, wary, cautious. Where was all this going? Felix suddenly saw himself in a midnight brawl, just as he had expected, despite what she had promised when she told him everything would be fine.

"So. Do you still love her!" the husband demanded.

"John!" Jean exclaimed. "What a question to ask!"

"Well, let's see if he has a ready answer! Why'd he come around after all these years? Probably wants to show us how grand he is — big time college man! What's he want, anyway! Get in your pants — finally — after all these years!"

"John! Stop it right now! You've been drinking! I asked him to come! And he was gracious enough to accept!"

"Still trying to keep your girlish dream alive! Well, it's about time you stop and understood those days are over! They're gone!"

"I'd better go," Felix said quietly. "Nice seeing you again, Jean. Take care of those lovely kids."

"You bet we will!" John said. He took Jean by the arm. "You about ready to go in?" He guided his wife toward the stairs. "I'm hungry!" he said, looking back at Felix. "And horny!" he added. "I can use some food and a piece of ass right about now!"

Then they started up the stairs, disappearing into the dark, leaving Felix alone watching them go. He wondered what the other man might find to eat or a bed clear enough to have sex, although that most likely wouldn't matter, and he noted with a droll smile that someone had dragged her away from him again.

Felix looked up the street one way then down the other along the lines of parked cars, the fully leafed trees, the signs and gleaming windows of the dark storefronts. Up the street at the corner he saw the welcomed, familiar shape and glowing green reader board of the electric trolley bus gliding toward the stoplight that had just changed from green to red.

Felix hurried to the corner, quickly crossed over to the other curb where he paused just before he swung up onto the bus that slowed almost to a stop, the doors flapping open, then flapping shut behind him as he deposited his coins, swayed toward the rear, collapsed onto a green vinyl seat at the same time the light turned green, and the trolley bus carried him off into the night, back to familiar territory he hoped had no surprises.

Even as he spoke with his old friend Jack on the phone when Jack called, surprising him, Felix wanted to inform his friend of how he felt changed. But Jack didn't want to talk long, informed Felix that he was on his way over, and that he'd be there soon. Then Jack hung up, so while he waited for his old friend to arrive, Felix sat alone in the dim light of his grandmother's quiet, dim attic beneath bare rafters using a dusty trunk for a seat while he reached into a large wood shipping crate from a former era bringing out one item after the other both once familiar yet now surprising.

Knowing them well from having used them, how many years ago, he couldn't say, he was surprised to discover they were still there, buried relics from his past: First the pair of long blade ice skates he had thought about on his walk to South Gate. Setting them aside, he reached for a sketchbook he leafed through restoring images of deciduous woods in full summer foliage and he at twelve or thirteen seated at the base of a towering oak, its leaves and branches shading him while he sketched the surrounding countryside with distant clusters of trees along a stream bordered by large rocks and grazing Holstein, high distant hills that rose above the remnants of ancient forest showing signs of being quarried from great gouges of brown and yellow earth that left palisades giving the hills a greater sense of grandeur and distance.

A worn dog collar he played through his fingers transfixed him as he stared at the stream of light through the window of the nearby doorway that opened to the roof of the sunporch. From shadows beneath the bare rafters of the antique house, he saw emerge the specter of the small black and tan mongrel terrier bitch once inseparable from him, imprinted as a pup roaming the woods, running to and from him while he sat absorbed sketching but still listening for the small brown and black form that foraged thick undergrowth and grass and matted leaves, the dog glad to be free but just as glad to return to find him still sitting there, her whole taut body twisting in delight, her stump of tail twitching.

One day after a pack of males tried repeatedly to mount her when she was in heat, Pa having refused to have her spaded because of the expense, Felix returned home from grade school to discover the dog no longer there. It was better for her, his parents claimed, but they never offered and he never dared ask what had become of that small, familiar form so much a part of his life that given him so much quiet, unexpected joy he rarely felt. Why had most of what he had cherished always vanished from his life?

He dipped in to draw out a microscope he had used as a boy when an insect wing had become a giant fan of iridescent color; inspecting specimens of his blood, almost delighting in jabbing his finger tip, seeing the red liquid ooze onto the glass slide, squeezing it thin between another glass plate revealing a reddish brown kaleidoscope of cells; urine revealing nothing; semen coaxed from his nascent testes he studied beneath the glaring light, he amazed those wiggling forms issuing from him would under the right conditions and circumstances duplicate part of him, be transformed and grow into a shadow record of himself.

From the stamp album inherited from Pa who, in turn, had received it from his father, Felix recalled his fascination with the panoply of colors, exotic scenes, exotic names, exotic symbols displayed while he worked on the collection, first with Pa, then alone, as he carefully mounted each display, sent off for bargain collections, visited the philatelist store downtown across from the domed museum, both an adventure. Imagine spending one's life selling stamps from around the world and from times past and never seeing those countries from which those stamps were issued.

In the high school yearbook of his senior year with slick pages now a bit yellow he leafed through slowly, he came upon D'Amico's senior year photo, then his own. How strange seeing the three-quarter profile of himself with a thin, somewhat smug smile, he in linen jacket, white shirt, and tie. When he came upon Jean's photo, he recalled his first meeting with her in Study Hall where she had sat in the seat before him. Overwhelmed by having her loose, gaping blouse so close right at his face, her hips and tight-skirted bottom right at his knees, he had met her later at a Homecoming game where she had invited him to the post-game sock hop at the school gym. They had hung around together almost constantly after that, until she had yielded to that college man, and she had dumped Felix twice, the third time for keeps. Soon after, Felix had become friendly with Nan who rode the same school bus. Felix studied Nan's sophomore year photo. How surprisingly mature she seemed. How sensual and knowing her studied expression. He recalled with stirred remembrance her having introduced him to eros in the mohair backseat of his brown, two-door, '49 Chevy with stick-shift on the steering wheel then recalled that morning he had arrived at Nan's house to find both her parents at work and she in bed asleep. Shedding his clothes, he had climbed into her small bed, his flesh already gorged from feeling her warm body beneath her gown. Waking, embracing him, she had removed her gown. He flushed now thinking of his flesh in full contact with hers rather than the confined, fully clothed struggles in the backseat of a car, her softness, her smooth warm skin, and how her small body opened to him, taking him in, how he had thrilled, quivering as they clung to each other beneath the close dormer of her room laced with frills soft and delicate and fragrant while they moved together to an explosive release that left them both limp. They had slept in each other's arms, and Felix had thought at the time that perhaps living together wouldn't be so bad, if it were anything like that.

A buzzer that once had woke him from sound sleep blatted waking him from reverie followed by a gruff voice.

"Anybody up there! Felix! You there, boy!"

Felix heard heavy footsteps, a tuneless whistle, a jangling ring of keys as a black Stetson hat appeared over the edge of the stairwell followed by a broad, puffy face, a stout, paunchy torso, then thick legs and wide hips in butt-tight jeans above pointed leather boots. Fat Jack with a wide grin, pushed back his Stetson exposing his vanishing hair as he planted his boots on the bare wide boards of the attic floor.

"Hey, Pilgrim!" Jack exclaimed in a drawl he had affected so long it was now a part of him. "Here you are, again!"

He came to Felix who rose to meet him from the trunk he sat on.

"Good to see you, boy! How the hell are you!" as Fat Jack locked Felix in a tight embrace.

"I'm fine, Jack," Felix said quietly as he withdrew from Jack's arms. "Sorry I didn't hear you at the door."

"Day dreamin' again? Thinkin' about pussy, I bet!" Then he quieted. "Your grandmother let me in. Nice lady. Let me see how your are!"

Felix stood back for his friend's inspection.

"You look a bit tired!" Jack said. "What you been up to! Too much booze! Too much tail!"

"Not much of either, lately. I've cut back on most of that."

"You not boozin' or chasin' pussy! You *must* be tired!"

"Just had enough for awhile. I've been traveling, mostly the West Coast. Just finished cutting wheat in Oregon before I hitched rides back here."

Felix unburied a chair from the recesses of the rafters, dusted it off, offered it to Jack, who eased himself with some caution onto a fragile piece of antique furniture that seemed almost overwhelmed by his bulk. Felix reseated himself on the trunk.

"So how was college?" Jack said.

"I didn't think you even knew I was gone."

"Well, you left in such a hurry, most of us thought someone was chasing you."

"How'd you find out?"

"From D'Amico before he left for California to find you."

The two men studying each other sat listening to the silence.

"I heard from him you got married." Felix offered.

"Yeah! Imagine that! I finally did it! Finally found someone who would put up with all my wild and crazy ways!"

"You married! Now, that is a surprise. I would have never thought that would happen. And who is this remarkable lady who would have enough patience to abide you for more than a day?"

"You'll have to meet her," Jack insisted.

The two men again studied each other.

"So what's all this business about changing? What you mean by change?" Jack challenged.

How, indeed, Felix thought. How could he explain what he felt now, his growing sense of awareness, the niggling sense of meaning, his life finally beginning to have focus. He beginning to perceive where he might be going, both the new world of knowledge and ideas and the actual world of living day to day on his own suggested how he might set out in the direction of his dream. How could he say all that and not sound pretentious. Even his use of the word 'pretentious' would sound strange to his friend, as it would have to him only a year ago, he with the arrogant pretention of an adolescent before he had left his father's house, gone off to school in California, now returned with the sense that now knowing more, having seen what he had seen, experienced what he had experienced, learned what he had learned, he had thought while he had waited for his friend to arrive and he had worried about how he could tell his friend about how he saw himself now. How could he make his friend understand that he was not the same naive youth whom his friend thought he knew, and that Jack shouldn't expect the same from him as before.

"I'm different, that's all," he said finally, breaking the awkward, heavy silence. "I mean. I think differently. I'm not the same person."

"So you said. How different? You seem about the same to me. Maybe put on a bit of weight that suits you well."

"I don't mean changed in that way. I mean changed."

"Sure," Jack said. "Don't we all. I think that's called 'aging'."

Felix studied his friend. Jack hadn't changed a bit.

"How come you didn't call when you got here?"

"I didn't have your number," Felix explained. "And you didn't leave it with my mother when you called."

"Sure," Jack said.

"Look," his friend insisted. "I just got in town. You moved didn't you? Got married?"

"That's true," Jack said, not yielding an inch.

"Look, I'm sorry!"

"Sure," Jack said. Then he saw Felix's troubled face. "Forget it, Pilgrim," he said, going into the swagger he always used to defuse uncomfortable situations. "We're here now."

"How'd you find I was staying at my grandmother's?"

"From D'Amico. He told me at the last Guard meeting a week ago. Said you called him. Guess you didn't forget his number."

"Not a matter of forgetting," Felix said. "His number's in the book. I'd forgotten about his being in the Reserve. I was surprised he still belongs."

"Yep, he still belongs. Doesn't come to many meetings, but he still belongs. How many other things you forget, Fella?"

Felix remained silent meeting Jack's intense gaze.

"Look," Jack offered finally. "There's a meeting tonight at seven. Why not come out to the armory and see some of the guys? I'll just go home and clean up and eat and I'll be back about six to pick you up. We can drive out together."

He looked at the watch on his thick, hairy arm.

"It's three now; meeting's at seven. Plenty of time. How about it?"

Felix looked out the window of the attic door at the asphalt tile roof of the sun porch below. Squinting against the glare under the heavy, overcast sky, he knew that later, the sky would thicken, the clouds darken, bringing thunder and lightning and rain that would roll across the hills and kettles of the moraine, maybe even this evening, heralding its coming for hours before it broke over their heads. Everyone would welcome the rain that would relieve them from the sticky, muggy heat that oppressed them now.

"Maybe you've got something better to do," Jack challenged.

"No, nothing." Felix insisted.

"Good! It's settled then! Maybe we can get some of the guys together. Stop for a few beers after the meeting, just like we used to." He relaxed in his seat draping his thick arms over the back of the fragile chair.

"Fine with me," Felix said. "I'd like that." Then he too sat and waited.

"You been doing any work?" Jack asked.

"Some. I've done a little when I've had time," Felix admitted. "But I haven't done much lately."

"You going to show me?"

"You really want to see?"

"Of course I want to see, fella!"

Felix scrambled from the trunk and started toward the open door of the room built beneath the raw rafters of the attic. "You'll see better in here!" he called back.

He turned to watch Jack ease his bulk from the antique chair and stomp across the attic floor, his boot heels hard on the wide, bare boards. Felix reached behind the worn, small dresser and drew out a small cardboard portfolio. Jack took the portfolio from his friend and untied the strings, studying Felix while he did so. Felix followed his every move.

"They're not very good," Felix suggested. Although he considered some the best he had ever done.

"We'll see," Fat Jack said.

He propped the portfolio against the wall beside the dresser and spread the sheets on the single bed. Then he picked up one sheet after another while pausing after every sheet to study Felix who held an intense scrutiny of Jack's expression while his friend inspected what he saw.

"They're good," Fat Jack conceded. "But I'm not sure I always follow what you're trying to do here or what you're trying to say."

"Let me explain," Felix offered eagerly.

While Felix began, Fat Jack went over to the single window to gaze down at his dinosaur Cad convertible on the street below while Felix talked to his broad back. Felix grew excited, gushing out his words as he tried to explain what he had seen, how he had tried to capture what he had lived. When he stopped, he stood with questioning eyes, studying Jack's back.

"I see," Jack said, finally as he turned and moved toward the door. "Look, I'll see you in a couple hours."

"Sure," Felix said.

"O.K., then" Jack said. He settled his hat and headed toward the stairs. "I'll catch you later!"

Then he was descending the steep stairs, his boots loud on the hollow wood risers. Felix went with him to the front door.

"You really think they're any good?" Felix asked as he followed his friend's Stetson, broad back, and cowboy boots reminding Felix a bit of the man in a small Oregon town who wore high-top sneakers and helped him find work.

"We'll talk later," Jack said over his shoulder.

Felix watched as Jack stomped down the gray enameled stairs of the wood porch to the concrete sidewalk, turned to look back up the stairs to where Felix watched him from the porch. Jack waved with the hand that held the jangling keys, then turned whistling without a tune, moved to the dinosaur Cadillac convertible at the curb, climbed in, settled his bulk into the seat, and fired the engine.

Felix lingered on the porch watching Jack pull away and roar up the street. Felix turned back into the house, went back to the attic room where he studied again — how many times before — the sheets that lay scattered on the bed and the rug in a sweeping collage of black and white. He bent to gather them, sort them, stack them, filing them again between the sections of the small portfolio. Then as he returned the portfolio to the dark space behind the dresser, he wondered from whom was he hiding it as he stood in the silent room thinking of his friend, uncertain about the night ahead.

As he waited on the front porch for his friend, Felix thought about their earlier encounter, how Fat Jack certainly had surprised him with that sudden phone call, Jack stating that he was on his way, and before Felix even had a chance to recover from surprise, Jack was there, climbing the stairs to the attic where Felix had sat in the dim light that helped conjure fleeting images of lost times. Felix recalled Jack's heavy countenance as Jack lumbered up the steps, the familiar whistle announcing his arrival along with the heavy sound of the boots ascending, the jangle of keys, and then the inquiring face above the bulk. Jack wore his hair short now that was the only change, probably because there was so little left, so Fat Jack seemed much the same. Even the studied indifference, the absence of expression that made Felix think Jack hadn't actually listened to him talk about what Felix had offered from the small portfolio. Felix recalled the wide back, the passive inspection of the sheets that were Felix's treasure. Fat Jack seemed not to have changed at all.

But Felix thought again of how he perceived himself as different. Even as he had recognized his friend's voice on the telephone, Felix had wanted to tell his friend of how he felt now, that he perceived himself differently now. He was not just simply older. More than that was Felix's sense that he had witnessed life. He had seen unexpected places and events that even now in thinking of them made him feel wiser and at the same time filled with a sense of wonder and humility that now those events were his, no matter how challenging some had been: what he had faced and met attending his first year of college, the first of his extended family; the trip to Oregon and his days of harvesting the fields of golden grain; the trip back here and the layover with the weird woman with mystic eyes and insatiable libido; the long walk to a small town and the troubling assault he had submitted to with a perverse tinge of pleasure. Having experienced them, all were now part of him, and Felix felt that they were his alone. He had lived them; he had tried to capture them in his own feeble way, freezing them in images through which he had tried to seize the moment. He had set out on his own to test himself, and now he had returned to explore the difference he found in himself and what that difference might mean for others. Wasn't that the reason for his return?

Jack's sudden appearance and departure made Felix think now of his taking leave the year before. How startled he had been at the ease with which he found himself setting off alone, he thinking, as usual, he would find it much more difficult. How surprised everyone else was that he could even think of going, some questioning whether he should while those last hectic days had kept him from changing his mind,

So now here he was again thinking of the possibilities in the night ahead, yet one thing he would insist on, one thing he must explain to his old friend Jack, one thing that he had hoped to explain that afternoon without being able to was that he had changed. He was no longer the same uncertain, naïve, anxious Felix who had hurried to catch that first plane ride the year before, nor did he want to be that same adolescent. He was sure now that if somehow he could explain the feeling of his change, then what might happen certainly would go differently that night. Oh, he was willing to go along with most of the old activities. In fact, he rather looked forward to some of them. He thought he might enjoy seeing some of his former weekend-warrior buddies, spend some time with them, have a beer or three with them, and then leave again as soon as he could. He most likely would be on his way again soon, so he saw little point in getting involved to any degree trying to resuscitate old friendships that couldn't actually be revived.

Then he thought of Fat Jack's attitude of this afternoon, and Felix knew that Jack considered nothing changed and that would mean that Jack most likely thought Felix was still fair game. Felix again thought long about what had happened in a small Illinois town after his long walk through the night. So with some uneasiness tinged with doubt, Felix shaved and showered on the wet wood slats above the concrete floor in the dark, dank basement stall of what once was considered the Fist family home. Then he dressed preparing himself for Jack's return, and Felix waited again for a chance to explain to his friend more clearly how he had changed.

When Jack returned, announcing his arrival in his typical fashion with tuneless whistle, jangling keys on thick, hairy finger, Felix waiting on the front porch sitting on the steps, his grandmother in her customary place behind him on a chair working on one of her endless projects, Jack stood on the walkway before the porch and tipped his Stetson to the old lady: "Evening, ma'm!" then turned to Felix. "You 'bout ready to saddle up?" then turned and went back around the car and climbed in.

Felix followed taking the front seat to ride shotgun, Jack started the car, both men waved to the woman who returned their farewell, and they were off in Jack's dinosaur Cad convertible toward the country and the distant town of Prairieville some twenty miles distant that held the armory where they would attend the weekly meeting of the National Guard Army Reserve unit, the trip out allowing Felix time to reconsider the somewhat unusual circumstances under which he and Jack had become close.

The beginning of their connection never had seemed auspicious and at first was quite typical. Belonging to the same Guard unit, they only on occasion had engaged each other. Felix a new enlistee persuaded to join by D'Amico who always seemed to need someone to accompany him in any new endeavor that held uncertainties, Felix, of course, self-absorbed by the newness of the situation and by all the various rituals and practices that were part of the institution in which he suddenly had found himself. Then because of the activities into which he was thrust, Felix had begun to notice Jack, older by ten or more years, one of the highest ranking non-coms, a Master Sergeant taking over whenever necessary for the company First Sergeant, a role and obligation Jack obviously relished from being frequently on display. Jack belonging to the unit longer than most officers and men, Jack considered an institution carried himself with a bearing that revealed his sense of self-importance and self-esteem derived from the status he had achieved.

Felix had watched Jack from the distance of his being of lowest rank and newest enlistee in the company. Felix also watched from the distance created by his own desire for acceptance, for success, for promotion that would establish for him a similar position of respect and self-worth. How he had needed that! Felix with growing fascination had watched Jack in his pressed, starched fatigues, polished boots, smart, blocked hat, insignias of rank all dressing the bulk that gave him the moniker which all his friends used to express their regard.

Felix decided that Jack wasn't really fat: perhaps he was stout. He was large, but his bulk seemed at the same time trim. His size helped his bearing, Jack moving quickly and with intense purpose like some large tank through the ranks of men who were under his firm command. His men held him in respect and liked him for his joking but decisive manner. Felix had held him in awe and as he watched Jack from a distance, he, however consciously or unconsciously, began to develop his own attitude while involved in unit activities after the model that Jack so conveniently and obviously offered him, Felix also mimicking others at roll call by shouting "Yo!" when his name was called. And Jack, for his part, in his typical deliberate but subtle way sensed from their contacts at weekly meetings, occasional weekends training, and summer camp Felix's silent growing adulation from his psychic need.

Their first close encounter, however, was as unexpected as their first contact was conventional. Riding now beside Jack who silently attended the road ahead, Felix recalled his other ride along another road he had driven with other friends, a road dark and narrow, passing scattered lights from homes with widening spaces between, the two lanes passing stands of thick trunks of full-leafed oak and a steady line of oncoming headlights, a slow bumpy, rocking ride over the high arch of wooden trestle under a massive cloth banner that proclaimed with huge letters: FRONTIER DAYS. He and his friends had entered the comparatively quiet end of town of old, brick buildings with turrets and round fronts that proclaimed their age in large, square granite blocks. Ahead, at the far end of the wide street, they could see the strung lights, the whirling neon of thrill rides as they turned down a dusty, graveled side street looking for a place to park, the narrow street made darker by the few circles of lights that led toward the blackness of the country at the edge of town. Finally struggling into a small, vacant place, walking back toward the brightened sky above the full-leafed treetops, the bright lights, the noise and whirl of the fair meeting them while they stomped from the dusty gravel onto smooth asphalt, they quickly blended into the press of people and booths and blaring twang of country music.

His friends going on ahead when he had lagged behind, abandoning him, disappearing into the crowd, Felix felt a bit of relief at being left alone, of not having to follow someone else's direction. He ambled on enjoying his sense of freedom and reached the broad main street transformed into a carnival, along with carnival rides, the thoroughfare rife with booths that held tiers of shelves with arrays of colored bottles, ashtrays, plastic dolls. An attendant in straw hat rasped out a challenge: "Ring any one and it's yours!" Another booth offered huge, stuffed bears in shrieking, iridescent colors. On either side, booths lined the thoroughfare offering a long string of throbbing lights that seemed to meld with the deep throb of music from the raised platform in the middle of a plaza. Stands at frequent intervals were filled with people guzzling beer poured from endlessly flowing spigots of full barrels dispensed by shouting men dressed as cowboys who served the multitude.

Felix had been astonished to see Master Sergeant Jack dressed in full western outfit: plaid western shirt, butt-tight jeans, spear-toe boots, Stetson pushed back exposing a high forehead as he stood hip slung at one of the beer stands expounding in his typical fashion to a group of attentive listeners. Jack apparently hadn't notice him, and Felix made no attempt to present himself for recognition and possible rejection. He ambling on his way, glancing back once to see if Sergeant Jack had noticed him, reaching the street end and the barricades, the glaring, sizzling flare blocking the road that lead off into the darkness ripe with the sweet-sour sting of barnyard, he returned along another row of booths much like the first, back again past the beer stand where Sergeant Jack still holding court had turned but gave no sign of recognition as Felix passed among the endlessly wandering, moving mass, Felix indifferently responding to the throb of crowd and lights, his mind passive, yet filled with interest until a snarling voice perceived dimly at first had cut through all the noise startling him, compelling him to turn.

"Hey, Fist!" a drunken voice had snarled as a large form had lunged at him, the drunken voice challenging him again, as it had before, surprising him at that high school dance Felix had attended with Jean whom he had won at the expense of other suitors. "Hey, son-a-bitch!"

Felix had tensed, the bloated, red-blotched, pocked face, like some carnival demon mask, thrusting itself at him, making him draw back.

"Where's your whore tonight?" the mask growled. "Should have brought her! We'd take care of her!"

As they would much later, Felix had learned, once she had abandoned Felix for the third time, offering herself for the pleasure of anyone who courted her, shaming Felix even more, since she had never given him what he had always wanted but denied because of his hesitancy from his fear of being rejected if he tried.

Felix had seen the others behind the demon who taunted him, the same hostile gang that had pursued him before, although he never understood what he had done to warrant their attention. Perhaps because he simply chose to remain apart from them, refusing to concede to their self-important insistence on dressing alike in the latest passing fashion, faddishly wearing the same current hairstyle, using the most recent coined cant phrases. He had refused to join in the overly loud laughter, the self-conscious adolescent horseplay. Or perhaps because she, whom the others pursued, had chosen Felix, rejecting the others, both choosing and rejecting for whatever reason neither Felix nor the others had understood.

Then as always he walked away slowly, telling himself as always: *"Walk slowly and pretend he doesn't bother you. Act calm even through your heart is pounding."*

They slowly following him, often tripping in their drunkenness, attempting to trip him, cursing him, snarling at everyone, the crowd parting before them, giving way to the vile hoarseness that pierced the throbbing clash of music and voices until reaching the street end where Felix had braced himself to bolt into the dark, make a dash for it, to where, he didn't know, hoping to outlast them, out run them in their drunken condition, when another voice, equally familiar, strong and assured, had stopped them all in their tracks.

"Hey, Pilgrim!" And there was Master Sergeant Jack in his plaid western shirt tight across his bulk, his butt-tight jeans and cowboy boots, his Stetson pushed back above his high forehead. He stood with thumb through belt loop, passively watching the crowd, sipping from a waxed paper cup. "Seems you got a bit of a problem."

"Yep."

"Need help?"

"Yep."

Then they had stood together to face the gang stopped up short, almost falling over each other in their continued pursuit, surprised by the unexpected challenge of two tall men who boldly faced them, Jack and Felix staring them down while they stood their ground watching as the gang turned back bursting in upon a beer stand, harassing and dominating the attendant, displacing their rage with loud shouts and cursing demands in response to the man's reluctant service.

From the safety of distance, Felix had relaxed with relief, turning to thank Sergeant Jack, but Jack had shrugged him off.

"What happened to your friends, Pilgrim?"

Surprised by Fat Jack's question, Felix wondered when Jack had noticed Felix was with friends?

"They always pull this," Felix had said. "They go off doing their own thing. They always forget me. I usually end up hitching rides home."

"So, you about ready to leave?"

"I guess. The guys I came with are gone now, or drunk, or both. No sense in me hanging around, not with that motley crew over there aching for trouble at my expense."

They both watched from a distance as the gang continued to dominate the beer stand.

"They'll only come after me once they see me alone again, and I've got no where to go!"

Jack had offered him a drink from his cup. Surprised and pleased, Felix accepted, taking a token sip of beer then returning the cup.

"You need a ride, then," Jack said.

"Guess I could use one."

"I was just leaving myself," Jack said. "You want to ride along with me, you're welcome."

"Thanks. I'd appreciate that."

"No problem. Let's go, then, Pilgrim," Jack invited. "Trusty steed's right over here."

So they had left together riding out through the scattering crowds in Jack's convertible, the one they rode in now, top down, as it was now, mocking those who had stood in drunken anger watching them go.

Felix looked up at the open sky above. He watched the splay of trees that rushed by alongside the road as they sped by. That other night they had moved through dark countryside with a stream of headlights coming at them, the clumps of trees rushing past broken by dark fields while above the familiar patterns of stars had led them on.

Stopping for something to eat at a place Jack recommended and where, of course, Jack knew everyone, and everyone greeted Jack on his entrance, Felix had tagged along in Jack's wake thrilled to be in Jack's illustrious company, filled with a sense of self-worth when those who greeted Jack also had welcomed Felix after Jack introduced Felix as his friend. Sitting at a table, ordering breakfast since it was past midnight, and therefore a new day, after they were served their food and began to eat, Felix had felt so exhausted from the night's challenges he found himself coming awake with his face almost in his plate.

"You must be tired," Jack said.

"Sorry," Felix said. "I didn't even know I dozed off."

"Maybe you better spend the night at my place."

"Really?"

"Save me having to go all the way across town and having to drive there and back."

"Sure," Felix agreed. "It probably would."

"You wouldn't mind?"

"No. That'd be great. If it's not a hassle for you."

"No problem, Pilgrim. Be glad to put you up."

Felix had felt a bit dazed at how quickly events transpired through the night, as if all that had happened and all that would happen seemed a dream.

They had left without finishing their food. Jack waving off Felix's offer to pay. Then as if in a fog, Felix following Jack out to the convertible and climbing in, he had quickly slipped into a doze once they pulled away from the curb and started towards Jack's place across town from where Felix had a room. Felix waking to find the car stopped and Jack helping him through the open car door, he had stumbled after as Jack led him up the path from the driveway to the front stoop, waiting chilled and shivering while Jack fumbled in the darkness for the key, managed to get the key in the lock, then opened the door.

Once inside, Felix had little chance to survey the darkened decor with which Jack had surrounded himself. But he had noted the blend of odors that closed in on him in the dark. Jack had led him to the bedroom, showed him the bathroom, offered him a towel. Felix used the facilities, then returned to the darkened bedroom where he undressed, slipped in between the sheets and immediately dropped into a deep sleep.

Waking to find his flesh gorged and a hand moving over him, caressing him, fondling him, he had felt a warm, wet mouth on him, stroking him, he wondering if he were still dreaming, but then more awake, in the dim light, his eyes accustomed to the dark, he could make out Jack's hairy shoulders, the scalp through his thinning hair as Jack's head moved in a steady, skilled rhythm. Laying back relaxed. "It's OK," he had told himself. He had done this before with his older brother Sonny. Placing his hand on Jack's head, Jack had increased his stroking, Felix giving himself up to the feel of Jack's mouth bringing him to a release that had him thrashing under Jack's insistent rhythm. When Felix had quieted, Jack had stretched beside him, continuing to caress him, holding him in his arms, coaxing Felix without a word to move down to do what Jack had done. Felix giving in, taking Jack in mouth, stroking him, he breathing in odors much like those he had noted on entering Jack's house, Jack with hardly a sign of release had filled Felix's throat, Felix had moved back to his place on a pillow, and they had spent the rest of the night in deep sleep.

In the morning, Felix waking found Jack emerging from the bathroom purged and groomed, settling his Stetson, ready to go out the door.

"Morning, Pilgrim!" Jack said, as Felix had pulled himself up to a sitting position in bed. "I'm running late. Make yourself at home. Have a shower. I'll see you at the meeting Monday next."

Then Jack was gone without a sign of what had taken place between them during the night, and Felix left alone with the quiet noises and Jack's lingering odors in the empty house. Felix had not moved to explore Jack's realm, although he was curious. Instead, after Jack left, the sound of his dinosaur Cad receding, carrying him off into his day, Felix rising, had used the toilet, wetted down his hair, gone back to the bedroom to dress, leaving the folded towel where Jack had placed it the night before, straightened the bed (Master Sergeant Jack would most likely have expected that) and left, walking to the nearest stop where he had waited for a bus that would take him across town to his room.

After that first close encounter, such sessions had become routine. But all through their involvement, reluctant to consider Jack as a lover, Felix had been certain he felt no love for Jack — respect, of course, but love? Why would he feel anything when Jack had shown no love and only allowed himself a display of casual affection for Felix as he would any of the other men under his command. What, then, might Felix consider the nature of his connection with Jack? Why would Jack pursue sex with young men? How often and how many were readily available?

Every Monday night after their meeting, they would stop at a tavern where they would meet others from the same unit. While quaffing pitchers of beer, they would begin to sing, Felix often urged to take the lead because of his strong, trained voice from singing in choirs when younger, the others joining him in harmony. Then after the tavern had closed, Jack would drive Felix to Jack's place where Felix would spend what was always a short night after they had quickly satisfied each other.

Felix had soon found a change in their routine: Instead of Felix being satisfied first, Jack would maneuver Felix so that Felix would be beneath him. Then Jack would pump himself to a brief shiver of release, rolling off Felix to rise from the bed and disappear behind the bathroom door. By the time Jack returned, Felix would find himself stirred from sleep but never satisfied, and he would turn away as Jack settled beside him. When Felix woke, he would hear the sound of Jack's Cad receding with distance, and he would rise, dress, and leave the empty house.

There were times when Felix had thought of breaking off the pattern, of not stopping for beer and song after the meeting, of making some excuse for not going to Jack's place, or before he found himself following Jack through Jack's door, he would try to find some reason for not staying the night. But Jack always had managed to maneuver him into staying by acting disappointed, almost rejected if Felix suggested he might want to do something other than what Jack wanted. Felix always finding himself yielding to Jack's quiet, firm direction, Felix began to wonder how he had turned into Jack's whore, his sense of being used increasing when Jack changed positions, satisfying himself by taking Felix from behind. Jack's size, or lack of it, had made it easier for Felix to accept the intrusion, he eventually finding Jack's movement and the feel of Jack inside him strangely exciting, so if he relaxed and gave himself up to the sensation, he too had been satisfied, pulsing into his palm to prevent soiling the sheets.

Their "affair" had ended almost as suddenly as it began. One Monday at their usual gathering at a tavern after their Reserve meeting, Jack had announced he was engaged to be married. Everyone was surprised. Felix was more than surprised. He was shocked without a clue Jack might be involved with anyone else, let alone a woman. But he had resigned himself to the turn of events, wondering what would happen now, expecting that he would no longer be invited to Jack's place, no longer expected to stay the night. At the gathering where Jack presented the news, Jack had excused himself early, pushing back his chair, settling his Stetson, rising, waving to everyone, turning, striding in his typical rolling determination past the bar and out through the door into the dark. Felix feeling abandoned, he had stayed for more beer and had bummed a ride with someone who was going somewhere near where he lived.

Soon after, when a young woman whom he had met by accident while cruising with former high school buddies offered to send him information about her school, Felix began considering leaving for California to attend college. Surprised by receiving that information, he impulsively filled out the application and just as impulsively had mailed it. Receiving an equally surprising letter informing him he had been accepted, he with growing excitement began making preparations to leave on what he came to consider his grand adventure.

Felix woke from reverie when the old Cad moved from country road onto familiar streets. Felix scanned the scene he knew well from the hundreds of times he had passed this way before but interested now because those familiar places held a tinge of change. Jack swung the car into the parking lot before the large domed building and pulled up along the row of cars already there in special designated spots for officers and non-coms. They scrambled from the Cad and joined the stream of men funneling through the open door and glaring light that drew them into the cavern underneath the dome and green steel girders of the armory.

Jack swaggered across the gray enameled concrete floor to the locker room. Felix followed met by a chorus of greetings he responded to in kind, exchanging wisecrack for smart-alec remark while Jack set about changing from Stetson, western shirt, jeans, and cowboy boots to combat boots and starched, creased fatigues bristling with stripes and insignia. Then he slammed the metal door, set his blocked fatigue cap on his head, and strode out to the floor to order his men into formation right behind the First Sergeant whose whistle shrieking beneath the cavernous roof brought the regimental command company to attention. The men shuffling into place, roll call began, and Felix lingered at the edge along the painted concrete block wall, conspicuous, made even more so by the First Sergeant's public recognition, then excluded, settling on a gray enameled bench to wait for a break from classes. At the break, he was overwhelmed by salutations and questions from those he hadn't seen in over a year. Even the regimental commander approached, the troops deferring to his rank, parting for him as he, stern as ever, quietly offered Felix his hand. "Glad to see you," the Old Man said, then walked off, allowing the men to fill in the gap most of them little more than late adolescents who had joined mostly from fear of being drafted.

One man from his old platoon with whom he chatted had a college degree. Felix was eager to share with the man an assessment of how he had changed through his leaving for California and having attended a year of college. Felix felt pleased that the man who had frequently chatted with him before Felix had left for Long Beach appeared to actually understood what Felix was saying as if the man also had experienced something similar.

"I feel as if I'm a different person. My mind seems different! I can actually feel it expanding!" Felix insisted.

"Exactly!" the man exclaimed. "You learn things you had never been aware of or had interest in or even imagined. Suddenly you find yourself in a world you never knew existed."

When the First Sergeant's whistle shrilled again calling the men back to their classes, Felix left alone again feeling suspended decided on a walk to pass the time by exploring the city he hadn't seen since high school. He informed Jack before Jack returned to his class. They agreed that Jack would meet Felix in the city center where Felix could easily walk to from the armory.

So after the men moved away, returning to class, Felix moved through the open door into darkness, crunched across the parking lot to the residential street of large, old homes nestled by tall oak thick and twisted with age. He crossed the asphalt street to the concrete walk and started down through the neighborhood he knew well from the years he spent here attending the nearby school. He had panted and pounded in daylight through these streets training for cross country in autumn, track and field in spring, or sometimes during winter gym class when the P.E. teacher had wanted them out of the way so he could help the teacher for women's PE inventory towels. Felix noted at the time from his growing stamina that they had counted towels a lot. Early on during his first year, Felix had trailed along behind others, relegated to that place as a freshman, bringing up the rear of the heaving, gasping pack. Later, as a Senior, he had led the pack along the route he found himself retracing now. Could he really follow that old route exactly?

The walk broke out from the houses to a parkway that ran along the river. The dark, roiling water bobbed the light of lampposts on the other bank. Then the street snaked underneath the railroad trestle and alongside the park thick with the black trunks of oak then back into an area of more modest houses where he saw above the trees and between the houses the shadowy bulking image of the school.

Having reached the campus of Prairieville High, its yellow sandstone building dimmed by night, the asphalt playgrounds secured by chain-link fence where he stopped and studied the dark windows crisscrossed by wire, the metal stairs and railings of the fire escape that rose to the third tier of windows for what he once knew as Study Hall. Behind those windows, assigned arbitrarily to one of the numerous seats in the long rows of linked seats, he had met what he considered his first love.

He overwhelmed by everything: the marvelous, new surroundings in which he had found himself, the crush of students in wide hallways with polished granite floors bordered with dark metal lockers trimmed in dark wood, a procession of dark wood classroom doors along the corridor ending in massive arched windows above vast stairwells with polished granite stairs, she, too, had overwhelmed him: How gorgeous she seemed, so physically immediate, so direct. Her smile of perfect teeth, the rouged luscious lips, her bright, blue eyes under short, dark hair cut in latest style, her fashionable clothes, her easy remarks to her acquaintances as if she knew everyone and everyone knew her. And she, for some reason, his innocence perhaps, his country bumpkin appearance from homemade, hand-me-down apparel that made him seem odd, singling him out, directing all her dazzling, sophisticated, suburban city, county seat charm toward him. She apparently courting him vied with others who similarly, for some reason, pursued him, perhaps because he was considered odd and not from the city, but mostly because, so it was whispered, he wrote poetry and was an artist. Yet she had won easily despite the competition.

Felix moved around to the front of the building to the expansive lawn canopied by tall oak, the wide walkway that led to the broad stairs and the large doors of the entrance, he, as others, rarely used. He moved on to the corner, to the side street where the line of yellow and black busses had waited for him and others to board for the ride through the countryside of hills with small farms and pastures, of county roads and lines of rural mailboxes, to one of the pocket lakes and his cottage home on the outer areas of Sunfish village.

He reached wide concrete sidewalks and Library Park two blocks from the city center and moved beneath the canopy of trees that rose above grass, the dark hulking burial mound of indigenous people Felix when a child had gazed at in transfixed wonder, the stony bulk of the granite-block Carnegie library, its yellow globes on black enameled iron posts dispelling the darkness, dispersing beams of light across the crisscross of asphalt pathways. Felix once had climbed those wide stairways, often entering that reverent hush where he had continued his passionate pursuit of books at the large, dark, gleaming wood tables in among the curved rows of stacks that followed the contour of the building. Here he had discovered poetry and great art: Keats and Wordsworth, Yeats and Arnold; Rembrandt and Vermeer and the Impressionists Monet, Pissarro, Renoir, and then, of course, Van Gogh.

Here he frequently had witnessed fistfights outside on the expansive surrounding park lawn, one or two in which he had been challenged because of his reading preferences and his revealed artistic aspirations raising questions regarding his sexual orientation. Yet he had held his own in such encounters, exchanging blow for jarring blow, always rescued finally by the librarian, a gray-haired, spectacled woman, or by an approaching patrol car. He considered how eagerly people had gathered to watch combatants circle each other like mongrel dogs, lunging at each other, landing thudding blows resounding like drums that drew blood and sometimes fractured bone or teeth, one time he receiving a chipped front tooth as a badge of courage.

Moving on into an area of storefronts, a department store, a movie theater, a drive-in diner, a jewelry store where one time having bought a hard-earned senior-class ring with fake ruby he had promptly offered Nan to wear on a chain, he reached the city center, a five-point intersection where roadways from all over the county came together, paved over from when the roads were dirt, this city then a town when farmers brought their crops and produce to market in horse-drawn wagons then in rattling, airy trucks with wood beds. The granite block buildings with their marble columns and vast, curved windows reflecting that long lost era, here from time to time while Pa and Felix's uncle visited a local doctor to have his uncle's work injuries attended, Felix, a ten-year-old, allowed to roam the area by himself as far as Library Park had confined by choice his movements to the sidewalks of the intersection before the grand facade of the bank, its stone-tiled floor a mosaic of a full-feathered Native-American chief. The time had passed quickly, so absorbed was he in the serious transactions of the well-dressed men and women who entered the open doorway and approached the gleaming brass teller's cage to conduct their business, he suddenly filled with wonder at the surprising sound wave of approaching students from nearby Prairieville High that had broke around him. How colossal and grand they had seemed towering above him as they passed laughing, yelling, chatting, dominating the scene, as he would himself a few years later when he would attend that same school, just as everyone did who lived in county townships and attended state funded schools. Here Felix with friends harassing local merchants, hanging out in drugstore booths or tables in restaurants, roaming from one to the other in a movable feast, here a more subdued Felix had shared those drugstore booths and fountain sodas first with Jean then with Nan to whom he had offered his senior-class ring. Here Felix had climbed the backs of buildings on iron rungs of fire escapes to reach tarpaper roofs and cornices from which he had gazed down at the continuous movement of vehicles and people, marveling at his wide perspective, the diminished size of all he viewed while he remained unobserved witnessing everything below him, he feeling somehow perverse and godlike.

Standing now transfixed, viewing the flow and ebb of passing scene, transported back to when he as a ten-year-old stood here before, curious that the person through whose eyes he once gazed in wonder seemed strange to him now, almost unreal, as if that person were someone other than himself, he spotted Jack's car at one of the points of the intersection, saw Jack's Stetson, Jack's thick arm raised in a casual salute. Felix hurried across to climb in the car just as the light changed, and they were off along the streets, heading for the open country along a dark road.

Felix and Jack entered a tavern. Jack, of course, waded in first, leading the way as always, greeting those along the bar and at the tables. The shouts and greetings he received in return showed Felix that Jack apparently knew all who were there, and Felix was not surprised. Jack yelled above the din of music and clash of voices.

"Look who I dragged in!"

A chorus of voices rose to greet Felix who faked a cringing response from the attention, he following Jack along the bar shaking hands, accepting the friendly poundings on his shoulders and back from those who greeted him. Felix and Jack took seats at a table opposite the bar after meeting the offered hands of the men already there.

"Long time no see!" one of the men said, a man with whom Felix had worked for the same company manufacturing industrial equipment for producing cement and concrete to build nascent interstates and the pads for tract homes.

"It has been awhile," Felix admitted.

"What you drinking?" the man asked.

"I think I'll pass for now," Felix said.

"Come on!" Jack ordered. "The man here wants to buy you a drink!"

"We've hit another other place before we came here," Felix explained.

"The night's still young! We've just got started!" Jack insisted.

"I'm trying to cut back," Felix insisted. "I hit the juice pretty hard before I left for California. After not drinking much while in school when I couldn't afford it, drinking again hits me pretty hard."

"You'll do all right!" Jack insisted, always the ranking non-com. "I'll get you a beer."

Jack rose and went to the bar. Felix and the man held a brief, awkward silence in the void left by Jack's absence.

"How you been?" the man asked. "You went out to California."

"Yeah, I did. Given the chance of going to college I thought I never had, I guess I got tired of hanging out in places like this, dreaming too much of what I wasn't able to do, not doing much of anything, not going anywhere, especially after I tried for a trainee position in the department you work, and there weren't any."

Jack returned with glasses and a pitcher of beer. He poured Felix a glass, freshened up the glasses of those already there. Then he sat while pouring himself a glass.

"What's wrong with doing what were doing now!" Jack argued as if he had overheard what they had said. "Friends here! We've had good times at places like this! Have a few beers! Sing a few songs!"

"I guess I want something more," Felix argued. "So must you. You got married, didn't you?"

"That's what you need!" Jack exclaimed. "A steady woman! She'd settle you!"

"Who'd marry him!" one of the men joked.

"Exactly!" Felix agreed. And everyone laughed.

"You'd find someone, you'd stay put long enough. Even I found the right one."

"Say, what about those California women?" another man asked. "What they like?"

"Not much different from here," Felix offered. "A lot of them are from the Midwest anyway. They seem to be running after some illusion, some impossible dream, hoping to become famous and rich. Some call it California dreaming."

"Just what you seem to be doing!" Jack accused.

"A man's got to dream!" one of the men advised.

"But that dream's got to have some chance of coming true. Otherwise just dreamin' won't get you anywhere. You wake up one day and realize you ain't got nothin!"

Jack poured more beer for everyone.

"But this party's getting way too serious! Let's drink to the prodigal return!" He lifted his glass, joined by the others. Then he began a song they all knew, Jack nodding to Felix to take the lead as he had so often before, and the others, as thy had before, joined in harmony.

Later that evening, Felix followed Jack from the tavern. Climbing into Jack's car, pulling out onto the street, they drove through the city to the park near where Felix was staying with his grandmother. Jack pulled into one of the spaces, shut down the engine, sat looking out through the windshield while the sound of the engine and the whine of western music on the car radio died in their heads allowing the night sounds to creep in. Then Jack opened the door, climbed out, slammed the door.

"I need some air," Jack said and started down along a gravel pathway that led through thick bushes. Felix followed, and when they moved to the edge of a pond, Felix studied the dim image of a boathouse across the pond. He felt lightheaded from the beer. He had not been here in a long time.

"We used to come here when I was a kid. There used to be an old boathouse where that new one is now. Not concrete and glass like that one. The old one was brick and wood, ripe and redolent with fragrances of passing seasons."

"Redolent?" Jack asked.

"We'd rent boats and paddle around on this old pond thinking we were something," Felix continued. "But we'd mostly fish from the shore with bent pins for hooks, bread for bait, string and a stick for a pole. We chased mud turtles. There were two huge white swans that would glide across the quiet, green water as if they ruled the world. In winter, we'd skate on the pond for hours, use the nearby hill for sledding. "Where are the snows of yesteryear!"

"What?" Jack asked.

Felix turned in the dark from where he stood studying the pond. "Where are the snows of yesteryear," Felix answered quietly. "A line from a poem by Francois Villon, a fifteen century French poet."

Jack came to Felix, put his arm around his shoulder.

"Did you ever think when you were a kid you'd be back here, having lived what you have lived?"

Felix accepted Jack's arm around his shoulder.

"Who ever does?" Felix said. "I left thinking I'd never be back. We never do until we find ourselves where we started. Then suddenly we seem to understand what it means, what we were, what perhaps we've lost."

"We don't have to lose everything," Jack insisted. "You can always renew something if you want it bad enough."

Felix felt the arm around his shoulder tighten, and he knew what was coming, then was certain when Jack turned toward him, gathering him into an embrace.

"Remember what we had?" Jack whispered.

Felix felt himself being directed, being maneuvered. Felix felt his hand on Jack's groin, felt his hand directed by Jack's, felt Jack unzip his butt-tight jeans, guiding Felix's hand, helping Felix expose him, then pressing on Felix's shoulders so that Felix felt himself sinking to his knees with Jack's now tumescent flesh at his face.

"Remember how it was?" Jack asked.

Felix felt Jack's hands behind his head pressing him in toward the hairy thighs and ridged flesh. Felix felt the flesh at his lips, his lips yielding, allowing the warm flesh to enter, and Jack's hips begin to move in a slow rhythm.

"You haven't forgotten," Jack moaned softly.

Felix sprawled back on the grass, leaving Jack exposed. "I don't want this!" Felix cried.

"You can't have changed that much!" Jack insisted.

Felix looked up at Jack from where he lay on the grass propped on his elbows.

"I've changed enough to know that I'm beyond this! I never really wanted this even before!"

"Well, you were certainly willing enough then!"

Felix pulled himself to his feet as Jack straightened his clothes.

"But I never knew why! I just went along because I didn't know what I wanted." Felix stood still defiant. "I couldn't see any reason not to. And there was something glamorous in being with you, given what people thought of you."

"They still think of me that way!" Jack insisted.

"I know they do," Felix conceded. "I could see that with the guys earlier. They haven't changed a bit." He hesitated, not sure whether he wanted to continue. "And neither have you."

"And you have!" Jack scoffed, indignant. "You claim you've changed so much, you think you're better than anyone else!"

"Not better. Just different than I was. And I no longer need to try to please anyone." He hesitated again. "Not even you."

"O.K., so I guess that's it!"

"Why does it have to be either/or?" Felix asked, softening his tone. "I thought we were friends."

"Friends!" Jack scoffed. "What the fuck you mean by 'friends'? I've got plenty friends!"

"No. What you have are people you can manipulate and control for satisfying your own self-interest, those who will build you up, make you think you're the big macho man."

"You think you're so superior! You go off a puking punk kid and come back a snob! You think going off to college in California makes you special? That you're better than anyone? That your experience gives you something we 'hometown' hicks don't have?" Jack moved off, then turned back. "You and your faggot art and poetry! You make me sick!"

Felix watched Jack's broad back as the man moved off through the bushes along the gravel path they had walked together. He heard Jack's car roar to life, the tires screeching as the car roared off, the engine sound diminishing with distance, leaving Felix alone in a darkness that again became quiet after the car was gone.

Felix began walking, leaving the park, moving through the dark streets past rows of two-story flats. He reached Clark Square and a wading pool. How small that greenspace seemed now, how small the flat area of lawn of which the pool was the center. Around the pool, green slat-board benches gleamed beneath the globed lamps that lit the walkways and the cracked painted concrete of the empty pool.

He had played here when a child, the shallow pool filled, the benches filled with mostly elderly who came to watch children splash and scream in delight in warm summer air beneath tall, ancient oak that crowned the park with a canopy of leaves, those trees now gone. He left the park and passed the dark brick building once an extended living facility for those so ancient they seemed immortal as they crept bent and feeble out onto the balconies to sit in warm sunlight. He reached a row of brick, one-story apartments that once appeared odd in their newness and design among the taller, older wood dwellings that were typical of the area. Here, while these structures were little more than foundations, a friend of his fell down an unfinished stairwell, stripping the skin from his arm and neck. Felix had watched as the fire rescue squad came to pull the boy up, take him off in an ambulance, leaving Felix in frightened awe. Here in these same apartments, once they were finished, a great aunt of Felix's had lived alone, abandoned by her husband, an alcoholic, whom Felix one day discovered begging before the bank on 16th and Greenfield.

Felix arrived at his grandmother's house. He climbed the front porch stairs then sat on the top step. He surveyed the dark row of two-story wood houses with balconies across the way, the lamplight on the tall trees that lined the street, the glow of signs from the window of the tavern at the corner, the screen door creaking then banging shut as some late patron finally emerged and swayed off unsteady into the night. He studied the brick facade of the pharmacy in streetlight across the avenue, the blank row of windows above, and the tan drawn blinds of his parents' bedroom.

He pulled himself to his feet, let himself into the dark house, the interior hot and stifling, close and redolent with his grandmother's fragrances, the furnishings dim and familiar, as he moved in and among them, making his way to the kitchen and the doorway that opened to the stairs winding up to the close, stuffy attic and the room he had slept in as a child when he was innocent through ignorance and open to the world.

While heavy traffic swept by on the busy avenue behind him, Felix stood outside the rusted, chain-linked fence before the massive abandoned building gazing at the high brick walls built by scores of laborers in the previous century. Seeing the structure from a distance, surprised that it was still here, as he had approached, drawn along by a wave of memories, he saw that not all the walls were whole. One was a pile of shattered bricks cascading to the weed-choked asphalt of what once was the parking lot he on a rare occasion had used. The windows of all the standing walls without glass, through the framed openings, Felix saw the high, heavy, light-green wood beams that once held up the ceiling and roof, those beams now soiled and darkened by the rain and wind and collected dirt of years. The section now without walls or windows, the floors gone, once held his desk at which he had toiled among the ranks and files of other desks through days of what had seemed endless, tedious drudgery.

One Saturday after working overtime for much needed funds, those rare occasions vivid because of the quiet: the foundry still, the phalanx of desks deserted, the large office space illuminated only from the overhead skylight, Felix upon leaving met D'Amico trying to thumb a ride. Why was that incident so memorable? Perhaps the mildness of the early spring day with its new warmth and freshness of thin sunlight after the dreary dark days of winter snow and hail and sleet, or the surprise of finding his friend without his beloved chariot, that '48 V8 Ford convertible, D'Amico walking just like other mortals, and Felix had not seen or heard from his former friend for sometime after they had finished high school. All those contributed to what Felix thought of while standing before this crumbling pile of bricks.

Pondering now those former days, Felix felt mildly amazed at how his eventual closeness with Gloria had evolved. That "affair," as Felix's father called it, with a less than auspicious beginning, more amazing to him that it had happened at all. She appeared so elegant, so striking, so confident in manner and stylish appearance that Felix just out of high school saw her as mature and aloof. In addition, their first encounters were contentious over something actually quite minor. So Felix found their later closeness curious and therefore even more compelling that she eventually was interested in him at all. Of course, the difference in their years and their lives also contributed to the unusual aspect of their eventual up close-and-personal involvement.

Felix now pondering those days suddenly understood how immature he must have been. Felix just turned eighteen found his first full-time job after working at various part time jobs summers on nearby truck farms he could peddle to on his bike, then setting pins evenings and weekends at a local bowling alley at the edge of the country town he had lived near, then evenings and weekends while a Senior at Prairieville High tending poultry on a farm he could drive to in his recently purchased black, two-door '48 Ford sedan. Once having finished high school he had driven into the city in a recently purchased '49 brown Chevy two-door searching until weary from looking but finally hired as an order clerk at a company manufacturing large industrial equipment for making concrete and cement for foundation slabs for tract housing and roadways for nascent interstates, he typing invoices for the sale orders of huge lime kilns and concrete mixers.

His work as an order clerk had appeared somewhat ironic since during the last semester of his senior year of high school taking a typing class just to fill out his schedule that would supposedly prepare him for college, instead of college, since he had insufficient resources, his parents not having the means to help him, and he not able to pay tuition or cover living costs, he found himself spending his days typing. After more than a year, bored with the work, despite his taking on the largest, most complex orders he would spend days compiling, submitting them to his supervisor who had worked in that position for more than two decades and had grown gray and worn with the passing of years, Felix one day looking up from his work and seeing that man bent over his task reviewing Felix's work, he knew the man one day eventually would be replaced by someone else, that someone else perhaps Felix, if he so aspired to that position. What else might likely happen that would keep him from moving in the direction of his dreams? Get Nan whom he had gone steady with his last year of high school pregnant? Repeat the pattern set by his father tied to a job as long as he could hold it? Working from pay check to paycheck to support a family with a so-called life style he barely managed now?

In response to this depressing vision, Felix had attempted to find a more challenging position as draftsman trainee, he considering drafting close enough to his grandiose aspirations for doing "real" art. But while he was commended for seeking such advancement and praised for his ambition, he was informed that no vacant positions were presently available and that until one became available he meanwhile could better himself by taking night school classes that would give him the foundation for the position he sought. How indifferent the man had seemed in his white shirt and tie and dark suit and dark-rimmed spectacles, so much the same as so many others Felix witnessed, he himself in white shirt and tie and dress slacks left over from a previous fashion era. Instead of night school, Felix sent away for a correspondence course in basic drafting techniques that he could study on his own. Why hadn't he tried such a career path in high school since the college prep program had led nowhere? Instead, Felix spent his days typing orders and invoices for kilns and dryers and concrete mixers while studying drafting at home when he wasn't doing something with Nan that took much of his time when not working since she was always so willingly available and his surging adolescent libido constant.

Gloria working in another section of the same department at the company where Felix labored typing invoices, she had started working at the company at about the same age as Felix had been hired and had worked there for several years, Felix eventually learning she was almost twenty-five, married, and Catholic. Of course, he noted almost at once from his first encounter what he thought were her exotic features: dark, fiery eyes, coloring that seemed a light, natural tan, auburn hair with natural curls she wore long, a lithe frame and graceful hips always sheathed in appropriate fashion for the world of work. He never able to decide her heritage was always too shy and polite to ask a question so personal. So he had resigned himself to studying her trim, shapely body that she adorned with simple elegance, her stature with heels reaching his shoulder.

Gorged with typical late-adolescent hormones, he, of course, watched as she with what he considered mature elegance and fashion moved slowly with purpose and focus about the office from her desk to the desks of others, to the corridors that led to the drafting and engineering departments to which Felix aspired, to the desk of her supervisor whose desk was near Felix's, a woman nearing retirement who had been with the company almost since its founding when it originally manufactured farm equipment. Gloria, of course, ignored him. Why wouldn't she, Felix so immature, despite his film-star features and tall stature? So he worked alone off by himself in his isolated corner while he paused from time to time to watch as she moved in her graceful way without even giving him a glance. He was not surprised or troubled by her ignoring him, he just out of high school, she a mature, married women. No wonder he was still surprised their "affair" had, even happened actually developing into a closeness that had challenged Felix's commitment to Nan and Gloria's marriage.

At lunch, after eating alone at his desk the sandwich and soda he bought at the line of dispensing machines down the corridor from his department, Felix had wandered the other corridors exploring the other departments with rows of desks similar to his, or sometimes he wandered back to a snack machine when tempted to indulge in a rare treat if he thought he could afford the expense when he considered his $188 monthly pay since he had his car payment and cost of fuel and services, pay room and board to Pa while he lived at Sunfish after high school then $11 a week for a room after he moved, the cost of paying for all his meals, and he had to keep himself in a dress somewhat appropriate to his position as a white collar worker, one level above Pa who had been blue collar all his life just as Grandpa Fist. Oh, how Felix aspired to something higher than where he found himself.

Most often during lunch break he found himself standing on the stairway above the entrance to the building that led to the foundry below and the parking lot, he gazing through a large window opposite the stairway allowing him a view of rows of idle, empty autos, the rusting chain link fence at the parking lot perimeter beyond which he parked his '49 two-door brown Chevy, the shrubs and bushes that lined the fence that sometimes gleamed in sunlight beneath the open sky after a rain or on clear days of sunshine. Now and again he tried to image what his being free to wander that world beyond the fence would be like. Then noticing the movements of others in response to the bell ending lunch break, he waking from his dream strolled back to his desk following the host of others to resume his isolated work throughout the afternoon, immersing himself in his task to keep from watching the clock whose hands seemed to always move so slowly. What a sense of release when his eight-hour shift ended at five.

If time allowed, he occasionally would stand and watch those seated around a large, vacant desk finishing a last hand of cards before the final bell ending lunch break sending them back to their own stations. He knew the game for some odd reason called Sheepshead that Felix later learned was regional, he having played endlessly with friends on rainy days and during the hottest days of summer, and the frigid, snowbound days of winter, their mimicking adults from whom they learned the game by watching. So he witnessed with interest the familiar gambits, the exaggerated or explosive moves, the exchange of remarks while the cards were being reshuffled and dealt. Then one day, one of the usual players absent, the man with two women seated around the perimeter of the desk, one of them Gloria, spoke to Felix who stood leaning against a light green pillar holding up the roof, Felix having returned early from his wanderings:

"You play?" the man asked.

"I have."

"Want to join us? We're short our usual player."

"I'm not that good."

"Great!"

The other woman laughed, but not Gloria, and Felix suddenly found himself seated directly across from her. The others each in turn introduced themselves even though he had been working with them in the same area for months. For the first time, Felix would meet Gloria's direct inspection with her fiery eyes. She didn't offer even a thin smile. Then he was dealt his hand and they began, and Felix soon confirmed the self-assessment of his skill at cards, such a lack of skill one source of Gloria's initial friction. The game involved playing with a partner selected by pairing a card of the same suit, and Felix — as luck determined — frequently found himself paired with Gloria, thus frequently resulting in their loss to the other pair. Gloria, of course, was less than pleased. The stakes not high, they playing for pennies, winning was most important, and any lose viewed as incompetence. So Felix concluded after having been paired frequently with Gloria and their losing, Gloria offering stern remarks that were less than kind, making her appear so much more a dominant adult. Felix squelching a typical adolescent response avoided further comments by declining any invitation to play again, his refusal leading to further caustic remarks from Gloria, he again suppressing a reply, Felix thus keeping his own counsel and once again resumed his wanderings.

Another source of more serious contention with Gloria had developed from rearrangements in department workstations: Gloria's desk moved for convenience near the desk of her supervisor, at the same time disrupting the Chatty Cathy group that had begun to annoy others, especially the department supervisor, that move placing Gloria's desk diagonally across from Felix. In addition, Gloria's supervisor now assigned and reviewed his work, and that change required he consult both women for advice and confirmation of his work, a requirement apparently rubbing him too roughly: He had worked alone, consulting with anyone only when he needed clarification or noted an inconsistency. Now required to work with others, had he been somehow slack or remiss before in completing his assignments? No one ever had challenged him, and even his now former supervisor had rarely commented on Felix's performance and then only favorably, so why now the change that made him uneasy since it meant working under the direction of two women, one slightly older but reserved, the other almost as old as his grandmother, the women too often having differing ideas on how Felix should do his work. No surprise that those differences had sometimes led to curt exchanges that consisted of his being reminded that they had worked there longer than he, the woman supervisor having started long before Felix first had seen the light of day, and he required to do his work however reluctantly but quietly under their mature, stern directives.

Then one day Gloria had startled him with a question he never expected. In a firm but quiet voice she had asked where he lived. He had paused before answering, scanning her face to detect some clue as to her curiosity. Why did she want to know? Then he told her. She responded by informing him where she lived on Sunfish Avenue and asked if he knew that area. He told her he did since for a year or two he had lived down the street with his parents on Sunfish when he was a child. "Last year?" she quipped, and he felt a sudden flush of embarrassment and quiet anger in noting her off-handed reference to his age that had often become an issue in how he did his work. But she overlooked or ignored his response as she explained the reason for her question: The fellow in engineering with whom she rode to work was going on a consulting trip for the following month. She would need a ride.

She wondered if Felix wouldn't mind coming by so she could ride with him. He paused before responding. She studied him, waiting. Then he replied he would be glad to help and wouldn't mind doing what she asked and where she lived wasn't that far out of his way to work since it was a direct drive from Sunfish village down Forest Home to where she lived on Sunfish Avenue. She thanked him and offered to compensate him for his going out of his way and accommodating her need, he quietly insisting he expected no compensation, even though he knew he could use whatever she offered since he was paid so little.

Then she offered a different compensation: The man with whom she rode had a permit for the company parking lot just outside the entrance to their building, that lot reserved for only a select few of advanced status and that she could use the permit while the man who worked in engineering was traveling. She suggested that Felix might use that permit if he chose. Felix readily accepted the offer and asked when he should start. She told him, they agreed on a time, and then both went on with their work, Felix occasionally looking up to glance at her, wondering what would happen next.

The following Monday, having woke early and prepared himself, aware of his new obligation that slightly nagged him, making his sleep restless, Felix leaving within sufficient time drove to the address she had given him and parked at the curb on the side street beside a dark brown, slatboard appliance store with apartments above, a somewhat refurbished relic from a previous era. Felix peered up through the windshield at the yellow glow of light from one of the windows above. He saw Gloria's face briefly appear in the window then turn away. Felix sat back and waited in the idling car. Soon a side door of the building opened and Gloria stepped out upon the stoop, closed the door, stepped carefully from the stoop in her high heels, and moved in her graceful manner to the side of the car. Felix leaned to unlock the door then on conditioned response hurried from his seat around the rear of the car to open the door and hold it while she moved by him, lowering herself backward onto the seat, feet together, swinging in her legs, while Felix studying her careful movements shut the door and came around the car to his seat.

"Thank you," she said, "You're such a gentleman."

"My pleasure," he offered, suddenly aware of her closeness and her fresh, morning warmth that enhanced her fragrance with a hint of musk.

"Thank you for taking the trouble to come by and being so prompt."

Felix ignored the bit about "being prompt" that seemed in character.

"Glad to help," he replied.

He put the car in gear then pulled away from the curb while she sat back to settle. He glanced at her quickly inspecting her typical, elegant attire. They stopped for a traffic light. He watched her open her purse, reach in, and retrieve a long card with large letters and numbers.

"The parking permit!" she said smiling, her eyes filled with delight. Again she searched in her purse.

"A clip to hold the permit!" she said, withdrawing it.

Then leaning against him to complete the task, she attached the clip and card to the visor above Felix's head. Felix felt acutely aware of her closeness and her firm, full, supple presence on his arm that made him stir. He felt her warmth, breathed her rich scent of cologne and talc and a lingering trace of something he couldn't name.

"What's that you're wearing?" he asked on impulse, prompted by her being so close and immediate.

"My cologne?" She offered a name. "You like it?" She offered her wrist and waved it beneath his nose."

"Exotic," he offered outloud. "*Just like you*," he added to himself.

"I've always used it. I don't remember how long. I use nothing else."

"Goes well with what you wear," Felix said quietly, again on impulse, expecting a rebuff.

"Thank you," she said, sounding pleased.

Thinking she might have been disturbed by his comment, he felt relieved by her response. But now what should he say? Had he said too much? Should he admit to having observed her throughout the day while he worked and while she went about her tasks?

"How do you manage on what we're paid?" he asked instead.

"I make most of what I wear," she said.

"Well, what you wear always looks nice."

"Really?" she exclaimed quietly. She sat back to look out the windshield as if his comment gave her pause.

Even more aware now of her immediate presence, Felix suddenly noted that the traffic light had changed after the car behind without surprise had honked. Felix silently attended to his maneuvering the vehicle through early morning traffic.

As he drove up the incline into the parking lot feeling a quirk of odd excitement at being admitted into this private reserve by a wave of the guard's hand, he found a place near the entrance to the building, set the handbrake, shut down the engine, and again hurried from his seat and around the car to open her door. She waited as if expecting the service and exited in the reverse order she had entered: legs together swung out to place both heels, pushing away from the seat, standing, then moving past him as he pushed the button and closed the door, locking it.

"Thank you, kind sir," she said and set off across the lot.

He followed her into the building and up the stairs to their department watching her straight, stately back and the slow movement of her sheathed legs and ankles, her shapely hips and bottom. But once they were at their desks and their work, their day preceded just as any other except for one difference. They slowly began to converse while they worked, often conferring on projects they now shared, Gloria now coming to his desk, standing beside where he sat, making him acutely aware of her swelling hip, firm thigh, sheathed leg, firm bosom as she leaned toward him to indicate a section of the document they examined while she also offered brief whiffs of her exotic scent.

On following days as they rode to and from work, they began to exchange events of their lives, their closeness within the vehicle perhaps contributing to their new sense of rapport. Felix, of course, thought he had little to offer but told her of his more immediate goal of becoming a draftsman trainee, his more grandiose ambition of becoming an artist and a writer, and she appeared to have an honest interest in what he said.

"Where did you learn to be such a gentleman?" she asked one morning after he again held the door to usher her into the car.

"My mother," Felix offered, pulling away from the curb. "She's always been strict! We've always had to help keep the house spotless, weren't allowed in the house without removing our shoes, and were never allowed in the living room except on special occasions!"

"She sounds like my grandmother who was born in Eastern Europe!"

"Really? What part?"

"Prussia. Now part of Poland."

"Our family origins are also in Prussia, but my mother was born in Berlin."

"That explains a lot."

Gloria's life, however, seemed more compelling, perhaps because what she told him seemed so personal: She never knew her father. She became a Catholic after having attended services several times with a friend and having become enthralled and comforted by the ritual of Mass: the tinkling bell that announced the transformation of the Eucharist, the hushed, dim setting from votives and candelabra and incense, the icons that lined the stations of the cross. She had met her husband David at a church activity for Catholic youth. They dated, became engaged, were married. One day, she offered Felix a photo of herself in white, elegant wedding gown. He stared, fascinated by what he saw. She, for some reason, allowed him to keep the photo, and he immediately considered it a lasting gift.

"You'll have to meet David," she suggested one morning.

"I'd like to," Felix said with honesty, curious, of course, as to what kind of man was able to persuade this elegant, exotic woman to submit to him. But he avoided considering her yielding to any man until he observed her at monthly intervals move from her desk, return to use the lotion she had in a drawer to anoint her hands, then use her desk calendar to count off days. Felix, of course, began to stir when he considered her informing her husband of those days in her cycle when he was allowed access.

Other mundane incidents helped develop a sense of closeness: She belonged to a bowling league sponsored by the company. Felix invited by his former supervisor to join a men's team that would bowl in a league following the women soon after work, Felix thinking himself a better bowler than playing Sheepshead, having bowled often with his parents and practicing during slow times during his years setting pins, he decided the social event would enhance his dull life of all work and no play and too much beer. More motivating was his thought that he could watch Gloria bowl while waiting for his men's league event to start.

During one of those times waiting while she bowled, Felix met David who came now and then to chauffeur her home. David was a complement to Gloria's elegance: as tall as Felix, solid, with brown, neatly groomed hair, sharp youthful features and an easy, open nature. How mature David seemed, how adolescent Felix felt meeting him. Felix observed with some wonder their exchange of affection and how David tended to her every whim. Whenever she wanted whatever she wanted, she had only to ask and David satisfied her desire for which he was rewarded with a quick kiss and thank you.

Felix one time also observed their veiled intimacy when Gloria returning from the restroom using hand lotion, David greeted her by asking matter-of-factly, "How'd everything come out?" Felix, surprised by the comment, of course thought the remark intended for his benefit, David intimating that he was the Alpha male regarding Gloria who offered only a contrived smile and a pat on David's cheek.

Why was Felix surprised by such a seemingly intimate exchange? Had he thought they weren't aware of each other as woman and man with basic bodily needs? Wasn't he aware of his own functions, his mother's, she one time asking Felix on the cusp of adolescence to fetch her a sanitary pad, and what about Nan who had introduced him to the throes of eros that always seemed to focus his attention and instigate too many of his actions promoted by unrelenting adolescent libido?

Then another time while he sat with David watching Gloria bowl, she approached from her turn on the alley:

"You should come to dinner sometime," she suddenly offered. She looked at David who studied her.

"I'd like that," Felix said. Felix had hoped in some way to continue their closeness after the man with whom she usually rode had returned to work. How empty the car seemed as he drove to work himself and he once again parked on the side street near the factory just beyond the rusted, chain-link fence. Now watching her bowl was something, but he wanted more. He suddenly knew he had always wanted more.

"You have a girlfriend?" she asked.

Felix revealed his connection with Nan.

"Something serious?" David offered.

"I guess," Felix admitted.

"Why don't you bring *her*." Gloria exclaimed.

"Sure," Felix said. "I guess I could."

So Gloria set a date for the gathering and looked at David for approval.

David seemed indifferent, "Sure. Why not?".

Felix, however, considered that event special, for it introduced him into Gloria's sanctuary and allowed him to inspect her possessions and observe her in her personal and intimate settings: The apartment where she lived with David above the appliance store was somewhat small where everything seemed dark and brown and antique consisting mostly of a large room with dark trim, high ceiling, a tan couch and matching upholstered chairs, three large bay windows with dark brown frames, and along one wall a galley kitchen area with sink and stove, another area set out for dining with a large, round table and antique chairs all dark brown. The bedroom to the right of the entrance he could glance into, inspect at length her double bed with white chenille spread and faux mahogany headboard, her faux mahogany dresser with oval mirror and curved drawers with bronze pulls, white crocheted doily, small flasks of her choice cologne with its hint of musk, her large dark armoire with full length mirror. Off the bedroom, her immaculate bathroom with walls and floor of small tile, ancient fixtures, darkly stained trim that matched that of the larger living space, along with the required closet for accessories of towels and tissue and soap, as well as the small hung mirrored cabinet for other more personal items. He inspected them all. He was, of course, acutely aware using the facilities as quietly as possible, having put off relieving the growing urge as long as he could, thus delaying having to acknowledge that he, too, had basic bodily functions.

The older couple warmly welcomed them. Felix was aware of the differences in age when he presented Nan who was still in high school. But both Gloria and David were gracious, offering the two young people adult drinks: Felix a gin martini, his first, and Gloria's favorite, Nan a glass of wine that with her cigarette held just so between two fingers made her manner and her responses to their questions appear adult.

What Gloria prepared for their meal was basic and simple: salad and pasta and fresh, crusty bread from a local bakery followed by dessert and coffee. While they ate, most of the discussion focused on Felix and Nan: how they had met, what were their plans. And Gloria and David shared their own experiences and dreams, some that Felix already knew. Gloria grew excited when she again stated her desire for a house. Where she now lived was as much a home as they could make it, but she needed a house to arrange into a true home of her own. The talk of plans for the future continued while they played Sheepshead, and Felix was no more of a winner than he had been when he had joined the game at work.

Felix again became the focus of remarks about his card playing that left him less than happy, and his chagrin was made worse by Nan proving to be the better player, frequently partnered with and learning from Gloria, with the two women frequently trumping the men. Yet, their play and chatting at the round table appeared to establish a relaxed rapport that resulted in a pleasant evening.

The following Monday at work, Gloria arrived to find a potted plant on her desk with a card reading "Thank you!" She studied Felix who briefly met her gaze then continued working. But he could tell from her slight smile that she was pleased, and she kept the plant in a prominent place on top gray file cabinets that formed a perimeter of their section. Their supervisor appeared amused and knowing. Some of those in other sections of the department were curious. Gloria increased their curiosity by claiming that the plant was a gift from a secret admirer, resulting in some admonishing exclamations about her being a married women.

Felix tried to recall when their phone calls started but was unsure. Perhaps after they exchanged their first embrace. Felix still felt the residue of that exchange, having been stunned, thrilled, his flesh tumescent.

David had not shown up to chauffeur Gloria home after her session of bowling, Felix offering her a ride after he finished his game, and she accepting since her teammates had already left. Felix recalled parking at the curb beside the appliance store. She had reached to turn off the ignition, the engine settling with typical quiet noises.

"What happened to David?"

"He went out with the guys. He probably lost track of time."

"I guess I'll see you at work." He reached to switch on the ignition.

"Why not come up for a bit," she suggested.

"It's late," he said. "Six o'clock comes around fast."

"I won't keep you long."

So he followed as she opened the car door herself and moved to the side door that led to her flat. He followed her up the stairs and into her apartment. She turned on the stove light but no others.

"Coffee?" she asked.

"Sure, if it's not too much trouble." But he knew he had agreed just to prolong precious time with her.

"Sit, Felix," she ordered softly.

He sat in a chair at the round table, the same place he had sat that evening he had come for dinner with Nan. Now here he was alone with Gloria, and as she turned to her task, he watched her every movement as she went to the sink for water, the cupboard for coffee, the stove to start and set the flame then place the pot.

She came to the table and sat in a chair beside him. The small light from the stove left the rest of the room in shadows. They sat silent. The pot on the stove began to perk heightening the stillness.

She reached for his hand and held it. "You love me, Felix?"

He studied her face in the soft light.

"Yes," he said.

"Tell me, Felix."

He studied her again. Then he told her.

She searched his face. "How did it happen? How did all this happen? Why?"

"I don't know. It just did."

"It must be a test."

"Of what?"

"My faith."

He had no reply. What about him? Was this also a test for him? Of what was this a test? Whatever faith he might have had was now lost since the death of his infant brother when Felix was still an unknowing child. How could he offer her an answer?

She studied him, her face anxious. She rose to move to the cupboard for mugs then to the stove to fill the mugs. She returned to the table and sat and placed a mug before Felix and one before her on the table.

"What happens now?" he asked.

"I don't know," she cried softly. She reached for his hand and held it. "Help me, Felix!"

"Help you? How?"

"Don't love me so much! Don't be so obvious about what you feel!"

"How can I hide what I feel?"

"You have to, Felix! You just have to! Haven't you seen people notice?"

He studied her. "Has David said something?"

She said nothing, but he knew from her expression.

"I think I better go."

He rose. She sat while he stood holding her hand. Then she rose and moved into his arms, and he knew he was lost for as long as he had life.

How could he ever forget the feel of her lips on his on their first touch with his? He had never known nor would he ever again know such a softness that spread a sudden surge that filled his soul. And as he held her and she clung to him, he folded her into his arms.

"Where is all this going?" he whispered in quiet amazement.

"I don't know," she answered as softly.

They held each other, and he sought her lips again, hungry now for their soft response, the lightness of their touch in contrast to his intense embrace that she answered. Then he quieted and held her with his head beside hers.

"I better go," he said again softly not ready to break the spell. She held him firmly in response then relaxed her hold and stepped back. She walked him to the door, reached up to pull him down for one last touch of her lips, then eased him out the door.

"Sleep well," she said.

"Fat chance!" he answered quietly. Then the door closed on him, and he went down the dark stairway to the curb and his silent car, climbed in, started the engine, and pulled away onto the street, passing the dark shape of someone about the stature of David who approached the doorway leading up to Gloria's flat.

That evening as Felix drove to the cottage where he still lived with his parents in Sunfish, he wondered how David might have responded to the aroma of freshly brewed coffee and the pot ready on the stove. How would she explain to David why she had made coffee? Felix supposed she could tell David what actually happened, save, perhaps, the part about the embrace, and Felix knew David would accept her story.

When he arrived at work the following day, he was eager but hesitant and quiet in asking about what happened after he had left her flat.

She smiled a thin smile. "Not much. David and I had coffee and then we went to bed."

He wanted to know more. Had she embraced and yielded to David while she thought of Felix? But, of course, he didn't ask, and she did not even offer a hint. She turned to her work, so he turned to his, and neither of them made any further reference to what had taken place.

Then one day as they left work together and parted in the parking lot, she to the car of the man from engineering with whom she rode, he to walk to his car parked on the side street outside the rusted chain-link fence, she handed him a piece of paper. He walked on to his car, unlocked the door, climbed in, sat, unfolded the piece of paper, and scanned the words:

Call me at 7:00. David bowls tonight.

The note included her number. He refolded the note, put it in his pocket, started the car, and drove home.

Later, just before 7:00, he drove to a convenience store on SR24 and Lannon Drive about a mile from his parents' cottage in Sunfish and used the outside phone booth to call. He was at first nervous waiting while the phone rang on the other end. Then he heard her voice.

"Hi! "How are you? Can you talk?"

"I'm fine," she answered quietly. "What's your number? I'll call you back."

When she returned his call, the ringing broadcast into the world at large startled him. Then they talked on and on, about what, Felix couldn't recall but all that he said seemed important at the time, his being able to talk to her alone and at length seemed even more romantic, especially since he stood outside in the cold, grimy booth that stunk of dried urine and he surveying people enter and leave the store, some glancing his way as he stood hunched in the cold, the receiver hot against his ear making it sweat. How noble Felix felt so steeped in her voice and his feeling. He recalled how dazed he seemed almost as if he were slightly drunk after they finally ended the call.

He called frequently after that, as often as he could, after she signaled him with a knowing smile he came to understand as her granting him permission. But one Friday night she surprised him by phoning the cottage near Sunfish Lake, he asleep in his bed in the unfinished attic, the hour late, the ringing phone part of his dream, waking him. He waited listening to the ringing, thinking the call for his father, foreman for maintenance who frequently received emergency calls from work. Then Felix heard his father's commanding voice calling in the dark.

"Hey, lover boy! It's for you!"

Scrambling from his warm bed, curious, apprehensive, chilled from not bothering to cloth his naked flesh, he hurried down the steep dark stairs to take up the receiver of the wall phone hanging by its cord.

"Hi!" she breathed. "I had to call."

"What's wrong?"

"I wanted to hear your voice."

"Where are you? It's after two."

"I'm home. David's asleep. We were out. We just got home. He's in bed." Her voice was quiet. She sounded a bit tipsy.

"You O.K.?" he asked.

"I've been thinking of you all evening."

He waited. "I'm always thinking of you," he said. He felt a bit odd but thrilled to be talking to her and he standing naked and chilled, his limp flesh stirring from the sound of her voice.

"Oh, Felix!" she cried, her voice hushed and restrained. "I want you!" she breathed in his ear.

He felt himself filling in response.

"What are we going to do!" she breathed.

But before he could answer, he heard his father's gruff, demanding voice from the dark bedroom.

"Who the hell is that!" his father yelled. "What she want?"

Felix ignored the question. "I better go," he said.

"I'm sorry," she said, most likely having heard the complaint his father had loudly launched into the dark. "Call me tomorrow. David bowls at ten."

He heard the click of the receiver being replaced. He crept back up the steep, dark stairs to his cold bed. He lay shivering, waiting to warm, pondering what had just happened, waiting for tomorrow, finally drifting to sleep without dreams.

The next morning, descending to the kitchen, he met the expected inquisition. His father sat at the table drinking coffee and smoking. His mother stood at the stove preparing breakfast. Felix poured himself a cup of coffee, sat at the table, lit a cigarette, and waited. He didn't have long to wait.

"Who was that woman?" Pa demanded.

"A friend."

"What she want?"

"She wanted to talk."

"At two in the morning! She woke the whole damn house!"

The whole damn house? Felix remarked. *Three people is a 'whole damn house'? Maybe the Old Man meant the dog and cat too.*

"She told me she was sorry," Felix offered instead.

"She damn well ought to be!"

Felix sipped his coffee.

"Who is she?"

"I told you. She's a friend."

"Where'd you meet her?

"We work together."

"She sounded drunk!"

Felix sipped his coffee, took a drag of his cigarette.

"She didn't sound like some girl."

"She's not."

"You can't find someone your own age?"

"We're just friends. I told you. We work together."

"She called at two in the morning to talk about work?"

"It wasn't about work."

"Then what'd she want?"

"I told you. She just wanted to talk."

"Well, tell her to try calling at some other time than two o'clock in the morning!"

"She won't call again."

"Good!" Pa snorted in response and lit another cigarette.

Felix's mother poured his father more coffee. Felix shook his head declining a refill.

He snuffed his cigarette, rose to use the bathroom, then climbed the stairs to his attic sanctuary.

Felix moved out soon after — not exactly from choice, partly due to Pa selling the cottage at Sunfish Lake planning on moving to Florida when he was laid off from his job at Rundle's after almost twenty years, so Felix moved mainly because he was ready, and he knew he would have to because of his growing involvement with Gloria. After that, whenever Gloria designated, he called her from the phone booth outside a convenience store near the room where he lived before leaving for California, he having rented the $11-a-week room a short drive from her apartment above the appliance store on Sunfish Avenue so he could have the sense of being close to her at least in spirit. Using that phone seemed to increase the sense of romance or chivalry, or something he couldn't label, perhaps commitment. Then he had a phone installed in his room, worried, of course, about the extra expense but telling himself it was necessary and, of course, more convenient since she could call him whenever she chose, and he had the comfort and privacy of his own room without the inconvenience and challenges to his health from a public phone booth. They never talked long, but such brief exchanges helped him survive what had become endless weekends once he had stopped seeing Nan because of his increasing commitment to Gloria.

Then one time Gloria called and quietly ordered him come meet her. She wanted to see him — needed to see him — and he should meet her at the church she always attended near her flat. He hurried to the church and went in. Having not been in a church for a long time, that church not anything like this one, the first difference that he had access, the other church always locked when not holding a service, the décor and atmosphere strikingly different: The one he had occasionally attended stark in daylight, cold and bare in contrast, this one warm with the yellow glow of flickering votive candles casting shadows in niches between thick, tall pillars toward the vaulted ceiling of the towering nave, the candles filling the hollow with their waxy aroma, their dim light reflected off the glassy eyes of the icons that flanked the walls between the tall windows of colored glass webbed with lead.

Felix understood immediately why she was so drawn to what seemed the closed, comforting ambience that caste a sense of mystery, perhaps of magic, maybe even of the occult through the lingering ambience of ancient rites and ritual. Only two others who knelt in prayer shared the nave. She was not present. Feeling illicit from his entering this foreign domain, more so given the reason for his visit, he took a seat at the very back just before the large doors that allowed him entrance. He waited, this place so different, he expected someone to challenge the legitimacy of his presence.

Then she appeared. He turned toward her, but she moved by toward the alter, knelt briefly without touching the floor, signed, moved to a niche where she paused to light a votive, deposit a coin, sign again, then turn and move up the side aisle and out one of the doors. He rose and followed. He found her waiting at the entrance. She moved into his arms, embracing him, raising her face to offer her lips. He clung to her until she stepped back.

"I have something to show you," she said.

She took his hand and led him from the church to her car. She climbed in and he took his seat beside her. She leaned toward him offering her lips in a slow, soft exchange. Then she sat back, started the engine, glanced back for oncoming traffic, and drove them off into the maze of city streets.

They arrived at a green space in a vast spread of antique, derelict dwellings.

"My favorite place!" she exclaimed.

He surveyed the small city park only a small portion of a city block. "Why is it here?"

"Someone built it, you silly boy!" she admonished pleasantly.

"But why?"

"Come look!"

Then she was out of the car and he followed. She waited to take his hand and led him up the small path in among young pine and fir to a small pond with a large willow that dipped its leafy branches into the pond stirred by the small stream of water spilling quietly from a low fall of rock.

He surveyed the scene. She squeezed his hand.

"Isn't it beautiful?

He sensed the tranquil beauty magically separated from the throng of engulfing city.

"You come here often?"

"Every chance when I have the car."

"You come alone?"

"David came once."

"Only once?"

She studied the scene without answering. She drew in a breath slightly lifting her shoulders, relaxing as if releasing a burden, then turning to him, she encircled him in her arms.

"I wanted to share it with you," she offered.

"It will be my favorite place," he said.

She laughed in delight. He joined her. She led him to a bench across the pond from the low fall of spilling, burbling water.

"It's so peaceful — so beautiful. I knew you'd like it."

"How could I not like it? It's yours."

"Now it's ours," she said.

He felt himself flush at her words. "Yes," he replied. "Now it's ours."

A few days following his close encounter with Fat Jack, the urban cowboy, Felix entered a tavern in a residential neighborhood on the southeast side of the city typical in its location on a corner across from another of the same kind. As he entered, Felix found equally odd that up the street a block or two yet another pair of taverns on opposing corners located in what people might consider a residential neighborhood. How any such establishments could make a go of it was part of the puzzle. Apparently, each attracted its own group of faithful patrons within a designated tribal territory.

Once inside, Felix moved across the black and white checked vinyl tile to the bar where he straddled a red vinyl stool trimmed in chrome, ordered from the man who came to greet him, waited for his beer, glanced at the group of men at the end of the bar gathered under the large window that displayed an arc of gold letters in reverse bordered in green. Felix recognized one of those at the other end of the bar by the window as Buster whom Felix remembered as David's closest friend. Felix also recalled that Gloria and Buster had carried on what seemed an almost continuous flirtation so that at times Felix seeing their frequent exchanges somewhat veiled and slightly suggestive, had wondered whether something more wasn't going on with David's tacit acceptance. Then Felix considered Gloria's commitment to her faith, she never allowing Felix anything more than passionate embraces and he either too naïve or too courtly and timid to try anything further for fear of being rejected and dismissed, but he wondered whether Buster was still pursuing Gloria and whether she still responded openly to Buster's attention.

Felix glanced the other way toward the pool table beneath the funnel lamp in an area of shadows near the hallway to the so-called restrooms (how much "rest" provided always in doubt), all this he observed as familiar along with the distinctive odor of beer, cigarette smoke, and floor wax from the highly polished black and white checkered vinyl floor.

The man whom he now recognized as Dan, the tavern owner, came back with the draft beer that Felix tasted while Dan went to the register then returned to lay change on the dark surface of the bar well.

"Place seems pretty much the same as when I last saw it," Felix said. He drank again, the liquid settling his stomach and beginning to clear a head made fuzzy by the residue of his continued over-indulgence in response to previous encounters with former friends.

"Not much changes around here," Dan agreed. "Those by the window have been coming here for years. Almost their second home for some. At least you'd think so from what most of their spouses complain!"

Felix, trying to appear good-natured, chuckled in response.

"What about the Harmons?" he asked, gathering his courage. "You know them? Gloria and David Harmon? They still come around here?"

"The Harmons? David and Gloria? Hey! They're as regular as rain!" Dan again nodded toward the group at the other end of the bar. "Just like them. Sure, David and Gloria come around here all the time. Most likely they'll be here since it's Friday. They almost always come around on Friday."

Dan looked at his watch then glanced at the large clock high on the wall opposite the bar. Felix could see its reverse face in the massive mirror that ran along the wall behind the bar, the mirror doubling the row of rainbow-colored bottles ranging in various heights on the shelf underneath the mirror. Felix thought of the tavern he had passed in the dark during his long night walk to the Illinois town.

"Right about now's the time they usually come around," Dan said, dispelling Felix's ghostly image.

Dan moved off down behind the bar to the group at the other end to answer the call of one who had signed. Felix slid from the barstool, turned, and ambled to the rainbow-colored jukebox set against the wall opposite the bar. He stood studying the selections, his face lit by a spectrum of color from the machine. Most selections were still those he remembered. Not much change here either. He turned and started back to his stool at the bar stopped by the screeching screen door as it swung open.

Felix knew immediately the man who entered. As tall as Felix yet heavier and with several more years, David Harmon greeted everyone with what Felix remembered as typical cheerful exuberance as David moved along the bar. Felix saw that David noticed him as Felix returned to his stool and his glass. Felix suddenly feeling a queasy stomach found comfort in the bitterness of the amber liquid, the music selections he had surveyed bringing back a rush of memories. David approached Felix, his manner typical.

"Well, look what the cat dragged in," David said with studied cheer. "Long time no see."

"How are you, David?"

"Fine. Just fine. Always have been. How about you?"

"I'm doing O.K."

"Well, that's just fine," David said, noticing Felix's glance toward the screen door. "Gloria should be here any second," he added, just as the screen door squawked open then screeched closed.

Felix and David turned at the same time, and Felix saw her as she stood in sunlight at the doorway much as before: Tall, trim, tan, and lovely, with a blend of heritage Felix had never been able to determine, her long auburn hair, her sharp, high cheek bones, large, almond-shaped amber eyes gleaming from the fullness of life drawing him in, as lively and exotic as ever.

Gloria strolled to the bar, her hips in tight skirt swaying, her torso held straight and taut, her full form firm beneath her summer blouse, her stiletto heels clicking on the checkered vinyl floor.

Felix witnessed the typical exchange between Gloria and Buster that he remembered well. Then he saw that she noticed him and he noted her husband's study of her silent, steady exchange with Felix. She greeted each man in the group, lingering with them, leaning into them to accept their friendly embrace as if she were deliberately putting off moving to where Felix stood with her husband.

She finally approached, her face set, but her eyes gleaming.

"Look who's here!" David exclaimed with faked enthusiasm.

Gloria studied Felix's face with an expression that revealed more than she may have wanted.

"I see that, Honey," she said quietly. "How are you, Felix?"

She moved toward him, perhaps from habit, as if she might be embraced, wanting to perhaps embrace him, but Felix held back, knowing she didn't want to be obvious about what she felt, especially with David and his good buddies watching. Felix noted the group at the end of the bar leaning together exchanging quiet comments, some in jest, and Felix felt relieved when he saw Gloria check her advance.

"I'm fine, Gloria," Felix said. "It's been a while."

"It certainly has," Gloria said as if trying to suppress her true feelings. "What brings you around here? Last I heard you were going to start college someplace out West."

Felix was sure she was covering what she knew. He had written her twice. Her replies had been brief and terse.

"California," Felix offered.

"Oh, of course, California. Now I remember."

She turned to her husband, giving him a sudden burst of her radiance.

"Honey, why don't you get us a drink? Can you do that?" She leaned to give him a quick, appreciative kiss.

"Sure!" David said, always pleased in satisfying her requests. "You want the usual?" He turned to Felix. "How 'bout you, Felix? You ready for another?"

"Sure," Felix replied. "Thanks."

"The same? Why not join us at our table." He turned to his wife. "You'd probably like that, wouldn't you, Gloria? Let the two of you talk about old times."

Gloria faked a grin of delight. "Felix? Come join us," she ordered while looking her husband full in the face, not backing down.

"Sure, why not," Felix conceded then moved from the bar with Gloria, while David signaled to Dan behind the bar.

Gloria and Felix seated themselves at a table along the wall next to the jukebox underneath the clock. David brought two drinks, set them down, went back for his, then came back and seated himself.

"Well, here we are again," he offered with his typical cultivated lightness. "Just like old times." He raised his glass. "Here's looking at you!" He drank, then studied the two people across from him. "Why don't I just go talk to the guys. Let you two get to know each other again, get you up to date. You'd probably like that wouldn't you, Gloria?"

Gloria studied him. David studied her then rose from his seat with his drink and moved to his buddies at the bar.

Gloria and Felix watched as David joined his cohorts, David and the others looking back at the two left alone at the table. Gloria and Felix sat in awkward silence, self-conscious at being set apart and observed. One waited for the other to speak.

"Nothing seems to have changed much around here," Felix finally offered.

"Why should it?" Gloria replied. Her voice and manner suddenly chilled, perhaps because of what David had said and now from the scrutiny she was getting from David and the others at the bar.

"No reason it should," Felix offered, sensing her mood. "You'd think eventually something would change."

"Not around here! We're just about the same as we've always been!" Now her voice seemed to have an edge that at one time had turned his blood to ice.

"I suppose," Felix said accepting her chill. "I noticed you seem to be as friendly with David's good buddy Buster as you always were."

"Well, you left. Buster's always been here. He knows what women want."

"What about your vows?"

"I've always kept my vows. You know that. Buster's just a good friend."

"I'm glad for you," he said.

"Why didn't you call?" she asked, her voice hushed and hard. "Or write?"

"I did phone once. I found that wasn't such a good idea. And I did write — couple times. I sent them to you at work. You sent a reply that suggested you weren't interested."

"Two letters! In how long! I needed to hear from you more. I needed to hear your voice! I thought you loved me!"

"I still do." Felix said quietly and firmly.

"Do you really!" Gloria accused. She studied him, as if wanting to believe but still doubting. Not allowing Felix to answer, Gloria rose from her chair, stepped to the jukebox, selected a number. As she returned to the table, the music swelled throughout the tavern, and Felix knew the song as one they had shared before, one that he had noted earlier raising memories.

"Nothing changes around here!" Gloria offered with a wry smile. "Same old crowd! Same old songs! You want to dance? For *old times* sake?"

"I'm not sure we should."

"Don't tell me you're shy? We used to dance here together all the time! Or have you been gone so long you've forgotten?"

Gloria strolled to the center of the floor and waited, the others at the bar watching. Felix rose reluctantly, self-conscious under the scrutiny of David and his chorus of cohorts. Felix slowly went to where she waited.

She moved into his arms, and as they began to move to the melody, their movement, their renewed closeness all caught them up again in a magic they once had. Gloria clung to him, Felix breathing in her familiar, exotic fragrance as they in a close embrace swept over the polished checkered vinyl floor round and round beneath the high, scrolled ceiling while Felix suddenly sensed being drawn into a scenario that would swell with grand emotions and passion and play out like a Harlequin romance.

"I missed you so!" Shelley whispered, her face flushed.

He pulled her closer, burying his face in her hair before he checked his desire, pulled back, aware of eyes studying them from the bar.

"You don't know how much I missed you." Felix answered.

"You should have come back sooner."

"I couldn't. I wasn't ready."

"Why not? Ready for what?"

"I can't explain here!"

"Where!"

"Somewhere quiet. Somewhere we can be alone!"

"When!"

"Tomorrow. Your church. We could meet there. Go to our park if it's still there."

"It's still there!" She pulled back to look at him. "Nothing ever changes around here!" Then she was back in his arms. "David has a game with the guys."

"I'll wait for you at your church."

The song ended. They walked back to the table as if nothing had changed.

Felix not wanting to be obvious sat and finished his beer. Then he rose and backed away from where she sat. "Tomorrow," he said quietly. He moved toward the door raising his hand to the silent chorus at the bar who watched him go, the screen door screeching open then slamming to behind him as he descended the concrete steps.

The following day, mid-morning, Felix waited in the church in the neighborhood where she lived, where he once lived as a child, where he once rented a room to be near where she lived only a few blocks from the tavern where they had danced the previous afternoon. Felix sat in one of the long, varnished wood benches studying the few worshipers at prayer scattered among the mostly empty rows ranged toward the altar, the icons displayed beneath the tall columns and high arches of the vaulted nave. A sudden movement at his shoulder made him glance to see Gloria in elegant yellow dress, white heels, pearl necklace, white gossamer mantilla veiling her rich auburn hair hurry up the aisle past where he sat, offer a votive at a small altar at the side, pause to offer a brief silent prayer, come back up the aisle without even a glance, and sweep on by out the heavy door.

Felix rose and followed her to her car, sleek and elegant, reminding him of the weird woman he had stayed with while on the road. He searched, surveying the streets, suspecting he might be suddenly challenged. Then he climbed in. Gloria gazed at him with an expression that seemed full of joy. Then she turned forward, spun the vehicle away from the curb, the powerful engine shooting them out onto the street. They drove in silence, Felix glancing at her, taking in her profile, admiring her typical apparel, a soft, light summer dress of rich, sleek material that clung to her in all the right places, she keeping her eyes on the road, sometimes glancing into the rearview mirror, he turning to see what she might have viewed, then turning back to study her, breathing deeply of her fragrance, so familiar, so stirring.

Arrived at the small neighborhood park, they climbed from the vehicle and strolled together in silence to the small pond bordered by flowering bushes, evergreens, and the willow that drooped long branches and dark green leaves into the pond frothed by the low fall of water over rocks. Felix took a deep breath then let it out slowly, relaxing, admiring the scene.

"I've always loved this place since you showed it to me," he said quietly. "It has a peacefulness that's healing."

"I've always needed its comfort," Gloria replied. "I've come here often all the while you were gone. I could think of you here, and I could feel you near, almost as if you were actually here with me."

"And now I'm here."

"Now you're finally here. Being here helped me not miss you so much."

Felix reached for her, turned her toward him, and took her into his arms. They embraced in a long, tender kiss until Gloria broke away, almost angry.

"Why did you have to leave!"

She moved away and sat on a small bench beside the pond. Felix moved to join her, pulling her to him.

"Nothing was happening for me here. I had no direction. I found myself waiting for you, running after you, and you were always some unattainable fantasy. Remember that Sunday morning after a night of drinking and dancing I followed you and David and Buster and his wife while you four drove to some all night café you couples always went to? It might have been the booze but more likely my not wanting to leave you. I even joined you at your table uninvited, and you and the others graciously made room for me despite the obvious reason for my being there. I sat while you and the others talked and ate while I drank coffee. Then all of you finished and went out leaving me watch you go, knowing you were going home to share your bed with David. I knew, finally, that nothing was going to change. You would stay with David, and I would always be waiting, always wanting you, never having you the way I wanted, always watching you leave with David."

"Felix! Honey!" she said quietly. "I told you before. I could never go against my vows, no matter how much I wanted you. You knew that. I told you then that you needed to find someone you could have the way you wanted to be with me. We still could have been friends."

"I didn't want someone else!" Felix said in quiet anger. "I did have someone else. Remember? I gave up everyone else so I might be with you. Remember Nan? I had her often the way I wanted you! I didn't want you only as a friend!"

"I know. I wanted you, too," Gloria admitted quietly. "You don't know how close I came to letting you have what you wanted. And I had to confess and do penance for that. So I couldn't. I just couldn't. And then you left so fast, it seemed as if you were running away."

"I was since you wouldn't be with me. I had to get away as fast as I could, especially when I saw you at work seeming so distant and the job growing so dull. Everything I did seemed a deadend and knowing you would never be with me the way I wanted."

"I couldn't. You know that."

"Yes, I know. You had to keep your vows."

"They're sacred!" Gloria cried. "I didn't want to sin! Loving you in the way I do might be bad enough, but I don't want to be damned forever!"

"So we live in our own kind of hell right here, right now! Who needs another?"

"It's how you see things," she offered quietly. "What you believe."

"What I believe?"

He sat back brooding. What did he believe when he had trouble believing in himself? Then he rose, walked to the pond, stood studying the still water, tossed in a pebble he had stooped to pick up, then watched the rings play out across to the other bank beneath the full-leafed weeping willow. He turned back to Gloria. He spoke to her from where he stood to where she sat on the bench, he using the setting as a stage.

"I never told you about the times I came here alone at night."

Gloria's face brightened in surprise. "You came here without me!"

"I came here to be with you when I couldn't actually be with you when you were with David. I used to pass your place at night, look up to see your light on, imagine you preparing to spend the night beside David, and I would come here. Well, the last time I came just before I left for California, a tiny owl attacked me."

"An owl attacked you!" Gloria laughed in delight.

"Right! And it wasn't funny! I heard him hoot at me right after I arrived. Then, as I walked around the pond, he dove at me, swooped down above my head. He finally dove right into me when I wouldn't leave. He hit me right in the skull. Knocked me dizzy."

Felix paused to watch her face, how her features moved, responding to his tale.

"I felt his small, hard skull crash against mine. Then he flew off, and I left." He paused again. "I took that attack as an omen and a warning."

"Oh, Felix! You were always the romantic!"

Gloria rose, came to him, folding herself into his arms.

"Perhaps I still am," he admitted. He held her, his face in her hair, breathing in her fragrance.

Gloria suddenly broke away, her face bright with excitement. "Guess what!" she cried. "I finally got my house!"

"Really!" he responded, trying to share her joy. "So you don't live above that appliance store anymore."

"No. Isn't that great! I now have my very own home! I want you to see it! You've got to see it, Felix!"

"I'd like to," Felix said quietly.

"Then come with me! Come with me now!"

"Now? You sure it's all right?"

"Don't worry! Everything will be fine!"

Felix studied her, recalling his recent experience with Jean and her husband.

"Do come with me, Felix!"

Then she took him by the hand, drawing him out of the park to her elegant new car, and he, as always, allowed himself to be led.

Gloria's house was in the suburbs near the airport, the dwelling one among many of the same kind, all built from one basic design with variations to give the appearance of being unique. But the houses were new and they were modern, with a two-car garage as standard and a driveway that splayed in new concrete before the brick and wood of the house and garage. Felix briefly thought of where he had stayed with the weird woman while on the road.

Gloria scrambled out and danced on the new lawn, along the walkway that led to the front door, her arms flung out, as if she were displaying the house as her dream fulfilled. Felix watched her in her yellow summer dress, taken up by her joy, more than his admiring the house that he found attractive but dull. He had seen hundreds of acres of similar dwellings in endless rows mushrooming from devastated California orchards and hills, men working 12-hour days building roads for endless tracts.

"It's lovely," he lied. "So this is why you wouldn't come away with me."

She studied him, opened the door, and led him inside, first through the living room then into the kitchen.

"I worked years for this!" she exclaimed.

Felix surveyed the bright pale fixtures and pastel furnishings that shouted "Modern!" so unlike the dark apartment he recalled.

"We saved! We gave up things we might have had then! Until now — it's mine!"

"So all your work and sacrifice was worth it."

She moved around the kitchen, opening cabinets, beginning to gather items for brewing coffee. "I haven't had a bad life," she said. "I've gotten most everything I've wanted. David's been good to me. He's spoiled me, really, allowing me to have whatever I've wanted — new house, new car."

"So you're happy."

"I'm all right," she said. Then she turned to prepare the coffee. Felix came to stand behind her, put his arms around her, press against her, his hands exploring her body through the thin, summer dress, stirred by the slide of his hands from what she wore beneath.

"You haven't had everything," he said, nuzzling her neck. "I bet something's been missing." He caressed her more urgently, running his hands over her, exploring her body beneath her dress so that she paused in her task, responding to his touch, his hands caressing her. "What's been missing?" he asked.

She remained silent, finished her task, plugged in the pot, pressed the button.

She turned to face him. "I've missed you!" she moaned, his hands having stirred her, awaking what she had worked so hard for so long to suppress.

He kissed her, his hands moving again, his movements becoming determined, his hands slowly undoing her, ignoring her pleas, he listening for the sound of vehicles while he worked slowly at her clothing, pushing the dress from her shoulders, working it down so that it slid to her feet, working the hooks and straps of her halter, thumbing the waistband of her briefs, pushing them over her hips and thighs, until they dropped, all the while his hands moved over her, touching her softly everywhere, she again weakly protesting, yet allowing him to ease her back onto the table where she lay open to his gaze as he knelt, her feet on his shoulders.

He breathed her scent as he slowly moved along her thighs, his lips brushing them softly, he thrilling from the fragrance and softness of her smooth skin, his mouth and hands moving until he buried his face in trimmed auburn hair.

He heard her soft moan and felt her hands on his head.

"What are you doing?" she cried softly.

"Loving you," he answered as softly.

"No one's ever loved me like that."

Having never had anything before except exchanges of soft, lingering kisses, having only imagined doing what he was now doing, having been so naive, so hesitant, he now went at her with a ferocious hunger, devouring her, his lips and tongue always moving, his hands caressing her legs, her thighs, spreading her so that he could bury himself more deeply into her, feel her start beneath his mouth and tongue.

She cried out softly, then more loudly as she gave herself to his insistent lips and tongue as her body spoke to him, her voice softly crying his name, urging him on, so that he rose from his knees, tore at his clothes until he stood between her splayed thighs his flesh gorged, moving toward her, holding himself to guide himself into that slick opening he had dreamt of for so long. Then at the moment of his entering, having placed himself, ready to thrust in, culminating his desire, she struggled back onto her arms.

"No, Felix!" she cried and moved to push herself away.

He pursued her, grabbing her legs, holding them apart, moving to gain full entrance. "I've waited so long!" he wailed.

"We can't!" She pushed away again.

"Why not!" he hissed.

"You know why! It's not right!"

Felix stepped back, studying her as she sprawled naked. He searched her face. "I could take you anyway! At least I'd have that!"

"But you won't," she said quietly. She lay back on the table, exposed. "That's not you, Felix," she said quietly. "That's not the Felix I knew."

"You're right," he admitted. "That's not how I wanted it to be." He stood above her, still gorged, taking in the sight of her there, spread open upon the tabletop, his mouth wet from her flow. Then he felt his excitement calm, his firm flesh soften.

"Coffee must be ready by now," he said quietly, turning to pick up her clothes, handing them to her, as she swung herself from the table.

"Thank you," she said quietly, placing her hand on him, smiling, stroking his face slick from her flow.

His first thought was that she meant his having retrieved her garments. Then she added, "Where did you learn all that?"

Felix stood mute and limp beneath her hand.

That afternoon, the day slowly fading toward evening, Felix pulled open the screeching screen door of the corner tavern he had been in the day before. He moved to the end of the bar away from the group of men at their usual place under the large window with gold lettering bordered in green. Waiting to order, he looked down toward the group where David stood with his cohorts, all of them still in team jerseys and matching caps, the colors matching those on the large window behind them. David, having watched Felix enter now approached along the bar.

"How's the big college man today?" David asked with typical cheer.

Felix thought the man a bit tipsy, and the way the others at the end of the bar were watching, Felix sensed that what was happening was staged for their benefit.

"Couldn't be better," Felix said, ignoring David's jibe. "How'd the game go?"

"We won," David said, studying him. "You waiting for Gloria?"

Felix tried to seem indifferent. "Not especially," he replied with some honesty knowing she would arrive. "She supposed to be here?"

"I bet any second now," David said. "Funny how that sometimes happens. You drop in someplace — just like you did now — looking for someone. And what do you know. . ." The screen door squawked. Gloria entering with her usual flair. ". . .that someone shows up just like that. Now, isn't that strange? I'd call that really strange!"

"Yeah," Felix agreed. "Strange."

Felix met David's inspection of mild disdain as if more was unwarranted and David turned and moved off to the other end of the bar where Gloria stopped to greet and chat with David's friends, exchanging remarks with veiled double meaning, becoming, as usual, the center of their rude, rutting male attention. Then she moved to her usual table, her hips swaying under her fresh summer dress almost penitential in contrast with the one she had worn earlier in the day. She sat sipping the drink she had carried from the bar while she studied Felix, then David.

Felix stayed at the bar, watching in the mirror as Gloria went to the jukebox, stood looking down, make a selection, return to her seat to sip her drink. Felix heard "Two Different World's" they had always referred to as "our song" swell into the room, sweep over him, filling him with sound and emotion. He choked back his response, then spun, slid from his stool, moved with purpose to where Gloria sat, and offered his hand.

Gloria rose slowly, moved with him to the center of the vinyl checkered floor where they came together renewing an embrace lingering from the one in which they had held each other earlier in the day. Feeling her body in his arms, Felix gazed out at the fading light beyond the large window with gold letters bordered in green.

He saw her again as she lay exposed to him in morning sunlight on the table as he knelt, placed her heels on his shoulders beginning to breathe in her scent as his lips slowly moved along her thighs brushing them softly, he thrilling from the fragrance and softness of her smooth skin, his lips moving until he buried his face in her auburn bush.

"Come with me!" Felix hissed in her ear, his urgent plea covered by the music that swelled and throbbed around them as they slowly twirled to the rhythm of the romantic melody they had always thought composed especially for them.

"Where would we go!" Gloria wailed softly with restraint, moved by his plea, by their renewed contact, by his having pursued her right there before her spouse and the whole world, by the lingering memory of his skilled movement of his urgent lips and tongue that had sent her where she had never been before.

"I don't *know*!" Felix cried softly. "Anywhere! I want you! I want you with me!"

"I know, Felix," she said. She stepped back still holding him. "I want to be with you. I really do. But you know I can't."

The melody ended, they stepped apart and moved to her table. Another one of their favorite songs welled into the hollow of the large space.

"Too much to give up," Felix said with quiet bitterness as they sat.

"You want me to give up my home? I might be able to do that. I might have the same with you. But I'd have to give up more than that. I'd have to give up my faith. And I can't do that. How could I do that? How could I call myself true to my belief if I did what you wanted? What I allowed this morning is bad enough! I'll have to do penance for that, especially since I enjoyed so much what you did and I didn't want you to stop. You made me feel more than I've ever felt. I can handle that! But leaving with you and completely breaking my vows would be something more. It would be giving up everything I believe in. Would you really want me to do that?"

Felix studied her seeing for the first time what he had previously been able to ignore, what she had conveniently helped him ignore by their supposedly innocent "relationship."

"No, I wouldn't want you to do that," he said finally. "What we might have wouldn't be enough to replace what you have."

"It never could! I would always feel guilty. I'd feel lost and damned without my faith. And then I would feel terrible and damned for what I had done to David who has always given me almost everything I've ever wanted. What could I give you if I felt that way? And then I'd probably start blaming you, and then where would we be!"

Felix studied her again, searching her face, her eyes, considering what she had said, his eyes welling in tears.

"It was a nice dream," he said, "while it lasted."

"Don't be sad, Felix! I want you to be happy!"

"I'll survive.," he said, trying to act resigned and sound adult.

She reached to cover his hand.

"I want you to have a good life, Felix. I do love you! I really do!"

"But you love David more!"

"Not more, Felix. Just different. You love me one way, he another. I love you one way, him another. I wish I could have you both, but I can't! Our lives don't work that way."

"Don't I know!" Felix replied.

"Try to be happy, Felix. Find someone who can love you the way you want to be loved."

"But I want you!"

"You can't have me, Felix! I can't give you what you want!"

He sat looking at his hands, considering what she had said.

"I guess I better go," he said.

"We could see each other now and then. You'll find work you like when you finish college. You'll write stories and poetry and do your painting and win praise for what you've done. You'll find someone who loves you the way I do."

"I may do all that but not here!"

"You're not coming back!"

"Most likely not. After a second year in Long Beach, I want to transfer to UC-Berkeley in the Bay area for at least two years. I have no idea what will happen, and there doesn't seem a lot left that would compel me to come back here."

Felix pushed himself up from his chair. "It was nice seeing you again, Gloria. Have a good life."

Then he turned and moved quickly to the screen door and out beneath the splayed light of the street lamp, the screeching screen door slamming to.

Gloria stopped him at the top of the concrete steps ignoring David's worried call.

"Don't be angry with me, Felix! Don't go away bitter!"

Felix descended the concrete steps and turned. "I'm not angry," Felix answered, his voice hard. "I'm not bitter!" he said tasting bile. "I naively thought I could come back here and have all my juvenile fantasies fulfilled! Well, they haven't been! I see now they won't ever be! So apparently it's time for me to grow up!"

She moved down to join him. "Don't forget me, Felix!" she said, her hand on his arm.

"How could I ever forget?" he said quietly.

He studied her; she met his gaze, both ignoring David who now stood on the other side of the screen door watching, his good buddies behind him at the bar silently witnessing the whole scene.

"I'm glad you have everything you want," Felix said. "I better go. Your husband's getting worried."

He looked past her to David who watched from behind the screen, the others at the bar waiting. Felix turned down to the sidewalk. Gloria followed, stopping him, taking him into her arms, turning him. She held him tightly, stepped back to study his face, took his head in her hands, pulled him down toward her, and touched her soft lips to his, her lips lingering, then releasing him, allowing him to move off, watching him go.

He turned to look back at her one last time as David came out onto the concrete stoop then down the steps to join his wife on the sidewalk underneath the street lamp. Felix watched the couple climb back up the concrete steps, David's arm around her shoulder, Gloria's arm around his waist as they ascended, moved back through the screen door that squawked open in the warm summer night then screeched behind them as it closed. Felix turned from under the yellow glow of street lamp splayed on full-leafed trees above concrete sidewalk and went into the dark alone.

Felix used his grandmother's phone with its rotary dial that he had seen her use since he was a child. He dialed the number. He waited for his mother to answer.

"Hi! You ready? O.K. I'll be right over. The cab will pick us at your place."

Then he replaced the receiver and went out onto the front porch where his grandmother sat in her chair working the needles on one of her continuous projects.

"My, don't you look handsome!" she said. "I haven't seen you so dressed up since you graduated from high school."

"Good that you still have some of my old clothes," Felix responded. She as everyone in the family never discarded anything that was deemed worth keeping just in case. "I'm surprised they still fit," he added.

"Guess I haven't fed you enough!" she laughed.

"I'll go meet them and the cab. You just relax. Don't worry, everything will work out."

"Not much use in worry. You go along and get them before your father gets impatient."

"Sure," he said. "We wouldn't want that."

Then he went down the stairs with care not accustomed to the dress shoes only slightly used and highly polished.

He noted the once familiar scuff of almost new leather soles and heels on pavement as he went down the street to the corner, paused, and turned to wave at the old woman who watched him go. He waited for a break in traffic before he crossed the avenue to the corner by the pharmacy then moved to the side door that led to apartments above. He entered the small hallway, pressed a button to buzz his parents then went back out to wait. Soon the door swung open and his parents dressed for the evening joined him on the sidewalk.

"Well, you look nice," his mother said smiling, apparently delighted at the prospect of an evening out.

"Do I know this young man?" his father asked, laughing through his words."

"He's your son!" his wife said.

"Is that so? Oh, I know him now. Then who was that other young man who visited us in faded denim jacket, faded jeans, and scruffy shoes?" he replied laughing. "What a change!"

Felix accepted the good-natured jibes as a hopeful indication that the evening might turnout pleasant even though he considered what he had in mind for the occasion. Regarding his change in apparel, Felix decided that what he wore felt odd, now even a bit strange when he considered that so many thought what he now wore the preferred formal dress for dining out.

"Here's the taxi now," he said as they watched the yellow cab with black lettering on the door and perfect timing turn from the avenue into the side street and pull along the curb. Felix opened the rear door and held it back allowing his mother to enter. Then he bowed to his father ushering him into the cab with a sweep of his arm.

"At your pleasure, sir."

Felix's father thanked him as he bent his long frame into the vehicle. Felix slammed the door, opened the front door and dipped in beside the driver.

"Great timing," Felix said.

"Where to?"

"Just make a U-turn, go across the avenue to the house just beyond the alley where you see a women in a chair on the porch."

He avoided even glancing back to note his father's expression.

"What's this?" Pa exclaimed.

Felix was not surprised that the light tone of his father's voice he had heard a few moments before was now absent. But Felix held his response until the cab pulled up to the curb before the house and porch where Felix's grandmother had risen from her chair, entered the house to deposit her knitting and returned just as Felix exited the cab and turned back to note the mix of surprise and sternness of his parents at being aware they were captives.

"You should know her," he quipped. "She's your mother. I've invited her to join us for what's suppose to be my welcome home."

Then he turned, hurried up the porch steps as best he could in his unaccustomed shoes to guide the elderly woman down the steps.

"You sit up front where it's safe, Grandma," he advised, helping her into the taxi then going around the rear of the cab to the left rear door that he opened and paused while his mother shifted to the center of the seat allowing him access. He slammed the door and sat back noting the ID card of the driver on the front visor. He cited the name of a celebrated restaurant.

"You know where that's located?"

The driver said he did.

"O.K., Ralph. Let's go!"

So they went within the warm afternoon of a warm summer day mellowing toward a mild evening. Felix gazed out the window at the passing scene that now seemed more familiar but still slightly foreign. His mother assumed the task of tour guide pointing out changes as they passed along the way.

A valet met them at the entrance, opened the front door of the cab, and helped the older woman struggle from the front seat. Felix's father opened his door, heaved himself out, straightened, and held the door while his wife slid across the seat to exit at the same time Felix issued from his side and bent at the open window of the driver's door to talk to Ralph, handing the driver a folded bill, requesting that Ralph return in about three hours. Ralph thanked him acknowledging both payment and request, then put the cab in gear and with a slight wave moved off as Felix went to join the others waiting silently at the entrance.

The valet held open the door allowing them to enter where they were met by the maître de who welcomed them, led them to a round table Felix considered appropriate for the occasion, helped the women with their chairs, and handed each a large menu. Then he left replaced by a middle-aged waiter in formal attire who asked their beverage preference before dinner.

Felix's father ordered his traditional whiskey and soda. Felix's mother ordered the same. His grandmother chose water with lemon. Felix ordered a martini, very dry and straight up.

"Where'd you learn all that?" Pa asked. "They certainly didn't teach you that in the Army Reserve. You learn that in college?"

"What?" Felix asked.

"That very dry martini business."

"I learned that from Gloria. She introduced me to martinis."

"The price's are maybe too high," Felix's' mother observed.

"Well, what you expect?" Pa responded. "This place has a rating of five-stars and five dollar signs! Your son's developed expensive tastes!"

"Perhaps we can now afford this one time since I now work," Ma offered.

"Well, I invited you so I could include Grandma," Felix offered, "so I'll pay. Order whatever you like. I made more money cutting wheat than I've ever had." Felix added.

"This outing is supposed to be a celebration!" Grandma Fist observed. "Let's just order! We can settle who pays when we're through!"

They studied their menu. The waiter returned with their beverages and took their dinner orders, and while they waited for their salads, they sampled their drinks.

"Shouldn't we toast Felix on his return?" Grandma Fist suggested.

"So we should," Felix's mother agreed.

The three raised their glasses.

"Welcome to the prodigal's return," Pa offered.

"How nice to have you home," Ma added.

"Yes it is!" Grandma Fist agreed.

Quietly thanking them, Felix raised his glass to acknowledge their toast.

"So you still haven't told us much about what you've learned in school," Pa asked, "or why you went off to college in California?"

"Wasn't sure where I was going. So I thought going to a college that wouldn't cost me much in a place I've always wanted to see might give me the direction I needed."

"Well, has it?

"I think so," Felix said finally after reflection. "But since I've already told you some of my college experience the day I arrived, I don't have much more to say right now. Maybe later once we eat."

"So we should talk about something else," Felix's mother said. "Besides, I think our food is soon ready."

Their salads, having arrived, Felix, following his mother's advice, offered a topic for discussion on which everyone would have something to say.

"We suppose to get rain?" he asked. "I'm no longer used to this heat and humidity. The California coast is warm after morning fog, but breezes off the ocean during the day helps keep it mild. I'm not sure I ever was or ever will be used to these hot, humid summers, or the winters I'm happy to leave behind.

"Yes, this year has seemed bad," Ma observed.

"It's always been bad," Pa grumbled. "We've never thought of living anywhere else, except that time we tried moving to Florida, so we just accept what we get here. Why complain about something you can't do anything about?"

That sour comment squelching any response, their entrees arrived in the nick of time with typical ceremony. Continuing on the somewhat safe topic of local weather, rarely having seen Pa so quiet, Felix reluctant to submit to dismay and wanting to prompt his father into talking, he asked about the heat where Pa worked.

"That's just part of the price having a steady job," his father replied, "something I haven't always had."

"But Henry, you have worked steady now for years," Felix's mother corrected.

Felix's father shrugged but said nothing, tilting his head in a gesture Felix knew well.

"Why'd you give up your cherished Buick?" Felix asked, deciding to try another topic. "I remember you always wanting a new one as soon as the one you had was paid off."

"Well, I finally got what I always wished for. Then I learned that I didn't need the so-called convenience having to pay for the required costs — gas, insurance, the hassle of permit street parking at night or the extra cost of renting a garage close enough to our apartment. So, I said, 'To hell with it!'. Now I just take the bus to work and back as I used to way back when before I could afford a car, so now I let others do the driving."

While he exchanged such small talk with his father, Felix noted his mother and grandmother conversing as if nothing had disrupted their shared interests.

"How is your garden?" Felix's mother asked. "One thing I miss so much. All the colors of the blossoms in the open air. Our apartment is so small and closed. I try to brighten it with fresh cut flowers, but that's not the same as having a garden."

Felix's father paused to inspect the two women and offered his usual complaint: "Our place is a cheese box! We should be living in a house!"

"You're welcome to move back anytime." Grandma Fist offered. "You should come see my latest project!" she said to Felix's mother. "It's a big one — a spread for the dining room table!"

"So when you going to retire?" Felix asked focusing again on his father.

"Why should I retire?" Pa responded. "I found out what that's like when I got laid off from my last job after twenty years at Rundle's. So much for job security! What would I do if I retired?"

"We could travel," Felix's mother suggested.

"I suppose we could. But not to Florida. We've been there. Once was enough for me!"

"So it was for me with all those bugs. But you also have your Sons of Norway service group for which you could do more."

"Sons of Norway!" Felix exclaimed. "No one in the whole extended family has Norwegian heritage!"

"So what? One day being nosey, I attended a meeting in the old Abby theater only a short walk from our place, enjoyed what I heard. I introduced myself and offered suggestions that might help them promote their programs. They thanked me, invited me back. Now I'm president of the local chapter. So, yeah, I have that too. I suppose I should consider retirement before I get too old, not like Pa who worked until his drinking finally killed him and he never had the chance to stop working and do something he really wanted?

"You should know, Felix, that your father has received several civic awards for his service!" Ma offered.

"Really! That's great!"

"So you see, Henry, you could devote more time to such work!" Ma said.

"OK! I'll have to think about whether we can afford it." Pa conceded.

They finished their meal in silence. The waiter came to take their plates and asked about desert. Everyone praised the excellence of the food and how they couldn't eat another bite.

"How about after-dinner drinks?" Felix asked, he needing a boost in courage for what he was about to attempt.

His mother tried to remember what she had the last time they dined out, that rare occasion in the distant past. Then she suddenly recalled something called a Grasshopper, so she ordered that.

Pa declined as did Grandma Fist. Pa instead lit a cigarette.

Felix suggested a California brandy. The waiter certain they carried that label went off to return with a snifter that Felix used with a flourish. The others watched his display.

"I once saw someone do that in a movie," Grandma Fist observed.

While he sipped his brandy, Felix thought of Gloria and how their *affair* had resolved itself. Although he hadn't been surprised, he felt saddened, and he knew what his father would say should Felix reveal what had recently taken place. Why had Felix expected something else? Felix considered what he could say that might change his father's attitude toward the choices Felix had made in his life. The martini, the brandy, and the somewhat quiet exchange over dinner had relaxed Felix's reserve, so he found himself ready to reveal what he had been considering:

"You might be surprised to hear that I have dreams — just as you did when you were my age. And that I also have ambitions."

"Dreams and ambitions?"

"I want to try developing my talent."

"You mean your artwork?" Ma asked.

"I haven't done all that much of my own, but I've leaned a lot of what others have done and why they're considered great, so I want to try to see what I can do."

"You were always so good at drawing," Ma observed. "I still have some of those early pictures you drew for me."

"Really?" Felix asked, not surprised that she had saved everything he had offered her.

"You want to develop your talent in art? Pa asked. "Where you think that will get you?"

"What about you?" Felix asked. "You always wanted to do something else working with wood, like that linen chest of cedar you made for Ma, not like what you've done all your working life. That dream must have dissolved into a more practical reality following Grandpa Fist's advice."

"You're right," Pa said. "He talked me into choosing work that would allow me more opportunity for a job at a time when just about everybody was out of work."

"So you chose that line of work because you thought it would get you a job that would allow you to support your dream of having a family."

Pa remained silent perhaps reminded of his dream deferred.

"I've also decided that while I'm developing my talent, when I've earned a degree, I might also try teaching."

"Well, that might get you work, but if teaching isn't your goal, what is? Do you have any?"

"I already told you. My dream is to develop art that people admire. So I just have to follow my bliss."

"Your what!" Pa asked.

What do you mean?" Grandma Fist asked.

Ma nodded in agreement.

"You read that in one of your books?" Pa asked.

"I did!" Felix admitted. "It means doing what you always dreamed of doing."

"You mean not like I did."

"You chose your option. You have mother. And you have me and Sonny. Weren't we part of your dream? Didn't you follow your bliss?"

His father studied him. Ma placed her hand on her husband's arm.

"Sure," Pa said. "But I had to give up something else I really wanted."

"The rate of exchange," Felix observed quietly.

"The what!"

"The cost of anything is determined by the amount of life you have to give in exchange for it."

"That's got to be from some book!"

"One of my favorites."

Pa slowly shook his head.

Encouraged by Pa's resignation viewing a son he apparently didn't know, Felix struck boldly following his plan.

"Let me offer something else I learned from another book. You ever hear of 'displacement'?"

"No. So what?"

"Then you should know it's a way of transferring your response to what happens to you to someone or something else. You take your feelings out on something or someone else. You're angry at your wife for not being available, so you fault your son for anything he's done, or you yell at your wife or someone else or everyone else. That's a form of displacement. An actual example of displacement that's called 'scapegoating' Ma surely must remember. Because of Germany's harsh economic difficulties due to the outcome of World War I, Hitler and the Nazis blamed the Jews and other "undesirables" for Germany's problems, and too many other people were willing to blame others for what had happened to make their own lives difficult."

"O.K., so what? Why bring all that up?"

"Your attitude and treatment of Grandma."

"What!"

Felix took a sip of brandy allowing Pa to calm.

"Grandma says that you no longer want to visit her because of what happened with the house."

"Your grandpa always said the house would eventually be mine."

"And your sister's," Grandma Fist added quietly. "You two were supposed to share."

"O.K., but I'd get to live there because she already had a house and didn't want to live in the city, and we'd work out a way for me to buy her share."

"But something happened that prevented all that," Felix offered.

"You're damn right something happened!"

Ma placed her hand on Pa's arm trying to calm his growing agitation.

"And what happened resulted from Ed's having made an unwise investment."

"Unwise! That's putting it mildly!"

"So you're angry at Ed because of what happened.

"You're damn right I'm angry!"

"How much good has holding that anger done for you since he's no longer here? What's the rate of exchange for that anger? And while you're justifiably angry at Ed for what happened, you blame Grandma. How has that blame helped you and equally important, perhaps more important, how has it helped her?"

Felix met Pa's stern inspection, the silence profound.

"Well, she brought him into our house!" Pa finally offered.

"But how could she begin to know what he might do? And from what I recall, you got along with Ed at first and even enjoyed doing things with him and going places."

"Then he moves in and takes over as if he owned the place and it was only his! And then he manages to make the situation so difficult he has her kick us out! My own mother kicking me out of my own house! One I lived in most of my life!"

"O.K., but you're still placing most of the blame on Grandma."

"Well, she always went along with whatever he wanted!"

"But she didn't know what he would actually do with the money he borrowed using the house as security. And you're still blaming her shows something else. A lack of respect."

"Lack of respect! What you talking about!"

"Blaming Grandma for marrying and bringing into what was still her house someone who would do something she could not have possibly foreseen, you're blaming her for what Ed did when she was not directly responsible for what happened. That displaced blame reveals disrespect for her values that in turn reveals an inconsistency with what you have always claimed you've believed and valued and have always preached and demanded from me. Respect for one's parents you claim is a universal edict: Honor your father and mother."

"Well, I still believe that."

"If you do, then the disrespect you show your mother by not wanting to have anything to do with her violates what you claim you still believe. So why am I supposed to respect you and honor your judgments if you don't show respect for your own mother?"

Pa's eyes searched Felix's face, his expression grim, but he remained uncommonly silent against his son's unexpected, uncommon, protracted prosecution.

Felix decided he had said too much and said it too harshly from anger, just as Pa always did. So he finished his brandy in a gulp, set down the snifter on the now soiled table cloth, and signaled the waiter who approached, asked if they required anything further, and when they declined, presented the bill. Felix reached in his jacket for his hard-earned traveler's checks.

Ma responded to his move. "We should pay. It's your homecoming!"

"But I invited you and Pa, and I invited Grandma, and I think what I've just said has obviously soured the welcome. So I think I should pay my share of the bill and Grandma's."

"O.K." Ma agreed. "We will share the bill," she said turning to her spouse.

"Sure, that's fine," Pa said with a resigned shrug finally breaking his ponderous silence. "Whatever you decide."

"Sure, why not?" his mother added. "We can now afford the expense with me working," she said smiling.

Felix was a bit surprised at Pa's subdued submission to his wife's decision, but Felix was delighted witnessing his mother's newfound sense of self-worth. So he signed traveler's checks that would sufficiently cover his and his grandmother's share as well as the waiter's gratuity. Perhaps, he decided, his contribution might help redeem the celebration of his return soured from the bitter aftertaste of words spoken in self-righteous anger.

The ride back in the cab was swift, they again chauffeured by Ralph. During that ride blessedly short, no one said a word and no one even seemed able to breathe, the heavy silence broken only when Ralph pulled up to the curb before the Fist family home and Felix helped his grandmother from the front seat of the cab then went around to the driver's side and paid Ralph, asking him to chauffeur his parents across the avenue and the door to their apartment above the corner pharmacy. But before Ralph could begin executing his move, Pa struggled to heave his large bulk from the back seat.

"We'll walk from here!" Pa exclaimed, ordering his wife to follow when she hesitated issuing from the cab, reluctant, apparently not surprised but obviously dismayed from how the evening was ending, Pa striding off without a word to either his mother or his son, his wife eventually following after bidding her mother-in-law and her son goodnight, while her husband charged on ahead, shouting back for her to hurry.

Felix and his grandmother watched the cab pull away, Ralph offering a knowing glance, a shrug, and a brief wave as he drove off.

"Well that didn't turn out the way I wanted," Felix said to himself. He went to his grandmother and embraced her. "Sorry, Grandma," Felix said. "I thought that might work."

"Well, you tried," Felix's grandmother consoled. "We'll just have to wait. He'll come around eventually."

"Maybe," Felix said. "But you know him. Who knows how long that will take? How long has it been since he's been angry over what he claims is his house?"

Then he helped his grandmother up the porch stairs. But when he opened the door, they were met by a heavy, stifling blast of heat from the dark, closed interior.

"Why don't we leave the door open and we sit out here for a bit while we enjoy the mild air?" Grandma Fist suggested.

"Good idea," Felix agreed. "It's still too hot up in my room to sleep."

"I could make coffee. But that would be too hot. How about a root beer float? You always used to like root beer floats on hot nights like this!"

"Thanks, Grandma. But you're right. It's too hot and too late for coffee, and I'm still stuffed from dinner."

"And most likely upset," she offered.

Felix remained mute brooding on the way the evening celebrating his return had ended. "Well, I hoped it might work," he offered again.

"It did for a while," his grandmother soothed.

Felix didn't respond, so they sat, she in her chair, he on the top porch step watching the intermittent evening traffic pass slowly on the avenue, the pharmacy closed for the night, the unlit shaded windows of the apartments above, the occasional exit of some reveler from the corner tavern, the screen door banging shut as a dark shape swayed off into the warm night.

"So what have you planned for tomorrow?" Grandma Fist asked.

Not much," Felix offered. "Maybe I'll just wander the neighborhood like I used to when I was a kid. I need to think about what's happened since I've been back and where I go from here."

"Well, I have lots of gardening to finish, so I thought I'd fix us a nice breakfast. Then you have the rest of the day to do want you want. How does that sound?"

"That sounds great, Grandma."

"OK, then. I think I'll go in now, turn on the fan, and prepare for bed. With all this heat, we'll probably have trouble sleeping."

Then she slowly rose from her seat and went into the dark house leaving Felix alone on the porch studying the dark windows above the pharmacy on the corner, brooding on what had happened during the time he had been back where he thought he had returned safely home.

In the morning after more than sufficient breakfast and with no one else to see and nothing else to do, the ritual ceremony of return over, and all he had was time to decide his next move, Felix set out to wander again the neighborhood he once roamed as a child and explore again old haunts, places so familiar to him and largely unchanged, it seemed as if he had never left or he had been absent only hours or days instead of a year. He upon his arrival had noticed changes, but most seemed minor: a structure here refurbished, a house with a color different from what he recalled, new metal awnings here, a new fence or carport there, all only helped remind him of what he had seen when they were making their day-to-day indelible record, showing him clearly through their continued existence tarnished with the patina of time that any significant change actually had occurred in him. Surely he had changed, but who had noticed? Certainly not those friends he now knew he never had.

So he set off to tour what he perceived as his origins, the events of the previous weeks having reacquainted him with its settings and locations, Felix having decided to explore what he once considered his home turf to which he had always returned from some adventure. Descending the gray enamel stairs of the sun porch from the kitchen, he went through the frosted glass door to the concrete stoop and walkway that led beneath the rose arbor through the front green gate to the street. There he turned down toward the avenue where he crossed, and here again the tan and pink brick pharmacy where for the last time he stepped inside past large display windows met by a wash of warm air that carried a panoply of fragrance from medications and cosmetics. He surveyed the soda fountain with its formica top and chrome trim, its vinyl stools, the large mirror behind that threw back images of crowded glass cases and shelves. How often had he sat on one of these stools when a boy, twisting and spinning, drinking sweet sodas made from syrups pumped from one of the curved spigots beneath the mirror, one, for some reason, called Green River? In the mirror, Felix saw people watching him watching them, he startled seeing his own image gazing back at him. So that's what he looked like to others. Did it matter?

He turned and left, crossing the side street beside the pharmacy to the tavern on the corner, its round facade and half circle of concrete steps mirroring Tess' tavern on the opposing corner across the avenue, but this one he passed lacked a wood bench of green enamel beside the cross corner tavern. From both taverns, his grandfather charged with drink and unrelieved lust had staggered home to assault his wife. On that green bench of the tavern across the avenue, Felix for hours had gathered both day and evening with cohorts to drink bottled soda from the smoke and hobby shop next to the tavern, spar with girls flowering into women to show them he was physically stronger and felt himself superior, run beer errands with small, galvanized buckets for those banished from the tavern for being unable to control their drinking.

Felix moved on down the block past the empty, green storefront of what once had been a small grocery and butcher shop where Ma once had gone almost daily to indulge her use of her native language. He having accompanied her then now imagined he heard the faint, ghostly echoes of bustling vibrancy from a foreign tongue, recalled the odors of bloody meats, spicy sausage, sawdust strewn floor. Passing Laynie's tavern his father had once frequented where Felix on occasion went along, allowed to climb up onto a bar stool and drink orange soda from a glass with ice while his father talked organizing a union. Here he had witnessed the wild celebration at the end of the Second Planetary War. Next to the tavern, a cindered lot for parking, now empty, then two doors from Twenty-third, a brown asphalt tiled duplex he had moved to with his brother and parents after living next to the Abby Theater.

He studied the gray enameled porch with lathe-turned pillars, the gray door with oval glass opening to a narrow stairway of tan enameled walls and tan enameled stairs with black rubber matting, the enameled walls with a thin line of dark brown fleur-du-lise leading up to where Felix had lived above in a two-bedroom flat with kitchen and dining area that had a large picture window overlooking a gangway and the large window of a neighboring flat, a walk-in pantry, a front room with tan flowery linoleum edged in a wide stripe of solid brown, and three tall, narrow front windows that looked out at the asphalt roof of the white-brick storage warehouse across the avenue and down onto the avenue below with endless traffic both vehicular and pedestrian.

At these windows Felix had often sat for hours on a low cedar chest Pa using all his skills with tools and wood had fashioned as a gift for Ma,

Felix watching the passing scene below: the tarred, rounded tops of trolley cars, the ever changing style of autos. Pa working swing shift, Ma ironing in the kitchen, Felix had sat alone in darkness at the window in the heavy, humid, stifling heat of summer, the kitchen light creeping to the edge of the front room and the tan, flowered linoleum trimmed with brown as one of the frequent summer storms swept in from the West, the storm's approach announced by distant thunder growing louder with increasing shocks as it moved closer until the storm broke overhead in crashing, sizzling bolts of lightning and booming bursts of sound that had made him think he was in a barrel, the wind billowing the lace curtains and finally the warm rain splattering torrents that washed streets and left great, dark streaks on the white brick facade of the warehouse across the way, the street and trolley tracks running in streams reflecting yellow street lamps and the bright red neon of the warehouse office and the tailor shop down toward Twenty-second with its intermittent billowing of steam, almost endlessly, day and night just before the flat he once lived in next to the Abby theater with its marquee of colored lights.

On the porch he now passed he had often played while digging fortifications for his war toys in the small plat of dirt at its side mimicking the great planetary war he had heard reports of on the radio. Beside the flat toward Twenty-third, the concrete gangway always in shadow where one time he had watched a robin totter, herald a single pure note, then topple over, its yellow beak in the white-pebbled black dirt. Taking up the body still warm, the neck limp, the mild spring wind ruffling feathers exposing white lice still scurrying, he had found a secret place and buried it with one white pebble to mark the place. Now after years, why did he recall that scene? Why was it so important? How had it shaped his spirit and his character?

At the rear, beyond the gangway between the asphalt tile duplex and the adjacent stucco flat, Felix glimpsed the concrete alleyway where he once had cultivated a small patch of dirt for a victory garden during the Second Planetary War, he proudly bringing in the always slightly unripened produce to the kitchen where washed, placed on a plate, he with ceremony had carried it to the table proudly feeling a provider when his family was most in need. Best of all, he had enjoyed watching his garden grow. Absorbed in preparing the small plot of soil, its rich, dark dirt alive with creeping, crawling things both bizarre and glorious, some with a grotesque beauty, the hard, compact patch he dug into with table fork and spoon turning up clumps of dirt revealing a wondrous cache of buried life. Clearing debris, allowing the exposed creatures to scurry off, he had pounded and raked the clumps into crumbled soil then laid out rows into which he shook seeds from packets vividly colored with illustrations of ripe produce he considered promises. Gently covering the seed, placing popsicle sticks as small stakes at each corner with strung string to mark the perimeter, this frail barrier, he believed, having so much faith, would ward against all possible threats from neighborhood brats who would want to destroy out of spite what he had taken so much pride in establishing, autos seeking off-street parking, stray animals depositing their turds. Standing back admiring his work, he had seen that it was good, received with characteristic shyness the praise of neighborhood adults who had watched him work, acknowledging what he had accomplished. Then waiting impatiently for the seeds to germinate, going out each day to assess their progress, he had been delighted to see the small green leaves in neat rows on the dark soil, watching the small sprouts rise above the earth into stemmed plants, then fan into sprays of leaves, some as delicate and expansive as the doilies or spreads his mother or grandmothers were always crocheting.

Felix moved on to the corner where he was confronted by the towering, red-brick massive church, its four-sided steeple narrowing to a peak and bronze cross that thrust toward a gray overcast. He always thought of this church as his, even after he had stopped attending when he had left the tall, barn-like school that despite its size seemed dwarfed by the brick structure in whose shadows it nestled.

How Felix loved to climb the spiral, narrow stairway to the balcony with its curved, sweeping rail. There at the edge he would sit beneath the peak of the high vault, the plaster ceiling ribbed with wood almost at his head, he poised before the phalanx of tubes from which had issued thundering blasts of glorious sound, melodies that had pierced his body, thrilling him to his core as he gazed down at the heads of the people below, their bodies fittingly reduced, small and humble. Here, too, he had sung solo in choir, selected, singled out, his clear, strong, soprano voice filling the hollow, broadcasting his faith and his praise before his voice had cracked and deepened, losing it about the same time he had lost his faith. In the schoolyard beside the church, he had romped with others over pebbled, packed earth, taken refuge from pursuit in the corner of a towering buttress. There, facing countless red brick that rose to the towering, slate-tiled roof, he would inspect the debris left by pigeons that cooed softly from their lofty nests above: fragments of delicate shells, soft, airy plumes, a featherless, dead chick, its blue-gray body naked and cold at his feet sheathed in black, high-top canvas shoes.

Here from beneath the towering redbrick church at 23rd, he started down the long, gradual incline of the avenue heading east toward the great lake, he treading the same path he had walked so often with Ma to the bank or bus stop on Sixteenth. Now he viewed the steep-roofed, barn-like wood structure that housed the classes Felix had attended his first years of school before he had moved out to Sunfish. Next to the school, the rectory he had been in only once when Pa went to fetch the key to the rear door of the church so Pa could ring the huge bell when the Second Planetary War had ended. Felix urged to pull the thick rope that rang the bell but failing to let go, he had been dragged up, burning his hands when sliding to the floor.

Beside the rectory that matched the redbrick church, its color dark with years of passing seasons, a line of two-story flats, some with rough, gray stucco siding, others gray slatboard, all with redbrick porch pillars he had once studied every day from the windows or porch of the lower flat beside the Abby Theater while he mended from being struck by a car while crossing the avenue to where his cousin David who had lived with their grandmother in a rear flat on an alley paved with granite blocks that sparkled in dazzling sunlight. Felix passed the flat he had lived in next to the Abby Theater, now the Norway House where Pa went for his service club meetings, and Felix wondered what might his parents have thought passing each time that two-story flat of gray enamel boards they had lived in on the ground floor, the gray enameled porch with its lathe-turned pillars, the front door with its oval, cut-glass window never used? Here Felix had helped celebrate his father's 27th birthday, the year Pa had tried out for the police force required to run the mile in seven minutes while a heavy smoker and have all his teeth pulled because they were so bad they would disqualify him from being hired. Here Pa had brought Felix and Sonny malted milks in a quart milk bottle for which he had paid a quarter when either fell sick with any disease that had quarantined them for undetermined length and where Felix had spent a year and a half, first in cast, then on withered leg mending from having it fractured when struck by a brown '37 Chevy when Felix playing a game he had invented tried running across the busy avenue in front of rush hour traffic. Standing for hours at the tall windows of the flat beside the Abby Theater, watching the passing scene, the round-domed trolley cars, the two-story flats across the way, he would gaze up the block to the tan slatboard, steep-roofed school and the towering pile of brick heaped toward heaven and watch the playground of small pebbles teeming with activity. He had felt sad not able to join all that turmoil and meet the challenges of facing other boys equally concerned with fashioning their identity.

The avenue down which Felix now strolled once had trolley tracks in the center until they were dug up, the street widened, and resurfaced. While that work went on, he could look down the incline of that long straight torn up street with heaps of dirt and rubble stretching for a couple of miles, the steam shovel some huge beast raising its long, jointed neck, its huge maw spilling a thunderous load of dirt and shattered brick and gravel into the monstrous steel dumps of trucks. In the evening, with the machines silent, the men gone with the softening summer light, the midday heat easing, the reddening sun still casting long shadows, Felix and cohorts had played war games among the trenches and the heaps of dirt and rubble, avoiding the Gestapo, the beat cops (one of them Pa) who patrolled the neighboring streets on foot, chasing them off, spoiling their sport. The street reopening with a ribbon cutting and a street dance, the new trackless thoroughfare remained closed while people danced to accordion bands and drank free sodas from glass bottles and wandered the length of the reconstructed avenue from Thirty-fifth down to First, surely two miles of virgin asphalt macadam with dazzling concrete curbing.

Nearing Sixteenth, Felix came upon the Natatorium with its blue, shimmering, amniotic pool where he had gone to swim every chance he could, returning, it seemed, to his source, he always challenging his courage by diving into the deep end and stroking to the tar-striped bottom,. He recalled the damp, grayish brown concrete floors, the balcony above with its yellow cubicles for changing, the lingering aura of echoing voices and pungent disinfectant. He passed the bank in front of which he had once seen Pa's uncle Earl after Earl had deserted Great Aunt May or she had thrown him out, he having become alcoholic. That time Felix had seen him when everyone had lost track of him, Earl grizzled and blood shot and grimy in a long tattered overcoat that had once been clean and tailored. His fingerless gloves, most likely a gift from his sister-in-law, Pa's Aunt Vi, he had held out his hand in supplication as Felix had passed, meeting Felix's questioning gaze, the derelict man turning away with feigned indifference when he had understood Felix knew him.

On this same corner before this bank, Felix had often waited with Ma for the bus that would take them to Mitchell Street and the doctor's office where Felix went for treatment for his slowly mending leg shattered by the car that had hit and dragged him until it had stopped. Two blocks up Sunfish Avenue, the front duplex flat his parents had lived in after they were first married and where Felix had experienced his first two years of life. Still further up Sunfish, the antique building with appliance store where in the flat above Gloria had once lived. Turning left up Sixteenth toward National, Felix passed the movie house where he and Sonny had once sat in rows of mohair seats through numerous Saturday matinee's of popcorn and ripe, heated bodies, and Hollywood westerns. Then a line of taverns along Sixteenth into which he as a boy would intrude from the doorstep on Halloween. Entering the thick roil of tobacco and booze and babble, Felix audaciously had begged for pennies from the host of patrons lining the bar grinning back at him in their cups. In one of these taverns his father had sat on occasion, sometimes with friends, one time in a uniform he had cherished and had been ordered to give up.

Felix took the long route on the way back to his grandmother's by continuing up Sixteenth to where it intersected National Avenue then crossed a viaduct over Menomonee Valley to the area of high-rise hotels and office buildings that marked the area he and others had always referred to as "Downtown."

Turning left off Sixteen, Felix headed up National Avenue past a four-story brick building with apartments, one his cousin David once had lived in for a time with his mother and her second husband, Felix visiting as often as Pa allowed, thrilled by sometimes even being granted permission to stay overnight, each stay an adventure. Ma's sister Erica notorious for her escapades and her marriages had cooked foods that to Felix were exotic, unlike the bare, basic meals of meat and potatoes with onions Ma always served, Pa always insisting, resisting anything foreign. What Felix's aunt had cooked and how she had cooked it reflected her life and her more than one union always brief.

Felix passed on by the square, weathered, redbrick buildings stark against the sky. A block up National he stopped. Nagged by compulsion, yielding to impulse, he went back. The redbrick duel buildings seemed the same as when he had last visited. Designed in the style of a previous era, a building on each side of a gangway, Felix moved cautiously toward the concrete courtyard. Gray porches loomed up cantilevered along side each building like ramps from some pinball game. Light from the open sky above the gangway played on the steel gray boards and railings, the edges of porches thrust out in rhomboid shapes.

At the end of the gangway, an old man hailed him, apparently mistaking Felix for someone else. The man gaunt from age, his skin waxy and yellow reminding Felix of the 84-year old man he often had served at Morey's Chevron in Long Beach. The old man here descended into a stairwell encased by a glass dome then stooped to busy himself beneath a bare bright bulb that glowed through billowing steam. When he emerged, he challenged Felix with dark, questioning eyes, "Who is it you're looking for?"

Felix explained that a friend had lived here long ago. "I'm just looking," Felix offered.

The man studied him, his face blank, his slightly worried eyes questioning. Felix turned and went back out under rhomboid ramps of porches feeling hurried, dissatisfied, annoyed that his quest had been disrupted, he not able to meditate on lost times and instead the everyday present passing moment having intruded, the sun bright on concrete walkway. What, or whom, indeed, had he been seeking? What had he hoped to redeem? Why?

Felix continuing his trek up National toward Twenty-seventh, suddenly, the flashing lights of a black and white patrol car roaring by with screaming siren. When he arrived at the scene, he studied a chalked outline on the roadway. A police officer spoke to a man with a camera prohibiting the man from taking photos. Nearby, a man lay beneath the rear of a car checking for a gas leak.

So it goes. Felix suddenly understood there is no such thing as life but only living for brief moments limited by what he had inherited and influenced by the places where he had lived. So what did all those lost years actually mean? Did they actually matter? And where did he go from here?

Felix moved on, turning left at Twenty-third to cross the avenue. Had he turned right, he could have walked a block to Mitchell Park where he had quarreled with his former friend Jack and where once upon a time his cousin David had fallen hands first into a refuse fire. There he like some small animal would creep through the warrens of underbrush, crawl the dark, damp places beneath the outdoor stage used on the Fourth of July eventually dismantled, he had boldly hung from iron railings of the boathouse pavilion eventually transformed from piled, red brick to sweeping concrete and glass, climbed the sinuous asphalt path up the hill he and his cousin David would sled down in winter, roll down over and over until they sat dizzy and laughing among the dandelions and ripe, green grass of summer. They had often climbed the weathered logs of Juneau's pioneer cabin on top that hill to gaze at the leggo-block towering skyline across Menomonee Valley where indigenous people once had met now filled with railroad tracks and boxcars. He and David had wandered through the Victorian crystal conservatory and along the adjoining yellow gravel paths and spouting lions heads beside the sunken garden with water lilies and gold and pink Coy.

Felix reached Clark Square at Twenty-third and Scott. Here the wide concrete pathways from each corner led in among the tall, numerous oak to the large circle of wading pool now drained, the bottom, stark concrete with squiggling lines of tar to seal the cracks. On one arc segment of the pool, a small brick pavilion now boarded once housed the dressing rooms, showers, and toilets. To one side, a yellow wood shack he now understood was once a senior center where men had gathered to play card games, the men so old they seemed ageless, their pipes and cigars filling the dimly lit room with billows of blue smoke, the shack now nailed shut, the door a blank wall of plywood.

Felix passed the Georgian style extended living home, its porches once filled now empty, its tall, classic windows with drawn shades. Then the tall, brown brick factory building he had witnessed through seasons of activity and decline standing empty at intervals of economic change, its high lattice-paned windows shattered by the merciless stones of small boys, then during other periods, the factory busy again, filled with the whine of machinery and power tools, the windows in summer open to the warm day letting out waves of hot odors of newly made plastic and hot electric motors.

Felix came upon the house where Pa's Uncle John and Aunt Tillie and their son Harvey had lived for years across the alley from the Fist family home where from the attic window, Felix could see their house, much like the one from which he gazed at night, its windows trimmed in green glowing yellow in the dark, In that house across the alley, Felix had witnessed frequent games of Sheepshead, these, too, mostly on summer nights, the air heavy with heat and humidity. Uncle John in ribbed undershirt, his braces down around his waist, the cigar stub in the corner of his mouth, Grandpa Fist, Pa, and Harvey, Pa's best friend, would gather around the kitchen table underneath the hanging shaded lamp with swirling clouds of cigar and cigarette smoke. Little talk went on while they played until the shouts broke out like attacks with the sudden slamming down of cards one after the other piling up in the center underneath the lamp. Then after the round ended, exclamations and discussion, serious remarks in grave tones, observations in clipped assertions while the cards were shuffled and dealt, as if some great battle had been won.

Felix and other kids had hung on the backs of chairs and whined for soft drinks they received then were banished outside into the heavy humid night alive with large, hard-shell insects that buzzed and hummed around their heads attracted by the light through the screen door against which they crashed and clung. Felix and the others would scoop them up in Mason jars and hold them captive until they tired of them, setting them free to whirl away into the dark. Felix suddenly thought of buzzing, hard-shell insects clinging to the screen door of a police outpost in a small Illinois town.

Across the street from Uncle John and Aunt Tillie's, a low line of one story brick apartments beside the alley. When seven or eight, Felix had watched as the old wood ward yard they replaced was demolished, he often visiting the yellow, clapboard structure with Pa who went there looking for work after being laid off from several jobs he had during the Great Depression and the following war years. The alleyway Felix now reached led to the backyard of the duplex flat he lived in next to the old Abbey Theater now the Norway house, the marquee of flashing colored lights gone, the doors on each side the ticket booth gone, the exterior now a bland beige, the brick sides still an aged, dirty brown.

A side alley from the main one he now gazed down once led to a slaughter house Felix had viewed from time to time with morbid, curious fascination as trucks with slatboard sides brought in loads of steaming, snorting animals. Following bloody water running down the center trough of tan concrete alleyway, Felix's childish curiosity guiding him, he had witnessed cattle driven in by men in long, white coats and tall, black rubber boots cursing and beating the wild-eyed beasts to get them moving up the wood ramp through gaping door from whence issued the raw smell of liquid dung and blood.

Felix recalled the shouts of men, the thud and clump of hooves on wood, the scrape and clatter of hooves on concrete, the blow of steel sledge on skull bone, the bellow of injured beast. Then after the hiss of water on concrete; the flow of blood down the center trough of concrete alley; the sticky, hot smell of butchered flesh; the raw, stark carcasses, headless, gutless, hung by shank from wicked, black hooks, Felix had watched while men heaved against black barrels of tallow and scraps, twirling them out onto the platform then pausing to light a tube of paper and tobacco before returning to their task that earned them their daily bread and portion of meat.

In a garage at the alley entrance, Felix had once attended two young men who were building a Model A hot rod from the frame up. Felix sent for snacks and sodas and fetched tools they couldn't reach, they had seemed to abide his presence, and his father on occasion dropping around to fetch Felix home in the dark, curious to know where his always wayward son was spending so much time without getting into some sort of trouble he was usually getting into that would warrant punishment Pa would always readily administer with righteous zeal. Felix again wondered why Pa had been such a control freak demanding that everyone conform to and follow what he thought was the only right way. Felix thought of the strange exchange he had experienced being abusively beaten supposedly to prevent him from committing acts that might lead to injury.

Felix recalled seeing the two young men roar past the Fist family car, their completed hot rod swerving in and out of traffic on the two-lane highway the Fists traveled on in a rare outing to visit a farm beneath Holy Hill outside Cedarburg, the farm maintained by a friend of Pa and former follow worker also an advocate of worker unions. Felix recalled his weekend stay at that farm where he had been challenged by unique experiences sleeping on a livening room sofa in a strange house; eating ripe apples direct from rain-drenched trees, many collected from the leave-strewn, rain-soaked tall grass of the orchard; the taste of venison from a deer hunted on the farm, a taste he found exotic but enjoyable and he a finicky eater from Pa always demanding onion in everything and Felix required to eat even though he always gaged; the blond, pig-tailed girl his age already flowering into a young woman raised on daily farm labor. Felix had found the girl with plastic-rimmed glasses bold and strong easily meeting and often dominating his own strength, he also surprised from feeling stirred by their immediate, physical contact as they wrestled in the hay of the musty barn, the close air filled with chaff in streaming sunlight. From such sustained contact with her trim, blossoming form, young Felix had felt his flesh fill in response and he suddenly aware that he had discovered an answer to something that once had puzzled him upon waking in the morning.

Felix shook himself from reverie, scattering the specters of his youth, turned into the alleyway beside the white brick warehouse and went up the alley toward his grandmother's house following the trough of redbrick that flowed away before him until it reached a concrete spur where he came upon Grandma Fist's yard fenced in green pickets set in concrete that raised the yard above the intersecting alleyways. He saw the concrete trash bin his grandfather and Pa had built decades ago, and cross corner from where he once had played Strikeout with bat and tennis ball against the white warehouse wall, he saw again his grandmother's garden crowded in full bloom: blue iris; red, pink and yellow tulip; white and red roses; pink peony alive with ants; fruit trees heavy with yellow plums, black cherries, pale green pears.

Felix used the wood gate to enter, closing it quietly unlike when he had lived here as a child always letting the gate snap back on its thick, black spring, he returning breathless and sweaty from some adventure, the loud report of the gate always bringing him a harsh reproof always too late. He went up the concrete path beside the painted gray poles with strung heavy wire washlines between, the delicate filigree asparagus bush he brushed with fingers as he passed, reached the frosted paneled door, twisted the brass knob worn yellow with use, and entered, climbing the gray enameled stairs to the kitchen past the sunporch crowded with green-leaf plants in pots of ripe, black dirt.

Slipping from his faded denim jacket, hanging it on a chair, he quickly took in again the kitchen much as he had always remembered furnished with utensils, appliances, silvered, cast-iron radiator with metal shelf that held a vase of cut flowers from the garden, the vase glowing translucent from the window behind, the caged, yellow bird, the flowered china in glass-front cupboards, dishes that had been in the house as long as Felix could remember and as long as the old woman had gathered them through the years, she who now greeted him for what most likely would be the last time.

"You're back!" the aging woman exclaimed.

She rose from the chrome and formica table upon which were spread rows of cards in yet another game of Solitaire.

"You're just in time for fresh coffee and kuchen I baked while you were out."

"More coffee cake!" Felix said. "I'm going to miss your coffee cake!"

"Then you better sit and have as much as you like while you're here!"

She served him again with a wide grin that wrinkled her round face and sparkled her eyes behind her wire-rimmed glasses while Felix dug in after she poured him a cup then helped himself to seconds, eating the cake more slowly between sips of fresh, strong coffee, obviously enjoying both, he most likely knowing he would not have any for what surely would be a very long time if ever.

At the end of August 1958, having experienced brief close encounters with friends he never knew or actually had, his brief reunion with Gloria resulting in his finally accepting their former closeness had altered at the best into something less, Felix decided without doubt to return to Long Beach to continue another year at City College. How might he do that? How else? He had hitched rides all the way to Oregon. He had hitched rides all the way from Oregon back to Milwaukee. If he left now, he'd have plenty of time to reach Long Beach, see if Morey needed help, find some place to lay his weary head, prepare himself for his second year of college by trying to remember what he had forgotten from his first. Then on a hot, humid evening, one of

his last sitting on the front porch of his grandmother's house on 24th just off Greenfield that once had been the family home, Felix thought of Hank and Amy.

Late afternoon, a bus took him to the edge of the city, depositing him, leaving him in a rush of wind and hot diesel exhaust, its wide rear swaying as it roared away, pale faces staring through clouded windows at the lone figure they left behind in faded denim jacket, faded jeans, worn shoes. Having inspected him with dulled eyes, they turned back toward their own lives, jostled, jolted against cracked vinyl seats inside their steel cage as the vehicle carried them away.

As Felix started walking, a light rain began blotching the pavement soon blending into one wet stain. He squinted at the overcast darkening the world. He passed spongy lawns matted with soaked leaves beneath a canopy of trees that shed their autumn harvest clogging culverts. Rain matted his hair. Rain drops kept falling on his head running down the side of his nose and the back of his neck. He shrugged from a sudden chill and pulled the collar of his faded jacket up around his neck. He breathed in the fresh fragrance of warm damp dust. Stopped beneath a striped canvas awning, a stream of water splattering to the pavement, he watched through a downpour young trees bent against a gust of wind. Vehicles like huge, wet snarling beasts splashed through standing water throwing up great spraying sheets as they passed, their headlights illuminating the curtain of rain. He stood chilled beneath the awning viewing the dark, steeped world.

Patches of blue in the overcast announced the shower's passing. Billowing white, majestic cumulus-nimbus gliding over the earth pushed back the overcast as they rose to meet gray overcast laced with black that fled before the approaching front. Bright sunlight suddenly filled the world with dazzling rays catching raindrops falling in thin sheets. A large bow of iridescent color curved high and graceful in the blue sky between massive billowing white clouds, the grand arching sweep of misty colors glistening in radiant sunlight. What an auspicious start to continuing his new life or a fitting conclusion to one he would soon leave behind.

Water cascading from the striped awning slowed to a stream, then a trickle, then drops that gathered, globed to a bead, fell to the wet pavement. He went out from beneath the awning and walked on into the steaming, brightening world.

Children in brief garments suddenly appeared running breathless into the wet world over wet pavement and lawn then stopped to gaze at the blue sky, billowing white clouds, soaring iridescent bow. Looking down, squatting to pick up paper scraps and sticks, they raced on bare feet and legs and thighs to drop debris in flowing culverts, dancing and shouting with glee as they watched their vessels sail away, they wading after, following the scraps and sticks carried by swelling, purling waters that reached a black steel grating, pouring into a dark pit, splashing in an echo far below, their voices shrill in excitement as they watched their accidental toys plummet into the dark hollow. They stared wide-eyed with wonder through thick, black, steel bars at the reflection of their own small faces in the dark pool far below mirroring their distant small, pale images far above. He left them sitting on their pale haunches beside the culvert.

Afternoon slowly fading toward night, Felix walked along the roadside that rose to the crest of a hill. Reaching the top, he turned, looked back. The sky, clear from the cleansing shower, lights of the distant metropolis glistened in the gathering dusk melding into colors rising toward clouds tinting them a soft neon red. He turned toward the horizon. There at the world's edge where a soft blue-green light still lingered, he studied the bright wanderer, its globed light cool and steady, its constant glow, the Love Star, his only companion. He walked on.

Felix imagined behind him among houses, in narrow streets and alleyways, beneath pale, yellow street lamps, the shrill cries of children echoing from his past.

"*Star Light!*"

"*Star Bright!*"

"*First star I see tonight!*" they cried, swinging around lampposts, just as he had, just as children he hoped always would but then doubted.

"*I wish I may!*"

"*I wish I might.!*" they cried as they dashed into shadows to whisper, huddling against dark walls, shivers gripping their frail bodies, their strident voices hushed in a brief moment filled with expectation. Then the next moment, the shivers vanished, releasing them as they ran back into the warm summer night.

"*First Light!*"

"Second Light!" children cried as street lamps winked on one following another, then all the lamps coming on to bathe the rain-fresh pavement in soft, yellow light.

Felix approached a dwelling on the edge of the town center of Greendale, a small, incorporated suburb of Milwaukee originally designed and built with the town center consisting of redbrick buildings enclosing a mall whose surrounding woods and gravel pits Felix had wandered as a boy. Climbing the short stoop of a tan clapboard dwelling where one night cruising with cohorts he had met Carrie, Hank's sister, who had sent him a catalogue of her college in Long Beach. Felix tapped on the wood frame of the screen door and peered through the screen as a small woman approached backlit by the wall lamp opposite.

"Felix! Felix Fist? You're here!" the woman beamed as she opened the door.

"Yep, I'm here," Felix said grinning at the lovely young woman with sharp features and short blond hair and blue eyes that displayed her delight, and he was suddenly aware of how often this small, Midwest village had been part of his life.

"Felix is here!" Amy called over her shoulder.

Then the tall man with buzz-cut hair came to stand behind the woman, his face in a characteristic smile that seemed more like grimace, his eyes squinting behind clear plastic-framed spectacles.

"Hey, Felix! You found us!" Hank exclaimed.

"Looks like I have," Felix agreed, delighted to see them again.

Then they stepped back, screeched open the screen door, and let him in.

"So what you been doing since we last saw you?" Hank asked as they made their way to the kitchen that appeared to Felix characteristic of a planned community as if someone twenty or thirty years ago had designed a dwelling as it might appear twenty or thirty years in the future but now looking antique, Felix again reminded of Disneyland and The World of Tomorrow he had seen with the man he had met on the beach his first trip out to Long Beach to take placement exams and register for classes.

"Where do I start?" Felix replied. "You know, of course, about my being fired from my first job in Oregon and I called Amy. Well, plenty happened after you two left and Bud remained."

"Right," Hank said. "How about offering us a synopsis while we continue packing getting ready to hit the road?"

"Where you off to now?"

"Right back where we started from!"

"California!"

"Where else?" Hank said, grimacing and shrugging in reply. "Seems I need graduate school to get a decent job."

"So where you think you might go?"

"UC Berkeley, if I can get in. Otherwise, it's back to Long Beach State where I got my B.A.

"So when you leaving?

"First thing day after tomorrow. Really early. Back on the road again. We need to make miles to get to the Bay Area in time so I can register at Cal before the 15th."

"You're leaving day after tomorrow!" Felix asked.

"So what are your plans? You about ready to cut the cord? Had enough of homecoming? You need a ride?"

"Day after tomorrow!"

"Felix!" Amy chided smiling, her blue eyes gleaming in delight. "You're repeating yourself!"

"And the answer's the same," Hank added.

"Day after tomorrow," Felix offered again.

And they all laughed.

Felix sat at his grandmother's kitchen table drinking coffee. His green duffle sat ready in the attic room, just as full as it had been the day he arrived. How long ago that had been, he couldn't say — too long, perhaps. His grandmother sat across from him. She had served him breakfast, insisting that he would need it if he were leaving. Another full meal would help keep him going and he unable to enjoy another with his leaving so early the next morning. When might he have another like those she had served him?

They sat quietly while the coffeepot slowly perked over the softly hissing blue flame. The yellow bird rustled in its cage. Felix and his grandmother looked up when the sun porch door suddenly opened, and Felix's parents surprised them by appearing in the doorway, starting up the stairs, their heads and shoulders appearing over the landing, then their torsos and then the rest of them as they reached the doorway and entered the kitchen.

Felix's grandmother rose and turned toward the cabinet for mugs.

"I just made a fresh pot," she said.

Her son waved her off. "We're on our way to work! We don't have all day! We have to catch a bus!" Yet he lowered his large frame into a chair facing Felix.

Felix's mother pulled up a chair beside him. "Well, I could use some when I'm facing another long day at work!"

Felix's grandmother retrieved green fireware mugs from the cabinet, placed them on the table then moved to the stove to fetch the pot. She filled one green mug with steaming black liquid and paused over the other.

"Well, O.K.," Felix's father relented, seeing his wife's admonishing look. "Maybe just a half cup. We don't have much time, but she insisted we drop by to see when Felix plans on taking off again since he seems in such a rush to get away!"

"I'm not in any hurry," Felix offered. "I'm not leaving until tomorrow."

Felix's mother reached to take his hand. "We are so sorry to see you go off again so soon. We've had so little chance to see much of you since you've been back."

"We've all had our own schedules," Felix said. "You both work. I needed to see people to learn where they were in their lives. Now I guess I've done that. There doesn't seem to be any reason for me to stay longer when I have a ride back out to California with Amy and Hank."

"So have you decided what you're going to do next?" Pa asked. "You have any idea of where you think you might be going?"

"We were hoping you would be staying here longer," Ma offered. "I know I would have liked to see you more. You have been gone so long. And now here you are leaving again. You have been here such a short time."

Felix covered his mother's hand with his. "We'll see each other when the time is right. Hank has to get back to California in time to register at UC-Berkeley and I have to get back to Long Beach in time to find a place to stay and get ready to start another year of classes."

"We are all not getting younger," Ma said.

"I know, Ma. I know you want me to stay. But I have to get back and find a place to live, see if I can get back the job I had before I went to Oregon."

"So when you think you'll find what you want?" Pa asked. "You've been wandering around all over the place. Seems to me you can just decide to make any kind of life you want, anywhere you want!"

"Maybe," Felix conceded. "But too many things here I'd just as soon leave behind."

"Don't kid yourself. You can never leave them behind," Pa advised. "You can't always just run away from them. You won't get anything settled by just running all over the place. You have to decide what you want, what you can do, what you want to do. No amount of wandering all over is going to help unless you know where you're going!"

"I understand that, Pa," Felix said quietly. "I guess maybe I'll see where I go next. After I finish City College in Long Beach, I'd like to transfer to UC-Berkeley if I can get in, especially if Hank can register for his first year of grad school. I would start there as a Junior the following year. Then I'd already know someone there when I moved to the Bay Area"

"And then what? You have any idea?"

"Sure." Felix said calmly, but his father's insistent attitude was beginning to nag him. Then he checked his response and quieted again. His father's inquiries suddenly seemed a sign of positive interest that Felix had not previously known. "I told you the other night at dinner. Maybe more schooling will help me find out."

"He's still young," Felix's grandmother advised. "He's got time."

"He doesn't know how fortunate he is." Pa said, his eyes seeming suddenly sad. "I wish I had half the chances he's had that he hasn't seemed to appreciate and that he's never used to his advantage."

"I know you think I'm not responsible," Felix answered. "But I have to decide for myself on my own life, my own direction, just as you did."

"What direction!" Then Pa grew quiet. "You should get more out of life than we've had."

"Well, sure, we could have used more always," Ma offered, "but we have had good times also with the bad. We just want you to be happy, Felix, just like us."

"Happy! How can you say you've been happy when you've had to struggle most of your lives, sometimes just to stay alive?"

"But it has not always been struggle. Sometimes yes at first, but we have managed, and we have had each other. And as for your father having wanted something more. Well, that is just his way. He wants only what is best for us."

"You don't have to defend me to him for what I've done," Pa grumbled. "Let him do what he wants! Seems to me nothing we say will keep him from doing that!"

"He'll be back!" Felix's grandmother offered. "He's come back this time. He'll be back again! Sooner or later all our children come back home!"

"Well, I'm not going to worry about that." Pa insisted. "He's got to do what he's got to do."

"Just like you've always done, Henry," Grandma Fist offered. "He's as strong-willed as you!"

"I'd like to leave knowing that at least you two have stopped fighting each other," Felix said. "I'd like to leave thinking that someday maybe all of us have stopped fighting each other!"

"Well, Felix, there's hope!' Grandma Fist said. "You see, here we are all together, at least for a while. And your father and mother have said they'll think about moving back here again to help me out!"

"Really!" Felix said. "That's great! How'd that happen?" He looked from one to another, searching their faces.

"What you said the other evening at dinner got me thinking," Pa said. "I'll at least give you that. I guess I realized after I calmed down that you were kinda right in a way. I guess I couldn't very well expect you to respect me if I didn't respect my own mother."

"I'm surprised what I said means anything to you."

"Well, you're my son! You can't just dismiss that! And neither can I!"

Felix studied Pa's face, searched his eyes, the first time he could ever remember facing Pa and meeting Pa's gaze without doubt or fear.

"I guess you're right. Neither you nor I can just write that off," Felix said quietly.

"So I guess we'll try to see if we can maybe make a go of it here," Pa said. "We'll see what happens. And who knows, maybe someday maybe even you and me will stop fighting each other."

"I don't want to fight you, Pa. I've never wanted to fight you. I just wanted to be able to find my own way — just like you've always wanted to find yours."

"You're right again. I never did stop fighting your grandpa, and I wish I had, so maybe it's time I should try something else with my son."

Felix's father rose, came around the table to where Felix sat. Felix's father offered his hand, and Felix rose to take it.

"I hope you find what you want," Pa said, and once again Felix found himself looking into his father's eyes, seeing there, for the first time, perhaps because he had never really been able to look, he found a warmth and a regard that he hadn't expected. "I only want the best for you," Pa added. "I've always wanted that."

Felix stood before his father filled with a sudden rush of feeling.

"I know that now. Thanks for your concern."

Then, on impulse, carried away by his own discovery, Felix enfolded his father's large bulk in his arms. He felt Pa tense at first in surprise. Then Felix felt his father yield, and finally, at long last, he felt Pa's strong embrace.

Felix's father stepped back from his son. "We better get going," Pa said. He reached in his pocket, drew out a kerchief, and wiped his eyes. "Time to be earning a paycheck!"

He moved toward the door, his wife rising from her chair, taking up her bag, ready to follow her husband. Then she stopped, turned back as if reluctant to leave.

"So when will you be going?"

"Tomorrow, early," Felix said. "Hank and Amy will pick me in front of Gildner's." Felix saw his father becoming impatient. "You better hurry," Felix advised. "You'll miss your bus and be late for work."

"Never been late for work a day in my life," Pa said. Then he started down the stairs and out the door.

"Very well, then," Ma said. "We will see you tomorrow early."

She went to him, embraced him, gave him a quick kiss, Felix surprised by his mother's sudden display of affection he had not often seen. Then she followed her husband, turning at the bottom of the stairs, her hand on the worn yellow knob for one last look before finally going out, closing the door behind her while Felix and his grandmother watched her go.

Having searched for and found them, Felix the last week of August left with Amy and Hank in their '38 Buick heading for the Bay Area and UC-Berkeley where Hank wanted to register for fall semester starting the second week of September. That morning early, as he stood apart from the others on the sidewalk outside the door to his parents' apartment above the pharmacy on 24th and Greenfield cross corner, a hundred yards or so from his grandmother's, the sun not yet above the horizon, the early morning light still cool tinting the brown and pink brick, Felix watched curious and surprised at how easily and matter-of-factly Pa conversed with Hank and just as surprised how easily the young man engaged Felix's father as they exchanged views on the challenging conditions of life and the world. But then Felix reminded himself of Pa's natural ability and cultivated ease dealing with people other than his son, and Felix had learned how readily Hank engaged others in conversation. Look how easily he had enlisted Felix into a way of life and a style Felix was eager to emulate. Wasn't that why Felix was so ready to set out, willingly accepting the offer of a ride? Felix, of course, had insisted he share the costs since he still had most of what he had earned cutting grain in Oregon.

Felix also noted with even more surprise how Ma always reticent with people whom she had just met seemed open and receptive to the smile and calm voice of Amy sharing a mother's concern for her son. Felix wondered whether the apparent attitude of his parents might have been due in part to the declaration of his intentions for the future, his decision to leave, and his somewhat assured means of transport toward his immediate objectives and therefore perhaps toward that goal he had declared at a gathering celebrating his return.

Then as the dawn brightened with growing sunlight, the young couple offered their regards to Felix's parents and turned toward the waiting auto while Felix faced his mother and father for the last time in years, Felix's mother now readily accepting her son's warm embrace.

"You write us now!" Ma said. "You have not been so good in doing that!"

"I know, Ma. I promise. I'll write."

"And don't stay away so long!" Pa ordered with typical stern countenance.

"I won't." he promised and meant it at the time.

Felix approached his father who had stood back witnessing Felix's exchange with his mother. Felix offered his hand.

"Let us know how you're doing," Pa ordered.

"I will," Felix agreed.

"Take care of yourself," Pa added.

Felix stepped back from his father and studied Pa's moist eyes.

Felix blinked against his own sudden response and turned away toward the antique car that stood idling, perking out a slow plume of blue exhaust. Amy and Hank bent to wave to the two older adults who stood at the curb as Felix entered the back with Hank's faded green bag, settled onto the seat, held up a hand to his parents who stood watching, receding behind, as the weathered '38 Buick pulled out onto the avenue, blending into the steady flow of early morning traffic taking it away toward the national highway heading west.

www.ingramcontent.com/pod-product-compliance
Lightning Source LLC
Chambersburg PA
CBHW020345180626
46812CB00001B/348